FORAGING FOR MURDER

A MARQUESS OF MORTIFORDE MYSTERY - BOOK 2

SIMON WHALEY

Copyright © 2021 by Simon Whaley

Print ISBN: 978-1-7398632-0-3

Ebook ISBN: 978-1-7398632-1-0

All rights reserved.

The moral right of Simon Whaley to be identified as the author of this work has been asserted by him in accordance with the Copyright, Designs and Patents Act 1988.

All characters in this book are fictitious, and any resemblance to actual persons living or dead is purely coincidental.

No part of this book may be reproduced in any form or by any electronic or mechanical means, including information storage and retrieval systems, without written permission from the author, except for the use of brief quotations in a book review.

For rights permissions email contact@simonwhaley.co.uk.

V 02,22

THE MARQUESS OF MORTIFORDE MYSTERIES

Blooming Murder

Foraging for Murder

CONTENTS

Chapter 1	1
Chapter 2	17
Chapter 3	35
Chapter 4	51
Chapter 5	69
Chapter 6	83
Chapter 7	99
Chapter 8	115
Chapter 9	131
Chapter 10	149
Chapter 11	165
Chapter 12	179
Chapter 13	191
Chapter 14	205
Chapter 15	219
Chapter 16	235
Chapter 17	253
Chapter 18	269
Chapter 19	283
Chapter 20	297
Chapter 21	311
Chapter 22	333
Stay In Touch	357
Enjoyed Foraging for Murder?	359
Acknowledgments	361
About the Author	363
Simon Whaley's Non-Fiction Books	365

CHAPTER ONE

Aldermaston peered through the camera's viewfinder as his finger caressed the shutter button in anticipation. Rays of October early morning sunlight fingered their way perfectly through the trees.

"Come on, my beauty." His tongue moistened his lips, his left hand grabbed the bottom corner of his lucky camouflage jacket, and his thumb stroked the hem from where a four-inch square piece had been ripped during a failed hit-and-run attempt. Originally, the jacket had earned its lucky status because of the wildlife photos he'd captured whilst wearing it. His wife, Lady Mortiforde, couldn't understand why he still called it his lucky jacket. The fact he'd survived a hit-and-run attempt seemed a pretty good reason in Aldermaston's eyes.

He rubbed its rough edge, as if conjuring up a genie to help him snare the image for which he was so desperate. There, sticking out from behind a tree in the densely forested Mortiforde Woods, about a hundred yards in front of the camouflage hide in which he was concealed, was a bottom. A bottom and two legs. Yet this was no ordinary bottom. It was hairy. To be precise, it was a long-haired hairy bottom. For these were the hindquarters of the rare, and unique to Mortiforde Woods, long-haired fallow deer. For the first time in ten years, since starting his quest to capture images of this shy creature, he was moments away from his goal. He just needed the doe to take a few steps backwards and come out from behind the thick Douglas fir trunk. A shaft of soft, amber dawn sunlight was ready to spotlight her among the browning autumnal bracken.

"Come on, girl," he whispered. "Let's see your face."

His finger half-depressed the shutter button. The camera focussed for the moment that was about to come any second—

Crack! A twig snapped.

The deer bolted.

"No!" Aldermaston hissed. "Come back."

He zoomed out wide, scouring the dense regimented Douglas fir trunks for any signs of the deer, or the idiot who'd frightened it.

"Lord Mortiforde! You in there?"

Startled, Aldermaston jumped from his folding stool, hitting his head on the hide's plastic frame, long before his own six-foot frame was upright. His thinning brown hair offered no cushion against the hide's harsh, plastic skeleton. He fell back onto his stool, rubbing the top of his head, and watched the hide's doorway unzip.

"Good. You are here, Your Lordship." A head pushed forward, topped by a green woollen cap, and sporting a white bushy handlebar moustache with ornately curved tips that looked strong enough to suspend a couple of fully stocked bird feeders. "Jock Trotter said he'd seen you setting up your hide here the other day."

Aldermaston sighed. What sort of camouflage hide was this when half the bloody town knew where he was? "Come in, Seth." Aldermaston beckoned to an empty corner.

Seth Shepherd zipped up the hide's door behind him and

pulled a crumpled sheet of paper from his cracked and heavily creased Barbour jacket. "This has to stop, Your Lordship. Can't you or the Borderer's Guild do something? I will *not* be intimidated." He thrust the note into Aldermaston's face.

Since unexpectedly acquiring the title of Marquess of Mortiforde nearly two years ago, he'd become used to his time being taken up by the local townspeople as and when they had a problem. Even if it was at seven-thirty on a Friday morning, deep in the heart of Mortiforde Woods.

He unfurled the document and switched on his head torch. His middle-aged eyes were grateful.

You have blood on your hands. The time has come for retribution.

Aldermaston looked up at the septuagenarian butcher stooped over him. Seth's white moustache and eyebrows gave added vibrancy to his sapphire eyes and the broken scarlet veins in his cheeks. "Who sent this?"

Seth waved his hand in the air. "Got to be that bloody Tibby Gillard from the Vegetarian Society. She's been giving us all grief recently."

"All?"

"Me. The Trotters. And Peggy Farmer." Seth shuffled awkwardly. "Jock Trotter was cursing Tibby the other day, and Peggy Farmer happened to mention Tibby was making her feel guilty about doing an honest day's work. We're butchers, Your Lordship. We'll always have blood on our hands. It's part of the bloody job. I've nothing against vegetarians. Just those who want to stop me earning a living as I have a right to."

Aldermaston folded the note and offered it back to Seth.

"Keep it. Can't the Guild have a word with the council? They'll listen to you. Environmental Health regulations apply to vegetarians just as much as us." Seth snorted. "Peggy tells me the Vegetarian Society is entering the Best Borderlandshire Burger competition this year. A *vegetarian* burger! Whatever next?"

Aldermaston slipped the note into his jacket pocket. "Her Ladyship and I occasionally eat vegetarian meals. You don't have to be one or the other. Look, Seth. I'm sure Environmental Health check every stall taking part in the food festival, and if the Mortiforde Vegetarian Society meets all the food safety criteria, then there's nothing I can do."

He checked his watch. It was approaching eight. Blast! He was supposed to be dropping Harry off at school today. "Sorry Seth. I have to go. This is probably Tibby Gillard just winding you up. With your longevity in the butchery business, I'm surprised you're even worried by a vegetarian burger."

Seth sneered. "Depends how poncey that celebrity chef is who's opening the food festival. We get inundated with tourists from down south when we get a celebrity chef. Bloody clueless, them southern softies. There's one London restaurant that charges fifty pounds for a cauliflower steak. Fifty quid for that stalk bit that most people throw away!"

Aldermaston chuckled. "And those Londoners buy a lot of your produce."

Seth winked. "That they do. And I charge them three times the price I charge locals, too."

Aldermaston grinned. "Just remember, without that huge influx of tourists, we wouldn't attract the celebrity chef. The festival is a huge economic boost to Mortiforde."

Seth nodded. "And for that, Your Lordship, we are forever grateful. Particularly to your father, God rest his soul. Amazing how it's grown over twenty years." He paused, then looked over both shoulders.

Aldermaston frowned. They were the only ones in the hide.

"Rumour has it," Seth whispered, "this year's celebrity chef is looking for suppliers. He's been awarded the catering contract for the Royal Garden parties."

Aldermaston rose from his stool, mirroring Seth's hunched position. "Bœuf Boucher has the catering contract for Buckingham Palace?"

"The garden parties," Seth clarified. "Think of the honour if Mr Boucher gave me a contract for my new burger I'm launching today. I could tell the world that royal teeth regularly nibble my award-winning meat."

A sharp, ear-piercing squeal penetrated the hide, followed by a loud, frantic snorting. Suddenly, the bottom zip of the canvas door rose, as a quarter of a ton of Gloucester Old Spot pig forced its way in.

"Maisie, I told you to stay outside!" Seth grabbed the leather collar around the black-spotted, pink pig's neck and pulled her to a halt, but not before her nose had ploughed its way through half the woodland floor of Aldermaston's hide, knocking his tripod, camera bag and stool.

Aldermaston caught his camera in both hands just before it hit the floor. "Why have you brought a pig with you, Seth?"

"This is no pig."

Aldermaston frowned. It looked like a pig. It sounded like a pig. He pinched his nose.

"This is Maisie," Seth declared, patting her smartly on the side of her rump. "She gets me out in the fresh air every morning. Clever animals, pigs." He tapped the side of his nose with the same hand he'd slapped Maisie's rear quarters. "There's more to pigs than bacon, you know. Come on, lass. We'd better let Lord Mortiforde get on. Cheerio."

Aldermaston stared in disbelief as Seth Shepherd walked Maisie out of his hide on a lead. He surveyed the churned up soil. Something glistened between the decaying leaves. He bent down and picked up a wide-angle lens that Maisie had trampled over. Broken glass dropped from its housing and fell between his fingers. Aldermaston seethed. He squinted at the butcher and pig waddling away through the woods and imagined a set of royal teeth sinking into Maisie's hind quarters. He retrieved Seth's note from his pocket and reread it. His stomach gurgled. Breakfast was calling. Or was it a sense of foreboding?

∽

"Bugger!" Felicity stared at the blackened contents of the pie dish on the oven shelf.

"Mummy, you swore!" sang seven-year-old Harry, before nibbling the crust of his granary toast in a clockwise direction.

Cartwright cleared his throat behind her. "Is everything all right, My Lady?"

Felicity swivelled on the spot, concealing her charred creativity. Their butler, with his white-gloved hands held behind the back of his neatly starched black, pin-striped jacket, diplomatically averted his gaze. His eyes latched onto a cobweb hanging from the ceiling of their private kitchen.

Felicity fixed her Marchioness of Mortiforde grin on her face. Despite nearly two years of practising, her cheek bones still ached whenever her face contorted in this manner.

"Yes, Cartwright. Everything's fine, thank you. Just a slight disagreement between me and the oven."

Cartwright's gaze caught hers. "If there's anything you need me to do, My Lady, you only have to ask."

The corners of Felicity's mouth dropped to a comfortable, natural smile. "Thank you, Cartwright. But I think the Mortiforde Ladies' Legion would think less of their President if she delegated her Bake Off entry to her butler."

Cartwright nodded. "In that case, I'll be in the West Wing attending to His Lordship's brother."

Felicity's nose wrinkled. "Dare I ask about Basildon's latest wheeze?"

"Canapés for tonight, Your Ladyship."

Felicity crossed her arms. "How does he think canapés will get him a job with the Secret Service?"

Cartwright turned. "Something to do with survival of the fittest in a post-apocalyptic world, My Lady." He slipped silently away.

"Mummy, what's post apocalyptic?" Harry snatched a second slice of toast from the silver rack.

"Something catastrophic." Felicity looked once more at the oven's contents. Whatever it was, it was charred and smouldered. And post-apocalyptic.

She reviewed the recipe for a clue as to where she'd gone wrong. It should have been a succulent example of the local delicacy, Boor Pie. This seventeenth century dish originated from Mortiforde Wood's plentiful wild boar population, hence the Middle English spelling of *Boor*. She'd followed the recipe, which involved marinading the meat in cider, then mixing it with sugar, diced apple, onion and turnips, and encasing it in pastry before cooking it.

She stared at the smouldering rock before her. Perhaps it wasn't meant to be eaten. Perhaps it was some sort of late-medieval weapon of mass destruction.

"Bugger!" Felicity dropped the recipe on the table. She'd have to start again.

"Mummy! That's the second time you swore." Harry nibbled the crust off his second slice of toast in an anti-clockwise direction.

"How many times have I told you? Do what Mummy says, not what she does."

Harry stopped nibbling. "But you said b—"

"Don't even go there!" She held up a finger without looking at him. Why were seven-year-olds too clever for their own good? She plucked a stray grey hair dangling in front of her blue eyes, and winced. Closer examination suggested it wasn't grey, just blonde and covered in flour.

"That's not tonight's dinner, is it?" Harry stared at the black brick.

Felicity shook her head. She checked her watch. Eight o'clock. "But it's all your father is having tonight, if he's not back from his dawn photo shoot to take you to school in the next two minutes."

She slipped her hands into the oven gloves and clamped them round the smouldering charcoal brick. Her face grimaced and reddened as she struggled to lift it out of the oven. Straightening her back, she clutched the pie close to her stomach. It was only five steps to the kitchen bin.

Suddenly, the kitchen door flew open with a flourish. Felicity flinched. The pie fell from her clutches, landing squarely on her left foot, crushing it. The resulting high-pitched scream shattered her favourite cut-glass vase in the cupboard under the sink.

Harry clapped both hands over his ears in preparation for more swearing.

As Lisa Duddon approached her office at Borderlandshire District Council, her smartphone rang. She pulled it from her royal purple trench coat pocket and saw who was calling.

"Morning, Aldermaston. You're doing well. I'm not at my desk yet."

"Do us a favour. Check with Environmental Health that the Mortiforde Vegetarian Society has passed all the necessary food regs for their Food Festival stall. Seth Shepherd's been bending my ear this morning."

"Will do. Where are you? You know you're supposed to be

here in…" she checked the time on her phone's display, "… ten minutes to meet Jillian Jones."

"I'll get there as quick as I can. I've just been attacked by Seth Shepherd's free-range Gloucester Old Spot pig."

"Pardon?" Lisa twisted her office door handle.

"Tell you later," Aldermaston muttered, then hung up.

Lisa checked her reflection in the glossy screen of her mobile and titivated her jet black hair as she stepped into her office.

"Good morning!"

A glamorous woman sat at Lisa's desk, wearing a black open-neck dress with a ruffled collar that fanned behind her neck like a peacock's tail. Her ash blonde hair was stylishly tussled, but long enough to cover her ears and the nape of her neck. She smiled, broadening her thick peach-pink lips, and lifted her head so she could scrutinise Lisa along her elongated nose. Although sitting in Lisa's chair, the woman's long, slender legs rose at an angle and were crossed at her ankles as they rested on the edge of Lisa's desk. The black figure-hugging dress stopped just below the knee. Then there were the heels. All four inches of them.

"Morning," Lisa finally replied. "I'm sorry. Do we have a meeting? Only I don't appear to have anything in my diary." She swiped her smartphone, checking her appointments.

"You are Lisa Duddon, Democracy Support Officer?"

Lisa nodded.

"Excellent." The visitor swung her legs and planted her feet securely on the floor. Then she rose from the chair: all six feet four inches of her, albeit the final four from her shoes.

"That dress is stunning," Lisa admired, as the woman stepped out from behind the desk.

"Thank you." A sleek hand at the end of a long arm thrust forwards. "Abigail Mayedew."

Lisa shook it. It was a confident, authoritative handshake.

Abigail looked late forties, but this was a woman who knew how to knock seven years off her age with the right make-up.

"You don't remember, do you?"

Lisa took off her coat and hung it on a hook behind the office door. "Sorry. Brain's not in gear yet."

Abigail smiled. "I'm you're new—"

"Chief Executive!" Lisa finished. She hooked her black hair behind her left ear. "But you're not due until Monday."

"I'm keen to get to know everyone before I start." She crossed her arms and paced the room. "Looking through my predecessor's files, before he was imprisoned for fraud, I see that the Authority's Chief Executive sits on a community group called the Borderer's Guild. What exactly is that?"

Lisa switched on her computer and pulled the blinds at the window. Sunlight flooded the office. "Lord Mortiforde can tell you more about that. I've just got off the phone from him. He'll be here soon."

Abigail stared at her. "You're the administrative support, aren't you? Why don't *you* tell me what it's all about?"

Lisa sat in her chair. It was still warm. A sense of unease stirred within her. "The Borderer's Guild is a historic community organisation, dating back to the mid-eighteenth century, when it was reformed by the First Marquess of Mortiforde. Its origins go back to the Norman Conquest, when the local Lord of the Marches, the King's representative, had a private army."

"A private army?"

Lisa nodded. "Skirmishes and attacks between the English and Welsh along this border region were common as recently as five hundred years ago. Things have calmed down a bit now. Although market day still has its moments. So, the private army became a ceremonial feature."

"That's comforting to know."

"When the title of Marquess of Mortiforde was first

bestowed upon the local Lord of the Manor, the First Marquess adapted the Borderer's Guild into an army of good for the community. Comprising representatives from various groups and businesses, it fights for the town's prosperity. This weekend's food festival, for example, is organised by the Guild."

Abigail sighed. "Sounds like a load of historical, sentimental claptrap to me. I can see this is all a waste of time and money. Not the sort of thing a modern local authority should be involved with." She crossed her arms. "You say the current Marquess of Mortiforde is in charge of the Borderer's Guild?"

Lisa nodded. "Lord Mortiforde is the Eighth Marquess of Mortiforde."

Abigail perched her bottom against Lisa's desk. "And the council, through you, acts as administrative support?"

Lisa bit her bottom lip and nodded.

"And you say Lord Mortiforde is due here soon?"

Lisa tried smiling, but her teeth still gripped her lower lip.

"Good. He needs to know I'll be introducing some changes at this authority. No longer shall we pander to the whims of an aristocratic twat and his private army."

Lisa gulped.

"Lady Mortiforde, are you all right?" A slender but muscular young man in a dark suit and light blue shirt hurried across the kitchen floor and dropped to his knees. He pulled at each suit jacket cuff in quick succession, and then placed his long, slim fingers around the Boor Pie. The tendons in his lower arms strained, standing proud of his smooth, pale skin, as he lifted the black weight off Felicity's foot.

Felicity bit hard on the chequered tea towel she'd placed in her mouth in an attempt to muffle any further profanities from Harry. As soon as Daniel heaved the weight high enough, Felicity whipped her foot out from underneath and hopped around the kitchen, clutching her painful toes in both hands.

Harry giggled.

"Let me look." Two hands grabbed her arm and pulled her down onto a kitchen chair.

Felicity watched her husband's personal assistant kneel at her feet, slide her fern-coloured suede slipper off her left foot, and carefully cup her bare heel in his soft-skinned hand. His fingertips traced her instep towards her toes. As he lifted her purpling toes for closer examination, an excruciating pain shot through her foot and up her leg.

The tea towel fell from her mouth. "DANIEL!"

"You need A&E. You might have broken a couple of toes. I'll get His Lordship." Daniel stood.

"He's still hiding somewhere," she moaned.

Daniel checked his watch. "But he's supposed to be meeting the Chief Archivist at eight-thirty."

Felicity looked at Daniel's angular face. He'd shaved yesterday and, therefore, had arrived earlier this morning because he didn't need to shave again until tomorrow. The paleness of his skin accentuated the darkness of his brown hair and eyebrows.

"He's supposed to be dropping off Harry at school on his way in."

Daniel pulled his car keys from his suit trouser pocket. "We'll do it."

"Sorry?"

"Come on." Daniel motioned Felicity to stand. He draped her arm around his neck. "Lean on me for support."

Felicity trembled as she placed her weight on her right foot and then leant into Daniel's youthful body. She caught a whiff of his sensual, earthy deodorant. After several hours in his camouflage hides, Aldermaston's aroma was earthy, with a strong hint of animal dung.

"Harry. Are you ready for school?" Daniel called.

"Coming!" Harry, already dressed in his yellow school sweatshirt, grey trousers and black shoes, jumped down from the kitchen table, grabbed his schoolbag, and headed for the door.

Daniel placed an arm around Felicity's waist. "We'll drop him off at school, on the way to A&E."

Felicity seethed. Being Lord and Lady of the Manor was more work than either of them had realised. Aldermaston's appointment of an assistant a few months ago was so he could delegate some of his administrative workload and spend more time with his family. Yet all Aldermaston had managed so far was delegating his fatherly and husbandly duties to his assistant.

With Lisa on the case, Aldermaston slipped his smartphone into the side pocket of his khaki camera rucksack, buckled up the leather strap, and then swung the heavy load onto his back. Standing upright, he surveyed the busy Market Square before him. With no mobile phone signal in Mortiforde Woods, he'd cut through the forest, crossed over the River Morte, and wandered around the side of Mortiforde's Norman castle, climbing to the centre of town where there was a signal… albeit when the wind blew in the right direction.

In front of him, four regimented rows of blue-and-white awninged stalls bustled as traders prepared for the annual food festival. As well as the regular food market traders, there were specialist artisan food producers. Multi-seeded loaves and baguettes jostled for space with fresh local vegetables, perries and ciders, oak-smoked sunflower seeds, rustic flapjacks, hot chilli dips, chutneys, marmalades, and succulent meat joints. The aromas of freshly roasting coffee beans, frying onions and beefburgers, and the sickly sweet fragrance of candyfloss assaulted Aldermaston's nose. Traders shouted panicked expletives as they readied themselves for the festival's official opening in under two hours' time. He could also hear *The Dam Busters'* theme tune.

"Oh, heck!" Aldermaston threw his rucksack back onto the pavement and unstrapped the pocket to retrieve his phone. It was Daniel.

"Daniel. I'm running late. Can you—"

"I'm at the hospital with Felicity," Daniel interrupted. "She's broken a couple of toes, and we're just waiting for—"

Daniel's voice trailed off. Suddenly, Aldermaston's ear was mugged with Felicity's irate tones.

"Aldermaston?"

"Yes, dear. Are you all—"

"No, I'm not! My foot's in agony! Where are you? You were supposed to be home ages ago. It's a bloody good job Daniel turned up when he did, otherwise Harry wouldn't have got to school on time and I wouldn't be here getting the urgent medical treatment I need."

"Sorry, dear. I was waylaid on Guild business and—"

"Sod the bloody Guild!" she screamed.

Aldermaston heard her pause and take a deep breath.

"You know I fully support your sense of family duty, but… sometimes I think you're more worried about the townspeople of Mortiforde than you are about your family."

Aldermaston looked at his feet. "How can I make it up to you?"

Felicity sighed. "You can start by going to Trotters and getting a kilo of diced wild boar."

"Diced what?"

"Wild boar. And if you don't, I'll—"

Aldermaston lost all sound from his ear and checked his phone's screen. No signal. The wind direction had changed. He closed his eyes and took a deep breath. His earlier gut reaction was right. It was going to be one of those days.

He turned and faced the warmth of the sun, hoping to encourage the frustration to drift away. Instead, it tapped him frenetically on his shoulder.

"Lord Mortiforde! I want a word with you."

He turned around and opened his eyes. It was Tibby Gillard.

CHAPTER TWO

Felicity thrust Daniel's phone back at him, grabbed the crutch, and limped towards Mortiforde's A&E exit. "Drop me off at the King James Hotel in town. I'm supposed to be chairing a Ladies' Legion meeting there, first thing. Cartwright can collect me afterwards."

"Yes, Your Ladyship."

She winced. She was about to reproach him for using her title, but… they were in a public area. That was their rule for close friends and good staff: first names in private, titles in public. Not that Cartwright ever used their first names. Against Butler Academy regulations, apparently. Felicity wasn't sure she'd ever get used to the title.

"And don't let Aldermaston forget my meat order!" She hobbled gingerly. With two broken toes, each strapped to its opposing neighbour for support, walking was uncomfortable but not impossible. The thick-soled plastic shoe provided by A&E encouraged an unladylike waddle when walking.

Daniel, whose hands hovered ready to catch her should she slip, yet not wanting to touch her as if she were the Monarch, was puzzled.

She stopped walking. "I need another kilo of wild boar meat. Apparently, as President of the Ladies' Legion, it is expected of me to demonstrate my home-baking skills and be judged on them, just like every other member of the Legion. Which would be fine if I had any baking skills." Her eyes narrowed. "Does Aldermaston ever mention my baking skills?"

Daniel licked his lips. "Er…"

Felicity began walking again. "Just make sure he gets me some more meat, so that I can have another go at making this bloody Boor Pie. It'll be the death of me, if I'm not careful." She stopped and looked down at her foot. Yes. In the battle between her life and making an edible Boor Pie, the Boor Pie was definitely winning.

Aldermaston stared at the elegant young woman in the light grey trouser suit standing in front of him. Tibby Gillard was chair of Mortiforde Vegetarian Society because she was young, intelligent and knew her brassicas from her solanum. She was as slim as a runner bean and as tall as the wigwam frames most gardeners grew them on. Her head, perfectly round like a savoy cabbage, was topped with cropped copper chestnut hair, and augmented with brown eyes, a button mushroom nose and a petite rose mouth. Her skin was as pale and smooth as a peeled Jersey Royal potato.

"It doesn't take a rocket scientist to work out who sent us this." Tibby held out a small, pine wooden box, the size of a shoe box.

Aldermaston took it. "What is it?"

"Mr Harcourt, a fellow society member, found it on our stall, over there, when he arrived to set up for the festival first thing this morning."

Aldermaston felt the trepidation running down his arm.

Tibby folded her arms and grinned. "Squeamish, Lord Mortiforde?"

Aldermaston smiled, but his heart wasn't in it. Lifting the lid, he saw the box had one, though. Fresh, too, judging by its vibrant pink flesh. A few drops of blood oozed from its arteries, congealing against the sides of the wooden box. It was large, although it probably wasn't human. At least, he *hoped* it wasn't human.

Written in permanent black ink on a piece of card stuck inside the lid were the words:

Have a heart: ditch the beef-less burger.

"Probably a pig's heart," Tibby explained. "They're anatomically similar in size and shape to a human heart. Meat-eaters seem to think vegetarians vaporise into thin air when we clap eyes on one of these things. Either that or they bombard us with freshly cooked bacon sandwiches."

Aldermaston's stomach gurgled at the thought of several slices of freshly cooked, crispy, salty bacon sandwiched between two chunks of lightly buttered, organic, white crusty bread.

Tibby interrupted his taste bud fantasy. "I know the butchers aren't happy about us entering the festival's Best Borderlandshire Burger competition this year. But I object to them abusing an animal's body parts purely for their pathetic scare tactics. Don't they realise that makes *them* the animals?"

She placed her hands on her hips. "This breaks environmental health regulations. It's not vacuum-packed or hermetically sealed. Who knows how many trillions of dangerous micro-organisms are on it? I'm sorry, Lord Mortiforde, but a butcher sent this. Who else has access to animal hearts? The Borderer's Guild must act." Tibby's mouth puckered as she crossed her arms again.

Aldermaston rummaged in his camouflage jacket pocket and pulled out Seth's note. "One of the butchers received this."

Tibby unravelled the scrunched up paper. "Don't tell me they think *we* sent this? How pathetic!" She threw it back at Aldermaston. "We would never stoop to these playground shenanigans, Lord Mortiforde. I want them stopped. I'll be in touch later to see how you're getting on. Good day."

Tibby turned on her inch-high court shoe heels and strutted across Market Square to the Vegetarian Society's stall.

Aldermaston peered down at the pig's heart and raised an eyebrow. Could he pass this off to Felicity as boar meat?

In the private kitchen of Tugford Hall's West Wing, Cartwright placed a small parcel on the flour-dusted breakfast bar. Two mixing bowls, heavily caked in flour, egg and baking powder, had been abandoned at one end. An electric whisk, still plugged in, lay neglected near the other.

"Light, you cretin!"

Cartwright frowned and leant over the breakfast bar, mindful to avoid contact between his dark grey, pin-striped waistcoat and the spilled cooking ingredients dusting every surface. A red corduroyed bottom stuck in the air, as if escaping from the gas oven.

There was a rasp as a match was struck, then a hand appeared, bent backwards, fumbling its way along the oven control panel. The fingers danced drunkenly between the control knobs, until they successfully captured one, and twisted. The hiss and pungent smell of escaping gas filled the air.

"Bloody light, old chap, will you? Ouch!" The oven's occupant flinched, clonked his head, and swiftly extricated himself.

"May I be of assistance, sir?" Cartwright ambled round the

breakfast bar, leant across Basildon still kneeling on the floor, and turned off the gas.

"Cartwright! What spiffing timing!" Basildon stood, pulled at his green and beige checked shirt, ruffled his salt and pepper hair, and handed him a box of extra-long safety matches. "Can't get the bloody oven lit."

"If I may, sir?"

Basildon stepped out of the way.

Cartwright's white-gloved hands twisted the central knob on the oven's facia and then pressed an ignition button beside it. A half dozen clicks were followed by the sudden whoomph of igniting gas.

"Golly gosh! I wondered what that button was for."

"What temperature do you need, sir?"

Basildon picked up an open cookery book from the breakfast bar and let his finger trace along the page. "Er, seven."

Cartwright adjusted the knob.

"That, Cartwright, is what we in the Secret Service like to call opportunistic teamwork."

Cartwright stepped back, closed the oven door, then gestured towards the small parcel on the breakfast bar. "I signed for it a few moments ago, sir."

Basildon clasped his hands together and rested his chin on them. His eyes flitted between the parcel and Cartwright, his thin-lipped grin growing with each flit. Suddenly, Basildon launched into a Highland jig, his arms creating an O above his head, as his knees leapt above his waist with each step.

Cartwright placed his hands behind his back. "Will there be anything else, sir?"

Basildon stopped dancing. "I'll say, old bean! Hold this for me." He lunged across the worktop, grabbed the box, and thrust it back into Cartwright's hands. Then he took a knife from the knife block and plunged it into the top of the parcel, slicing it open in one swift movement.

Cartwright gulped.

Basildon ripped open the parcel and pulled at the white polystyrene packaging, revealing the contents. He paused briefly, peering at all twelve of them, and then carefully slipped his hand inside and pulled out a tall, thin phial containing a clear liquid.

Cartwright gulped again, as Basildon's eyes latched onto his.

"Don't be scared, Cartwright. There's nothing to worry about." He held the phial up to the light. "This will get me into the Secret Service, once and for all."

Cartwright moistened his lips. "If I may, sir. What exactly is it?"

Basildon grinned. "Sodium thiopental. The truth serum."

Aldermaston barged into Lisa's office, gasping for breath. "Sorry I'm late." The door swung closed behind him as he bent forwards, bracing his hands on his knees. His rucksack reassessed its grip on his back and slid to one side. Sometimes the weight of his townspeople's problems shifted similarly on his shoulders.

"You're only ten minutes late, Lord Mortiforde." Lisa rose from her chair, collected a mug of coffee from the tray on her desk and handed it to him. "Black because you're going to need it," she whispered.

Strange. She'd used his title. Not something she'd normally do when they were alone. He stood upright and relieved Lisa of the coffee. Her head made an almost imperceptible nod behind him. Slowly, he turned to see a woman hiding behind the door.

"Lord Mortiforde. Pleased to meet you. I'm Abigail Mayedew, your new—"

"Chief Exec," Aldermaston finished. "But you're not due until Monday."

Abigail thrust a hand forward and practically snatched Aldermaston's free hand to shake it.

He marvelled at the stunning sight before him. Abigail Mayedew would be a shock to those people of Borderlandshire more used to grey-suited chief executives. Round here, most thought dressing up merely involved the removal of the latest splatters of rural mud from one's clothes. Abigail looked like a model who'd graced the front cover of one of Felicity's celebrity gossip magazines.

Lisa interrupted his thoughts. "Mrs Mayedew—"

"Ms," Abigail interjected.

"Sorry. Ms Mayedew is keen to get to know Mortiforde before she officially starts next week, and thought you'd be the best person to show her around town."

Aldermaston glanced back and forth between Abigail's expectant gaze and Lisa's look of fear. The former had no idea what she was letting herself in for, while the latter, although still relatively new to the local authority herself, had complete comprehension of what was being asked. "Erm… today's not really a good day, what with the food festival being launched in…" Aldermaston checked his watch.

"Come, come, Lord Mortiforde. What better day to get to know a town than when it throws open its doors to the world and invites them in to experience one of the best food festivals held anywhere in Britain?"

Aldermaston sipped his coffee, suddenly aware of how Abigail's standard of dress compared with his camouflage jacket and jeans. "You'll have to excuse my attire. I was accosted by a local businessman earlier, and I haven't had time to go home and get changed."

"I'm sure as the lord of the local manor, you stand out in many ways, don't you?" Abigail smiled. Or was it a smirk?

The door to Lisa's office sprang open. A short, plump woman in a beige two-piece suit dashed into the room and planted an oblong parcel on Lisa's desk.

"It's here! It's finally arrived." The woman clapped her hands and stamped her feet as she stared at everyone in turn, then froze when she saw Abigail. Her hands clasped her cheeks. "I'm terribly sorry! Have I interrupted another meeting? I have, haven't I? I know I'm late but—"

"No, you're fine." Lisa placed a reassuring hand on the woman's shoulder. "Jillian, this is Abigail Mayedew. Abigail, this is Jillian Jones, our Chief Archivist."

"*Only* archivist," Jillian clarified, cricking her neck to look Abigail in the face.

"Forgive me." Abigail clasped Jillian's hand. "But it is *I* who is gatecrashing *your* meeting."

Aldermaston stared at Jillian's package on Lisa's desk. Its shape and size concerned him.

"Jillian's been waiting for this package from the Royal Palace's Collection," Lisa explained to Abigail. "As part of this year's food festival, we have a Food History Marquee in the grounds of Mortiforde Castle, depicting food throughout the centuries here in Mortiforde and the Welsh Borders."

"Yes," Jillian interrupted, "Mortiforde Castle used to be a royal residence in the sixteenth and seventeenth centuries. The chef at the castle maintained a recipe book containing the favourite meals of the royal family when they were in residence. After many months of negotiations, the Royal Palaces Collection has kindly agreed to lend us the recipe book for the exhibition."

Jillian turned to gaze at the package and allowed her hands to caress it. Her voice dropped to a whisper. "For the first time in four hundred years, the Mortiforde Royal Recipe Collection has come home." She pulled a pink handkerchief from the cuff of her beige suit jacket and dabbed her eyes. She turned to Aldermaston.

"Thank you, Your Lordship, for helping with the negotiations. I couldn't have done this without you." Jillian turned to Abigail. "When I first approached the Royal Palaces Collection and enquired if they might lend us the book for the weekend, I was told that wasn't possible. It's a popular document for researchers, apparently, regularly requested in their reading room. However, His Lordship persuaded them to let us have it."

Aldermaston smiled. "I merely emphasised the historical importance of this document to the town, and how the festival was a perfect opportunity for a wider audience to see it."

Jillian stared at the package. "This is the pinnacle of my thirty-year career."

Aldermaston's stomach griped. Something wasn't right.

Lisa handed Jillian a pair of standard issue local government safety scissors.

Repeatedly, Jillian scored the package's tape with its blades, then discarded them and used her fingernails instead. She tore away the brown paper, revealing a small wooden box.

The unease in Aldermaston's stomach rose to his throat.

Jillian clutched the wooden box to her chest, closed her eyes, and inhaled deeply. Finally, she opened her eyes and lifted the lid.

Her scream penetrated the bowels of the council offices, including the contents stuck inside the bottom drawers of the filing cabinets abandoned in the basement. The box crashed to the floor, disgorging its contents.

There, at everyone's feet, was a pig's hock and trotter… and a note caught between its hooves.

Daniel hurried across the vast council car park, checking his watch every few seconds. Being late always guaranteed getting a parking space furthest from the main entrance.

He strode up Borderlandshire District Council's entrance steps, two at a time, and threw his entire bodyweight against the revolving door, which was heavy enough to prevent all but the most determined members of the public from entering the building. Eventually, he overcame the door's inertia.

"Daniel!"

"Can't stop, Sheila," he bellowed to the receptionist.

"But there's another package for Jillian Jones. You're meeting with her and Lord Mortiforde, aren't you?"

Daniel's black brogues skidded across the polished reception floor, slipping as he changed course towards Sheila's dark, imposing, wooden reception counter.

"Do you need me to sign for it?"

"Yes. Now, where did I put my pen?"

Daniel watched the fifty-year-old step back from the wooden counter and survey her work area. Her grey knee-length skirt was back to front, and the thin cream jumper she was wearing had the label sticking out under her chin. Even the fastener on her nine-carat gold chain necklace was resting on her breastbone. He spotted the chewed, black-plastic biro lid poking through her auburn hair.

"Behind your ear, Sheila."

She clasped her hand to the side of her head and giggled. "I'd lose my head if it wasn't screwed on. Mind you, knowing me, I'd lose those screws too." She giggled again. "Sign there, please." She handed him the black biro and pointed to a dotted line on a sheet of paper. She dropped to her knees, reappearing moments later with a large cardboard box.

"Jillian's popular today. That's the second package she's had. Luckily, the first one was already waiting on the reception desk for her when she arrived this morning."

Daniel's running-late signature barely used any ink. He grabbed the box.

"Be careful with that!" Sheila yelled. "The delivery man said it was precious. It's from the Royal Palaces Collection."

Aldermaston bent down and picked up the thin strip of paper, bloodstained at the edges from the hacked pig's hock, and turned it over.

The retribution starts here for your forefather's sin.

Abigail clicked her fingers and held out her hand for the note.

Aldermaston held it up so she could read it, but he kept hold of it.

"Whose forefather's sins?" Abigail enquired.

Aldermaston swallowed. His momentary hesitation was enough.

"It was addressed to me," Jillian whispered, her eyes widening as they fixed themselves on the note in his hands.

"Call the police!" Abigail strode across Lisa's office and grabbed the phone.

Lisa's hand slammed down hard on top of Abigail's. "No!"

Abigail flinched.

"In due course." Aldermaston's heart sank. These were not the best circumstances to introduce the new Chief Exec to Mortiforde's one and only policeman. "Lisa, call Ajay in Environmental Health. I'd like his view on what we have here."

"It looks bloody obvious from where I'm standing!" Abigail snatched her hand back from underneath Lisa's.

"Get many pig trotters in the post in your last position, Ms Mayedew?" Aldermaston looked expectantly at her. He turned to Jillian, whose eyes were now fixed on the bloodied trotter, while her fingers clasped the sides of her face.

"Abigail," Aldermaston continued. "Make Jillian a strong coffee. She's in shock."

"But we should be calling the police!"

"When the time's right. The last thing we need moments before the food festival opens are rumours of the police investigating dead animal body parts turning up all over town. That's not the impression the Borderer's Guild would want the public to have of the food festival, or of the local authority."

Abigail's face softened. He allowed himself a wry smile. Yes. Abigail Mayedew was a woman concerned about image. All Chief Execs needed steering and image was the wheel to steer her. "The kettle's behind you." He nodded towards the desktop behind her.

He dropped to his knees and took a closer look at the pig's trotter. Glance at it quickly, as most of them had when it first fell out of the box, and it looked like a human limb. Even the two large hooves, with the third, smaller, thumb-like hoof tucked behind them, had a hand-like quality about them.

Aldermaston heard Lisa chatting on the phone, while Abigail stirred metal spoons inside china mugs. He reached across to his rucksack and retrieved his mobile phone. Zooming in, he took several pictures from different angles.

"Sorry, I'm late," wheezed Daniel, hurling himself into the room at breakneck speed, taking everyone by surprise. "I had to collect this package for Jillian."

Everyone watched Daniel place the parcel on Lisa's desk. Their eyes remained latched onto it as he stepped back to take off his suit jacket.

Aldermaston relaxed when he saw the parcel looked nothing like Jillian's earlier delivery. For a moment, he, along with the rest of the room's occupants, feared another pig part had just arrived.

"What's going on?" Daniel scanned the room and noticed Aldermaston on his knees. Then he saw—

"Is that… real?"

Lisa put the phone down. "Ajay says he'll pop down and take a quick look."

Aldermaston stood. "Right, nobody else is to come into this room. The fewer people who know about this, the better." He glanced down at the pig limb on the floor. If nothing else, at this rate, he'd have Felicity's kilo of porcine meat in no time.

Outside the King James Hotel, Felicity struggled to negotiate the burgeoning visitors gathering in readiness for the official opening of the food festival in an hour. Having a crutch was a handicap in a crowd. It was easy identifying tourists for they looked up at the intricately carved, three-storey, timber-framed, leaded-window seventeenth century hotel, with jutting first and second floors overhanging into the street, as they walked by.

To stop tourists inadvertently treading on her broken toes, Felicity swept her crutch in an arc ahead of her, as if it were a blind person's white stick.

"Oi! Watch what you do with that, luv!" sneered one chap, stumbling over the rubber ferrule.

"Sorry!" Embarrassed, Felicity spotted a gap in the passers-by and lunged towards the main entrance of the hotel. As she did so, she collided in the doorway with a hotel guest heading out. Her crutch clattered to the floor.

It was his shoes that caught her attention first. The bright red, leather lace-ups screamed attention against the soil-coloured hotel carpet, and his duck brown denim jeans were from a Parisian outfitters, not the country clothing store on the outskirts of town frequented by the local farmers searching for shit-coloured boiler suits. The white shirt was ruffled in an enigmatic way, and the top three buttons were undone, revealing a few dark chest hairs against the gently tanned skin. He also wore a light green suede jacket, unbuttoned to accentuate his suave style. The healthy-looking tan continued across his face, which sported some day-old stubble, and a small dimple in his chin. His dark, dishevelled hair looked sophisticated as it tumbled over his forehead into his big brown eyes. Surely, it couldn't be?

"*Excusez moi, mademoiselle!*" He bent down and picked up the crutch. "Zis is yours, I believe."

The heavy French accent caused Felicity's heart to skip. Bœuf Boucher! He looked younger than the mid-fifties all the women's magazines claimed he was.

"I'm terribly sorry," she gushed. "It's my fault." She took her crutch from him. "Haven't learned how to drive one of these yet."

He frowned. "You use zis to drive?"

Felicity placed her hand on his forearm. "Sorry. I'm confusing you."

He tutted. "I am all in a tizz zis morning. I need to be somewhere and ze lady on reception showed me where we are on a map, but not where I need to go."

Felicity smiled. "Where do you need to be?"

He shuffled uncomfortably in his red leather shoes. "I… er… how you say?" His hand gesticulated, trying to pull the words he needed from thin air.

"*Le marché de beurre…* er… market of butter… Non, er…"

"Buttermarket?" Felicity suggested.

"*Oui*! Ze Buttermarket. Do you know where I will find it?"

Felicity's eyes lingered on the relief washing across his face. His chocolate eyes gazed directly at hers, and his grin broadened. She'd forgotten how charming the French could be. She'd been at the centre of Frenchmen's attention on several occasions during her marketing career. Another life.

"It's not far," she said, pointing with her stick. "I'll show you the way."

He beamed. "I am a lucky man," he concluded, "to 'ave such a beautiful woman to guide me." He glanced down at her foot. "But are you sure? I could not let a woman endure pain just to help an idiot like me."

She waved her hand in the air. "It's nothing." Felicity was suddenly aware of the coolness of the air against the heat of her skin.

"But I am interrupting you, am I not?" Bœuf enquired. "Surely you were coming here for a reason?"

Felicity turned her nose up and shook her head. "Nothing that can't wait."

"But what if you are needed while we are off gallivanting?"

The thought of gallivanting with this famous French chef appealed. Aldermaston never took her gallivanting. Perhaps it was a French thing. "I'm sure they can manage."

"In zat case," he said, holding out an arm for her to cling to, "lead on."

～

Tibby took two delicate steps back and admired their stall from the public's perspective. It was a voracious variety of vegetable delights, arranged in a rainbow of colours: red tomatoes, peppers and radishes; orange pumpkins and butternut squashes; yellow sweetcorn, peppers and lemons; brown onions, potatoes, parsnips and turnips; green broccoli, savoy cabbages, peas, leeks, celery and apples; then purple carrots, aubergines, grapes, and beetroot. She snatched a red grape and popped it into her mouth.

"Oi! You're not supposed to eat the produce before we open to the public." Ashton Harcourt's Black Country accent floated across the stall. His spivvy black moustache mirrored his grin. "But can I tempt yow to a vegetarian burger?"

Tibby nodded. "I think we've earned breakfast, especially after that stupid prank the butchers played earlier." She watched him stoop slightly under the blue-and-white striped awning. Despite it being higher than his six-foot two frame, he was conscious of how close his head was to it, as he busied himself behind the stall. He straightened the white mesh food hygiene hat covering his thick, coarse, black hair by pulling at its white peak, then wiped his hands across the dark green apron protecting his light green waistcoat, blue shirt and red tie. His bulbous eyes searched for something, then found their prey as his large hands engulfed the bread roll.

He titivated a couple of burgers with a stainless steel slotted turner on the commercial griddle hotplate. An explosion of sizzling expectation filled the air, followed by a sweet aroma.

"Smell that burger." His nostrils flared and his chest expanded as he sucked in half the air of the entire Market Square. "God, that's bloody marvellous." He opened his eyes. "Who needs meat when you can have a Borderlandshire Blue Burger?"

"Let's hope we can tempt the public into buying them." Tibby glanced around the other stalls, now a frenzy of activity. There was only an hour to go until the official opening and stallholders were applying the finishing touches. Even the nut man was pimping his pistachios. Members of the public browsed slowly, and the hard-core festival attendees were noting down prices and bargains.

"Get your gnashers around that."

A Borderlandshire Blue Burger bap was thrust in front of her. The aroma was wonderful. Parsley and thyme mixed with the creamy fragrance of Borderlandshire Blue cheese. Tibby sank her teeth into it and savoured the moment. "Mmmm. This," she said, pointing what was left of her burger roll at

Ashton, "is bloody fantastic!" She took another bite, enjoying the crispiness of the fried organic wholemeal breadcrumb coating, the flavoursome leeks, sweet potato, aubergine and walnut filling, and the surprisingly soft Borderlandshire Blue cheese centre oozing across her tongue.

She wiped a crumb from the corner of her mouth. "If this doesn't win the Best Borderlandshire Burger competition, nothing will."

"We've clearly got the butchers rattled." Ashton grinned. "And if we play our cards right, we could win a tasty little contract."

Tibby frowned.

Ashton beckoned her closer. "Bœuf Boucher, the celebrity chef, has won the catering contract for the Royal Garden Parties at Buckingham Palace. He's looking for suppliers. That would upset the butchers if we won the beefburger contract, wouldn't it?"

Tibby grinned. Wouldn't it just?

CHAPTER THREE

Aldermaston offered his hand to Ajay, who was struggling to get up off the floor.

"Thank you, Your Lordship." Ajay pulled his belted chinos up under his paunch, smoothed his black, receding hair behind the back of his head, and then grasped his chubby jowls. "If I'd known I'd be on the floor to look at this, I'd have sent one of the younger lads." He looked down at the severed leg joint, then returned his gaze towards Aldermaston. "It's definitely real, but it's been hacked about a bit."

Aldermaston sighed. "Not a butcher's cut, then?"

Ajay shook his head. "It's a rear leg, but it's been cut too high into the shank. Any trained butcher would cut here," he pointed further down the limb, "at the top of the hock, and then again here, for the trotter. No butcher would waste that much shank end meat."

Aldermaston's stomach gurgled. He could murder a ham hock sandwich now. Or any food, for that matter. "How... er... fresh is it?"

Ajay rubbed his jowls again. "Rough guestimate… between three and six hours."

"How can you be sure?" Abigail folded her arms across her chest, and stared at Ajay. "Anatomically trained, are you?"

Ajay returned Abigail's stare. "I'm an Environmental Health Officer, madam. We see a lot in our jobs. And I'm also a first aider for the second floor offices on Thursdays. So, I can tell you categorically, there's no point in me giving *that* the kiss of life." He pointed to the floor.

Aldermaston encouraged Ajay towards the door. Now wasn't the time to introduce him to his new boss. Leave that for Monday. "Thanks for coming down, Ajay. Means we can probably keep this local then." Aldermaston nodded to Lisa. "Better give PC Norten a call now. Cheers, Ajay. I take it you'll stay shtum about this?"

Ajay tapped the side of his nose. "Environmental Health never mentions the bad stuff. We only praise the good." He leant closer to Aldermaston's ear. "But we've just downgraded the Border Bird public house near the bypass from a five-star hygiene rating to a zero-star. You don't want to know what they were putting into their chicken nuggets." He turned and left the room.

Lisa picked up her phone again and called the police.

Abigail stepped forward, her arms still crossed. "Right, nobody is to touch anything because forensics will still need to scrutinise this. It could have fingerprints on it. Who's in charge of PR because we need to be prepared for when the press picks up on this? And wouldn't it be good if—"

Aldermaston raised his hand. "Sorry Abigail, but this isn't London and, with the greatest respect, technically, you don't work here yet, so you're in no place to issue instructions."

Lisa raised an eyebrow as she chatted on the phone. Daniel shifted uncomfortably on his feet.

Abigail held up her hands in surrender. "Fine. But your

failure to call the appropriate authorities as soon as possible is just one of many points that I'll put in my report."

Aldermaston frowned. "Report?"

"At the London Borough of Thameside, every incident was followed up with a detailed scrutiny report, which led to the development of new local authority policy. Within two months of implementing that policy, every member of staff followed procedures to the letter." Abigail pouted and raised her eyebrows. "They were sacked, if they didn't."

Aldermaston stared at Abigail. "Here in the Welsh Borders, such a dogmatic approach isn't always the most appropriate response."

Lisa put the phone down. "PC Norten says he'll pop round soon. He's just having his favourite breakfast. Cocoa Pops."

Aldermaston smiled at Abigail's puzzled look. Welcome to Borderlandshire.

He stepped across the room and grabbed the box the pork part had arrived in, turned it upside down, and covered the offending limb. Out of sight was out of mind, if only temporarily. He turned to Jillian, still nursing the strong coffee Abigail had made. "Perhaps we should open this other package while we wait for PC Norten."

Jillian shook her head. "No. I… I can't. There might be…"

Aldermaston grabbed the box. "I'll do it." He took a penknife from his camouflage jacket pocket and scored the Sellotape seal. Lifting the flaps, he found a large, thick, white envelope addressed to Jillian, and a bigger ledger-shaped package wrapped in white tissue paper.

"Don't!" Jillian lunged forward, grabbing his arm. "Here, let me." Carefully, she took the precious box from his hand and placed it on the desk.

"At least that doesn't look like the other back leg." Daniel stepped forward. "Perhaps we'd better check." He picked up the box and turned it upside down. An inverted mushroom cloud of polystyrene balls billowed to the floor.

"You can clear that lot up right now!" There was strength in Lisa's Mancunian accent.

Aldermaston nodded at Daniel. She meant it.

"This is it!" Jillian whispered. From her beige jacket pocket, she pulled out a pair of white cotton gloves, quickly slipped her hands into them, and gently unwrapped the tissue paper.

Only the faint rustling of the tissue paper could be heard as Jillian unwrapped the historical document. A slip of paper fell from the ledger to Aldermaston's feet.

He bent down and grabbed it. It was a Royal Palaces Collection reader's pass bearing the name *A Truff*. Somebody had doodled a beard and spectacles onto the photograph.

Jillian admired the green and brown leather ledger. Its condition was impressive, considering its four-hundred-year age. The base of the spine was worn, and the corners of the ledger were a little tatty. Aldermaston had seen recent Borderer's Guild agendas in a far worse state. And they were of no interest to anyone. But this? This ledger had been used by Royal chefs daily in the hostile environment of a seventeenth century kitchen.

Using both gloved hands, Jillian slowly opened the ledger cover, revealing a display of intricate calligraphy. "Just as I thought."

"What language is it in?" Abigail enquired. "French? Early Modern English?"

Jillian looked up from the text. "Latin."

"Latin?" Abigail stepped closer. "But that doesn't make sense. If this book is early seventeenth century, surely it should be in Late Middle English?"

Jillian bristled. "Latin was still used by certain sections of the community, particularly the Church and the legal profession. It was also commonly used for international documents and treaties. You have to remember that European Royal families regularly visited palaces across Europe, bringing their head chefs and their cookbooks with them. Recording recipes in Latin meant most palace chefs could read and understand them. For many years, Latin was the language of cooking."

Aldermaston remembered the thick white envelope addressed to Jillian, still in his hand. "Don't forget this." He passed it to her.

Ripping it open, Jillian extracted a thick spiral-bound document, then sniggered. "It's a translation." She flicked through its pages. "The Royal Palaces Collection has assumed nobody in the Welsh Borders understands Latin."

Aldermaston considered her point. Round here, if anyone saw a confusing language, they'd assume it was Welsh. Compulsory bilingual road signs were only a few miles away.

Jillian's fingers suddenly stopped page-flicking.

Aldermaston peered over her shoulder. "What is?"

"Stella was right, Your Lordship. This isn't *just* a recipe collection. There's a diary section, too." She clutched her chest with one hand. "These are the personal recordings of the Head Chef, Oswyn Cooke. At one of my *Trace Your Ancestors* evening classes a few months ago, I discovered Oswyn Cooke is one of my distant ancestors. This is amazing!"

Suddenly, a loud knock at the door interrupted them. Everyone turned in unison to the upturned box on the floor.

Aldermaston tiptoed across the office. Cautiously, he pulled the door open enough to see who was there. When he saw the excess white shirt material hanging over the trouser belt, he let out a deep sigh. "PC Norton. Do come in."

The lanky seven feet ten inches tall policeman dropped to his knees to clear the top of the door frame and shuffled into the room. Once inside, he stood, then smoothed his blonde hair sticking up near his crown. Aldermaston hurriedly closed the door and smiled when he saw Abigail stretching her neck to look up at PC Norton.

"Abigail, can I introduce you to our one and *only* policeman here in Mortiforde? This is PC Norten. PC Norten, this is Abigail Mayedew, our new Chief Exec, who starts on Monday."

A slender hand with six-inch-long fingers stretched forward and grabbed Abigail's hand. "Nice to meet you. I hope you won't be getting up to any mischief like the last Chief Exec. He was a very naughty boy, wasn't he, Lord Mortiforde?"

Abigail managed a smile.

"Abigail comes from London," said Aldermaston.

PC Norten scowled. "I didn't like London when I did my police training."

Abigail pulled her hand from the policeman's grip. "Why not?"

"Kept hitting my head on all the CCTV cameras there. Now, Lord Mortiforde." PC Norten clapped his hands together. "I understand you have some lost property."

Abigail stifled a laugh. "I'd hardly call it lost property." She stepped forward and picked up the upturned box, revealing the severed pig's leg lying on the carpet.

"That's a shame." PC Norten bent over and picked it up.

Abigail grabbed his arm. "Shouldn't you be wearing gloves? You're contaminating the evidence!"

PC Norten laughed and inspected the trotter. "I know lost property when I see it. It's worrying how absent-minded people can be sometimes."

Aldermaston frowned. "What's a shame?"

PC Norten pointed the trotter at Aldermaston. "Farmer Bell rang me last night. One of his pig's has gone missing. But this is only a pig leg, so it can't be his." He sighed. "Then, this morning, Peggy Farmer called to say someone had left a front right pig's shoulder and leg in the middle of her butcher's shop floor." He scratched the back of his head with the hoof. "I reckon it's going to be a pig of a day, today, Your Lordship!"

PC Norten laughed, and nudged Aldermaston with his elbow. "Get it, Your Lordship? A pig of a day!" He waved the trotter in the air.

"Any pig limbs been found at Shepherds or Trotters?" Aldermaston was doing the maths … and the biology.

PC Norten shook his head. "Don't think so. But Mrs Trotter called earlier. She's only mislaid her husband. Not seen him since last night, she said." He chuckled. "It's a good job forgetfulness isn't a crime. Think of the paperwork then!"

∽

Seth Shepherd unlatched the rear gate of his butcher's premises and held it wide open. He placed an encouraging foot on Maisie's rump.

"Go on now, girl. Don't make too much noise. We're late! Evie won't be happy."

Maisie squealed as she trotted into the rear yard, the sound of her hooves muffled by the fresh straw Evie had thrown down across the yard while they were both out.

Seth looked towards the back door of the three-storey Georgian building. An hour late, and today of all days. Evie would give him what for. First, he needed to hide his little beauties. His hands checked the contents of his Barbour jacket pockets. His smile broadened to a grin. Even the curly corners of his white moustache curved upwards, too. A good day. Perhaps it was because he'd not bumped into the others.

Maisie scampered off to her brick sty, part of a small extension once housing the outside privy of the butcher's premises.

Seth unlocked the door to the coal shed, adjacent to Maisie's sty, and slipped surreptitiously inside. He didn't bother with the light of the windowless outbuilding. His hands slipped into his jacket pockets, retrieved their quarry, and then carefully placed them into a plastic container on a shelf on the side. Evie would sort them later. He resealed the lid and stepped backwards into the rear yard. He shut the door, flipped the latch across, and secured the padlock.

Seth wandered over to Maisie's sty and pulled the waist-high wooden gate shut, locking it in place. "Good girl, Maisie. Rest up. You've earned—"

A black-gloved hand came from behind and pulled his chest backwards. Seconds later, another gloved hand, holding a crumpled wodge of material, forced itself against his nose and mouth. He couldn't breathe. His feet kicked and scuffled against the freshly laid straw. Muffled panic echoed in his lungs along with a faintly sweet chemical aroma. His chest tightened and his legs felt weak. Then everything went black.

～

PC Norten departed with the offending pork joint and Lisa shut the door behind him. Aldermaston relaxed. With one idiot out of the room, that just left Abigail.

Jillian burst into tears. "For a moment, I'd forgotten about that threatening message," she sniffled. "Why me? I haven't done anything." She blew her nose on her pink hanky.

Abigail turned to Lisa. "Where are the Ladies?"

"Along the corridor, third door on the left."

Aldermaston saw his chance. "I need to go home and get changed for the festival's official opening in forty-five minutes. Abigail, perhaps you could tag along to the official opening with Lisa, and I'll meet you there."

Abigail nodded. She turned to Jillian. "Come on, dear. Let's go somewhere private, and we'll sort you out."

As soon as the door shut behind them, Aldermaston picked

up his rucksack and planted it on Lisa's desk. "Right, Daniel. You and I need to take a quick trip into town, but before we go there's something else I need to show you."

Lisa brushed her hair behind her ear. "By the way, when I spoke to Ajay earlier, he said the Vegetarian Society had a clean bill of health for their festival stall. They wouldn't be behind this, would they?"

Daniel laughed nervously. "I didn't think vegetarians touched meat of any kind. I went out with a girl at university who was vegetarian, and she didn't like touching my—"

"I don't want to know, thank you!" Lisa's Mancunian accent kicked in. "Some of the nicest customers Mark and I have staying at the bed and breakfast are vegetarians."

Daniel's skin flushed. "I was only going to say she wouldn't even touch my breaded chicken goujons."

Aldermaston smirked as he rummaged in his rucksack. There were only eight years between Daniel and Lisa, but sometimes Lisa acted more like his mother than the thirty-year-old she was. "Anyway, children," he said, finding what he was looking for. "Thank heavens I know you two aren't vegetarian, otherwise you wouldn't take a look at this."

He pulled out Tibby Gillard's small wooden box and placed it on Lisa's desk. Then he flipped the lid.

"That's disgusting!" Lisa stepped back.

Daniel bent closer to inspect its contents. "Is it real? Not human, is it?"

"Tibby Gillard thinks a butcher placed it on their stall. It came with this." Aldermaston pointed to the note attached inside the lid.

"Have a heart, ditch the burger," Lisa read out. "I've heard the Vegetarian Society are launching a vegetarian burger this year, but are the butchers really *that* scared of a bit of competition?"

Aldermaston flipped the lid shut. The fleshy contents made

his stomach churn. He was desperate for some breakfast. "I'll leave this with you."

Lisa took two steps back. "Do you have to?"

Aldermaston nodded. "Get Ajay to check it. Tibby thinks it's a pig's heart. In light of Jillian's first package, there's a pretty good chance it is." He pushed the box towards Lisa.

Daniel perched himself on the corner of Lisa's desk. "Why would anyone do this? Tibby assumes the butchers are behind this, but if so, why would Jillian have been sent a pig leg?"

"Double-bluff? Throwing suspicion away from themselves," Lisa suggested.

Aldermaston shrugged. "When we get back from the festival's official opening, do some digging around into the butchers. I want to know what financial impact the Festival's Best Borderlandshire Burger competition has on their business."

Lisa ran her fingers through her hair. "But they're private family businesses. Their accounts are not in the public domain."

"There are ways and means," Aldermaston winked. "One never knows when a shopfront grant scheme will come in handy."

"A what?" Daniel asked.

"When town centres look tired and unloved, a fresh lick of paint on the shop frontages can transform them. Makes the place feel more welcoming. Two years ago, one of the last things my father instigated, as head of the Borderer's Guild, was a shopfront grant scheme. The local council tempts business owners to spend a bit of cash on improving the look of their shop premises by offering them a grant that covers half the costs of the refurbishment."

Daniel remained puzzled. "What's this got to do with—"

Lisa interrupted. "The applicants had to supply a set of accounts."

Aldermaston nodded. "Five years' worth. Applicants had to show they were a viable business and not just about to go under. Some councillors objected because the businesses didn't need the grant money. But sometimes business needs a little guiding hand. Luckily for us, all three butchers applied."

"I suppose as soon as one applied the others…" Lisa surmised.

"Exactly." Aldermaston zipped up his camouflage jacket. "Which means that somewhere, deep in the bowels of the council's basement, are the shopfront grant scheme files with five years' worth of accounts for each of the butchers. It'll be interesting to see what they throw up."

"I'll throw up, if I don't get that box off my desk soon," muttered Lisa, throwing her copy of The Mortiforde Chronicle over it.

∽

"Zis is a popular festival, is it not?" Bœuf commented, as Felicity guided him through the burgeoning crowds towards the Buttermarket.

"Extremely." Felicity's cheeks ached more than her broken toes, such was the width of her grin. As they politely pushed their way between festival-goers, she savoured the moment when they spotted she was clutching the arm of the famous chef. Many took photos of them both on their smartphones.

"Are you his wife?" a woman enquired.

A little taken aback, Felicity blushed and grinned, deftly shaking her head. Most people in Mortiforde knew who she was. Being the Lady of the Manor was a celebrity status in itself around town, but today, when another twenty thousand visitors from across the country were in town, she was unknown again. It was liberating. Just like the old days.

They approached the top of Southgate Street, dominated

by the yellow-stone Buttermarket, its portico main entrance to the covered open-air market hall looking straight down the wide Georgian street, and its south-facing, square sash windows on the first floor basking in the morning sunshine. The town clock, sitting under a white cupola, chimed the quarter-hour.

Felicity pointed. "That's the main festival information point there."

"You 'ave been so helpful, er… I'm sorry," said Bœuf, "but here you are helping me and I do not even know your name. It is rude of me."

She gazed into his beautiful brown eyes. "Felicity."

"Felicity," he repeated, although his French accent pronounced it as *Vee-liss-itee*. "Such a beautiful name. Do you love cooking?"

Her toes throbbed. "I don't think cooking loves me."

Bœuf brushed his black fringe from his eyes, then took Felicity's hands in his. "A woman should enjoy cooking as much as she enjoys making love to her husband."

Felicity bit her bottom lip. If her next attempt at Boor Pie didn't work later, then Aldermaston would have to make do with chicken nuggets tonight. "Tell me," she said, her eyes still staring deeply into his, "how do you ensure the meat inside a pie is cooked through without burning the pastry casing?"

Bœuf smiled. "A little preparation goes a long way. Brown ze meat first in ze frying pan. But remember the love-making. Start off with a slow-burning, smouldering heat for ten minutes, and then erupt into a passionate, frenzied flame for a few climatic minutes." He tapped the side of his nose. "Zen you can put your meat into your pre-prepared blind-baked pastry casing and create your perfect pie. Another hour in the oven and… mmwwaa!" He kissed his fingertips. "Perfection!"

Felicity's heart pounded. Was it all this talk of food, or the way Bœuf spoke of love and passion?

"I 'ave taken enough of your time," Bœuf continued. "You must get back to ze hotel. I interrupted you, did I not?"

Felicity smiled. She'd enjoyed the interruption. It had been a long time since a man had given her this much attention.

∽

"Turn right!" Aldermaston yelled, thrusting his arm in front of Daniel's face and pointing out through the driver's window. Daniel hit the brakes of his small twelve-year-old silver Toyota. The tyres screeched, and both men's heads gently kissed the windscreen.

Daniel indicated right and turned into Curtain Wall Road. "I thought you wanted to go home and get changed."

"I do but, if you remember Felicity's phone call from A&E, I have to pick up—"

"Some boar meat."

"Follow this round and it'll bring you out near Morte Bridge."

Curtain Wall Road was a narrow single track residential lane skirting the northern and western edge of Mortiforde town centre, passing the perimeter walls of Mortiforde Castle, towering above their heads. They passed Norman Foundations on the right, the two-starred Michelin restaurant on the banks of the River Morte, before reaching the junction with Castle Avenue.

"Turn left and follow it uphill. Park outside Lisa and Mark's bed and breakfast."

Castle Avenue rose steeply, itself only wide enough for a car and a bike to pass each other in places, as it followed the castle's southern perimeter wall. At the top of the hill, the road levelled and Daniel snuck his Toyota into a small space between a Land Rover Defender and a Mercedes. On their left, beside the crenelated castle walls, were several rose beds and lawns, punctuated with an occasional wooden bench, which festival-goers were making use of. On their right was a row of large, three-storey Georgian properties.

Aldermaston and Daniel got out of the car and strolled round the corner into Market Square, now heaving with expectant tourists.

"What time do the butchers start selling their new burgers?" Daniel enquired.

"When the festival officially opens at ten." Aldermaston glanced at his watch. "Half an hour. Come on, let's see if Mairi has any boar meat."

Aldermaston stepped into Trotter's Butchery. Immediately, his nose twitched at the smell of raw meat.

Mairi Trotter appeared from the rear of the shop in a white apron, wearing blood-red lipstick. Wisps of black curly hair escaped from under her hairnet.

"Lord Mortiforde, what can I do for you?"

"Lady Mortiforde wants a kilo of diced boar." Aldermaston turned to Daniel. "It was a kilo, wasn't it?"

Daniel nodded.

"Making Boor Pie for the Ladies' Legion Bake Off, is she?" Her chubby face grinned, causing her cheeks to squash her eyes half-shut.

"Attempting to," Aldermaston sighed. "You don't sell anything for indigestion, do you?" he muttered under his breath.

Mairi shuffled her way along the counter toward the shop window, searching the various cuts of meat; from the chicken and beef joints, through to the veal, goat, and pork. Behind her, hanging from S-shaped hooks, were pheasants, rabbits, squirrels, and pigeons. Her hand hovered over the diced pork. "Gavin! Have you sold any boar this morning?" Her yell echoed around the tiled floor and walls.

"Yeah," called a voice from out the back. "Last lot about fifteen minutes ago."

Mairi placed her blue latex gloved hands on her hips. "How many times have I told you, Gavin? Replenish, replenish, replenish!"

"Check the freezer," Gavin yelled.

Mairi shook her head. "What would your father say if he were here?" She turned to Aldermaston. "Shan't be long." She waddled along the counter and parted the steel fly-screen separating the shop from their rear preparation area. "Where is your father? On today of *all* days. PC Norten was a waste of bloody time, but what's new there? We'll be rushed off our feet when the festival kicks off." She disappeared through the metal curtain and it clattered closed behind her. Her voice permeated through the steel fly-screen. "He can't just wander off when he feels like it. Not this weekend. We're going to be—"

A piercing scream penetrated the shop. The fly-screen shivered.

Aldermaston dashed round the counter and through the still-vibrating steel fly-screen.

In the rear of Trotter's butchery, Aldermaston smelt the tempting aroma of cooked burgers. His stomach gurgled with anticipation. Gavin's rotund figure was wrapped in a blood-stained apron. Both his hands were in butcher's chain-mail gloves, as he flipped rows of ferociously sizzling and spitting burgers on an open cooking hotplate. On the worktop in front of him were mountains of uncooked beef discs waiting to join the hotplate throughout the day.

Gavin, though, wasn't cooking. Instead, he was staring. Staring at the other side of the room, where his mother stood, open-mouthed.

Mairi's left hand remained clasped to the freezer room door she'd opened. Inside were several pig carcasses, along with an array of shelving units holding at least a week's supply of joints, burgers, and sausages.

But as Aldermaston continued analysing the scene, he stumbled across the cause of Mairi's scream. There, on the floor of the freezer, was a front left pig's leg. If this were pig bingo, he only needed one more to have each of the four corners. Literally.

Mairi took a huge intake of air and issued another carcass-shuddering scream.

Aldermaston stepped in front of her, grabbed both her shoulders and shook the shock from her.

"Mairi! Calm down." It was only an unexpected porcine appendage in the freezer area. "Listen to me. It's probably some joke in poor taste. Another butcher has had one, as has the council."

Aldermaston watched her eyes flit between his eyes and the pork leg over his shoulder.

"Are… are you sure?" she whimpered.

Aldermaston nodded. "Somebody, somewhere, is playing a stupid prank. It's nothing to worry about."

Mairi blinked, failing to suppress the tears. "Are you sure?"
"Yes."

Her eyes stared at the leg over his left shoulder. "Then why is my husband's wedding ring wedged between its toes? And where is my husband?"

CHAPTER FOUR

"There you are, darling!" In a side room of the King James Hotel, Lavinia Farquhar-Cordell rose from the red leather armchair and air-kissed Felicity's cheeks. "We thought you'd got cold feet, as this is your first food festival as President of the Ladies' Legion. I was about to step into the breach. Again."

Felicity eyed Lavinia cautiously. She'd stepped into the role of President of the Ladies' Legion after the sudden death of Felicity's mother-in-law. And she'd enjoyed it. So when the Ladies' Legion voted a few months later for Felicity to be President, Lavinia made no effort at hiding the fact that her nose had been put out of joint. Although, such was the size of Lavinia's nose, hiding that was nigh on impossible.

Felicity held up her crutch. "Not cold feet, but broken toes."

Lavinia looked aghast. "Darling! How awful! Whatever happened? Here, take my seat."

She helped Felicity ease into the chair, which groaned more than her as she sank into it.

"Stubbed them against a piece of furniture," Felicity lied.

"Amazing how much damage a walnut Chippendale sideboard can inflict."

Lavinia perched on the end of a matching three-seater sofa, already occupied by three other Ladies' Legion members.

"You should sack Cartwright," Lavinia suggested. "All furniture should be returned to its rightful place after dusting behind it." Her staccato laugh machine-gunned her joke.

Felicity smiled politely. "Now, ladies. Time presses on. Remind me, where are we in the running order?"

Heidi Yail, at the other end of the three-seater, shuffled forward on the cushion. She peered at the clipboard on her lap, through her half-moon reading glasses. "The Ladies' Legion tent will serve home-made refreshments during festival hours. Kitty here," Heidi gestured to the young, long brown-haired farmer's wife sat beside her, "has made enough mouthwatering scones to feed everyone attending the festival twice over."

Lavinia snorted. "We'll scone them to death!"

"This afternoon, in the Food Theatre Marquee," Heidi continued, before Lavinia could take another breath and drown her with a second round of high-pitched laughs, "the celebrity chef, Bœuf Boucher, will run a cookery demonstration on three different ways to stuff a petits pois, and then tomorrow we'll host the traditional Festival Bake Off at 4pm."

Margaret Hillbrow, sandwiched between Lavinia and Kitty, leant forward, pulling at the hem of her navy skirt as she did so. "Have you decided which Bake Off categories you'll be entering, Your Ladyship?"

Felicity wrinkled her nose. "Baking isn't really my forte—"

"But you *must*, Your Ladyship!" Margaret interrupted. "It's tradition."

Heidi peered over her reading glasses. "The President of the Ladies' Legion is expected to win at least one category."

Felicity's toes throbbed. *Win?* At least *one* category? "I've been doing some baking," she began, "but I'm sure you ladies are of a far higher standard than I ever will be."

Margaret cocked her head to one side. "That's for the judge to decide. A Ladies' Legion President is expected to lead. Your late mother-in-law, God rest her soul," Margaret signed a cross against her chest, forehead and shoulders, "was a dab hand at a Mortiforde Sponge. She won that category every year for fifteen years. One year she even won the pork pie category, too."

Felicity's toes throbbed. She didn't like the way this conversation was going.

"Look, I do not expect to be given preferential treatment as President. I may be the Marchioness, but when it comes to the judging, I expect it to be impartial."

Heidi shifted to the edge of the cushion. "If I may, Your Ladyship, the judging of each category in the Ladies' Legion Bake Off has always been blind and, therefore, impartial. Indeed, the celebrity chef is our judge, so there's no opportunity for impropriety at all. The previous Marchioness was a legitimate winner in at least one category *every* year."

Margaret patted Felicity's knee. "And we have high expectations for you! So, which categories were you thinking of entering?"

"Er …" Felicity's stomach wrestled with the unease growing inside it. "As it's my first year, I thought best to start small. Just the one category."

Margaret clapped her hands excitedly. "One category! What confidence. What true strength to put all of your eggs in one basket."

"Or mixing bowl!" Lavinia screamed, before firing off another round of laughter.

"I thought," Felicity gazed at the ornate plasterwork on the ceiling of the King James Hotel, "of entering the savoury pie category."

Suddenly, all four ladies gawped silently at her for several seconds, until Lavinia rose to her feet and turned to those sitting on the leather sofa.

"You heard her, ladies. Her Ladyship has opted for the savoury pie category. That can mean only one thing."

All four ladies declared in unison, "Boor Pie!"

Felicity's eyes widened. Her stomach gurgled. Her broken toes pulsated painfully.

Heidi scribbled on her clipboard briefly, then stood. "Your Ladyship, only a true leader would contemplate tackling such an iconic, historic dish. We are honoured to have you as President."

Margaret and Kitty also stood, whereupon all four curtsied simultaneously.

Lavinia leant close and whispered, "Muck this one up, My Lady, and you won't be President for long."

∾

Aldermaston peered back through the chain curtain and came face-to-face with Daniel.

"What's happened?" Daniel looked over Aldermaston's shoulder.

Aldermaston pushed him back into the shop. "Another pig leg. But with Jock's wedding ring wedged between its toes."

"Definitely his ring, is it?"

Aldermaston sighed. Only an unmarried young man would ask such a question. "Shut the door, and turn the sign round to closed. Mairi's shaken. She won't be serving any customers today."

A powerful pressure in the small of Aldermaston's back shoved him forcibly from behind. Mairi pushed past and wagged a bloody finger under Daniel's nose.

"You'll do no such thing, lad. This is *our* business, and *we* decide when to shut up shop." She returned behind the counter and put her hands on her hips. "I'm sorry, Your Lordship, but we're out of wild boar at the moment. I can probably get some more in for Her Ladyship on Tuesday. But that'll be too late for the Ladies' Legion Bake Off tomorrow afternoon."

Aldermaston leant against the top of the glass counter. "Mairi, you've had a shock. Close the shop. We must call PC Norton."

Mairi lunged. Her hands grabbed Aldermaston's camouflage jacket collar, and she pulled him up onto tiptoes. Her face was so close he could see that the small lamb-chop-shaped mole on the left of her chin had four thick black hairs sprouting from it. "In twenty minutes' time, our busiest trading weekend of the year starts. It's what keeps us financially afloat for the rest of the year. If we close now, then Seth Shepherd or Peggy Farmer will win the Best Borderlandshire Burger competition, and *I'm* not letting that happen. Not when we're the defending champions for the last three years running. The only way Seth Shepherd will get his hands on the Best Borderlandshire Burger Trophy is if he cuts off my hands so I can't serve customers. Got that?"

Aldermaston nodded. Mairi released her grip, and his heels returned to the red-tiled floor. She straightened her hairnet. "I'm sorry, Your Lordship. I didn't mean to manhandle you so publicly."

"You're in shock." He paused. "Could Seth be behind Jock's disappearance?"

Mairi untied the strings on her blue and white apron and then retied them again, tighter. "Wouldn't put it past him." She checked outside the shop window. "He approached us a few months ago, wanting to fix the competition."

Daniel leant against the glass counter. "How do you fix a competition that's judged by twenty thousand festival-goers?"

Mairi turned and disappeared out the back. She soon returned with a small paper plate with an inch-thick piece of cooked beefburger and handed it to Daniel.

Daniel looked at Aldermaston. His Adam's apple bobbed.

"Go on, then," Aldermaston encouraged.

Daniel took the burger piece between his finger and thumb and hesitated.

"Just eat the damn thing!" Mairi snapped.

Daniel closed his eyes and threw it into his mouth. Slowly, he chewed, then his face contorted, and he spat it back out into his hand. "Eurrggghhh!"

Mairi grabbed his hand and shook the masticated contents back onto the paper plate. "Sorry, did I put a bit *too* much salt on that?"

Daniel's tongue tried desperately to wash away the excess sodium chloride.

She turned to Aldermaston. "*That* was Seth's idea. Maybe not quite as much salt as I put on that bit, but you get the point. Be heavy-handed with the seasoning and you can influence the voters' decision."

"I don't understand." Daniel frowned. "Seth Shepherd planned to over-season his competitors' burgers. How?"

Mairi stared at Aldermaston, but nodded at Daniel. "He for real?" She looked Daniel straight in the face. "No. Seth wanted us to come to a gentlemen's agreement where we would decide which of us would win each year, leaving the other two parties to over-season their burgers."

"Would that have worked?" Daniel rubbed a handkerchief across his salt-soaked taste buds.

Mairi sighed. "Doesn't matter. Jock and I weren't interested. We've won the last three years on the trot. Peggy Farmer was interested. But she's not won the competition for five years."

Aldermaston checked his watch. "The festival is about to

open, and I haven't changed. We're going to have to dash." Aldermaston grabbed Daniel's arm. "Mairi, much as it pains me to say this, tell PC Norten about Jock's wedding ring. There's no rational reason why Jock would take it off, is there?"

Mairi shook her head. "Thirty-six years ago, it was the perfect fit. We've both filled out a bit since then. Couldn't take it off if he wanted to." Her eyes moistened.

"When did you last see Jock?" Aldermaston asked.

Mairi blinked back the tears. "Last night, in bed. When I woke up this morning, he was gone."

"Gone?" Aldermaston frowned.

"He often gets up early and goes for a walk. He loves the solitude before a hectic day in the shop."

"Does he walk in Mortiforde Woods?" Aldermaston remembered Seth's comment about Jock knowing where his hide was.

Mairi nodded.

"What time does he usually get back?"

Mairi wrung her hands, nervously. "Usually six-thirty. We have breakfast at seven, and are out the back here by half seven, ready to open the shop at eight. Technically, he's not been missing for four hours yet, but his wedding ring…"

Aldermaston glanced at his watch. The festival was minutes away from its official opening. Mairi was right. Jock should be here, ready for the busiest trading weekend of the year. So, where was he, and why was he no longer in possession of his wedding ring?

～

"The least she could have done was offered me a glass of water," Daniel complained as they stepped out onto the pavement.

Aldermaston sighed. "There's no time to go home and get

changed. I'll have to do the official opening dressed like this." He pulled the hem of his camouflage jacket taut and zipped it up to his chin. His hand flattened his thinning hair. "Go find yourself a bottle of water somewhere. And try Shepherds for some boar meat, will you?" Aldermaston slipped Daniel a twenty-pound note. "Meet me in the hospitality marquee, over in Market Square, after the official opening."

Daniel took the cash and pushed his way through the crowds, struggling to move as festival-goers shouldered their way past, jostling him from one tourist to another, until they spat him out, like a piece of gristle, in front of the convenience store on the corner of the Square.

It was quieter here. Tourists weren't interested in the chain store's offerings when over two hundred artisan stalls filled Market Square and the castle's grounds. He grabbed a bottle of mineral water, collected the change, and hurried out of the store. Shepherds was along the High Street, a grand name for a narrow road, wide enough only for one vehicle and a set of yellow lines on either side. But it was the main thoroughfare linking Market Square with Southgate Street and the Buttermarket.

Daniel battled through the flow of tourists heading in the opposite direction, until he reached the doors of Shepherds Butchers, on the corner of Southgate Street and High Street.

He paused briefly by the entrance, away from the flow of people, with his back to the door and unscrewed the water bottle. His eyes closed in ecstasy as he tipped back his head and gulped mouthful, upon wonderful, thirst-quenching mouthful of salt-swilling water.

SMACK! Somebody collided with him from behind. The bottle flew high into the air, showering its contents across the gathering crowds. Daniel fell to the pavement, but he looked up in time to see a young athletic woman in black leggings, a pink sports bra and a pink baseball cap running away. She stopped momentarily and glanced back at him, her blonde, shoulder-length ponytail flying high as her head spun. Her right hand grabbed her left wrist, then her eyes fixed in his direction. Daniel followed her gaze.

On the pavement, a metallic bracelet with shiny trinkets sparkled on the flagstones. Grabbing it before a passing tourist inadvertently trod on it, he turned towards the runner, holding aloft his find. But she was gone. Digested by the crowds.

Daniel stood and dusted himself down. His bottle of water was nowhere to be seen, kicked away by festival-goers' feet.

A calming atmosphere enveloped him as he stepped into the butchers.

"Can I help you?" An elderly woman peered over the counter. Her white hair was tied tightly in a bun and covered in a netted head garment.

"Do you have a kilo of boar meat?" Daniel enquired.

The woman shook her head. "Sold out, I'm afraid. Be a couple of days before we get any more stock." She suddenly spotted a small cardboard box perched at the other end of the counter. She looked at Daniel and pointed at it. "Was that here when you came in? I only stepped out the back a minute ago."

"I think so."

The woman frowned before picking it up and examining it. "There's no delivery name or address." She looked up at Daniel again. "Try Trotters, or Peggy Farmer. They might have some." She turned and then disappeared into the back of the shop with her delivery.

Daniel pulled the bracelet from his suit packet. He was convinced the runner had come out of this shop. Had she left the parcel? He inspected the bracelet and spotted the clasp was broken. The simple silver chain was studded with a selection of small silver charms: a bunch of flowers, a spade, a pheasant, a pig, a toadstool, and a plain silver disc, about the size of a penny. Engraved across it were two letters: MB.

∼

"How long until it all kicks off?" Tibby perched herself on the edge of their prep table.

Ashton checked his watch. "Fifteen minutes." He grabbed a water bottle from under the stall and swigged several mouthfuls.

Tibby pulled her phone from her pocket. Time to chase Lord Mortiforde. She called the Festival Committee office.

"Can I speak with Lord Mortiforde, please?" she began, as soon as it was answered. "It's about an urgent issue I was discussing with him ninety minutes ago."

There was a rustling as the mouthpiece was covered, before it suddenly cleared.

"Ms Gillard. Can I call you back after the official opening?"

"No, you can't. I want to know what action has been taken concerning the pig's heart dumped on our stall first thing this morning."

A deep sigh echoed in her earpiece.

"Lord Mortiforde, there are reasons why the local authority issues food hygiene regulations. I asked you in your capacity as Head of the Borderer's Guild, and therefore, in charge of this food festival, to get the culprits shut down for breach of regulations, and you haven't done it!"

"We don't have proof yet that the heart was left there by a butcher, Ms Gillard," Aldermaston clarified. "I'm sorry if things are not moving as quickly as you'd like, but I have asked the local authority to investigate. Once they've determined where they think the heart came from, then we can determine the most appropriate action, if any—"

"What do you mean, *if any*? It was a deliberate attempt to disrupt our sales today because the butchers are worried about our vegetarian burger."

"Ms Gillard, if you could just—"

"No, I bloody won't! Only a butcher could have sent that. The safest course of action would be to shut down all three butchers while the local authority carries out its investigations."

"Ms Gillard, I'm sorry, but I've got to go. I can assure you the matter is being looked into."

"You're not shutting down the butchers, Lord Mortiforde, because the Best Borderlandshire Burger competition is an integral part of your precious food festival, and—"

The line went dead.

"He's hung up on me!" Tibby stared at her phone.

Ashton tutted. "Everyone knows the butchers are up and about early. I was here at six to set up and it was waiting for us then."

"Where exactly did you find it?"

Ashton pointed. "Right where you're sitting. On the food prep table."

Tibby jumped off the table corner she was perched against, grabbed a cloth and some disinfectant, and began cleaning again.

He sighed. "For what it's worth, Tibbs," Ashton drawled, "I think you're spot on. The burger competition is what draws the huge crowds. They like the competition, you see. Tourists love traipsing round this historic town, finding the butchers and testing the new burger flavours. It's in Lord Mortiforde's interests to keep the competition going."

Tibby paced the floor. "It's a flagrant bias towards meat! This means war!"

∽

Felicity shut the door of the telephone cubicle in the King James Hotel reception area. No larger than a cupboard, it contained a comfortable green-suede upholstered Georgian chair, a list of useful telephone numbers typed on a sheet of paper pinned to the wall, and a collection of tourist attraction leaflets. Beside her, on a small telephone table, stood a working Bakelite phone, much to the amusement of many American tourists. Most guests, however, did what Felicity had done and pulled out their mobile phone.

The call connected. Through a small window in the door, Felicity watched Lavinia, Kitty, Margaret and Heidi laughing and giggling as they made their way out onto the street. How come nobody had mentioned anything about the President winning categories in the Bake Off event at the Food Festival before? Aldermaston's mother had never mentioned her baking success at the previous fifteen food festivals.

The ringing stopped and Felicity was about to vent her frustration when the dulcet tones of Aldermaston's voicemail filled her ear, followed by a short beep.

"Aldermaston, ring me when you get this. Somehow, I've just been shafted by your mother. I never knew she was a dab hand at conjuring up the best Mortiforde Sponge in town. Something she managed fifteen years in succession, apparently. How come we never saw a slice?"

She drew a deep breath, held it momentarily, and then let it out. Slowly.

"Anyway, regarding the boar meat I asked you to get. I know I asked for a kilo, but that was before I knew that I was supposed to win this bloody Bake Off category. Get me five kilos, please, if not more. Got that?"

She hung up. It was times like this when she begrudged her parents-in-law's fatal accident nearly two years ago… and her mother-in-law's dalliance with a mystery admirer some forty-seven years earlier. If it wasn't for those two facts, she'd still be the ordinary Felicity who married Aldermaston twenty years ago, in the belief that Basildon, as the older brother, would inherit the Marquess of Mortiforde title.

But now her mission in life was, apparently, to make the perfect Boor Pie to maintain tradition. Because that was important to the people of the Welsh Borders. Tradition. A sense of passing on the baton from one generation to the next. But the way her culinary skills were operating at the moment, the Boor Pie baton would only be passed on if she could cook something that was physically possible to lift.

She glanced at her painful foot. Cartwright would have to come and collect her. At least he could be relied upon, even if her husband couldn't.

⁓

"There you are!" Lisa cried as she grabbed Aldermaston's elbow.

Together, they negotiated the stuffy and audibly oppressive environs of the hospitality marquee, packed with festival volunteers, dignitaries, and members of the press.

"Abigail is introducing Bœuf to the press, festival volunteers and the Borderer's Guild,"␣Lisa explained, "or rather, she's *trying* to do the introductions. Not great when she doesn't know who anybody is yet."

Aldermaston sighed. Chief Executives always slipped into leadership mode when there were dignitaries, celebrities, and press about.

They squeezed through the press pack, most of whom were already sampling the local ale in plastic pint glasses, and arrived beside Abigail, standing next to Bœuf, just as Cissy Warbouys was introducing herself. She'd stopped knitting briefly and tucked her size eight knitting needles and ball of blue wool under her left armpit.

"I'm Cecilia, although everyone calls me Cissy," she declared, taking Bœuf's hand and curtseying.

"What are you knitting?" Bœuf pointed to Cissy's armpit.

She retrieved her creation, tucked the ball of wool into her orange cardigan pocket and held aloft her creation. It was an unusual shape, with numerous edges and many large holes. "Sometimes these things take time to evolve."

Aldermaston stifled a smirk. Many of Cissy's creations were undefinable.

Bœuf, though, clearly knew how to handle such people. He nodded. "Like you, sometimes I know not what I am making, but I just throw some ingredients into a pot and see what 'appens. Sometimes it is a masterpiece, and yet other times…" he held his hands in the air and shrugged his shoulders, "… it is not. Experimentation is the soul of creativity."

Cissy's cheeks flushed. "In that case, Mr Boucher, whatever my creation turns out to be, it is yours."

He bent forward, took Cissy's hand, and lightly kissed the back of her fingers. "That is an honour. Thank you."

"Your Lordship. What perfect timing." Abigail hooked her arm through Bœuf's and pulled him away from someone she clearly thought was mad. "Mr Boucher, may I introduce you to the Marquess of Mortiforde?"

Aldermaston shook Bœuf's hand. "Mr Boucher, thank you for coming all this way to be our guest of honour. We're delighted to host you for our two-day event, and trust you will be amazed at the produce we have to offer here."

Bœuf bowed. "Your Lordship, it is an honour to be here."

"Have you met everyone from the Borderer's Guild?" Aldermaston enquired.

Lisa cut in. "Everyone except Gerald." She turned and waved across the crowded marquee, beckoning a rotund man in his mid-fifties with black hair. "GERALD!"

He waved a pint glass high in the air and pushed his way through the throng.

"Gerald Lockmount is the local estate agent," Aldermaston explained to both Bœuf and Abigail. "Family business. His grandfather established it. Gerald has run it for the last twenty years."

Bœuf nodded. "Such threads through time are important, *n'est-ce pas*? Makes one feel part of something much bigger."

Abigail sighed. "Not everything is about the past. We must look forward. Change is inevitable. Continuous improvement, we call it. Get rid of the dead wood on a frequent basis."

Aldermaston turned to Bœuf. "Ms Mayedew is originally from London, but has only recently moved to Mortiforde. She is yet to experience the essence of traditional rural life in the Welsh Borders."

Abigail glanced sideways at Aldermaston.

Gerald Lockmount blundered into the group, spilling some of his beer at everyone's feet. "Terribly sorry about that. Didn't pay for it, so all's not lost. What can I do for you?" He looked at them one by one, but his eyes lingered on Abigail.

"I say, you've got yourself a fine catch there!" He nudged Bœuf with his elbow and then winked at Aldermaston.

"Gerald," Aldermaston gestured to Bœuf, "may I introduce you to our celebrity guest of honour, Mr Bœuf Boucher, and this is Ms Mayedew," his hand took Gerald's gaze up from Abigail's chest, "who is the new Chief Executive at the council, starting Monday."

Gerald ignored Bœuf and shook Abigail's hand. "Our new Chief Exec, heh? Well, you're a gorgeous turn-up for the books. Come far?"

Abigail pulled her hand out of Gerald's grip. "London. Borough of Thameside, to be precise."

Gerald sucked air between his teeth. "Thameside, heh? Bet you made a killing there." His free hand rummaged in his jacket pocket and pulled out a business card. "Must mean you've a nice tidy sum to spend on a property round here, then. Give me a call, and I'll sort you out something special." He looked over both shoulders and then leant closer to Abigail.

"And for the right client, I'm happy to discuss property options and viewings over dinner. I know a nice little place down by the—"

"Gerald, we must get on," Aldermaston interjected. "The festival is about to start and Mr Boucher is needed."

"Yes, of course, Your Lordship." He winked at Abigail. "Call me," he mouthed. Then he turned to Bœuf. "Tell me, do you know Saint Benno? Got a wonderful little gîte there I use in the summer. Fantastic little fishing village."

Bœuf threw his hands in the air, as if praising a higher deity. "*Mais oui*. Saint Benno's seafood is magnifique! Ze Mediterranean coastline there is out of zis world."

"Forgive me, but time is pressing," Abigail interrupted. "Perhaps we should grab our seats, while Lord Mortiforde takes Mr Boucher up onto the stage for the official opening."

"We need you on stage too, Abigail," said Aldermaston.

"Me? Whatever for?"

"The food festival is a partnership between the Borderer's Guild and the local council. As the authority's new Chief Exec, I'm sure you appreciate the merits of exploiting all good media opportunities." Aldermaston grinned. He decided to go in for the kill. "Part of the job, isn't it? Or are you not playing at Chief Exec until you officially start on Monday?"

Abigail sneered. "This way, is it?" She pointed to some steps leading up to the stage area.

Aldermaston nodded, then watched as she gestured to Bœuf to follow her on stage, where Jillian was already waiting.

Gerald belched right beside Aldermaston's ear. "Better out than in, as my grandfather always used to say." He slapped Aldermaston hard on the back, then leant close to Aldermaston's ear again. "Weird chap, that French bloke."

"Oh?"

"My gîte in Saint Benno."

Aldermaston frowned. "What about it?"

"He seemed to think Saint Benno is on the Mediterranean."

"Isn't it?"

Gerald shook his head. "Brittany. You'd think a Frenchman would know that, wouldn't you?"

Aldermaston pondered. Ask anyone in Britain to identify Mortiforde on the map and most would struggle. Yet, instead of shrugging his shoulders in true Gaelic fashion, Bœuf had said he knew Saint Benno intimately, when clearly he didn't. Why would someone do that?

CHAPTER FIVE

Tibby Gillard grabbed Ashton's broad shoulder and pulled herself onto an upturned wooden fruit pallet. That was better. She could now see over the crowd's heads, all staring in the same direction. Beside the hospitality marquee was an awninged mini-stage, where a single microphone stand failed miserably to claim the centre of attention. Bœuf Boucher stood a few feet behind it, and to his left, was Lord Mortiforde. Also onstage were the council's Chief Archivist and another tall woman hovering in the background.

Tibby nudged Ashton. "Who's the beanpole in the fancy dress? Looks like she should be on some Parisian fashion show."

Ashton stoked his chin. "Bœuf's wife?"

Tibby shook her head. "Divorced. Apparently."

"Mind you, I'd be one happy runner bean racing up that."

Tibby watched Ashton's facial muscles twitch as his imagination ran riot. Was there a Mrs Harcourt?

Bœuf tapped the microphone. "Ladies and gentlemen!" His voice echoed through the loudspeakers and rebounded off the Grade II listed buildings lining Market Square, before continuing its journey into mid-Wales. "It is with ze greatest of pleasures that I now declare ze Mortiforde Food Festival officially open!"

Jillian and the Beanpole dashed to the front of the stage and suspended a long string of pork and chilli, with a hint of coriander, sausages between them. Aldermaston handed Bœuf a pair of round-ended safety scissors. The celebrity chef grabbed two of the sausages in one hand and attempted to slice through the connective collagen. The scissors wrestled with the rubbery skin protein and lost. Frustrated, Bœuf grabbed a sausage in each hand and slipped the connective tissue between his teeth and chewed. Seconds later, the collagen broke, and he dropped both sausage ends to the floor with a flourish. The Beanpole dropped her end of the sausage string and stared at her hand with disgust. Then she sniffed her fingertips.

Tibby cringed, remembering the last time she'd touched a sausage. Then she grinned. The Beanpole was one of *them*.

A huge cheer rose from the crowd, followed by a raucous applause.

Aldermaston stepped up to the microphone. "Ladies and gentlemen," he began. The frenzied bubbling crowd noise diminished to a low background simmer. "Firstly, I'd like to thank Bœuf Boucher for coming here today, all the way from France, to open our great festival. We're honoured to have such a distinguished chef here."

Another cheer rose from the crowd.

"Bœuf will run some cookery demonstrations in the Food Theatre Marquee inside the castle grounds today at two-thirty and four-thirty. So if you've always fancied flambéing a fig, or blowtorching a Brussels sprout, you know where to head. He'll also be judging the best home-made produce in the Mortiforde Ladies League tent tomorrow afternoon at four o'clock."

Ashton snorted. "Sod what's happening tomorrow. We've got veggie burgers to sell today." He clapped his hands together and rubbed them in anticipation. "Bloody Lord of the Manor never knows when to shut up."

"And before I let you go," Aldermaston's tannoyed voice boomed through the market stalls, "although she doesn't start until Monday, please give a warm welcome to Ms Abigail Mayedew, Borderlandshire District Council's new Chief Executive." Aldermaston held out his right arm, directing the audience's gaze towards Abigail, who was still sniffing her fingertips.

Tibby watched the Beanpole raise a hand high in the air and wave royally. There was a polite smattering of applause. Tibby beamed. Even better if they could get the Council's new Chief Exec to join their cause.

"And finally," Aldermaston's voice permeated the air again, "our Chief Archivist, Jillian Jones, has something she'd like to say."

Ashton's chin dropped into his chest despondently. "Whatever has that woman got to say that could be of the slightest interest to any of us?" He started mock snoring.

"Good morning, ladies and gentlemen." Jillian's voice wavered slightly, unused to public speaking. "At four o'clock this afternoon, our Food History Marquee will open, in the castle grounds. There are lots of fascinating objects and information to be seen relating to food in Mortiforde over the centuries. And I'm especially delighted to announce that the Royal Palaces Collection has lent us an original recipe book, used here at Mortiforde Castle during the seventeenth century, which gives a real insight into the food the chefs cooked here for the Royal family, when this was a royal residence."

Ashton stopped snoring.

"What's really exciting," continued Jillian, "is the diary section, written by the head chef, about life in the castle during this time. This is the first time this wonderful historic document has returned to Mortiforde in four hundred years, so if you'd like to see it unveiled, then visit our Food History Marquee at four o'clock today. Thank you."

Ashton rummaged in his pocket and retrieved his smartphone. His thumb danced across the screen.

"Problem?" Tibby enquired.

"I've… er… got to nip home. Family emergency." He shrugged his shoulders. "Family is family." He rammed his phone back into his trouser pocket. "Won't be long." He untied the green apron and pulled it over his head.

"You can't leave me now!" Tibby grabbed Ashton's wrist, but he yanked it straight from her grip. "We're just about to face an onslaught of customers."

Ashton avoided her gaze and pushed his way through the people crowding the stall. Seconds later, they swallowed him.

Tibby fumed. Bloody men! Sometimes they were as much use as eating rice noodles with a cocktail stick.

∽

"How dare you!" Abigail's incredulous face stared at Aldermaston. "That's *not* how a new Chief Executive should be introduced to the local community! These things have to be staged-managed, usually by an outside management consultancy rather than the council's own internal PR department, but definitely not by some bumbling aristocratic twat!" She paused and took several deep breaths. "You do know that as a result of your actions, there'll be a photo of me, on this stage, sniffing my fingertips, on the front page of the local newspaper before the day is out, don't you?"

Aldermaston watched Abigail's nostrils flare as wide as the ruff round her neck. She wagged a finger in front of his face. His nose twitched.

"My office, eleven o'clock sharp." She turned and stormed off the stage, albeit a little cautiously, as she hobbled down the steps in her four-inch heels.

He sighed. She was definitely concerned about image. Hers. Especially if it involved an outside firm of public relations consultants whose fee would warrant an additional ten pounds on the local council tax bill for the next four years.

Aldermaston gazed out across Market Square and saw the crowds thronging the market stalls and surrounding shops. At least the festival was underway. This was the first year he'd been involved right from the start. His father had already organised most of last year's festival before his untimely death.

A warm sense of comfort enveloped him. Who'd have thought over twenty years ago that a food festival with fewer than a dozen stalls would develop into this? It had grown exponentially… much like portion sizes generally.

Rural communities had to work hard to survive these days. Events like this were crucial. It wasn't just the butchers relying on this weekend's trade. The whole town needed the food festival to be a success.

Lisa grabbed Aldermaston's arm. "Daniel's just told me about Jock Trotter's wedding ring."

Daniel suddenly appeared beside him. "No boar meat at Shepherds, by the way."

Lisa crossed her arms. "This isn't just about threatening notes now, is it?"

Aldermaston brought his finger to his lips and then pulled them away from the microphone on stage. "Where's Bœuf?"

Lisa indicated left. "Festival volunteers are looking after him."

"In that case," Aldermaston continued, "start looking through those shopfront grant scheme applications. After what Mairi told us earlier, there's clearly some rivalry between the butchers to win this bloody burger competition." He pointed at

Daniel. "Go back to Mairi. Find out where Jock goes for his early morning wanders in Mortiforde Woods. Then, head to the council offices and help Lisa."

"Lord Mortiforde," gasped Jillian, behind him. "Sorry to interrupt. Can I give you this?" She handed him the thick white envelope he'd originally pulled out of the Royal Palaces Collection parcel earlier.

"What is it?"

"It's the English translation of the Royal Recipe Collection. It makes such fascinating reading. Might help with your speech later." She clasped his arm with both hands. "The chef's diary section is a revelation! I've only read a few pages, but I'll tell you more at lunchtime."

Aldermaston folded the envelope lengthways and slipped it inside his camouflage jacket. There wasn't time to read it now, but he knew how important it was to Jillian that he looked excited about reading it.

"Excellent! What time are we lunching with Bœuf?"

"One fifteen. Shall we meet here?"

Aldermaston nodded.

"Must dash, Your Lordship." She disappeared into the ever-mushrooming crowd of visitors mingling among the stalls.

At least the Mortiforde Royal Recipe Collection had taken her mind off the earlier parcel's contents. Perhaps Jillian had the right approach to life. After all, she only focussed on the past and, although that included some pretty obnoxious characters, at least they'd usually been dead for a century or two. For him, being Lord of the Manor meant dealing with the present's problems. And the way today was going, the present had several big problems that needed dealing with.

He checked his mobile, saw Felicity's missed call, and gulped as he digested her message. Five kilos? His gut grumbled. Would Peggy Farmer have five kilos of the stuff? He sighed. Sometimes, the local Lord had to be seen going through the motions, even though it was a waste of time. Something his father referred to as constipated action: a lot of energy for very little movement.

∽

"I've told you what you want to know. Now get out of my shop!" Mairi Trotter flung her hand holding the meat cleaver in the direction of the shop doorway. "These customers need serving, and I wish my husband was here to help me!"

Daniel sprinted from the shop, not easy now it was packed with festival-goers eager to try the Trotter's all-new Woodland Burger.

Pavement space was at a premium too, as the crowds hovered around the Trotter's butchery window, mingling with those sauntering round Market Square. A flash of pink caught his eye. His double-take confirmed it was *her*. The runner from Shepherds. Black leggings, a pink sports bra, and a pink baseball cap. Was she talking to someone? She leaned closer, and offered a cheek for a kiss, but to whom he couldn't see.

His hand rummaged in his suit jacket pocket for the silver charm bracelet as he stared at her. She looked early twenties, average height, with a fit body in both senses of the word. The lightly tanned bare skin on her upper arms was silky smooth and taut. The firmness of her thighs, wrapped in those black Lycra leggings, only confirmed she was a regular runner, and her abdominal muscles flattened her bare stomach without revealing themselves. His eyes lingered…

"Excuse me!" he yelled, clutching the bracelet tightly in his fingers and holding his hand high in the air.

Several passing festival-goers stopped and turned, wondering what the commotion was. But he remained focussed on the pink-capped runner. She glanced towards him and spotted the bracelet between his upheld fingers.

She bolted. The pink sports bra blurred as her supple body weaved its way between the crowds.

Daniel soon lost sight of her. He twisted awkwardly, attempting to see round and between pedestrians walking up Weir Street. He propelled himself through the thronging crowds, dodging tourists and visitors like a football striker snaking his way through the opposition's defence. Weir Street dropped steeply towards the River Morte, which should have quickened his speed, but he was travelling in the opposite direction to the main flow of tourists, heading towards Market Square.

Occasionally, he jumped into the air, scanning for her pink baseball cap. But on this bright, sunny October morning, all he could see in the split second of extra height were the first and second storeys of the fine Georgian properties lining both sides of the road.

Dejected, he turned and wandered back up Weir Street, swept along by the crowd. Why had she run? She was definitely the same girl who'd run into him outside Shepherds Butchers. Or rather, she was the girl who'd run into him as she was running away *from* the shop. So, had she delivered that parcel to Shepherds? If so, that begged another question. What was in the parcel?

∽

Aldermaston wagged his finger at the full-length mirror in his dressing room at Tugford Hall. "You have to understand, Ms Mayedew. Here in the Welsh Borders, things work differently than in London. You'd do well to get to know our ways first, before imposing the law of London upon us."

He hooked his thumbs under the waistband of his navy boxer shorts and pulled them higher, narrowing the gap between the top of the waistband and his belly button. Then he pulled in his stomach. A bit. Aldermaston stared at his middle-age sag reflection. It was nowhere near as bad as other men, but the sag and spare tyre were definitely setting up home together.

He relaxed and his stomach dropped, as did the waistband of his boxers. What should he wear for his meeting with Abigail? It ought to be the full tweed jacket and tie set. If she could dress to impress, then so could he. Dress code was about respecting oneself, but also those with whom you were meeting. *Respect your stakeholders*, his father had always said. *Respecting someone is not the same as liking them.* He'd only known Abigail for a couple of hours. He hadn't had a chance to get to like her yet.

"Somehow, Abigail," Aldermaston said to the mirror as he slipped on his beige-checked shirt and knotted his Radnor green tie around his neck, "gut instinct tells me the two of us just aren't going to get on."

"And they have the audacity to call me the eccentric one, little bro'."

Aldermaston spun round to see Basildon leaning against the doorway of his bedroom.

"What can I do for you, Basildon?"

"You can stand still while I straighten that for a start, old bean." Basildon stepped forward and wiggled Aldermaston's tie, then pulled it taut. "That's better. So, who's Abigail?"

Aldermaston crossed his arms. "How long have you been standing there?"

Basildon beamed. "Long enough. Who's Abigail?"

"The council's new Chief Exec."

"Is she now? Where's she from?"

"London Borough of Thameside."

His eyebrows arched. "Could be useful."

Aldermaston sighed. "Basildon, she led a London borough local authority. She won't have connections with MI5 or MI6."

"How would you know?" He turned and slowly walked back to the door. "Is she coming tonight?"

Aldermaston slipped a finger between his shirt collar and pulled. "We hadn't issued an invitation. Weren't expecting her until Monday. But I'm meeting her shortly, so I'll issue an invitation then."

"Black tie?"

Aldermaston nodded. "We are dining at seven."

"Can't wait." Basildon grinned.

Aldermaston's eyes narrowed. "What are you up to?"

Basildon turned to leave. "I'll let Cartwright know there'll be one more for dinner then. When he gets back from town having collected Lady Mortiforde, that is. Something to do with broken toes." He left the dressing room.

Aldermaston called after him. "You didn't answer my question."

The phone on his Sheraton dressing table interrupted him.

"Thank heavens I've found you, Your Lordship."

"Mrs Shepherd. Whatever's the matter?"

"Did you see Seth this morning?"

"Yes. A couple of hours ago."

"Was Maisie with him?"

"Yes." Aldermaston sneered, remembering the financial cost of this morning's encounter. "Are they not back yet?"

"Not really."

Aldermaston stared at his reflection in the mirror. "What do you mean, not *really*?"

"I know Seth's been back here. He left this morning's harvest in its usual place. But they've both disappeared. It doesn't make sense. We can't cope in the shop. I'm worried."

In the background, he heard a constant droning of customers in the butcher's shop. Then he heard a sniff, followed by Mrs Shepherd blowing her nose. "We had another delivery about half an hour ago."

That sinking feeling gurgled in Aldermaston's stomach. "Sorry. Did you say *another* delivery? Did you get a pig trotter earlier?"

"Did Seth not say? It came with the note he brought to show you."

Aldermaston closed his eyes. Why hadn't Seth mentioned the trotter? "Have you had another pig part delivered?"

"Not a pig part, Your Lordship. This one's human."

Aldermaston gulped. Human?

"It's Seth's!" Mrs Shepherd screamed. "Something terrible has happened. I know it has."

Aldermaston collapsed onto a chair. "Evie, what was in this second package?"

A huge wail blared down the earpiece. "Seth's moustache!"

∽

Once Felicity was safely ensconced in the rear of the silver Jaguar F-Pace, Cartwright slipped into the driver's seat.

"Tugford Hall, Your Ladyship?"

"Yes, please, Cartwright. I need a plan of action."

Cartwright eased the Jaguar through the barely wide-enough tunnel leading from the parking area at the rear of the King James Hotel to the main road. Now the festival was in full swing, pedestrians were coming at them from all directions.

Felicity bit her lip as she gazed through the window. Whatever made her think she could cook a decent Boor Pie?

"Anything I can help with, Your Ladyship?" Cartwright sped up as they reached the outskirts of town where pedestrian traffic was lighter.

Felicity tutted. "I never realised the Seventh Marchioness had such culinary finesse when it came to a Mortiforde Sponge."

"There are always ways and means, My Lady."

"Yes, but she was judged blindly, as I've learned today, to produce the best Mortiforde Sponge for fifteen years. Fifteen years!" Felicity shuffled in the leather seat. "Lavinia Farquhar-Cordell is itching for me to mess up. She wants me ousted as President. How the hell am I going to—"

She fixed her gaze at Cartwright's reflection in the rear-view mirror. "What do you mean? *Ways and means*."

Cartwright focussed on the road ahead, indicated, then turned off the main A492 towards Tugford Hall.

Felicity leant forward. "Cartwright, are you telling me the Seventh Marchioness cheated?"

Cartwright's eyes widened. "In forty years of service, I have never insinuated that a Lady of the Manor has ever—"

Felicity held up her hands. "Cartwright, I apologise."

Cartwright turned off the narrow single-track lane, in through the main gates of Tugford Hall. "Rarely does anyone achieve anything on their own, Your Ladyship." Cartwright pulled up outside the main entrance.

Felicity frowned. "I don't see where you're going with this."

Cartwright looked at her via the rearview mirror. "Some of the world's most outstanding individual achievements have involved teamwork."

Felicity shook her head. "Your point is?"

He looked over his shoulder. "Gold medal winners at the Olympics rarely achieve such success on their own. They might collect the medal. They might stand alone on the podium. But they don't get there on their own." He slipped out of the driver's door and wandered slowly round the rear of the Jaguar.

Felicity gathered her crutch. What was the man wittering on about? Cartwright opened the rear door as wide as it would go.

"Coaching, Your Ladyship."

Felicity swung her legs out of the car and awkwardly transferred her crutch through the doorway. "Coaching?"

Cartwright nodded. "Olympians are coached, My Lady. They have someone to guide and encourage them to deliver what they're capable of achieving. A true Olympian succeeds because they know they can't do it alone."

Felicity slid easily off the leather seats and onto her good foot and her crutch. "So, the Seventh Marchioness was coached!"

Cartwright smiled.

Felicity waved her crutch at him. "You coached her!"

Cartwright's smile broadened.

"Well, the bad news, Cartwright, is that I need a lot of coaching."

Cartwright closed the Jaguar's door. "Of course, My Lady. If I do say so myself, my grandmother's Mortiforde Sponge recipe is the best in the county."

Felicity hobbled towards the steps of Tugford Hall. "That may well be, Cartwright, but I'm not entering the Mortiforde Sponge category."

"You're not, My Lady?"

Felicity stopped at the bottom of Tugford Hall's steps and turned. "No. I'm entering the Boor Pie category."

She watched the colour drain from his face.

CHAPTER SIX

Aldermaston hovered outside the door to the Chief Exec's office. He knocked twice, then placed an ear against the door.

The previous Chief Exec, Nigel Hughes-Banes, occasionally shouted so loudly when beckoning staff that the entire county knew the comings and goings of his office.

Was Abigail a shouter or a delegator? Delegating would require her to buzz the Chief Exec's secretary, Pamela, on the intercom system. Aldermaston glanced at the empty desk to his left. Pamela had, quite understandably, assumed that as the new Chief Exec didn't officially start until Monday, this would be a sneaky opportunity to take an extra day's unauthorised annual leave.

Suddenly, the door swung open and Aldermaston found a considerably shorter Abigail eyeing up his earhole.

"Lord Mortiforde! Come in." She extended an arm into her new domain.

He realised why he hadn't heard her approaching, and why she was now shorter. No shoes.

"Take a seat." Abigail gestured towards her desk.

The offered chair was not the bright orange, plastic, child-sized school chair that Nigel had, which put victims at a height where their chins rested on top of the Chief Exec's desk. Abigail's was a comfortable-looking, black leather chair on a tubular chrome frame. He sank into it. It rocked backwards and forwards, if he didn't sit perfectly still.

Abigail slipped elegantly into her high-backed leather executive chair, with its perfectly positioned headrest and smooth-gliding castors. A few minor adjustments with her little toes, and she manoeuvred herself into position with an authoritative pose: elbows and forearms flat on the desk with both hands clasped together. She smiled. "Your Lordship."

"Please, call me Aldermaston when we're in private. The title still sits rather awkwardly with me."

"I think formality is an appropriate method of establishing boundaries and hierarchies, don't you, Your Lordship?" She smiled. Again.

Aldermaston took a deep breath. "Seeing as you're not officially Chief Executive until Monday, I believe first-name terms are more appropriate. Here in the Welsh Borders, we prefer a friendlier approach to life. It's more conducive to co-operative partnership working, wouldn't you say… Abigail?"

Her smile shrank and her eyes focussed on her clasped hands.

Aldermaston cast his eyes around the office. She'd only been here for a couple of hours and already it bore no resemblance to Nigel's den of deceit. While his desk had been a constant mess of files, papers, Post-it notes and a computer screen displaying the current game of Solitaire, Abigail's was clear, save for a new flatscreen monitor in the right-hand corner of the desk, a low, sleek keyboard, and a wireless mouse sitting on an official Borderlandshire District Council mouse mat. Borderlandshire District Council's logo comprised two rounded green hills, each a slightly different shade. When used the wrong way up, they looked like a bare bottom… quite appropriate considering the crap many council staff had to deal with in the line of duty.

Adjacent to the mouse mat was a silver wire mesh pen pot containing two Cross fountain pens, and in the left-hand corner of the desk was a silver photo frame. Aldermaston couldn't see the photo, but assumed it was probably of Abigail accompanied by the Prime Minister, or a member of the Royal family.

Abigail's head rose. Her pale blue eyes latched onto his. "I think we need to get one thing straight, Your Lordship." Her thumbs rose from her clasped hands, creating a triangular spire. "I detest the aristocracy."

Aldermaston crossed his arms. "But you don't know me yet."

Abigail's hands separated, and her fingers danced across the keyboard. She turned to her computer monitor. "You're the Eighth Marquess of Mortiforde, forty-four, married to Felicity, for twenty-three years, and have one son, Harry, aged seven. You reside at Tugford Hall, the ancestral family home, which you inherited less than two years ago when your father and mother were tragically killed in a road traffic accident involving a farm vehicle on the Mortiforde bypass."

Aldermaston was about to speak, but Abigail held a finger against her lips as her eyes remained fixed to her computer screen.

Her other middle finger trampolined on the keyboard's down arrow key. "Everyone assumed your older brother, Basildon, as your father's firstborn, would inherit the title. But he didn't, did he? He wasn't your *father's* firstborn, was he?"

Her eyes sparkled.

"In your spare time, you run a little wildlife photography business, and you also head up some quango called the Borderer's Guild, which uses a disproportionate amount of

Lisa Duddon's time." She stopped and looked up at him. "How am I doing so far?"

Aldermaston shuffled in his seat. It wobbled. "Whichever website you're viewing has the basic facts correct, although I'd recommend *Debrett's Peerage* for a less sensational summary. And I've never knowingly taken Lisa away from more of her council work than—"

"So why is she currently looking through five-year-old Shopfront Grant Scheme applications when Councillor Renwick is expecting her to minute the current meeting of the Highways Drainage (Seepage and Sewerage) Improvement Planning Sub Group?"

Aldermaston sat upright. "Lisa is an excellent Democracy Support Officer, who is more than capable of managing her workload. I know she takes a lot of work home with her to ensure she meets her responsibilities. The time she gives to the Borderer's Guild is an agreed partnership arrangement between this council and the Guild—"

Abigail sat back in her chair. "A partnership arrangement I shall be reviewing, first thing Monday morning."

Aldermaston felt his chair's rocking increase. He stood, to stop the sense of seasickness, and wandered over to a window overlooking the council car park. "There's a Borderer's Guild meeting at three o'clock this afternoon. We'll be assessing how the food festival is going so far. Come along. See for yourself what can happen when a community comes together. As Chief Exec, you have a partnership seat at the table."

"I'm all for bringing people together, Your Lordship. But it's *how* you lead that's important. I've been leading local communities in the public sector for nearly twenty years. Whereas you…"

Aldermaston turned away from the window and stepped closer to her desk. "Whereas I have over forty years of watching the seventh Marquess of Mortiforde lead by example.

I may have fewer than two years under my belt, and I've made many mistakes in that time. No doubt I'll make many more in the future. But with the support of the local community, I will guide them to draw upon their strengths."

Abigail took a Cross pen from the pen pot and scribbled on a sheet of paper. "Three o'clock, you say?"

Aldermaston nodded. "In the Buttermarket community room on the first floor. Before I forget, there's a formal dinner tonight. Seven o'clock, at Tugford Hall for Borderer's Guild members. It would be lovely if you could join us. We didn't issue an invitation because we weren't aware of your early arrival."

Abigail smiled. "And it would be an opportunity for you to interrogate me on your home ground, wouldn't it?"

"I'm sure you'll appreciate the chance to further your knowledge of the local community." He turned to head for the door, but stopped. "Forgive me, but I need to confirm numbers with Cartwright. Will you be bringing anyone with you tonight?"

Abigail briefly glanced at her bare ring-finger. "I find when working in such demanding leadership roles, it can be unfair to inflict such a lifestyle on partners who may not have the skills to cope. It's a business decision. You learn from your mistakes. Continuous improvement is the ethos these days. We should always look to the future."

She took a deep breath, then looked squarely at him. "And that's why the Borderer's Guild has no place in a modern, democratic society. You're an archaic, anachronistic organisation that should have been extinct decades ago. And as this authority's newest Chief Executive, I shall drag Mortiforde, kicking and screaming, out of the seventeenth century and into the twenty-first."

Aldermaston nodded and turned. He sensed her gaze running along her nose into his back as he walked towards the door. He twisted the handle, pulled the door ajar, then faced her one more time.

"I only wish for one thing," he said.

She crossed her arms and leant back in her chair. "Yes?"

"That you quickly come to terms with whatever it is you're running away from in London."

For a brief second, her face flushed.

∾

"Where the brassicas have you been?" Tibby yelled, as Ashton slipped back behind the stall. She handed two Borderlandshire Blue Burger baps to her waiting customer with one hand and took his money with the other.

"Sorry about that, Tibbs," his Black Country accent drawled. "Family emergency. All sorted now." He tied the apron strings around his chubby midriff.

Tibby served another customer, while turning the current batch of vegetarian burgers onto the hotplate to ensure they didn't burn. A frenzied sizzling and spitting exploded into the air. Their burgers were proving popular, and this aroma had people salivating several stalls away. In the past hour, she'd sold over two hundred.

"Who's next please?" She glanced up at the crowd thronging the aisles. Their stall frontage was more tightly packed with customers than the seeds in a sunflower.

"Two of your veggie burger baps please, love." A woman thrust a ten-pound note into her hand.

"Coming right up." She turned to Ashton, still titivating with his apron strings. "Are you stopping? Or might you have another family emergency later?"

Ashton placed his hands on his hips. "Family is important. If you haven't got family, what have you got?"

Tibby bit her bottom lip. Having been left on her own to

deal with a crowd of customers for an hour, she wasn't looking for a philosophical debate. "I wouldn't know," she spluttered. She stopped and pointed the spatula in his face, inadvertently swiping his bulbous nose.

He flinched and pinched his nose.

"Perhaps it allows me to a focus on the job in hand?" she suggested.

She threw the spatula into a box of other dirty utensils hidden under the counter and picked out a clean one to agitate the burgers in the heavily spitting oil. Her mind was spitting furiously, too. How dare he desert her like that. Perhaps she should drop him in the lurch.

Her hand froze. Yes! She grabbed an organic soft white roll in a serviette and slipped a Borderlandshire Blue Burger into it. Then she untied her apron and threw it at him.

"What are you doing?" said Ashton, catching her apron with one hand.

"What does it look like? I'm leaving you on your own. Think of it as a family emergency."

With the wrapped veggie burger bap in her hand, she stormed off into the crowds. If her plan was to stand any chance of working, she needed to strike while the iron was hot. Or rather, while the burger was still hot.

～

Aldermaston pushed his way through the visitors into Peggy Farmer's shop, much to the annoyance of the festival-goers.

A ginger-haired woman grabbed his forearm. "Oi! There's a queue here!" Her other hand waved at the line of people in front and behind her.

"Bora Da!" Aldermaston grinned, nodded, and pushed his way further into the shop. A bit of Welsh always flummoxed the tourists. His stomach was flummoxed by the aroma of freshly frying pork and thyme burgers.

He heard Peggy's voice among the cacophony of customer orders and requests, as her three assistants, all wearing the shop's branded olive-green aprons, dealt with them in a haphazard fashion. Aldermaston feared Peggy was serving, but noticed her nip out the back. Moments later, she returned carrying a large tray of freshly cooked burgers and placed them down on a counter along the far wall.

"Peggy!" Aldermaston hissed.

The five-foot five, white-haired-owner turned and spotted him. Underneath her branded overall, she wore a purple blouse, topped by a blue jumper and a white cardigan.

"I'm a bit busy, Your Lordship," she replied. "Can't it wait?"

"It's about the extra delivery you had this morning. The one you mentioned to PC Norten."

She paused.

"Came with an interesting delivery note." Aldermaston stared at her.

Peggy bit her bottom lip, then nodded to the doorway to the back of the shop.

Aldermaston squeezed between two large American tourists, who were explaining to one of Peggy's assistants that an American hamburger came with at least three burgers in a bun rather than the one thin disc they'd been offered. He slipped around the far end of the counter and through the doorway Peggy had passed earlier.

He nodded to two other members of Peggy's team busy, chopping meat carcasses into joints, and cooking more burgers. At the far end was a doorway leading to a staircase, where Peggy stood.

"Come upstairs." She disappeared upstairs more quickly than he expected of the septuagenarian.

Aldermaston followed, taking two steps at a time, and was soon on the landing of Peggy's private residence. A small, circular wooden table bore a rather dishevelled aspidistra and a black-and-white photo of her and her husband, Walter, standing outside their shop.

"Through here, Your Lordship," Peggy called from another room.

Aldermaston entered a cosy living room, an oasis of calm compared to the storm downstairs. Two winged armchairs, in green suede, stood either side of a log fire, the embers of which were gasping their final breaths. In an alcove stood a tall glass-fronted cabinet, full of silverware, some of which were commemorative plaques and plates, trophies from their industry peers. More photos of Peggy and Walter adorned a sideboard, one of their wedding day outside St Julian's Church here in Mortiforde, one of them sitting on a bench eating an ice cream on the promenade at Aberdovey, and another of them both dressed smartly outside Buckingham Palace, Walter proudly holding his MBE. A large wooden mantel clock echoed the seconds of time around the room.

"Take a seat." Peggy stood in the doorway to her kitchen and pointed to one of the armchairs. "Can I get you anything? Tea. Coffee? Bacon sandwich?"

Aldermaston's stomach somersaulted in anticipation. "Peggy, I could *murder* a bacon sandwich. Been up since five and I haven't had breakfast yet."

Peggy beamed. "I'll sort you something out. Then we'll sit down and have a chat." Her smile dropped from her face and her eyes searched the room. "I have a confession to make."

∼

Tibby knocked on the Chief Executive's office door and took two paces backwards. Had she been at school, she'd have licked the palms of both hands and wiped them downwards from her crown to behind her ears. Instead, she held the Borderlandshire Blue Burger bap in her hands and rocked back and forth on her heels.

The heavy wooden door creaked ajar.

"Can I help you?" Abigail peered over Tibby's shoulder for witnesses, then looked directly at her. "Should you be here?"

Tibby held aloft the bap. "As President of the Mortiforde Vegetarian Society, I would like to formally welcome you to Borderlandshire."

Abigail frowned. "I'm sorry, but I'm not in a position to accept gifts. It goes against the council's code of conduct." She made to close the door.

Tibby winced as her right foot absorbed the crushing force. "Please," she whispered, trying to disguise the pain. "I think you're more understanding of our cause than Lord Mortiforde." She held up the bap a little higher. "I think we share the same values. And anyway," Tibby's eyes narrowed. "I didn't think you started officially until Monday, so all that code of conduct crap doesn't apply today, does it?"

Abigail's pensive features relaxed.

Tibby felt the pressure on her foot dissipate.

Abigail opened the door and extended an arm. "Come in. I'm particularly intrigued to know how Lord Mortiforde isn't as understanding as you'd like him to be."

∽

Aldermaston's teeth sank into the softest granary bread and crispiest bacon he'd ever tasted. A slightly smoked aroma teased his nostrils as a single drip of fat ran down his chin. He rolled the bite of bacon butty around his mouth, allowing his taste buds to enjoy the cessation of this morning's starvation. His stomach gurgled and somersaulted with delight.

"Peggy, you're a star." He wiped his chin, then devoured another bite. "This is…" he continued, between chewing, "…absolute heaven."

Peggy relaxed into the green suede armchair opposite. "You can't beat a bacon sandwich for instant gratification. Walter's grandfather never left the house until he'd had a freshly cooked bacon sandwich on a slice of white, crusty bread. Doorstep sized, of course." She beamed at the memory. "And you'll only get decent bacon from us independent butchers in town. I can't vouch for any of that imported stuff the supermarket down Watling Street sells at a third of the price."

Aldermaston popped the remainder of the sandwich into his mouth and sucked the fatty juices off each fingertip in turn. "What do I owe you for that?" He rummaged in his trouser pockets for some change.

"Don't be ridiculous, Your Lordship. Wouldn't hear of it. Not with what you and your father have done for this town over the years."

Aldermaston stared at Peggy. "This extra delivery you had this morning. What did the note say?"

Peggy stood and wandered over to the cabinet. "The front pig's leg had been poorly butchered. Hacked would be a more accurate description. Waste of a good joint there. Here we are." She handed him a small, folded piece of paper. "I kept it because it was hand delivered to the flat address, not the shop downstairs."

Aldermaston recognised the typeface. Just like the others.

Peggy continued. "I thought it was some silly marketing claptrap."

"What did you do with the leg?"

"Industrial waste bin. Couldn't use it. No traceability. Don't know who's handled it, or where it's come from. Complete waste. I'm a butcher's wife. We respect our animals, and whoever sent that doesn't." She pointed at the note in his hand.

Revenge is a dish best served cold.

"I don't understand." Peggy returned to the armchair. "Revenge for what? It has to be a marketing gimmick, doesn't it? It's the food festival. Every business is trying to launch some new product."

Aldermaston folded the paper. "Can I keep this?"

"You could have had the pig leg too, if I hadn't disposed of it."

"Actually, I've seen enough pig parts today." Although, if it had been a boar's leg Aldermaston might have thought differently. It could have helped him back into Felicity's good books. He sighed. If only Felicity's good books were cookery books.

"Both Trotters and Shepherds had pig limbs sent to them, and the Mortiforde Vegetarian Society got a surprise package too."

Peggy looked shocked. "I know the Vegetarian Society doesn't like our line of business, but sending them an animal part must have been deeply upsetting for them. We might have different views of what's right to eat, but I still respect the Vegetarian Society for their beliefs. It is a free country."

Aldermaston nodded. "There is something else." He took a deep breath. "Jock Trotter is missing."

"Missing?" Peggy clasped both hands to her mouth.

"He's not been seen since first thing this morning."

The colour drained from Peggy's papery-thin skin.

"And," Aldermaston continued, "I have reason to believe that Seth Shepherd has disappeared, too. Neither butcher is in their shop. Worrying, on this weekend, isn't it?"

Peggy nodded, her hands remaining fixed to her face.

Aldermaston leant his elbows on his knees and clasped his hands together.

"I know about Seth Shepherd's plan to fix the Best Borderlandshire Burger competition. A plan, I understand, you were extremely interested in."

Peggy's head dropped into her hands. She tried stifling a sob, then plucked a tissue from the sleeve of her white cardigan and wiped her eyes. "It's getting so hard. *Too* hard. Since the supermarket opened on the outskirts of town seven years ago, we've struggled. As have Shepherds. Well, most of the independent retailers, really. If I don't win the Best Borderlandshire Burger this year, I'll have to close before Christmas."

She stood and wandered back over to the cabinet and picked up a photo of her husband. She stroked his cheek. "When my Walter passed away five years ago, he was the fifteenth generation to run the family butchery in Mortiforde. His family can trace their roots back to the seventeenth century. And we're not the only ones. Jock Trotter and Seth Shepherd have similar family butchery heritage."

"Here in Mortiforde?"

Peggy nodded. "That's what makes Mortiforde so special. If only that blooming supermarket wasn't here—"

She clutched the photo frame to her chest. "We'll be the generation that failed. There'll be no family business to pass on to our two sons. Can you imagine how that feels, Your Lordship? After nearly four hundred years?"

Her worried expression changed to a smile as she straightened a couple of other family photos on the same shelf. "Of course you can, Your Lordship. What am I wittering on about? Your family has been here longer than anyone's."

Aldermaston smiled. "The longer the history, the greater the weight on one's shoulders." He pointed at Walter's photo. "And four hundred years is a considerable weight for yourselves." He leant back in the chair. "What are you confessing to, Peggy?"

Peggy stood behind and gripped the top of the chair. "Seth's plan to share the success of the competition might have saved us. But the Trotters weren't having any of it. They always have been self-centred. But then, business is business."

Aldermaston's eyes narrowed. "There's something you're not telling me."

Peggy moved across to the living room window. "Come here."

Aldermaston went over and stood next to her. Being in the centre of town, on the hill, meant the view from this first-floor window extended over the tops of the surrounding roofs and chimneys and out onto the idyllic rolling hills of Borderlandshire. Although, as Aldermaston knew, a rural idyll was not all that it seemed, once you scraped away the summer beauty.

"What am I looking at?"

Peggy pointed into the backyard below.

Space at the rear of town centre properties was small, a reminder of Mortiforde's medieval history when it was first established with small burgage plots behind each dwelling. Historically, residents rented them to grow vegetables, or keep a pig, to be self-sufficient. Peggy's cobbled rear yard had a small stone outbuilding in the far corner. What Aldermaston hadn't expected to see were two pigs, one on its side, lying on some straw, having a nap, while the other rooted around a muddy corner with its nose.

"The one sleeping is Miss Piggy. She's a Gloucester Old Spot."

"What's the other pig called?"

"Technically, it's not a pig, for a start."

Aldermaston squinted.

"It's a boar," she clarified. "I found it wandering Mortiforde Woods this morning."

Aldermaston stared at the animal. "We don't have wild boar in Mortiforde Woods, do we?" He'd never seen one during his wildlife photography shoots.

"If that animal is wild, I'm a pole-dancing circus clown."

Aldermaston worked hard to clear that particular image from his mind. "Someone's pet, then?"

"Sort of."

Aldermaston placed his hands on Peggy's shoulders. "Spit it out, Peggy. What's the significance of the boar?"

She closed her eyes. "It's Jock Trotter's. And he would never let that animal out of his sight. Not unless his life depended on it. And even then, he'd wrestle with the decision for some time." She inhaled deeply, then turned to face Aldermaston. "That's no ordinary boar. That's Jock Trotter's pride and joy."

CHAPTER SEVEN

Abigail caught the crumbs from her Borderlandshire Blue Burger bap as her teeth sank into the succulent savoury burger and soft roll. An explosion of rich creaminess assaulted her taste buds and her eyes closed in ecstasy. She inhaled deeply, captivating the herby aromas. Nobody in London ever bought such an exquisite delicacy to her desk. At Thameside, once you'd eaten one shrink-wrapped mass-produced blueberry muffin three months past its best-before date you'd eaten them all. And had the indigestion to prove it.

Abigail's eyes opened, ready for the next bite, and caught Tibby's beaming smile. "This is absolutely divine."

Tibby blushed. "It's my dream to show the world that vegetarian food can be truly outstanding. There are some amazing flavours to be had. And the Welsh Borders is one of the best places at producing them."

Abigail swallowed her second bite and studied the half bap left in her hand. "I honestly thought when I moved here I'd be stuck with eating anaemic nut roasts and monotonous mung bean salads."

"When I saw you holding those sausages at the official opening, I knew you were vegetarian," said Tibby.

Abigail leant back in her office chair and swung her feet and four-inch heels onto the desk. "If I'd known I'd be holding one end of some pig's intestines this morning, I wouldn't have shown up until my official start on Monday." Her nose twitched as she took her penultimate bite of burger. "Three times I've sterilised my hands, and I can still smell the bloody stuff on my fingertips. Lord Mortiforde certainly caught me out with that one."

Tibby fell back into the chair, which rocked. "He wasn't particularly bothered by the threatening message we found on our stall this morning."

Abigail popped the final piece into her mouth, savoured the moment, then took a wet wipe from the top drawer of her desk. "Message?"

"There was a pig's heart waiting for us on our stall first thing this morning."

Abigail swept her feet off the desk and sat upright. "What?"

Tibby nodded. "Dumped on our stall in a small wooden box."

Abigail leant on her desk.

"I brought it to Lord Mortiforde's attention. Told him we weren't having it. It was obviously one of the butchers trying to frighten us. They're scared about *that*." Tibby pointed at Abigail's stomach. "Our vegetarian burger."

Abigail licked her lips. "So they should be!"

"I thought as the head of the Borderer's Guild, Lord Mortiforde would take this matter seriously. The heart hadn't been hermetically sealed in plastic to prevent cross-contamination. It was a blatant disregard of food hygiene regulations. Whichever butcher sent it should be shut down with immediate effect. But all three butchers are open and busy serving extremely long queues. Clearly, neither Lord Mortiforde nor the Borderer's Guild give a stuff about the vegetarian society, or the council's food regulations. It's not fair! We pay our local taxes too, Ms Mayedew!" Tibby thumped the top of Abigail's desk.

Abigail flinched, then rose from her chair. "I wonder… I'm dining at Lord Mortiforde's tonight. It's a Guild event. Seven o'clock. He asked if I wanted to bring a guest, but I'm so new here I don't know anyone. Would you be interested in joining me? We might make a more substantial force, working together."

A flash of fear passed Tibby's eyes. "Oh, er… I'm not sure."

Abigail waved her hands in the air. "Forgive me. You're running a festival stall. You'll either be busy prepping for tomorrow or collapsed on the sofa, exhausted from today's efforts."

Tibby giggled nervously. "It's far busier than I thought it would be."

Abigail grabbed her Cross fountain pen from the pot and scribbled something on a Post-it note. "Take this. My mobile phone number. In case you change your mind, or want to bring anything else to my attention about Lord Mortiforde. I've dealt with my fair share of aristocratic numbskulls." She handed it to Tibby. "Lord Mortiforde's days of running his own private fiefdom are well and truly over."

∾

Aldermaston stared at the boar, pushing its snout into the deepest corners of Peggy's backyard. If that boar was Jock Trotter's, and Peggy's assertion that he'd never part with it at any cost was true, then Jock's disappearance was deeply troubling. It didn't bode well for Seth, either.

He turned and sat on the windowsill. "What's going on, Peggy?" He took her trembling hands in his. "What are you confessing to?" His eyes narrowed. "Do you know where Jock is?"

"No!" A tear rolled down her cheek.

"Talk to me, Peggy."

She sighed. "I was out walking Miss Piggy in Mortiforde Woods—"

"What time?"

"About a quarter to seven."

Aldermaston nodded. A good hour before Seth stumbled into his hide then. "Go on."

"I heard this rustling in the undergrowth. I knew immediately what it was. Bound to be Seth and Maisie. He regularly walks her in the woods, too. But when I couldn't see anyone, I thought Maisie had wandered off. Once a pig gets the scent of something, it's off. They're determined animals and big beasts. You don't argue with them. Walter always told me to let go of the lead if ever Miss Piggy shot off, otherwise I'd end up being dragged for miles. I assumed that's what Seth had done."

"Let go of Maisie?"

Peggy nodded. "They're easy to track. Just follow the trail of destruction."

Peggy sighed. "So I hung about, waiting for Maisie to come out from the thick bracken, thinking I'd grab hold of her lead and wait for Seth to find us."

"But it wasn't Maisie, was it?"

Peggy paused. "I've never seen Jock's boar before. Seth and I often joked it was some mythical creature. But as soon as it stumbled out of the undergrowth, I knew. We haven't had wild boar in Mortiforde Woods since the eighteenth century. That and the fact that wild boar don't have a lead and collar round their neck."

"So you grabbed it. Then what? How long did you wait for Jock?"

Peggy pulled her hands from Aldermaston's grip and wiped her cheeks. "I thought it was my chance. My *only* chance." More tears cascaded down her face.

Aldermaston leant closer. "Chance? For what?"

Peggy sniffed, turned to look at the photo of Walter on the cabinet momentarily, and then looked at her feet.

Aldermaston gently lifted her chin with his finger. "Come on, Peggy. How long have we known each other? I can't help you, if you won't tell me."

A brief smile flashed across her face. "My first thought, and that's what upsets me most, was not for Jock's safety, but that this was an opportunity."

"An opportunity?"

"Jock worships that animal. I thought that if I took it home with me, then perhaps I could see how much Jock would pay to get his pride and joy back."

"Hold it to ransom?"

Peggy bit both lips and nodded as she fought back another wave of tears.

"How?"

Her shoulders shrugged. "I don't know. I hadn't thought about any of that. I told you. It all happened so quick. I saw an opportunity. Perhaps he'd pay enough to tide me over for another year. Give us more time. Give my boys a chance to keep the shop going. Or maybe I could persuade Jock to reconsider Seth's plan — perhaps favouring me this year." Her eyes pleaded with understanding.

Aldermaston hugged her. "No wonder you looked shocked when I said Jock was missing. Asking for a ransom would have made you a prime suspect for his disappearance."

Peggy nodded. "I have no idea where Jock is. You have to believe me!"

Aldermaston watched the boar push its nose through the soil and straw towards Miss Piggy, asleep on her side in the far corner. "Why do you all keep pigs?"

Peggy stepped back and wiped her face with her tissue. "In our line of business, Your Lordship, it's important to remember that what we sell in our shops were once living, thriving animals. Respect an animal when it is alive, and it teaches you to respect it when it is dead." She tucked her tissue back under the sleeve of her cardigan. "They're also intelligent creatures with fantastic personalities."

A series of ear-splitting shrieks, squeals, snorts and grunts erupted outside as the boar attempted to rummage through the straw upon which Miss Piggy lay.

Peggy went to the living room door. "Then again, there are times when they can be a right pain in the ruddy neck. I'd better go and sort them out. Probably best I take the boar back to Mairi, anyway."

"No, don't!" Aldermaston interrupted. "Not for the moment. It'll only worry Mairi further about Jock's disappearance. Could you look after it for the time being?"

"Of course."

"Thank you."

Another bout of squeals and grunts ripped through the air as the two animals continued their standoff.

"I'd better go," said Peggy.

Aldermaston watched her disappear downstairs. Through the window, he saw her grab Miss Piggy's collar and drag her into the covered sty and bolt the gate. Then she turned to Jock's boar and wagged a remonstrative finger at it. Aldermaston couldn't determine what she was saying. But he was certain of one thing. Peggy *had* lied. Not about finding the boar, or thinking it might be a way of blackmailing Jock. But about why all three butchers kept pigs.

Felicity stared at the abandoned blackened brick on the kitchen floor where Daniel had left it. Her toes throbbed at the memory of this morning's events.

"I'll sort that, Your Ladyship." Cartwright bent down and wrapped his hands around the remains. The veins in his temple strained, his foot slipped twice as he attempted to raise the charcoal dish off the floor. Beads of sweat burst through his reddening forehead as his aching arms eventually hoisted the dead weight onto the kitchen table.

It thudded onto the tabletop. Cartwright collapsed alongside it, wheezing and coughing. His beetroot face glistened, as his gloved hand retrieved the starched handkerchief from his jacket breast pocket.

Felicity prodded the remains with her crutch. "All the boar meat I had has been cremated in *that*."

Cartwright wiped his brow. "Perhaps one could enter a different Bake Off category, Your Ladyship?"

She leant on her crutch. "Impossible. The Ladies' Legion expects me to win this class in the competition. They're salivating with excitement. Although, I suspect Lavinia is salivating the most. But I'm stuffed without any more boar meat!"

She thumped the kitchen tabletop.

Cartwright flinched.

"If only we could do *something*," she continued. "When I was chatting to Bœuf Boucher this morning, he said … that's it!" She hobbled over to Cartwright. "Do we have enough flour, eggs and butter in the main house kitchen?"

Cartwright nodded. "I would not be doing my job properly if we didn't."

"We can make the pastry case! Bœuf mentioned something

about blind-baking the pastry first. Please tell me you can coach me in blind-baking."

"I can do that blindfolded, My Lady."

Felicity scowled. "I'd rather you didn't."

∽

Aldermaston paused at the bottom of Peggy's stairs. Ahead was the rear door to Peggy's backyard. It was half open and Peggy's muffled tones were interspersed with short, sharp grunts and squeals.

He crept along the hallway and hid behind the door. Through the gap, he watched Peggy sitting on a bale of straw with one hand around the boar's collar, the other scratching behind its ear.

"Lord Mortiforde's done me a favour." She chuckled. "Might as well make the most of you, while I have you, mightn't I?" She tickled the boar under its chin and a raft of contented grunts filled the air.

Aldermaston frowned. He leant closer to hear better, knocking his nose against the edge of the door. The hinges creaked. Peggy looked up.

He held his breath momentarily. Her attention returned to the boar. She rummaged in her cardigan pocket and pulled out something Aldermaston couldn't quite see, but the boar squealed excitedly.

"Sit!" Peggy instructed, holding up her hand containing the prize. With her other hand, she pushed down on the boar's rump. "I want you to sit. You'd do this for Jock. I know you would."

The boar gave in, her eyes transfixed on the contents of Peggy's hand high in the air, as its bottom dropped to the floor.

"That's it." Peggy scratched its forehead and handed the boar the treat. Loud snorts and frenzied squeals filled the air.

"Tonight, young lady, we're going for a little walk in Mortiforde Woods. And you can show me all the places where Jock takes you. Then, for once in my life, I might actually be ahead of the game." Peggy giggled, then grabbed the boar's head, bent down and kissed it on the snout.

The high-pitched squeal hurt Aldermaston's ears. It broke free from Peggy's grip and ran around the backyard. Peggy chuckled.

Aldermaston shuddered. Not because he'd just watched Peggy kiss a boar on the snout, but because it proved there was more to the butchers' woodland walks than merely exercising their pet pigs.

∾

Tibby checked her watch as she battled her way through Market Square crowds. It was approaching noon. Ashton wouldn't be happy at her length of desertion. Still, as recruitment went, getting the council's new chief executive involved could open many doors for them. Her interest in Lord Mortiforde's lack of action over the pig's heart was… heartening.

"Sorry!" Her apology became more frequent as her shoulders clashed with those of the crowd. Was it her imagination, or were there more people? Peering between shoulders and heads, she could just make out the society's stall a few feet away. She shouldered her slight frame through the onlookers, many of whom tutted or gazed disparagingly down their noses at her as she inched her way closer. Suddenly, she heard Ashton's Black Country accent.

"—and we source all our ingredients from a thirty-mile radius of Mortiforde. We could ramp up production at a moment's notice."

Tibby was confused. Production?

"Hmmm. Eet is very flavoursome, and ze quality is magnifique!"

Tibby froze. *Bœuf!* Bœuf was tasting their vegetarian burger. And Ashton was on his own. Sodding hell!

"Excuse me, please!" She pushed harder this time. "I need to get to my stall."

Scowling faces sneered as she forced her way through the smallest of gaps until, finally, she reached the slender gap between their stall and the one adjacent. Seconds later, she stood next to Bœuf and Ashton, and threw a green apron over her head.

"Sorry to have left you so long, Ashton. I see we have a special guest." She tied the apron string behind her back, then thrust a hand out to shake Bœuf's.

Ashton poked his tongue deep into his cheek and raised his eyebrows. "Tibby. *At last.* Mr Boucher, may I introduce you to our president, Tibby Gillard?" Ashton's eyes crossed, allowing him to look down, and around, his bulbous nose at her. "I was just explaining to Mr Boucher here the merits of drawing upon local produce when creating our vegetarian burger."

"Madame, it is an honour to meet you. You 'ave an exquisite burger. In fact, I would go as far as saying this is one of the best burgers, if not the best vegetarian burger, I 'ave ever tasted."

Tibby flushed with pride as a smattering of applause around their stall grew into a long sustained ovation of admiration from the onlookers. "That's very kind of you, Mr Boucher. To be appreciated by someone of your calibre, after we," she gestured to Ashton, "and the rest of the Vegetarian Society have worked tirelessly to create a truly scrumptious product, is so rewarding."

Bœuf smiled. "Zis burger will go a long way," he winked, "if I have anything to do with it."

Tibby's heart pounded. She turned to Ashton, just as he

punched the air victoriously, ripping a large hole in the blue-and-white striped awning above his head.

∼

Lisa hooked her hair behind her ear as she bent forward and picked another buff-coloured file off the basement floor. Aldermaston was right. These shopfront grant project files made interesting reading. She sat on the abrasive carpet flooring, legs outstretched, and leant back against one of the beige, metal four-drawer filing cabinets. This wasn't a basement filing room, but a graveyard of discarded files no one had the confidence to cremate, just in case someone wanted them exhumed. There wasn't a chair to sit on, and the energy-saving lighting was so weak even the shadows it created were half-hearted.

She checked the file reference of the two-inch thick folder: *SFGS/Farmer*. Peggy Farmer's application. Flicking through the initial pages of the form, she stopped at her audited accounts for the five years before her application. Lisa ran a finger along the net profit column. All positive, but definitely a downward trend, except for the fourth year before the grant application, when her profits were tenfold. Tenfold? She checked the dates. Nine years ago. Lisa stretched across to reach her notepad, where she'd written down the list of winners of the Best Borderlandshire Burger competition, and counted back. Yes. Nine years ago was the last time Peggy won.

Lisa turned a couple more pages. Peggy's bank account summaries showed the tremendous boost, followed by regular withdrawals over the following three years. Although her business was making a profit, it wasn't enough, and she was drawing on the capital accrued during the year she won the Best Borderlandshire Burger competition.

It had been the same for Seth Shepherd, except he'd won

four years ago, and then six and eight years ago. The Trotters were doing well, winning in all the other years and—

A door banged, its anger rumbling around the room like thunder.

"Hello?"

No answer. She detected the dull thud of footsteps against the carpet.

"Can I help you?"

The footsteps stopped, then started again, although this time they seemed to be heading in a different direction.

Suddenly, from the corner of her eye, she spotted a pair of trousered legs come around the corner of the filing cabinets she was leaning against. She screamed, clutching her chest.

The legs stopped abruptly. "There you are!" Daniel held his smartphone in one hand and pulled out his earphones with his other.

Lisa smacked him across the shins with Peggy Farmer's file.

"Ouch! What was that for?"

"You scared me witless, you prat. It's not exactly a soothing ambiance down here."

Daniel slipped his smartphone into his suit jacket pocket and sat down on the floor, cross-legged. He picked up a file and flicked through it. "Found anything?"

Lisa threw Peggy's file on the floor and crossed her arms. "There's money in beefburgers," she began. "All the butchers do well, financially, during the food festival."

Daniel picked up another file. "Makes sense. There's an additional twenty thousand customers in town."

"Yes, but," Lisa continued, "if you win the Best Borderlandshire Burger competition, you get a significant financial boost. If you *don't* win the competition, the general increase in trade is like having a Christmas bonus equal to one week's salary. Nice, but it doesn't last long."

Daniel nodded.

"Win the competition," Lisa continued, "and it's like getting a bonus equal to your annual salary."

Daniel whistled.

Lisa held up a spreadsheet printout. "The income trend for all three butchers is deteriorating. They took a big hit when the supermarket on the edge of town opened seven years ago, and they've not recovered." She rubbed her forehead as she flicked through the file. "Based upon these figures, I'd say Mortiforde is only big enough for two, not three, independent butchers. That's why winning the competition is so important. The publicity gives the winning butchers a huge boost in online orders for months afterwards. Sales for the other butchers' competition burgers shrivel up and disappear. It's all about the winning. And Trotters have been doing a lot of winning recently."

"Enough to make the other butchers jealous?" another voice enquired behind them.

Both Lisa and Daniel jumped.

Aldermaston stepped out from behind a bank of filing cabinets.

"How long have you been there?" Lisa rubbed the back of her neck.

"Long enough." Aldermaston bent down and took the file from her. "So, could the Trotters' success incite the other butchers into taking more drastic action? We know Seth attempted some sort of gentleman's agreement."

Daniel's face contorted. "I can still taste the bloody salt now. But Seth's plan," he shook his head, "wasn't a long-term strategy."

Aldermaston nodded. "I agree. And it needed one butcher to agree to play by the rules for two consecutive food festivals until they saw any benefit from the plan. Which made me wonder if Seth decided to up the ante."

"Seth?" Daniel rose to his feet. "But he gave you the first note this morning, didn't he?"

Aldermaston dropped Peggy's file on top of the filing cabinet with a thud. "He did. Then again, it could be a nice little bluff, making out he's a victim too. But now, I'm not sure. Evie Shepherd rang me earlier. Seth's missing."

"Missing?" Lisa pulled herself up and rubbed the stiffness from her calf muscles. "When was the last time she saw him?"

Aldermaston half-snorted. "She's not seen *all* of him since he left to do his walk this morning in Mortiforde Woods, which is when he bumped into me."

Lisa's eyes narrowed. "*All* of him?"

"Evie had another package this morning. Seth's moustache."

"That's his pride and joy!" Lisa stretched out her legs as the numbness eased. "He wears that face mask when serving in the shop because he won't shave it off. He wouldn't give that up lightly."

"That's what concerns me." Aldermaston turned to Daniel. "Did you get any information out of Mairi about where Jock goes walking?"

"Yes." Daniel glanced at his smartphone and swiped it several times. "I made a note. Here we are. He takes Tess for a walk every morning, through Vinnalls Coppice usually."

Aldermaston sighed. "Not far from where my hide is set up, and where Seth ambushed me this morning."

"So, what do we do now?" Lisa picked up the other files from the floor and handed them to Daniel. "Give us a hand with these."

Aldermaston stared at her. "First, you've got the Highways Drainage (Seepage and Sewerage) Improvement Planning Sub Group meeting to take notes for in the next ten minutes."

Lisa sneered. "Don't remind me."

"I'm only doing so because the new Chief Exec thinks the Borderer's Guild is using too much of your time."

"What?" Lisa's chin dropped, briefly. "Says the woman with so much time on her hands she can start her new job a day early."

Aldermaston turned to Daniel. "And I hope you weren't thinking of having an early night tonight."

Daniel frowned.

"You've got some tracking to do in Mortiforde Woods."

Daniel scratched his head. "Tracking? But long-haired fallow deer aren't active at night."

Aldermaston grinned. "Not long-haired fallow deer."

Daniel scratched the back of his head. "What then?"

Aldermaston grinned. "A boar."

CHAPTER EIGHT

Basildon peered round the thick wooden door of Tugford Hall's main kitchen. Below stairs. Cartwright's territory. It was light and spacious, despite being half underground. The squat south-facing opaque windows were seven feet above the kitchen floor, but ground level outside, and gave little light. Still, the glare from four huge fluorescent strip lights bounced off the many gleaming stainless-steel surfaces, forcing all shadows into obscurity.

Even a non-chef could see everything was in its rightful place. Cartwright's full set of copper-bottomed saucepans and lids hung from S-shaped steel hooks suspended above the main preparation area in the centre of the room. Not exactly an island, more of a continent in this vast kitchen. A vast three-door metallic silver fridge and freezer unit occupied half of one wall, the rest taken up with Meccano-style shelving, groaning under the weight of crockery for official functions. Even Cartwright's knife collection, stored on a metallic bar against the opposite wall, was in a strict size order, from what looked like a machete on the far left, down to what could have been a toothpick with a handle, some forty-three knives later.

Against another wall were two large electric ovens, three gas hob units capable of heating a half a dozen pots and pans each, and an industrial-sized dishwasher. In the far corner stood a green Rayburn oven, which Cartwright used when cooking for himself.

Standing at the main preparation area in the centre of the kitchen, with their backs to him, were Cartwright and Felicity.

"It's heading in the right direction, My Lady, but it may be a little dry." Cartwright peered over Felicity's shoulder. "A couple of drops of water should do the trick."

Basildon crept up behind them and peered between their shoulders at the large mixing bowl in front of them. "I agree, Cartwright. Spot on, old chap."

"Aaarrrggghhh!" screamed Felicity. She punched his upper arm. "Basildon! Don't creep up on people like that. I could have been holding a sharp knife."

He stepped backwards, crossing his arms in a martial arts defence pose. "Not a problem for those of us in training for MI5, Your Ladyship." He jumped, throwing both arms wide, then spun round and kicked out his right foot. His red moccasin slipper flew high into the air, collided with a brass saucepan hanging from the ceiling, ricocheted across the room, and landed in the Belfast sink. A plume of water erupted two feet into the air.

Cartwright stared at Basildon. "Is there anything I can help you with, sir?"

"Do you have any rosewater, old bean? Only, I'm doing Mother's Mortiforde Sponge recipe for the Bake Off tomorrow, and suddenly remembered she always liked to add a few drops of the stuff."

"Let me see what I can find for you, sir." Cartwright headed across the kitchen to the vast pantry and stepped inside.

Felicity leaned against the preparation area. "*You're* entering Mortiforde Sponge category?"

Basildon nodded. "Mother's recipe always served her well. Although, I believe," he nodded in Cartwright's direction, "it wasn't originally Mother's recipe."

Felicity's eyebrows rose. "So I've recently learned."

Basildon glanced at the pastry mixture on the dusted worktop before them. "You're going savoury, then?"

Felicity nodded. "The sponge was your mother's *pièce de résistance*. I need my own."

"Good for you. Spiffing idea." Basildon leant against the work surface, knocking a wooden spoon to the floor. "Sorry, I…"

Carefully, Felicity bent over to retrieve it.

Basildon glanced at the pantry door. Cartwright was still inside. Rosewater wasn't an everyday ingredient. Down at his feet, Felicity fumbled as she struggled to retrieve the spoon, which had slid part way under the kitchen unit.

Surreptitiously, Basildon pulled a small phial from his cardigan pocket. He checked the pantry. With a deft twist of the rubber bung, he poured four drops of sodium thiopental onto Felicity's ball of pastry. Seconds later, the phial was back in his cardigan pocket.

"You're in luck, sir," Cartwright called, stepping out of the pantry, holding a small glass bottle in his hand.

Felicity stood upright again, clutching the wooden spoon.

Basildon took the rose water from Cartwright. "I knew you wouldn't let me down." He took the spoon from Felicity and wandered over to the sink, dropped it in, then retrieved his slipper. He turned to Felicity. "Good luck with your entry. I don't know what's worse. Doing the actual baking, or waiting to hear what the judge has to say about your efforts." He smirked, then walked out of the kitchen.

Aldermaston entered the Portakabin that was Mortiforde's police station. The counter was waist height, but came somewhere between the knees and thighs of PC Norten, who simply overcame this problem by remaining seated on the other side.

"Be with you in a minute, Lord Mortiforde." PC Norten sat beside his inkjet printer, catching the paper it churned out. "Mrs Trotter's been nagging me, demanding to know how my investigation is going with finding her missing husband."

Aldermaston leant on the countertop. "Actually, that's why I popped in. Any news on Jock?"

PC Norten shook his head. "I'm not having a good day. I've used up all the *MISSING* posters with Farmer Bell's pig." He pointed to the wall where a photo of a pig's face looked down at him. "I'm having to use these *WANTED* ones instead."

He held up the latest poster the inkjet printer had churned out. *WANTED* it read. *Dead or Alive… but preferably alive.* Beneath this were two photos of Jock Trotter: one sideways on, the other facing forwards. He was holding a board with his name and a Powys Police identity number. "I know Mr Trotter is technically missing, but Mrs Trotter wants him back, so *Wanted* posters aren't completely inappropriate," the constable continued. "But as soon as I stick them up, someone rips them down. This is the third batch I've printed off. It's as though someone doesn't want the town to know that Mr Trotter is missing."

Aldermaston stared at the small A4 poster with faded red and blue vertical stripes on it. "Your ink cartridge is running out."

PC Norten clasped his forehead. "No! Today just gets worse." He stood quickly, banging his head on the Portakabin ceiling.

Aldermaston winced at the loss of yet another of the

policeman's brain cells. And PC Norten needed all the brain cells he could lay his hands on.

"Has Evie Shepherd called you?"

PC Norten shook his head as he rubbed it.

Aldermaston chose not to say any more. That was Evie's call to make. He pointed at the poster. "Is that an official police photo of Jock?"

PC Norten nodded, then checked over both shoulders. "I shouldn't say, but... as it's you, Lord Mortiforde. I called my Welsh colleagues after checking Mr Trotter's file."

Aldermaston's eyebrows rose. "Jock has a file?"

"Criminal damage."

Aldermaston chuckled. "What did he do? Cut up a joint of beef the wrong way?"

"Heritage crime. Damaged a scheduled ancient monument."

"What?" Aldermaston leant in closer and whispered, "Jock wouldn't hurt a fly." He paused. Technically, that was wrong. Environmental Health regulations insisted he had electronic fly killers is his establishment. "Which monument?"

"Offa's Dyke. Six years ago. Got picked up by Powys Police. I called to check he wasn't up to his old tricks again." PC Norten handed Aldermaston a *Wanted* poster. "Didn't want to waste all that paper and ink if he was enjoying a cup of Welsh tea with my Powys cousins."

"Sensible idea," said Aldermaston, shocked he was directing those words to PC Norten. "I don't remember reading about his arrest."

"Only mentioned in The Powys Gazette, I think."

Aldermaston scratched his neck. "So what did Jock do? Can't imagine him smashing a scheduled ancient monument up for the fun of it."

PC Norten tapped the side of his nose. "Sorry, Your Lordship. Can't disclose that information."

Aldermaston sighed and straightened up. "Okay, but if you find Jock, let me know, will you?"

"Yes, Your Lordship." PC Norten unwrapped a fresh ink cartridge and opened up his inkjet printer.

Aldermaston stepped outside. What had Jock been up to? And was it connected to his disappearance?

~

Lisa threw her minute-taking notebook onto her desk. The resultant thud of despair echoed around her office. The Highways Drainage (Seepage and Sewerage) Improvement Planning Sub Group meetings were, literally, a complete waste. All they achieved was making you older on the way out than you were on the way in. The seepage was of one's life.

The phone on her desk trilled.

"Lisa Duddon, Democracy Support."

"It's Ajay. Aldermaston's heart."

"What about it?"

"It's not human. Well, *his* is, obviously, but you know what I'm talking about."

Lisa sat down in her chair. "Do you know where it's from?"

"It's a swine."

Lisa tutted. "We all have challenges in our job, Ajay. You should try minuting the Highways Drainage (Seepage and Sewerage) Improvement Planning Sub Group meetings."

"It's a pig's heart."

"Oh. Makes sense." Lisa scribbled down a note. "Had it been as expertly extracted from its donor as the limb you saw earlier?" Presumably, all these body parts were from one animal.

Ajay sighed. "Someone's taken a bit more care here. Have any more body parts turned up anywhere?"

Lisa chewed her lip. Probably best not to tell Ajay about

Seth Shepherd's moustache. "All three of the town's butchers have received pig packages."

"The butchers?"

"Yes. And they all come with messages. Something about retribution."

"Retribution?" Ajay whispered. "Hang on a minute."

A rustling noise echoed in Lisa's ear as Ajay shielded the mouthpiece briefly. Suddenly, clarity returned.

"Lisa, you didn't hear this from me, okay?"

She picked up her pen again.

"About five, maybe six, years ago," Ajay continued in a low whisper, "one of the butchers was involved in a short measures case."

"Short measures? Quarter-pounders a bit light, were they?"

"No. The butchers were the whistleblowers, not the culprits."

Oh. *Retribution*.

"There's a file. In the basement."

Lisa's heart sank.

"It was a new company. I can't remember why it was a butcher who tipped us off. But this company—"

"What was the company's name?" Could she google it? Anything to save a trip to the basement of despair.

Ajay exhaled. "Sorry. All I remember is that the company was a start-up. Claimed they didn't know the rules. Which is hogwash. They were maximising profits as quickly as possible. Magistrates fined them five grand. It was enough to put them out of business."

"Thanks." Lisa finished scribbling down her notes.

"Check our files in the basement," Ajay continued. "The food regs cabinets go on for miles, but the short measures cases are few and far between. It's why I vaguely remember the case."

"Thanks, Ajay." She hung up and sat back in her chair.

The basement was the most soul-destroying place in the council, if not Mortiforde. Typing up the minutes of the Highways Drainage (Seepage and Sewerage) Improvement Planning Sub Group suddenly looked inviting.

Lisa's office door swung open and Daniel walked in, carrying a pile of papers. "Finished photocopying those shopfront grant scheme files. Glad to get out of that basement." He dumped the copies on her desk. "Right. If there's nothing else you need me to do, I'll go looking for some boar meat for Aldermaston."

Lisa fluttered her eyelashes. "Actually, there *is* something you could do for me."

∽

Ashton handed two burgers and some change to the waiting customer, then leant across to Tibby, who was also serving. "If we play our cards right with Bœuf, we could become the official suppliers of vegetarian burgers to the Buckingham Palace garden parties."

Tibby handed her customer their change. "There's a lot to get done before then. We've started selling the burgers we'd provisionally made for tomorrow. You said Mrs Hargreaves was making extra today, just in case, but they'll all need packing and pricing up for tomorrow. We'll have to do that tonight."

Ashton nodded. "Good idea."

The bell in St Julian's tower chimed one o'clock. Ashton slipped his overall over his head.

"Where are you going now?" Tibby watched Ashton fold his overall and place it in a box under the stall.

"Lunchtime."

Tibby's mouth dropped. "But…"

Ashton clasped her head in both hands, then kissed her forehead. "We're all entitled to a lunch break, dear," his Black

Country accent making entitled sound like *intoitled*. "Won't be long. Thirty minutes max. You can nip off when I'm back. Okay?"

He didn't wait for an answer, slipping out from behind the stall and disappearing into the thronging crowds, most of whom were now trying to get her attention and be served.

Tibby seethed. He'd done it again! She thrust her hands into her overall pockets indignantly, and felt a scrap of paper.

She recognised it as soon as she pulled it out. Her eyes narrowed. If Ashton was going to leave her in the lurch at a lunchtime, then why shouldn't she leave him in the lurch tonight?

"I'll be two seconds," she called to the long line of hands offering money, desperate to be served. "Need to make a quick phone call."

"I hope you're calling for more staff," jeered a voice from the crowd.

Tibby smiled apologetically and dialled the number. It rang four times and then cut to voicemail.

"Abigail, it's Tibby." She turned her back to the crowds. "About tonight. If the offer's still there, I'd love to join you."

∽

"Mr Boucher, I hope you've had an enjoyable morning." Aldermaston grabbed the celebrity chef's elbow and prised him away from Cissy Warbouys, who'd clearly held him captive to the vagaries of creative knitting for longer than anyone should be. Aldermaston half-waved at Cissy. "See you at the Guild meeting this afternoon, Cissy."

She nodded and waved a knitting needle.

Aldermaston pulled Bœuf towards a quieter corner of the hospitality tent. "Cissy is enthusiastic about her knitting."

Bœuf sighed deeply. "I admire 'er enthusiasm, but sadly

knitting with ze needles does not appeal to *moi*." He clutched his chest. "Food, on ze other hand, is a different matter. Everybody is passionate about food, do you not you think?"

Aldermaston's stomach rumbled. Peggy's bacon sarnie had filled a hole two hours ago, but it was ready for lunch. "I'm certainly passionate about food at lunchtime." He peered across the crowded marquee. "The sooner Jillian turns up, the sooner we can go."

He checked his watch. She was only five minutes late, so far.

Bœuf chuckled. "Zis is one of those events when everyone is so busy they lose track of time. It is an amazing festival. So many stalls, and such wonderful produce."

"I'm hoping we can tempt you with a local dish at our oldest hostelry." He paused. "Perhaps I should give Jillian a call."

He pulled his phone from his pocket and dialled. Four times it rang, as he scoured the busy marquee before going to voicemail. "Hi Jillian, it's Lord Mortiforde. It's gone quarter past one, so it looks like you've been waylaid. Mr Boucher has to be at the demonstration food marquee for two-thirty, so we'll head straight to The Nooseman's Knot now. Join us there when you can."

He returned his phone to his inside pocket. His stomach gurgled. Hunger or unease? He wasn't sure.

~

Felicity stared at the bedroom mirror. How did she always end up with several ounces of flour in her hair? She brushed it and watched a fine dust of plain flour drift to the floor.

Downstairs, the grandfather clock in the East Wing hallway chimed the half hour. Cartwright said her blind-baked pastry case would be ready at two. That gave her thirty minutes. No.

Make that fifteen minutes. With her broken toes, she needed to treble the usual five-minute stroll from their East Wing apartment to Tugford Hall's basement kitchen.

Aldermaston's camouflage jacket lay crumpled on the floor by his side of the bed. She bent down, grabbed a sleeve, and pulled it up off the floor. Something dropped against the carpet with a muffled thud. A white envelope.

The flap lifted as she picked it up. Inside was a thick document. Emblazoned on the front cover was the crown-shaped logo of the Royal Palaces Collection, and the title: *Mortiforde Royal Recipe Collection. (English Translation.)*

Recipe Collection? What was Aldermaston doing with a recipe collection? She turned the page.

This is a certified English translation (from the original Latin) of the seventeenth century Mortiforde Royal Recipe Collection. This document comprises two sections: a diary, by the chef (Oswyn Cooke), followed by a large selection of recipes…

Felicity flicked through the pages hurriedly. The left page contained a facsimile of the original document, while the English translation was on the right. She skipped forward a half-dozen pages or so, then read the translation. Diary entry. She skipped another batch. Diary entry. Then a third. Diary entry. Followed by a fourth, then a fifth and…

Just as she was about to throw the whole document over her head, she hit the jackpot. A recipe. The Latin on the left caught her eye. *Porcus Crustum* On the right, the Royal Palaces translator appeared to have hedged their bets. *Pig/Boar Pie.*

Bingo!

There were similarities to the recipe she'd been following. Diced apple. Onions. Sage and… oh. Oh! Her finger tapped the page. *That* wasn't in her recipe. She glanced over her shoulder, hesitated, then…

At least she had the deference to wince as the ripped page came away in her hand. She dropped it onto the white, satin,

La Perla duvet, so she could stuff the translated document back into the envelope and return it to Aldermaston's camouflage jacket inside pocket.

She grabbed the torn recipe and kissed it. *This* could be just what she needed. Well, that, and some boar meat.

∼

The reserved table hid in what appeared to be the darkest corner of The Nooseman's Knot public house. Barely illuminated by three sets of twin plastic candle-shaped lights casting an eerie amber hue, and a tiny, stained-glass window depicting a man hanging by a gibbet, The Nooseman's Knot certainly had an atmosphere.

"Compliments of The Nooseman's Knot." Cynthia, the septuagenarian barmaid, carefully placed a small tray with two pint glasses down on the table.

"Thank you, Cynthia." Aldermaston handed a pint to Bœuf sitting opposite and took the other for himself.

Cynthia, whose stature naturally suited the low-ceilinged hostelry, beamed. "There's no need to look at the menus. It's not every day we have a celebrity chef in the building." Her voice dropped to a whisper as she leant closer to Aldermaston's ear. "To be honest, Your Lordship, it's not everyday we have *any* chef in the building." She stood upright again. "I've arranged for two of our Last Suppers to be brought to you." She turned and disappeared into the darkness.

"Two warnings, Mr Boucher," Aldermaston warned. "The Nooseman's Knot Last Supper is three meals in one. Don't feel you have to eat it all. I'd hate for you to spoil your appetite for tonight's dinner at Tugford Hall."

"Thank you for ze advice, Lord Mortiforde." He picked up his pint glass. "And ze other warning?"

"The Hangman's Anaesthetic you have in your hands has a bit of a kick to it."

Bœuf brought the glass to his lips and chuckled. "There is little a chef's taste buds can't handle, Your Lordship. I 'ave sampled some strange concoctions over the years."

He supped a large mouthful, which immediately induced a vein-bulging, eye-popping, blue-cheeked coughing fit.

Cynthia returned with a large jug of tap water and two more pint glasses. "Looks like I brought these just in time, Your Lordship."

Aldermaston grabbed a glass, filled it with water and planted it in Bœuf's other hand, wrapped his fingers around it and then carefully brought it up to the celebrity chef's mouth.

Half a pint of tap water disappeared down Bœuf's throat in three gulps. Slowly, his breathing settled and his voice returned, albeit a little croaky.

"*Merde*! That certainly 'as a kick to it!" He raised the pint of Hangman's Anaesthetic to eye level and scrutinised the liquid. "I feel as though my insides 'ave been chemically cleansed, yet… somehow, I can see why people enjoy this."

Aldermaston sipped his glass of tap water. He needed a clear head. "Traditionally, it was the last drink given to a condemned man before he was hanged. It cut off all senses from the neck down."

Bœuf laughed. "In France, we 'ad something similar. It was called ze guillotine."

Cynthia returned with a trolley carrying two three-foot long planks of wood, piled high with sausages, bacon, fried eggs, black pudding, baked beans, two slices of toast, a selection of cold meats and cheeses, baby salad leaves, with mixed peppers, raw onion and cucumber, and a single-serving of Boor Pie, mushy peas, with a side bowl of triple-cooked chunky chips. "Your Last Suppers."

The trolley was the same height as the table, enabling the

septuagenarian to slide the planks straight across. "Bon appétit!" She disappeared into the darkness again.

Bœuf inhaled deeply. "Hmmm. Zis smells wonderful."

Aldermaston relaxed. "There used to be a gibbet just outside the window here." He pointed towards to the stained glass window of locals applauding a man hanging limply from the noose.

"Trials were held in a room upstairs," he continued, "and if a judge dished out a sentence of death by hanging, the prisoners were locked in the basement overnight. Hangings were at midday, so the Last Supper was their last meal, given the night before. It represents a day's three meals in one: fried breakfast, a ploughman's lunch, and a cooked meal for the evening."

Bœuf nodded as he savoured his first mouthful. "A man's last meal should be a good one. And if zis is what they had, then the people of Mortiforde knew how to send a man to his death with a full and happy stomach."

He forked more food towards his mouth. "Our eyes are the first part of our body to devour our meal, yet in here I can hardly see the end of my nose."

"I thought it might offer us some privacy. I hope you're enjoying the festival so far."

"*Mais oui*." Bœuf placed his cutlery down, leant his elbows on the table and gesticulated with his hands. "There is such a beautiful arrangement of food and drink here. I 'ave been blown away by the flavours my taste buds have encountered. I am looking for suppliers to help me with my new contract I have for ze garden parties at Buckingham Palace. I thought I might just find one or two wonderful, flavoursome products here, but I was wrong. The huge choice of first class food you have here is overwhelming."

Aldermaston wiped his mouth with a paper napkin. "We might not lead cutting-edge lives out here in the Welsh Borders, but we have traditions and customs that date back centuries. We know our place in the world. And food is a big part of that. Historically, the town has always harvested what it can from its environs."

Bœuf gathered his next forkful. "And when you know where your food has come from, you respect it, and savour it all the more, do you not think?"

"Exactly." Aldermaston sipped more water. "That history and traceability is important. We have traders here running family businesses going back four, perhaps five, centuries. There aren't many places that can boast that. That goes back to the time when Mortiforde Castle was a royal residence."

"A royal residence? What? Here?"

Aldermaston nodded. "During the sixteenth and seventeenth centuries, Mortiforde Castle was a royal residence, mostly used by royal children, but also royal honeymoons."

Bœuf sat back in his chair. "*Mon dieu*! So in some ways your food festival is like one giant Royal Garden Party."

Aldermaston chuckled. He'd never thought of it like that.

"Lord Mortiforde!" screamed a woman.

Aldermaston dropped his cutlery onto the table as Mairi's face and bloodstained apron emerged out of the shadows. She thrust a sheet of paper in his face.

"Thank heavens I found you. I heard it drop to the floor, as if someone threw it over the counter."

Aldermaston turned the sheet around and held it closer to the electric plastic candle lighting to read it. "Did you see who threw it?"

"No. The shop is heaving. Could have been anybody."

"When did it arrive?"

"About five minutes ago. I rang the Hospitality Marquee, and they said you were here."

Aldermaston stared at the note. Same font as the others. But this one was longer.

If you don't want your husband to be dead meat, deliver 5,000 packs of your Woodland Burger to the Food Marquee by ten o'clock tomorrow morning, to be given away free to members of the public. Fail to do so, and Jock Trotter becomes burger meat.

Aldermaston turned to Mairi. "What's your Woodland Burger?"

"Our burger competition entry for this year. And 5,000 packs are my entire stock for tomorrow. Nearly thirty grand's worth. If we work through the night, we might be able to produce enough for this demand, but…"

"Can you do it?" Aldermaston enquired.

"Oh, for heaven's sake, Lord Mortiforde!" snapped a voice behind Mairi.

Abigail Mayedew stepped into the half-light. "The Hospitality Marquee said I'd find you here." She grabbed the ransom note from Aldermaston's hand. "This is a death threat! Mr Trotter's life is in danger. This is not the time for parochial probing. This is now a police matter!"

CHAPTER NINE

Felicity hobbled into Tugford Hall's main kitchen, just as Cartwright's timer exploded into an ear-piercing alarm. She clamped her hands against her ears.

Impervious to the noise, Cartwright stepped out of the pantry and gently placed a white-gloved hand on top of the alarm, silencing it.

Felicity released her ears. "Please tell me that wasn't the fire alarm because my pastry is going up in smoke."

Cartwright spun round. "Your Ladyship. Perfect timing. The alarm is a tad loud, but there are times when needs must. Especially when one is up to one's elbows clearing the latest blockage in the West Wing waste disposal system."

Felicity grimaced. No one really knew what Basildon got up to in his private quarters, nor did one ever want to know either. But she sincerely hoped Cartwright washed his hands thoroughly afterwards.

A blast of hot air enveloped them when Cartwright opened the oven door. He clasped the pie tin between some oven gloves and brought it out onto the preparation area in the middle of the kitchen. He shut the oven door with a deft kick of his highly polished brogues.

Carefully, Cartwright tipped the beige ceramic baking beans into a Pyrex bowl, revealing a gently tanned and perfectly cooked pastry base.

"It doesn't look burnt." Felicity's nose twitched. "Doesn't smell burnt either."

"That, My Lady, is because it isn't." Cartwright removed the oven gloves and checked the pastry base with the back of his pale-skinned hand. "Spot on."

A frisson of excitement ran through her. It actually looked *edible*. "Right, Cartwright," she said, pulling a sheet of paper from her pocket and then flattening it out on the work surface. "I want to try this recipe for Boor Pie, as my original recipe wasn't working."

Cartwright inspected it. "These ingredients appear…"

"Traditional?" Felicity suggested.

Cartwright nodded. "Half a *pottle* of cider…" Cartwright tapped the paper. "A pottle. If my memory serves me right, My Lady, there were four pints to a pottle. So, we'll need two pints of cider."

"Oh." Felicity frowned. "I thought it was a translation error. Not half a bottle, then?"

Cartwright shook his head. "No, a pottle was equal to two quarts, four pints, sixteen gills, and thirty-two jacks." His finger ran down the list of ingredients. "I have the rest of these ingredients in the pantry, although …" He tapped the recipe again.

"Problem?" Felicity peered at his fingertip.

"The lovage. I think we have some in the walled garden, My Lady."

The archaic clatter of an old telephone bell erupted, echoing around the vast room.

Cartwright stepped across to a black Bakelite telephone

mounted on the wall behind the kitchen door, and lifted the receiver.

"Mortiforde 425738. Framlington! How good to hear from you." Cartwright picked up a pen, purposefully placed beside an awaiting pad of paper. "You have? Marvellous! Her Ladyship will be delighted. Courier it? Five o'clock? Perfect. How are Lord and Lady Greville-Sykes?" Cartwright nodded. "The Countess of Chester hospital? Nothing serious, I hope." Cartwright's eyebrows rose. "Oh. His Lordship was always one for the stable lads." He nodded again. "Perhaps he'll ensure his blunderbusses are kept out of Her Ladyship's reach in future. You'd do well to make the necessary arrangements before His Lordship is released from hospital." Cartwright put the pen down. "Thank you, Framlington. I must return the favour sometime."

Cartwright replaced the receiver.

"Is Lord Greville-Sykes alright?" Felicity queried. "Should we send flowers?"

Cartwright shook his head. "Best keep that to yourself, Your Ladyship. It's not common knowledge."

"What isn't? That Lord Greville-Sykes is in hospital, that Lady Greville-Sykes shot him, or that Lord Greville-Sykes enjoys the company of his stable lads?"

"All the above, Your Ladyship. Framlington's call is good news." He rejoined her beside the preparation area.

"It didn't sound good news for Lady Greville-Sykes. Or Lord Greville-Sykes, for that matter."

"Boar meat," Cartwright declared. "Framlington has five kilos. He's couriering it down to us. Should be here by five o'clock."

"Cartwright, you are a star!" She went to hug him, but stopped herself. Physical expressions of gratitude were not to be encouraged. Against Butler Academy regulations, apparently.

Cartwright blushed heavily. "As I explained, My Lady. Ways and means. And I refuse to stoop so low as to use the Head Butler Private Facebook Group."

Felicity closed her eyes and pictured her first proper Boor Pie, sitting on the table in the Ladies' Legion tent tomorrow afternoon, waiting to be judged.

Suddenly, she opened them and glared at Cartwright, busy covering her pastry case with a fly-screen. If Framlington shared gossip about his employers with Cartwright, what sort of gossip did Cartwright share about her and Aldermaston?

∼

At his desk in the West Wing, Basildon replaced the red Bakelite telephone receiver and scribbled down the details.

So, Felicity's boar meat was due at 5pm. That could be useful. He feared the few drops of sodium thiopental he'd slipped into her pastry earlier would be insufficient. The judge wouldn't eat enough pastry for the sodium thiopental to take effect. He should have spiked the pie's filling.

Basildon bent down, pulled open the bottom drawer of his desk, and counted the number of phials left. Seven. One should be enough for five kilos of meat.

∼

Aldermaston grabbed Abigail's wrist and pulled her onto the seat beside him. "Don't talk about death threats so loudly in a public place."

Abigail jabbed his arm with her finger. "If you don't take this to the police, then first thing Monday morning I shall withdraw all council support from the Borderer's Guild with immediate effect. And I'll ban you from all council premises. Tell the police everything now and I'll reconsider. And when I say everything, I mean *everything*. Including the heart found on the vegetarian stall earlier." Abigail's eyebrows rose two inches up her forehead. She nodded. "Yes, I know all about *that*. Is there anything else I should know?"

Aldermaston shrugged. "What you do Monday morning is your choice. But at this precise moment, you are not the Chief Executive of this authority. Nor do you have any jurisdiction over me or the Borderer's Guild. If you think now is the right time to inform the police, then why don't *you* take that note to the police station?"

Suddenly, the note was whipped from Abigail's hand.

"Like hell she will!" Mairi Trotter stared defiantly at Abigail. "This threat is aimed at me and *my* husband. It's *our* business. It's *my* decision when, or if, I decide to tell the police. Is that clear?"

"I didn't mean to—"

"You're not from round here, love, are you?" Mairi placed her hands on her hips.

"No, but the law is the law, and—"

"Let me give you your first lesson in working with a rural community. Trust. If you trust someone to help when you have a problem, and they deliver that assistance, then that trust magnifies. Ask someone for help, and they go all bureaucratic with form-filling claptrap, then that trust doesn't flourish. But when trust thrives and a community comes together, amazing things happen. This food festival hasn't been going for nearly two decades because of some fancy form-filling. It's happened because the local community and businesses trust one another. They also trust Lord Mortiforde, as they did his father before him."

Mairi waved the note in front of Abigail's face. "Now, I don't trust the person who sent this. There is mistrust somewhere in this community, and we need to sort it. What you need to remember is that I brought this note to Lord Mortiforde because I trust him."

She folded the note twice, turned her back on Abigail, and offered Aldermaston the note. "We need your help, Lord Mortiforde. But, please don't go to the police. You won't let me or Jock down, will you?"

Aldermaston shook his head. He hoped The Nooseman's Knot's poor lighting hid the fear in his eyes.

∼

"You said thirty minutes!" Tibby handed her customer their purchases, then scowled at Ashton. "That's twice you've left me on my own today." She slipped half a dozen more Borderlandshire Blue Burgers on the hotplate and allowed the sizzle and aroma to tantalise passersby.

"Oi'm, sorry, Tibbs," Ashton drawled. "Lost track of time. I'll make it up to you tonight."

He crouched down and peered under the stall at the dwindling stock boxes. "Blimey. You've been busy. We've only half a dozen boxes of tomorrow's supplies left." He rose to his feet. "We'll be flat out tonight, making tomorrow's stock."

Tibby bit her top lip. "You'll have to start without me tonight. I should be with you by ten o'clock."

Ashton grabbed her arm. "What d'ya mean? Ten o'clock?"

"I've been invited out." She pulled her arm from Ashton's grip. "Be with you in a minute," she reassured a customer.

"Look, darling." Ashton tied his apron strings. "I know you're cross, but tomorrow's stock preparation is far more important than a date night with some bloke who's hoping you're going to fondle his root veg at some point."

Tibby's jaw dropped. "I've been invited to tonight's festival dinner at Tugford Hall as the guest of the new Chief Exec."

Ashton stepped back. "The beanpole woman? At Tugford Hall?"

Tibby nodded. "Ms Mayedew is a strong advocate of vegetarian food. Having such a high-profile supporter at the council, and on the Borderer's Guild, could really help our cause."

A grin broke out across Ashton's face. "I wish I were coming with you now. You couldn't get me in, could you?"

Tibby wagged a finger at him. "You'll be too busy making a couple of thousand burgers for tomorrow."

"We'll see," he muttered. "My family has been pushed around enough as it is."

She frowned as she turned to greet the next customer in line. What did he mean by that?

~

In the council basement, Daniel pulled out the next file from the cabinet drawer. Typed across the top of the paper in bold print were the names of the case parties: *Foraging Mortiforde vs Borderlandshire District Council*. Unlike the previous half dozen files, this had potential. It was dated five years ago. He turned the cover.

Defendant: Miss M Bryan trading as Foraging Mortiforde.

Claimant: Borderlandshire District Council Environmental Health and Trading Standards.

Following a public complaint, Borderlandshire District Council undertook a six-week investigation, purchasing and sampling a wide range of products sold by Foraging Mortiforde and proved the business was regularly failing to meet standard weights and measurements legislation.

The complainant, a local business…

Daniel's eyes widened at the name of the business. This was it! And this put a whole new perspective on *everything*.

"Thanks for checking, Sheila." Aldermaston terminated the call and slipped his phone into his tweed jacket pocket.

Abigail threw her hands in the air. "What is it with you people? A local businesswoman hands you a ransom note, and you all conspire not to call the police, quoting some community trust claptrap issues, and now you're phoning round trying to locate the local authority's Chief Archivist. What's she going to do? Rummage through her archives and find the culprit is actually a fourteenth century ghost?" She slumped into the chair, disappearing into the shadows of The Nooseman's Knot.

Aldermaston inhaled deeply. "No. Jillian was supposed to be joining us for lunch. I was trying to establish where she is."

"Per'aps she is engrossed in ze Food History Marquee preparations," Bœuf suggested.

Aldermaston smiled. "Probably. Her big moment takes place there in…" Aldermaston checked his watch. "… ninety minutes."

Abigail leant forward. "Talking of appointments, there is someone I'd like to bring with me to dinner tonight at Tugford Hall."

Aldermaston smiled. "Of course. May I ask who?"

"Tibby Gillard. President of the Mortiforde Vegetarian Society." Abigail smiled. "You met her this morning."

His official how-lovely smile beamed at her. "I'll let Cartwright know." He stood. "Ms Mayedew, could you escort our celebrity guest back to the Food Festival Committee Marquee? I'll join you as soon as I can."

"Why? Where are you going?" Abigail enquired.

Aldermaston took a deep breath. "To see a butcher about a moustache."

Abigail looked bemused. "Please tell me that's a country bumpkin euphemism for something really important."

Aldermaston smiled. It should be. But it wasn't.

∽

Basildon stopped at the top of the rear stairway in Tugford Hall and leant over the banister. There were footsteps. A woman's footsteps. Footsteps comprising two heels, not one heel, and the awkward rubber-soled shoe that Felicity was wearing.

Two flights down, a shadow fell away from bottom rung.

Suddenly, Felicity called out. "Lavinia! Whatever are you doing here?"

The clipped heels on flagstone steps stopped abruptly.

"Felicity, darling!"

Basildon smirked. It *was* Lavinia. What was *she* doing downstairs in Tugford Hall?

"Fancy seeing you here!" Lavinia squealed.

Basildon's right eyebrow rose. She sounded flustered.

"I don't see why you should be surprised," Felicity replied. "It is *my* house."

Lavinia's staccato laugh ricocheted around the stairwell. "No, darling! That's not what I meant. You're *here*. Downstairs."

The creaks of a crutch taking the strain echoed up the stairwell. "Cartwright wanted my opinion of something for tonight's dinner. The Borderer's Guild is entertaining here tonight."

"I'm surprised at Cartwright." Lavinia's heels danced her weight from one foot to another. "Making Her Ladyship struggle down two flights of stairs when she is incapacitated seems a little unprofessional, in my opinion."

Basildon could almost hear the smugness across Lavinia's face.

"It was easier for me to come down than for him to

disconnect the industrial gas ovens and haul them upstairs to me in the Morning Room. Sometimes, one just has to be practical about these matters, don't you think?"

Basildon's left eyebrow rose to mirror his other. He'd never heard Felicity be so forthright before. The Lady of the Manor had guts, it seemed.

"You haven't answered my question. What are you doing here? Are you spying on my Ladies' Legion Bake Off entry?"

Lavinia's nervous laugh rose an octave. Or three. Basildon winced.

"Spying! Felicity, darling. Don't be so silly. No, I was… I was…"

"Yes?"

"I was just…"

"Lavinia!" yelled Basildon. "What the devil are you doing down there, my dear?" He hurried down the stairs, two at a time, coming face to face with both ladies within seconds. He smiled at Felicity, then air kissed Lavinia's cheeks.

"I thought my instructions were clear. Come round the back, and then take the servants' staircase up two flights of stairs and I'll meet you there."

Lavinia frowned, glanced at Felicity, then returned her gaze to Basildon. "Oh! *Up!* I could have sworn you said down!" Her chortle returned to its usual octave.

"Come along, darling. This way." He put an arm around her waist and pulled her upstairs quickly. "There's something I would like your opinion on."

Lavinia waved to Felicity. "Lovely to see you, dear."

Basildon led Lavinia up the stairs, then took the side door into his private West Wing kitchen. He pushed Lavinia into the room, then shut the door quickly. He fell back against it and crossed his arms.

Lavinia smoothed her beige jodhpurs. "That was good of you, Basildon. Making out was here to see you."

"So, what were you *really* doing downstairs?"

Lavinia shrugged. "Don't know what you mean."

Basildon took two steps forward. "You *were* spying on Felicity."

Lavinia guffawed. "Basildon! The trouble with your MI5 infatuation is that you think everyone is up to mischief."

He stepped closer and slid his hand into the front pocket of Lavinia's black and grey herringbone Harris tweed jacket. Gazing into her hazel eyes, he smiled as his fingers pulled out a syringe.

"Ooh, these look nice," Lavinia suddenly exclaimed, picking up a small Stilton and chutney rarebit canapé from a cooling tray on the side of the worktop. "Someone's been busy this morning."

"Help yourself." Basildon stepped back and held up the syringe to the light. The liquid was clear.

Lavinia popped the canapé into her mouth. Within seconds, she was squealing with pleasure. "Basildon, these are seriously good!"

"Why, thank you."

"These for tonight? Felicity said something about a Borderer's Guild event."

Basildon nodded. "I told Cartwright I'd do the canapés. Poor chap has enough to do as it is."

Lavinia popped another one into her mouth. Her eyes narrowed. "Speaking of motives, why would *you* help Cartwright?"

Basildon clutched his hands to his chest, the syringe still within his grasp. "Lavinia, darling! You wound me! But your appreciation of my culinary skills redeems you. You cannot taste the sodium thiopental?"

Lavinia frowned. "Sodium what?"

"Thiopental."

Lavinia shook her head. "Wouldn't know what sodium thio… whatever tasted like. What is it?"

Basildon beamed. "A truth drug."

Lavinia smirked. "It clearly works because I've just told you the truth. I can't taste the sodium thio…"

"Thiopental…" Basildon leant against the kitchen worktop. "So what were you doing downstairs at Tugford Hall when Felicity caught you?"

"About to squirt all of that ammonium chloride into Felicity's Boor Pie." Lavinia clasped her hands across her mouth. Her eyes widened as she stared at Basildon, then glanced at his canapés.

"Ammonium chloride, you say?" Basildon nodded.

Lavinia pulled her hands away from her mouth. "Gosh! Did I just say that out loud?"

Basildon folded his arms across his chest. "Why do you want to sabotage my sister-in-law's Bake Off entry?"

"I want her to fail spectacularly in front of everyone!" she blurted. Her hands shot up and covered her mouth.

Basildon shook his head, grabbed her hands, and pulled them away from her face. "You can't stop the truth from coming out, my dear. Not with sodium thiopental. Why do you want to shame my sister-in-law so publicly?"

Lavinia tensed, her face contorting as she fought the urge to speak.

"Spit it out, darling. You know you want to," Basildon encouraged.

"I hate her!" Lavinia spluttered. "Twelve months I deputised as President of the Ladies' Legion. Nobody thanked me." She threw her hands in the air. "I kept the organisation going after your mother's tragic death. Without me stepping up, the Ladies' Legion would have folded. Then Felicity joins us and everyone wants her as President." She wagged a finger in Basildon's face. "It's not fair! They should have voted for me."

Basildon hugged her. "That's so enlightening, darling. I thank you for being my guinea pig. Don't worry. Its effect will wear off within a few minutes." He stared at the remaining canapés. Tonight's dinner party was going to be such fun. "I say, Lavinia, darling. Would you like to be my plus one tonight? Now you've tested them, it only seems fair that you see the consequences of my new secret weapon."

She beamed. "But what about what I've just told you?"

Basildon shrugged his shoulders. "Doesn't bother me who's President of the Ladies' Legion. You might find you're doing Lady Mortiforde a favour. My brother is involved with several local societies he'd rather not be involved with, but he's the Marquess. There are times when I'm thankful my mother had an affair. Means my little bro' has to do all the high society stuff, not me."

He grabbed her upper arms. "So, come on then, old gal. What do you say? Be my plus one."

Lavinia's face softened, then smiled. "I'd be delighted." She traced the side of his cheek with her finger. "Always have found you an interesting character, Basildon."

Basildon gazed longingly at Lavinia's chortling expression. Suddenly, he was looking at her in a new light. This was a woman on his wavelength.

∽

Daniel staggered into Lisa's office with an eight-inch-thick beige-coloured file under his arms and collapsed into the chair opposite her desk. "This makes interesting reading, but I don't understand everything in it."

The noise of clattering keys as Lisa finished typing up her

meeting notes echoed around the room. "So, what was the name of the company? Ajay couldn't remember."

"Foraging Mortiforde."

Lisa shook her head. "Never heard of them."

Daniel thumbed through the file. "Five years ago. Way before our time. From what I can make out, Foraging Mortiforde were focussed on plant-based products."

"What do you mean, from what you can make out? Surely, that degree from Durham University means you've some brains in that head of yours," she teased.

Daniel poked his tongue at her. "Seeing as you've worked here for nearly a year, I thought you might know what some of these abbreviations mean. You must learn something when you're typing up all those minutes." He turned the page of the file and scanned the contents.

Foraging Mortiforde is a small business selling foraged foodstuffs harvested from Mortiforde Woods and its environs. Produce is collected, washed, positively identified by a second foraging specialist, before being packaged for sale and distribution to local retailers, restaurants and mail order. Typical seasonal foodstuffs include wood sorrel, wild garlic, blackberries, chestnuts and fungi, including chanterelle, oyster mushrooms, and common mushrooms.

These items fall under the Weights and Measures (Packaged Goods) 2006 Act, which stipulates that items should be sold in sealed packets with the weight clearly displayed.

The consumer bringing this case to our attention, Jock Trotter, reported that on three occasions, packages of wild garlic bought online had failed to weigh the declared weight on the packet. Two of their one hundred gram packets only contained ninety grams of produce, while the third contained eighty-eight grams.

Over a two-week period, both Trading Standards and Environmental Health bought a total of fifty-two products, of which six fell under the TNE as a percentage of quantity.

Daniel tapped the sentence with his finger. "What's TNE?"

Lisa curled her bottom lip and shook her head. "No idea. Hang on." She pushed the speaker button on her phone and dialled an internal extension. It rang three times.

"Ajay, Environmental Health."

"Ajay, it's Lisa. TNE. What's that in English?"

"Tolerable Negative Error. You've found the file?"

She clicked her fingers at Daniel. "Daniel, read out that last sentence again."

Daniel moved closer to Lisa's phone. "Over a two-week period, both Trading Standards and Environmental Health bought a total of fifty-two products, of which six fell under the TNE as a percentage of quantity."

Ajay cleared his throat. "When it comes to products sold in sealed packets, businesses have a choice as to which weighing system they use. There's a minimum system or an average system. With a minimum system, the contents in *every* packet must weigh *at least* the figure printed on the packet. It can weigh more, but it can never weigh less. Now, there are some products where the average system works better. This system allows for the *occasional* packet to weigh less than the figure stated, but the vast majority *must* weigh at least the printed weight. The number of *occasional* packets must not exceed the tolerable negative error. This tolerable error varies depending upon the size of the packets."

"How do you police something like that?" Lisa interrupted.

Ajay sighed. "You don't. You do spot checks, but we don't have the manpower, time, or budget. We're reliant upon the public raising the issue with us and asking us to investigate."

"It would never cross my mind to check the weight," said Daniel. "I assumed that it had to be that weight by law."

"It does, generally," Ajay replied, "but this averaging system means there's a margin of flexibility, albeit a small one. Wild leafy material, like salad leaves for example, can't always be packaged to a precise weight. That's why the averaging system exists. Daniel, what does the file say about the underweight packets?"

Daniel's finger ran across the page. "The claims made by Jock Trotter were that two of the one-hundred gram packets they bought only weighed ninety grams and eighty-eight grams."

"The tolerable margin of error for a one-hundred gram packet is four point five grams. Technically, it means a couple of their bags could weigh ninety-five point five grams and it would be treated as a one-hundred gram packet. However, the percentage of bags that is permitted to fall within this weight is low. It's something like four and a half per cent. You said earlier that we bought fifty-two packets and found six that failed to meet the TNE. My maths isn't good, but six as a percentage of fifty-two is higher than ten per cent, which is way more than the legal TNE threshold. So, not only were their packets below the tolerable negative error, but the number of packets below this level was excessive, too. What was the name of the company?"

"Foraging Mortiforde," said Daniel.

"That's it! Family business, if I remember rightly. Unusual. Uncle and niece setup. They foraged in Mortiforde Woods daily. Caused a few problems with Mortiforde Forestry who'd asked them not to harvest from certain areas. Anyway, with our sample purchasing proving they were failing the tolerable negative error by such wide margins, we had to take them to court. Proved to be the end of the business. The fine crippled them financially."

Daniel returned to his chair. "So Jock Trotter's complaint ruined the Foraging Mortiforde business."

"Yes," said Ajay. "And it takes a business involved in weights and measures to understand those regulations."

Lisa placed a finger on her phone's keypad. "Thanks, Ajay."

"Hang on." There was more rustling on the line. Ajay's voice dropped to a whisper. "I've just remembered something. How long ago was this?"

"Five years," said Daniel, checking the date on the front of the file.

"Right. I need to check some other records—"

"Other records?" Lisa leant closer to the phone's microphone. "You mean everything isn't in this file?"

"I've a private notebook somewhere. I write down my thoughts and stuff that can't be backed up with evidence. Can you meet me in the King James Hotel at, say… five o'clock?"

"Why the subterfuge?"

"I'll explain when I get there."

"Thanks, Ajay. We'll see you then." She terminated the call.

Daniel closed the file. "This could be the motive. Whoever ran Foraging Mortiforde are seeking revenge on the Trotters."

Lisa leant back in her chair. "And what better time than by sabotaging a butcher's business during their most profitable weekend of the year?"

CHAPTER TEN

The crowds swept Aldermaston up Southgate Street towards the centre of town. At the corner of the High Street, he sidestepped in through the wide open doorway of Shepherds.

"Psst! Evie!"

Evie handed a customer a beefburger in a bun. "There's your change, dear, and a voting slip. You have until 2pm tomorrow to vote." She turned to Aldermaston. "Have you found him?" Her eyes widened with hope.

Aldermaston shook his head.

Evie nodded despondently. "Follow me," she said, wandering to the back of the shop and taking a door out to a cobbled courtyard.

"I take it you want to see the package?" Evie shut the back door behind them and headed for the rear store beside Maisie's sty.

"Was there a message with it?" Aldermaston asked.

Evie unlatched the outhouse door and stepped inside, then picked something up off the floor. "Once I saw Seth's…" She stepped back outside with a large box in her arms and a tear in her eye.

Aldermaston squeezed Evie's shoulder. "We'll find him. I promise." He took the box and was surprised at its lightness.

Evie wiped her eyes with a handkerchief. "What's this all about? I don't understand."

Aldermaston sat down on a wooden bench near to Maisie's sty, and carefully opened the lid. "There have been developments."

"Developments?" Evie's hands covered her mouth.

"Mairi's received a ransom note."

"A ransom?" Evie stumbled on her feet and clutched the side of the brick sty. "But that's good news, isn't it? Jock must be alive."

Aldermaston acknowledged the point. "Hopefully."

Carefully, he lifted the lid and peered inside. Hiding in the corner, stuck to a piece of card, were the two long, unmistakable twirls of Seth's flamboyant moustache.

Gingerly, he picked up the card between his finger and thumb, and found a small sheet of paper folded twice underneath. He took it in his free hand and gently replaced Seth's pride and joy in the box.

Evie stepped forward. "What's that?"

Aldermaston unfurled it and recognised the font immediately.

If you don't want your husband to be dead meat, then deliver 5,000 packs of your Baa Burger to the Food History Marquee by ten o'clock tomorrow afternoon, to be given away free to members of the public. Fail to do so, and Seth Shepherd becomes burger meat.

Evie hovered close by. "Is it a ransom?"

Aldermaston folded it quickly and slipped it into his tweed

jacket pocket. He placed the box on the bench beside him, then stood and grasped each of Evie's arms. "We'll sort this."

"It is, isn't it? It's a ransom! How much do they want? When do they want it by? What do I have to…" Tears streamed down her face.

"They, whoever these people are, want you to give away thousands of your burgers in the Food History Marquee at ten o'clock tomorrow morning."

"Give away? But… it'll ruin us!"

Evie collapsed, but Aldermaston's grip tightened instinctively, saving her from falling.

"Sit down." He perched her on the bench beside the cardboard box and crouched down in front of her. "I'm not going to say don't worry."

"Fifty-seven years we've been married. I worry about him all the time. But, this business. Butchery. It gets harder every year. Ever since that supermarket opened…"

Aldermaston nodded. "I need to ask you something."

Evie's watery eyes stared straight at him.

"Do you want me to call PC Norten?"

Evie shook her head. "Couldn't cope with his incompetence."

Aldermaston nodded. "Mairi feels the same. When did you last see Seth?"

Evie thought for a moment. "I watched him from our bedroom window up there," she pointed to a second-floor window, "when he left to take Maisie for her walk this morning at about seven o'clock."

"I saw him just before eight." Aldermaston paced the small, cobbled courtyard. "You haven't seen him since?"

Evie shook her head. "I don't think he got back." She paused. "Just let me check." She hobbled over to the outhouse door again and disappeared inside. Moments later, she reappeared, her face white with shock.

"What's the matter?" Aldermaston's hand took her elbow again.

Evie stared at Aldermaston. "He's definitely been back." Her hand covered her mouth.

Aldermaston frowned. "How do you know?"

Evie went to say something, but stopped.

The muffled tone of *The Dam Busters'* theme tune escaped from his jacket pocket. He ignored it. His eyes narrowed. "Come on, Evie. How can you be sure he's been back?"

"Sometimes he brings stuff back from the woods."

"What kind of stuff?"

"Whatever's in season. Wild garlic. Bit of sorrel. That sort of thing. There are some beech nuts in a container in the outhouse that definitely weren't there last night."

"Beech nuts."

"Maisie likes them. We use them as treats." Evie bit her bottom lip. "They weren't there last night."

Aldermaston glanced at the straw-covered cobbled floor. He crouched down and ran his fingers along a relatively clear line on the cobbles. Six inches beside it was another line running parallel through the straw.

Now he'd spotted them, he followed the obvious tramlines across the courtyard to the tall back gate. He stepped across and unlatched it. "What's through here?"

"Back alley."

He peered round the gatepost. To the right was the High Street, a short-distance away, via an alleyway wide enough to take a small van.

Aldermaston sighed. Seth had been kidnapped from his own backyard.

∽

Lisa stared at her phone's screen. "It's going to voicemail. I'll text him." Her thumbs danced across her phone's screen.

Daniel flicked through the *Foraging Mortiforde* short measures file. "I don't understand. If this is some sort of revenge by Foraging Mortiforde because the Trotters destroyed their business, why is Seth Shepherd missing too? He's not mentioned anywhere in this file."

Lisa dropped her phone onto her desktop and leant forward. "And why would someone send threatening notes and pig body parts to the Mortiforde Vegetarian Society and Jillian?"

Daniel flicked back to the main page of the file. "This should simply be a spat between the Trotters and Foraging Mortiforde, which is why this Miss M Bry—"

Lisa leant closer. "What's up?"

Daniel chucked the file on the floor and stood.

"Careful!" Lisa hurried around her desk and picked up the file, collecting the few loose pages that had bid for freedom. "What are you doing?"

Daniel frantically searched every pocket in his suit trousers and jacket. "It's here somewhere. Aha!"

His hand flew out of his trouser pocket, clutching a silver bracelet. Picking through the various charms, he found the disc.

"Gotcha! I think I know who's behind all this."

"Who?" Lisa leant against her desk.

"Miss M Bryan of *Foraging Mortiforde*. This is her charm bracelet. It has her initials. MB."

Lisa peered closer. "How can you be sure that's Miss M Bryan's bracelet, and not some random person whose initials are also MB?"

"She crashed into me coming out of Shepherds this morning. It fell off, and I picked it up. I tried chasing after her, but she disappeared into the crowd."

Lisa returned to her desk. "How can you be sure it was her who collided with you? And I still don't see how that connects her to our ransom notes."

Daniel paced the room and smacked his forehead. "The package!" He stared at Lisa. "I reckon she delivered the package containing Seth's moustache."

"When?"

Daniel collapsed into the chair, and he stared at the floor as this morning's events replayed through his mind. "While you were at the official opening of the food festival, Aldermaston asked me to check Shepherds for some boar meat for Felicity. Just as I reached Shepherds, a young woman dashed out and collided with me. She hit me with such a force I fell to the ground. Something on the pavement caught my eye. This."

He held up the bracelet.

Lisa shook her head. "That doesn't prove it was hers."

"Later, I saw her in the crowds again, and called after her. I held up the bracelet for her to see, but as soon as she saw it, she ran off."

"Perhaps she's heard what a crap date you are." Lisa grinned.

Daniel stuck a middle finger up at her. "When I went into Shepherd's, there was a parcel that had been left on the counter. Evie Shepherd came out from the back and asked me if I'd seen who'd delivered it."

"And had you?"

"Well... I didn't see this woman *leave* the parcel on the counter."

"Did you see her *with* the parcel?"

Daniel wrinkled his nose. "But if she had delivered that parcel with Seth's moustache, it would explain why she ran out of the shop so quickly."

Lisa ran her fingers through her jet black hair.

Daniel stared at the bracelet. "You've got to admit. Miss M Bryan is definitely a person of interest."

Lisa nodded. The bracelet connection was tenuous. But the *Foraging Mortiforde* link was undeniable.

∼

Cartwright placed the walnut tray down on the coffee table, and unloaded the china cup, saucer, milk jug and teapot, bearing the Mortiforde crest.

Felicity sank into the dark brown leather sofa in their private lounge at Tugford Hall and picked up the latest issue of *Country Life*.

"I'll let you know when the boar meat arrives, My Lady." Cartwright poured the tea.

"Thank you, Cartwright. When would be convenient to continue making my pie?" Felicity enquired. "You've enough to do with tonight's dinner in the main hall. I don't want to get in your way."

Cartwright stirred the tea, the spoon caressed the china occasionally as he did so. "If it arrives promptly at five o'clock, then we may be able to do something this evening. If not, first thing tomorrow morning will be fine."

Felicity flicked through the pages of *Country Life*. "I'll be guided by you, Cartwright. I appreciate your mentoring and… good heavens!"

Felicity stared at the magazine.

"Is everything in order, My Lady?" Cartwright stood upright and returned his gloved hands behind his back.

"It says here the Earl of Dartbury jilted his bride on their wedding day, four months ago. Left the poor woman standing at the altar."

Cartwright rocked back and forth on his shoes. "I did hear something, My Lady."

Felicity reached for her tea.

Cartwright continued. "The Earl of Dartbury's butler resigned. He no longer wished to be associated with the family."

Felicity sipped her tea. "But it was hardly the butler's fault." She paused. "Are you happy here, Cartwright?"

"It's an honour to serve the family, My Lady."

She returned the cup back to its saucer. "Have you ever considered leaving us?"

Cartwright's gaze remained fixed on the Stubbs portrait hanging behind Felicity. "It is an honour to serve this family, My Lady."

"That's kind of you, Cartwright. But… what about all that business nearly two years ago? When Basildon's true parentage came to light. Can't have been easy for you."

Cartwright's gaze remained fixed on the Stubbs. "I'm sure it wasn't easy for anyone, My Lady."

Felicity held up the magazine. "No, but there's clearly more concern about the family than the loyal staff. Our family revelations can't have made life easy for you."

"The Earl of Dartbury's head butler is a fine fellow, My Lady. He quickly found suitable employment elsewhere. The Earl of Dartbury, on the other hand, has struggled to fill that post. And therein lies the difference between his situation and your situation, My Lady."

Felicity frowned.

Cartwright's gaze dropped to meet hers. "The Earl of Dartbury brought his fate upon himself. The fate of His Lordship, his brother and yourself, was through other people's actions, not your own. And, if I may, My Lady, I am still honoured to have served the Seventh Marquess and Marchioness of Mortiforde. They were good people who did a lot of good for the community."

Felicity smiled. Cartwright's loyalty was admirable. Perhaps it was best that the revelations about Basildon's illegitimacy had only become known after the sudden, tragic death of both Aldermaston's parents.

"Thank you, Cartwright. Stepping into the Seventh's Marchioness's shoes hasn't been easy, especially as I wasn't expecting it." She sipped some more tea. "I know His Lordship and I get things wrong, which means we rely on you far more than we probably should. But we are truly grateful for your support and loyalty, Cartwright. We couldn't do any of this without you."

Cartwright's eyes moistened. "Thank you, My Lady. And tomorrow, you will knock them dead with your Boor Pie."

Felicity looked at her toes. "I'd rather not cause any more physical pain with my culinary creations. I'd much rather they simply enjoyed the taste and found it edible."

∽

The distracting hubbub of the festival died away as Aldermaston climbed the stone steps from the Buttermarket's open air ground floor up to the enclosed meeting room above. The bells of St Julian's, tucked behind the Buttermarket, chimed three clipped, hourly notes.

He was about to switch off his phone for the Borderer's Guild meeting when he spotted Lisa's text.

URGENT! Meet us and Ajay in the King James Hotel at 5pm. May all be connected with a Short Measures case.

Strange. Why did Ajay want to see them in the King James Hotel? *Great work. See you then.* Aldermaston replied. He was about to hit *Send* when he stopped. He typed another instruction. *Find out what you can about Jock Trotter's arrest six years ago for criminal damage. Check The Powys Gazette.* Then he hit *Send*.

He pushed open the heavy wooden door and stepped into the cosy meeting room.

"Ah! Lord Mortiforde. You made it." Gerald Lockmount gestured towards the seat at the head of the table.

The substantial wooden table filled the room, with six heavy chairs along each side and then a chair at each end. Gerald took the chair immediately to Aldermaston's left.

Next to him sat Cissy Warbouys, her knitting needles clacking as the pale blue ball of wool danced around the table with each tug of her hand.

The Revd Emlyn Makepiece sat next to her, his black wavy hair doing nothing to cover his humongous ears, although the hairs sprouting from his earholes made a valiant attempt. Aldermaston smiled an acknowledgement, which was half-heartedly reciprocated.

To Aldermaston's right sat Stella Osgathorpe, from the Historic Borders Agency, whose silver bob hair cut accentuated her tanned facial skin and blue eyes. Thoughtful, measured, fair-minded but principled, Stella's historical knowledge of the area brought context and reason to the discussion table.

Beside her was Martin Crookmann, manager at the West Mercia Bank, who nodded a welcome, as did his wife beside him, Jane from Crookmann and Co solicitors. Both in their late-thirties, it always concerned Aldermaston how much knowledge of the town's private affairs was known in that household. Martin knew most people's financial affairs, while Jane knew of all their legal and, in some cases, illegal matters. Frequently, the two were connected.

At the far end of the room, standing beside one of the large stone-framed windows overlooking the bustling South Street, stood Abigail Mayedew.

"Abigail, please join us." Aldermaston indicated to the chair next to Jane Crookmann.

Abigail smiled and took the chair at the far end of the table, directly opposite Aldermaston.

"Ladies and gentlemen," Aldermaston began. "I know we

all met her briefly this morning, before the festival's official launch, but let me formally introduce Abigail Mayedew, our new Chief Executive at Borderlandshire District Council." He gestured to the far end of the table. "I'm sure you'll all join me in giving her a warm welcome to the town and to the Guild."

There was a polite smattering of applause. Gerald picked up The Mortiforde Chronicle and shook the creases out of it. "She's already made the front page of the afternoon edition."

There, just as Abigail predicted, was a photo of her on stage this morning, sniffing her fingertips. The headline didn't help.

Mortiforde's New Chief Executive Gets Whiff Of What's To Come.

Gerald dropped the paper and Aldermaston's eyes fell immediately upon Abigail's disdainful face at the far end of the table.

Aldermaston clapped his hands. "Let's crack on with this short update meeting, shall we? We all need to be in the Food History Marquee in an hour's time for the grand unveiling of the historic Mortiforde Royal Recipe Collection."

Abigail cocked her head to one side. "Had any luck locating my missing Chief Archivist?"

Aldermaston shook his head. "Not yet, but I'm sure she's busy preparing for her big moment at four. Festival volunteers have assured me her displays are all ready and prepped." He offered a reassuring smile to the rest of the group. "Jillian was supposed to join our celebrity guest, Bœuf, and me for lunch, but was obviously waylaid with other work."

Cissy stopped knitting. "Jillian missed lunch with Bœuf? I'd have taken her place. I could have given him these." She pulled out an unusually shaped crocheted pouch and suspended it in the air.

"What exactly is it?" asked Martin Crookmann.

"A fruit holder!" Cissy declared, trying not to look hurt. "Look, you slot an orange in here, and another one in here, and this long thin bit in the middle holds a banana."

Aldermaston rested a hand on her elbow. "Keep it safe for now. You'll be able to give it to him at tonight's dinner at Tugford Hall." He turned to Jane Crookmann. "Jane, any legal issues we need to worry about?"

Jane's finger swiped her tablet screen. "We've only had one reported incident of a traffic violation in Watling Street. Maggie Alltarn parked her diesel four-wheel-drive vehicle in an electric car charging bay. It took longer than anticipated for her to move it. She had a flat battery."

Aldermaston turned to Martin. "Any money issues?"

Martin shook his head. "Had a couple of forged twenty-pound notes handed in by traders. The increase is proportionate to the increase in visitors, so I'm not duly alarmed. And, anyway, I've stuffed them back in the cash machine. Most visitors make a cash withdrawal before catching the train, so they might as well take their forged notes back home with them."

Abigail's chair scraped across the wooden floor. "When will we deal with the elephant in the room?"

Cissy stopped knitting, placed her needles down on the table and wagged a finger at the new Chief Exec. "That's no way to talk about Gerald. He's lost a lot of weight recently. It's just from places you can't see so easily, isn't it, Gerald?" She whispered to Aldermaston, "His earlobes have definitely shrunk."

Aldermaston smiled at Cissy. "Ms Mayedew is referring to another matter."

"Too bloody right, I am!" She placed her elbows on the table and leant forward. "At least one, if not two, of our butchers are missing. Not only that, but all the butchers, including staff at the council and the Mortiforde Vegetarian Society, have received threatening letters that were accompanied by a porcine body part of some description. The Vegetarian Society was particularly upset."

Cissy frowned and whispered in the Vicar's hairy ear. "What's a porcine body part?"

"Probably a sausage," replied the Reverend.

Cissy nodded. "Free meat isn't to be sniffed at," she said.

The Reverend pointed to the photo of Abigail on the Chronicle's front page. "I think you'll find it is."

Abigail stood. "The butchers have been threatened with dire consequences if they don't freely give away their competition beefburgers tomorrow morning. This should be a police matter! And I don't mean your local bobby. We need to go higher. Let me chat to the Chief Constable. I guarantee that within an hour, the town will be swamped with uniformed officers and specialist hostage negotiators."

Cissy leant to her right this time and whispered to Gerald, "Did she say free beefburgers?"

Gerald nodded.

"Which butchers?" Cissy asked, hopefully.

"If I can just interrupt you there, Ms Mayedew." Aldermaston raised his hand. "Immediately before this meeting, I was advised that we are close to identifying who may be behind these threatening letters and pig body parts, as well as the ransom note sent to Mairi Trotter—"

Cissy stopped knitting again. "Trotter? Is that where the free beefburgers will be, then?"

Aldermaston smiled. "There won't be any free beefburgers because we'll have this all sorted by then. However, Ms Mayedew thinks going public will resolve the situation."

"Public? With what?" questioned Stella Osgathorpe.

"Sorry, you are?" Abigail enquired.

"Stella Osgathorpe. Historic Borders Agency. We manage

Mortiforde Castle. And I can tell you categorically that if we went public with disappearing butchers, threatening notes, ransom demands and animal body parts being sent to venues across the festival town, we'd be devastated. Visitors would leave within minutes. We'd be left with an economic disaster that a small market town like Mortiforde couldn't recover from. The income we generate from entry fees to the castle over the weekend in itself is enough to finance the upkeep of this historic building for six months. We simply cannot afford to lose this cash cow. Lord Mortiforde's father spent twenty years developing the food festival. It's been the making of many of the independent shops, and the saviour of our tourist attractions in this town. Any potential threat to such a vital part of our economy would be catastrophic. Is that what you want to be known for, Ms Mayedew? As the local authority Chief Executive who killed a vibrant border town community?"

Abigail settled back into her chair. "Well, no, but…"

"So," Stella continued, "if Lord Mortiforde believes that progress can be made locally that will resolve this situation, without the need for outside resources being drafted in, then I think that's the right course of action."

Jane Crookmann raised the pen she was taking notes with. "Can I query something, Lord Mortiforde?"

Aldermaston nodded.

"What does Mairi want?"

"She wants this kept local," Aldermaston advised.

Stella collapsed back into her chair. "Well, there's no point discussing this any further, then. We have to respect the families' wishes."

Aldermaston seized the opportunity. "All those in favour of Ms Mayedew getting in touch with the Chief Constable now, raise your hand."

Cissy leant across the table towards him and whispered, "Is this the option that gets me free beefburgers?"

"There won't be any free beefburgers, Cissy," Aldermaston clarified.

"Pity," she sighed, tugging her ball of wool and freeing up another six feet of yarn.

Aldermaston looked around the room. Only Abigail had her hand up. "One vote. And all those in favour of keeping things between ourselves for the immediate future, raise your hand."

Seven hands rose in the air.

"In that case, Guild members, the motion to keep this between ourselves for the immediate future is carried. Should anything happen that warrants changing our position, I'll be in touch."

Abigail rose from her chair. "I wish it put on record now that, as a public authority, Borderlandshire District Council cannot condone this action. When I take up my position officially on Monday, I shall begin proceedings to withdraw the council's support from this community group. And that includes all the administrative assistance. We cannot be seen to be in partnership with a private fiefdom of which the local community has no say, input or control over. When will this town realise that feudalism ended in the Middle Ages?"

She stood upright, then stomped as well as her four-inch-high heels would allow, along the side of the meeting room, passing behind Cissy and Gerald, and left the room. The door slammed in its frame, causing the sixteenth century single glass panels within the leaded-light windows to shiver.

"She's new, bless," said Jane Crookmann, switching off her tablet and slipping it into her briefcase. "She'll soon come round to how we do things round here."

Aldermaston inhaled deeply. He hoped so.

CHAPTER ELEVEN

Tibby wiped her forehead with the back of her arm, overwhelmed by the queue still waiting to be served.

"Come on, lass," Ashton whined. "Stop slacking. Who's next please?"

An elderly woman passed him a couple of kohlrabi and some mange tout for wrapping.

Tibby slipped another four burgers onto the griddled hotplate and savoured the aroma that burst from them. Her mobile phone burst into life, too.

"Hello?"

"It's Abigail Mayedew."

"Oh, hi! Did you get my message?" She bit her lip, worried that the Chief Executive had now changed her mind.

"I'm delighted you can join me," Abigail replied.

Tibby smiled.

"Although, I should warn you, after the meeting I've just walked out of with Lord Mortiforde and his bloody Borderer's Guild, I'm not sure how welcoming he's going to be. If you want to back out, I'll quite understand."

Tibby's head shook. "No, I'd love to come, if you still want to go."

Abigail snorted. "I'm expected to go. In this job, one has to schmooze with everyone, no matter how big an idiot they are."

Tibby smiled. "I'm keen to go. It's an opportunity for us vegetarians to remind Lord Mortiforde that we won't be swept under the carpet." Tibby flipped each of the four burgers over.

Abigail chuckled. "I might enjoy it, knowing I shan't be on my own. The sanctimonious little dictator really got under my skin this afternoon."

Tibby giggled. "He *has* annoyed you, hasn't he?"

"I'll pick you up from outside the Buttermarket at a quarter to seven. I drive a white Audi TT."

"Perfect. See you then."

The call ended. Tibby grinned. That free Borderlandshire Blue Burger she'd given Abigail was opening doors for her. Tonight, it was opening doors at Tugford Hall.

～

Abigail leant back in her office chair and planned her next step. Her computer screen displayed a professional photo of Marchlands Constabulary's Chief Constable Colin Stoyle, in full police uniform, standing next to the current prime minister. She scrolled through his career history on the police force's website. He'd been in his current post for ten years, which probably explained the remains of his greying hair, and the bald patch that he covered with his uniform cap.

She grabbed the landline handset on her desk and dialled the Marchlands Constabulary number found at the bottom of the webpage.

"Marchlands Constabulary, operator speaking."

"Good afternoon. I'm Abigail Mayedew, the new Chief Executive of Borderlandshire District Council. Is Chief

Constable Stoyle available? I'd like to introduce myself as a fellow public service leader."

"Thank you caller. Connecting you now."

Abigail continued browsing Stoyle's career information. Her eyebrow rose. According to his CV, the Chief Constable spent an early part of his career in the Thameside Division of the Metropolitan Police. It was a couple of decades before Abigail's time at the local authority there, but any connection was better than nothing. Suddenly, the line crackled into life.

"Ms Mayedew! I'd heard you were starting soon."

Abigail leant back in her chair. "Technically, I'm not in post until Monday, but… well, you know how these things work."

Stoyle chuckled softly. "At this level in the public sector, one rarely has defined working hours, just a working way of life."

She heard him typing on his keyboard. "Exactly. It's vital to get one's feet under the table as soon as possible." Abigail swung her feet up on top of her desk.

"Make yourself comfortable," Stoyle suggested, "but a word of advice — don't fill your predecessor's shoes. His were corrupt, which I'm sure you were aware of."

She rotated her right foot in circles, as if showing off her four-inch heels. "When it comes to shoes, I'm in a league of my own. As for corruption, one of the reasons I was selected is because of my reputation for procedures. Down at the London Borough of Thameside, we were praised for our procedural accuracy in all areas of life."

"Thameside, did you say?" The clattering of fingers against lettered keys stopped.

"Yes. Do you know it?" Abigail grinned.

"Spent a few years there as a Sergeant."

"Really? Small world."

"Served me well, as an apprenticeship. But to get any career progression, I had to move around the country a bit. I'm not sure there's much career after Marchlands Constabulary, though. It's a relatively quiet region. Gives me an opportunity to indulge in plenty of golf, and—"

"Sorry to interrupt," Abigail feared she might be invited to join him for a round, "but I do have another reason for getting in touch."

"Oh?"

"We appear to have an issue here. A kidnapping."

Stoyle laughed. "It's called sheep rustling where you are, although they rarely demand a ransom. Most of the time, the thieves sell on their hostages after forging the traceability documentation."

"No, not animal kidnapping. Human kidnapping. A butcher has gone missing, and a ransom has been demanded."

She heard Stoyle's body shift in his chair.

"Really? Do we know about this?" He tapped at his computer keyboard again. "What manpower do we have in the area? Oh. You're in Mortiforde."

"Yes," Abigail confirmed.

"PC Norten's jurisdiction." Stoyle sighed. Deeply. "Abigail, policing works differently here than that of London's Metropolitan force."

"So I'm learning. But we only have one full-time police officer for the *whole* town? A population of ten thousand, and all we get is one copper? One copper who is so lousy the locals are loathe to report any crime to him."

"Every cloud has a silver lining," Stoyle sighed. "You do have an exceedingly low official crime rate in Mortiforde. I have the statistics to prove it. And there are some market towns with no police presence, who would kill to have just one police officer. Literally… even if it were PC Norten."

"Well, we have a serious situation over here, and I need a decent police presence." Abigail swung her feet off the desk and planted them firmly on the floor. "Can you divert any of your other officers to us, please?"

There was another huge sigh. "Ms Mayedew, when I said this isn't the Met, I meant it. Marchlands Constabulary covers nearly twelve-hundred square miles with fewer than 2,000 officers, of which 900 are on duty at any one time, and only 130 of those are on patrol. The nearest officers on duty are twenty-five miles away. There are two of them serving a city of fifty thousand. If there's a road traffic accident on the A492, which there frequently is, I can't pull those two officers from their city base. Instead, I have to draw upon road patrols from forty miles away. Heck, last month I had to ask neighbouring Staffordshire Police to help out with some house-to-house enquiries following a spate of burglaries in the north of the region."

Abigail tutted. "But that's ridiculous!"

"That's rural policing." Stoyle shuffled in his chair. "Look, I'll call PC Norten and tell him to go out on patrol. It's amazing what seeing a police presence on the streets can do."

"It'll do bugger all round here. Nobody has any confidence in the man." Abigail stood and paced behind her desk, aware of how the body language could change the tone of her voice. "I've witnessed a local businesswoman show a ransom demand to Lord Mortiforde, and when I suggested notifying the local constabulary, they both insisted that I do no such thing. Clearly, this town has no confidence in the Marchlands Constabulary."

"Ms Mayedew, let me assure you—"

She sensed she was ruffling feathers. "The only way you'll assure me is by taking this seriously. Can I report a kidnapping, or will you only accept it from the victim's family?"

"In theory," Stoyle explained, "anyone can report a crime—"

"Well, I'm reporting one to you now. And if you don't have any men to send, then I suggest you come over yourself. One thing I learned about leadership is the need to get your hands dirty from time to time. Sounds like now's the time to roll up your sleeves. How long will it take you to get from your HQ to Mortiforde?"

"Er… it's a quarter past three now, I'm a little over thirty miles away, it's October, so the potato harvest is in full swing round here, which means they'll be plenty of tractors causing long tailbacks, there's no trunk road connecting the two of us, so…"

Abigail threw her spare hand up in the air.

"… just after four."

"What? Can't you use your lights and sirens? People's lives may be at stake here."

"That *is* using blues and twos. Welcome to life outside of London." Stoyle hung up.

~

Lisa led Daniel through to the snug at the back of her and Mark's bed-and-breakfast establishment and switched on the kettle.

"Tea?"

Daniel nodded. "Why couldn't we do this in your office?"

"Aldermaston wanted us to look into Jock Trotter's arrest in Powys."

"So?"

She picked a couple of mugs off the mug tree. "Not really sure I want the search being recorded on the council's servers. Now it's clear Abigail is anti-Borderer's Guild, I don't want to give her any further ammunition for cutting support."

Daniel collapsed into one of the comfy leather armchairs situated either side of the wood-burner. The creaking leather stirred Esme, asleep on the two-seater sofa opposite, strewn with blankets to protect it from the moulting coat of a muddy golden retriever. Her excited tail drummed the soft cushion.

Lisa made a quick fuss of her. "Go back to sleep. Daniel's not here to play. I'll take you out for a walk later."

The kettle boiled, and Lisa made two mugs of tea. "There you go." She handed one to Daniel, then sat in the chair opposite, put her mug down on the flagstone wood-burner surround, and picked up her laptop.

Daniel flicked through the Short Measures case file. "There's no personal address for Miss Bryan in this Foraging Mortiforde file, only a business address."

"Where were they based?" Lisa's laptop issued its startup chime.

"Industrial estate. Unit 3b."

"If the business folded, I doubt there's a forwarding address." She tapped away on her keyboard as she searched The Powys Gazette website for *Jock Trotter*. Five results were returned. The first three announced the Trotters as the winners of the food festival's Best Borderlandshire Burger competition for the last three years. The fourth and fifth were more interesting.

"Come and have a look at this. It's from six years ago."

Daniel went and stood behind Lisa's armchair, peering over her shoulder.

ENGLISHMAN CHARGED WITH CRIMINAL DAMAGE

Jock Trotter, 50, of Trotter's Butchery, Weir Street, Mortiforde, Borderlandshire, was sentenced by Newtown Magistrates' Court for criminal damage to the Offa's Dyke ancient scheduled monument. Trotter, who has no previous convictions, pleaded guilty and agreed to pay a £500 fine. He was also banned for three years from visiting the ancient linear earthwork, first built in the 8th century as the border between the Anglian Mercia region and the Welsh kingdom of Powys.

"But that doesn't make sense," said Daniel. "Why would he intentionally damage a scheduled ancient monument?"

Lisa scrolled back to the top of the screen. "Offa's Dyke is a 150-mile-long earth embankment. It's so worn away in places you don't even know you're walking on it. What was he doing?"

Daniel pointed to the bottom search return. "What does that one say? It's dated a week earlier than that last page."

Lisa clicked it.

ENGLISHMAN CAUSES TRENCH WARFARE ON DYKE

Police have arrested Jock Trotter, of Trotter's Butchery, Weir Street, Mortiforde, Borderlandshire, and charged him with criminal damage to an ancient scheduled monument. The damage occurred last Tuesday when a passing hiker on the Offa's Dyke National Trail saw Mr Trotter encouraging a pig to churn up a forested section of the 8th century soil embankment. The hiker claimed the animal bulldozed its way through a six-feet wide stretch of the ancient earthwork, almost completely obliterating it in the process.

'It looked like something out of the First World War trenches,' said Mr Brian Southmall, from Penzance, who was walking the entire Offa's Dyke National Trail. 'There was so much churned up mud, I couldn't see where the right of way went. When I complained, he just laughed at me and told me to bugger off!'

Mr Trotter is scheduled to appear before Newtown Magistrates' Court in ten days' time.

Lisa twisted round to look at Daniel. "Why would Jock Trotter incite a pig to do that sort of damage?"

∼

Inside the industrial, plastic-walled Food History Marquee, the cacophony of chattering anticipatory voices hung in the air, trapped by the PVC roof, like cling film covering proving dough. The air was stale, like most of the exhibits Jillian had curated for the exhibition. Around the perimeter of the white, plastic-walled marquee stood huge metal display units topped with heavy-duty Perspex lids, housing small LED lights spotlighting a variety of historical objects: wooden cutlery, cooking utensils, pots, pans and ornately carved wooden plates, all remnants from Mortiforde Castle's Royal Palace days over four hundred years ago.

At the far end, where Aldermaston was heading if he could negotiate his way through the thronging crowd of expectant festival-goers, was Jillian's *pièce de résistance*. Currently, shrouded in a thick black cloth, was a six-foot-tall cabinet display case, housing the recipe book on loan from the Royal Palaces Collection. Its official unveiling was due to take place in… Aldermaston checked his watch… ten minutes.

The uneasiness in his stomach threw a few punches. Where was Jillian? *This* was her moment. He glanced around, yet couldn't see her.

Abigail stepped out from behind Jillian's star cabinet. "Lord Mortiforde. I wondered when you'd finally show up."

Abigail's perfume of sweet, mandarin orange and amber briefly smothered the marquee's heady aroma of heavily trampled grass and trapped body odour.

"Have you seen Jillian?" He peered around the glass cabinet to be met with a continuous blur of moving heads, all jostling to get a clearer view of the main cabinet.

"No." Abigail bent closer to his ear. "Do council staff often chicken out of the main event, right at the last minute? This would be a disciplinary matter at Thameside." Her lips pouted disdainfully.

Aldermaston searched the crowd frantically now, willing for

Jillian to appear. "Jillian wouldn't let us down. Not if she can help it. This took months of negotiations. She'll be here for the announcement at four o'clock."

The bells of St Julian's began their hourly peal.

Abigail's eyebrows rose. "You were saying?" She gestured to the black-clothed cabinet. "The crowd is waiting. I think you'd better crack on, don't you?"

Aldermaston surveyed the room, desperate to spot Jillian pushing frenetically through the crowds. But she was nowhere to be seen.

A sense of dread overwhelmed him. *Jillian wouldn't let us down. Not if she can help it.* Why had he said that? *Not if she can help it?* What was his subconscious telling him?

A sickening sensation swirled in Aldermaston's stomach. Jock Trotter had been threatened and was now missing. Seth Shepherd had been threatened and was now missing. And first thing this morning in Lisa's office, Jillian had opened a package that contained a threatening message. Aldermaston closed his eyes. It could only mean one thing. Jillian Jones had been kidnapped, too.

∽

Cartwright entered Basildon's private study and placed the silver tray down on the end of the paper-strewn, green, leather-topped desk.

"I say, Cartwright." Basildon looked up from the spread of papers sprawled across his desk. "Bit early for afternoon tea, isn't it?"

Cartwright picked up the teapot and poured. "Normally, sir, I would agree, but in light of this evening's gathering, and slightly earlier dining time, I thought you might like your afternoon tea proportionately sooner."

Basildon leant back in his chair. "Good thinking,

Cartwright. One should not let afternoon tea spoil one's dinner."

The butler dropped a dash of milk into the tea-laden china cup.

"Especially as I've gone to so much trouble with my canapés."

Cartwright placed the cup and saucer closer to Basildon. "Your assistance in that matter has been gratefully appreciated, sir."

Basildon sipped some tea. "And by helping you, I've been able to help Her Ladyship, haven't I?"

Cartwright stepped back a pace and placed his hands behind his back. "You have, sir?"

Basildon leant forward. "If I hadn't made the canapés, you wouldn't have had time to assist Lady Mortiforde with her Bake Off entry, would you?"

Cartwright avoided eye contact. "Like the Seventh Marchioness, she only needs some reassuring guidance. Her Ladyship is doing it all herself and—"

"I'm making an observation, Cartwright, not an accusation," Basildon interrupted. "My main observation is that of teamwork."

Cartwright smiled. "That is how I explained it to Her Ladyship."

Basildon picked up a small photograph lying among the confusion of papers and wandered round his desk to Cartwright's side. "Can I ask you something in confidence, old chap?"

Cartwright pursed his lips.

Basildon slapped him on the back. "Forgive me, Cartwright. Turn of phrase, not a direct question. You see, this is where I think I've been going wrong all these years."

He held the photo in front of Cartwright's face.

"What do you think? Lavinia's a wonderful specimen, isn't she?"

"In my experience, sir, we all see something different in everybody."

"Exactly! Something happened earlier, and I saw Lavinia in an entirely different way."

Cartwright looked at the photo again and hoped so. Lavinia was partially naked, and frolicking about in the River Morte, somewhere on the Mortiforde estate. Her nappy sagged and the inflatable armbands she wore were far too big for her.

"I've literally grown up with this woman, yet today I truly saw her for the first time," Basildon continued. "This is where I've been going wrong. MI5 and MI6 see me a lone wolf. A single man in his mid-forties. Unattached. Nobody to act as a sounding board. And that, I think, is what scares them. Whereas, if I were married…"

"Ah!" Cartwright nodded. "Teamwork, sir."

"Exactly!" Basildon pointed at the infant Lavinia in the photo. "If I were to approach the Security Services as a married man, they are bound to look upon me more favourably."

Cartwright smiled. "If you say so, sir."

"I do! I do!" Basildon laughed. "And that's what I need her to say to me when I ask her to marry me."

Cartwright's eyebrows rose momentarily. "Anticipating a short courtship, are you, sir?"

Basildon returned to his chair. "You're right, old bean. Got to woo her first, haven't I? Well, that starts tonight. Did I mention I'd asked Lavinia here tonight as my plus one?"

Cartwright took a deep breath. "No, sir. You hadn't."

"Not a problem for someone like you, is it, Cartwright?"

"No, sir. There are never problems in life, only memorable highlights to one's day."

Basildon leant forward, his arms crushing paperwork

beneath them. "I say, Cartwright. I've not done much of this wooing lark. Couldn't give me any pointers, could you?"

Cartwright nodded and smiled. The highlights of one's day were really mounting up.

∼

"Get a move on!" boomed a male heckler. "I'm losing serious drinking time here."

A ripple of laughter ricocheted around the PVC walls. Aldermaston glanced at Bœuf, who shrugged his shoulders. Abigail tapped her wristwatch.

The sickening feeling in his stomach tightened. He should stall the official opening somehow. This was Jillian's moment. But… if he delayed any further, the crowd would become too agitated and disperse. As his father once told him, you never get a crowd back once you've sent them away.

His eyes swept the mass of faces before him, desperately searching for Jillian. She wasn't there. He inhaled deeply. The show had to go on. That's what he'd seen his father do. In times of struggle or uncertainty, people clung to any sort of normality they could find. Not that many people would call Mortiforde *normal*.

A finger prodded him sharply in his back. Abigail held up both hands in the air, despairingly.

It was no good. He had to get on with it.

"Ladies and gentlemen!" His voice boomed across the marquee, and nearly two hundred other voices suddenly fell silent. "Apologies for the slight delay, but it appears one of our party is caught up with the festival elsewhere, and is unable to get to us. I've been asked to step into the breach."

A kick stool suddenly appeared near Aldermaston's feet. Abigail nodded at it. He climbed on, his face now clearing even the tallest of heads in the crowd before him. Automatically, he scanned the gathered faces for Jillian.

"Jillian Jones, Chief Archivist at Borderlandshire District Council, has curated this amazing display of food items from Mortiforde's historic past, some of which have not been on public display before." He stretched out a hand, waving at his surroundings. "The castle, the grounds of which you are standing in now, played host to many a royal banquet. The chefs working here recorded several of the royal family's favourite recipes, creating a unique recipe book."

He turned to face the black velvet shrouded display cabinet. "Contained under here are the results of Jillian's dogged determination at tracking down this document, and her success at securing its loan for today's event. For the first time in over four hundred years, I'm delighted to announce that the Mortiforde Royal Recipe Book has come home."

Aldermaston turned and gestured to Bœuf. "And we'd be most grateful if our celebrity chef, Bœuf Boucher, could do the honours and unveil it."

A smattering of applause rippled through the marquee as Bœuf initiated a countdown, waving his arms at everyone, encouraging them to join in.

"*Cinq, quatre, trois, deux, un …*"

With a sharp tug, the black cloth tumbled to the floor.

Three of the closest women emitted blood-curdling screams, and a man holding a half-consumed pint of cider passed out and collapsed to the floor.

Horrified, Aldermaston turned towards the display cabinet and came face to face with his worst nightmare: a severed pig's head. And there, in its mouth, was a pair of white, cotton inspection gloves. *Jillian's gloves.*

CHAPTER TWELVE

"Please go and enjoy the rest of the festival," Aldermaston chivvied, ushering the remaining visitors out of the marquee. "It's all some mischievous misunderstanding, that's all."

He beamed at the last woman to leave, who took one final glance over her shoulder at the porcine head, then hurried out through the marquee door. Aldermaston slammed shut the plastic door, sending shock waves along the industrial marquee's rigid plastic walls, and locked it.

"I want a word with you," Abigail hissed in his ear.

He turned round. "Just the one?"

"We have three women being treated for shock over there." She indicated over her shoulder with her left thumb.

Aldermaston peered round her to see six St John's Ambulance volunteers, two to each unconscious woman, waving white handkerchiefs in front of their faces and patting their wrists in an attempt to revive them.

"I'm more worried about Jillian." He marched over to the display, where the pig's head sat, its eyes gazing over the space filled moments ago by at least two hundred expectant festival-goers.

Abigail crossed her arms. "We need the proper authorities involved, and I'm not talking about that lanky dipstick you introduced me to this morning!"

Aldermaston stared at the pig's head. From this angle, it looked like it was grinning. Smirking at him for being so foolish. Teasing him for not having acted differently earlier. "I don't understand," he muttered.

She threw her hands up in despair. "Is everyone around here a complete imbecile?" She placed a hand behind his back and pushed him forcibly closer to the display unit. "You did that! You did that because you didn't go to the police when that butcher woman showed you the ransom note in the pub earlier. You did that when you failed to escalate the issue to the proper authorities first thing this morning when porcine body parts began turning up all over town!"

She flung her finger at the glass display cabinet and pointed to the pig's snout. "You did that, because you're just like all the other pretentious, egotistical, supercilious, condescending, patronising upper-class twits who think they run this country."

Abigail clasped her forehead. "When will you realise that it was *your* action, or rather your *lack* of action, this morning that effectively sealed Jillian's fate? If anything has happened to Jillian Jones, Your Lordship, *you* are culpable. You have blood on your hands too."

She stood there, nostrils flaring, chest heaving, eyes staring.

Aldermaston shook his head. "That's not what I meant. I don't understand Jillian's note."

Abigail scowled. "What? What note?"

Aldermaston stepped closer to the display cabinet. "Seth Shepherd's note mentioned having blood on his hands. But Jillian's note was different."

He paced around the display cabinet. "It was about retribution."

Abigail threw her arms in the air. "Who cares *what* it was about? She's missing! Lord Mortiforde, there comes a moment in every crisis where someone has to lead with authority. And so far, you have failed to do so."

Aldermaston went to raise a finger, but Abigail raised hers first.

"No! I won't tolerate it any longer. You're failing to lead this town through this crisis. In fact, you're making a complete pig's ear…"

She paused, bit her bottom lip, and looked down at her shoes. "This situation is deteriorating drastically, and if someone else doesn't take control, things will only get worse. A council employee is missing, so from now on, I'm in charge of this food festival. Got that?"

Three short, sharp, ferocious bangs against the plastic marquee door made them flinch. Abigail peered over Aldermaston's shoulder and beamed.

"At last! Reinforcements."

She strode the few paces to the door, unlocked it, and threw it wide open.

"Colin, do come in."

Chief Constable Stoyle stepped into the marquee, removed his cap, and slipped it under his arm.

Abigail locked the door behind him. "Thank you for coming," she began. "There have been some further developments since we spoke on the phone."

Stoyle saw Aldermaston, grinned and held out his hand. "Lord Mortiforde. Always good to see you."

They shook hands. Aldermaston nodded. "Always lovely to have the police presence in Mortiforde doubled."

Abigail marched past them both and stood next to the glass

cabinet. "Chief Constable Stoyle, the local authority's Chief Archivist is missing. She should have been here to unveil this."

Stoyle frowned. "Why was she unveiling a pig's head?" He turned to Aldermaston. "I wouldn't show up for that, either!"

"She was supposed to be unveiling the Mortiforde Royal Recipe Book," Aldermaston clarified. "When she didn't turn up, I took over proceedings."

Stoyle stepped closer to the display and examined its contents. "Yes, I can see this is a grave matter indeed. It raises several questions."

Aldermaston caught Abigail's knowing look. "Yes! Like where's my Chief Archivist?"

Stoyle turned to face Abigail. "And where is the Mortiforde Royal Recipe Book?"

∞

"What's going on?" Tibby peered over the festival-goers mingling around the stalls. The general hubbub around Market Square had suddenly increased.

Ashton placed his hands in the small of his back and arched it backwards. "Don't tell me it'll get busy again. I haven't stopped all day."

Tibby stared at him. "You stopped at least twice when you naffed off and left me on my own. You haven't forgotten you're helping Mrs Hargreaves tonight, have you? There are several thousand Borderlandshire Blue Burgers to be made tonight."

Ashton's shoulders dropped. "I'll be sick of the bloody things by the end of the evening."

Tibby waved a spatula in front of his nose. "You heard what Bœuf said. This is the best vegetarian burger he's ever tasted. Play our cards right, and we could have a contract to supply the Buckingham Palace garden parties."

Ashton nodded, then waved in the direction of Trotter's

Butchery in Weir Street. "Can't wait to get one over those bloody butchers!"

"You and me, both." Tibby turned to a potential customer browsing their stall. "Can I help you?"

He scratched his forehead, just below his bright orange turban, as he deliberated. "I'll take one of your Borderlandshire Burgers, please, love." His West Midlands accent caught Ashton's attention.

"Come across to the Welsh Borders for the day, have *yow*?" Ashton's Black Country accent suddenly strengthened.

The customer nodded. "No point stopping now, though."

Tibby selected a freshly cooked burger and sandwiched it between a soft roll. "Why? What's happened?"

The customer shrugged his shoulders. "That historic recipe book has disappeared. Bœuf unveiled it, but it wasn't there."

Tibby stopped titivating the burgers on the hotplate. "What? The display case was empty?"

The customer chuckled. "Oh, it weren't empty. But you don't want to know what was in it. They soon cleared everyone out of the marquee, I can tell you." He handed Tibby a five-pound note.

She handed him his burger, took his money and then watched him disappear into the crowds. She turned to Ashton. "I bet the council's Chief Archivist is panicking."

Ashton chuckled. "Who wants to look at a dry, dusty, boring old recipe book written in Latin? People want today's food! Modern food! Like a bloody tasty vegetarian burger." He collected a fresh packet of burgers from under the stall and stabbed the plastic seal with a knife.

Tibby frowned. "How do you know it's written in Latin?"

Ashton crimsoned slightly, shrugged his shoulders, and sliced open the packet. "Bound to be. It's like, what, four hundred years old?" He turned and sliced open half a dozen more white, fluffy rolls.

Aldermaston walked around the rear of the display cabinet. The pig's head was suspended four feet in the air on a glass shelf, giving the impression it was floating.

"Presumably, whoever put this here," he pointed at the display case, "has taken the recipe book."

Abigail crossed her arms. "Not necessarily. That could have been placed there before Jillian had a chance to install it."

Chief Constable Stoyle perused the cabinet. "Both scenarios are plausible. There's no evidence of tampering." His fingers tugged at a small padlock securing the clear rear door. "How many people were in here setting up earlier?"

"This has been Jillian's domain," Aldermaston explained. "She's had a week to set this all up. A couple of festival volunteers were helping her, but that's it. The doors opened to the public at three-thirty, ready for the unveiling at four o'clock."

Stoyle nodded in thought. "And what time, Your Lordship, was Jillian scheduled to place the food diary in the display case?"

"Not until shortly before the doors opened to the public," Aldermaston explained. "The recipe book only arrived this morning. Ms Mayedew and I were present at the time. Since then, Jillian kept it safely in her office—"

"Was that the most secure place?" Abigail interrupted.

Aldermaston inhaled deeply. "Ms Mayedew, when you get your guided tour of Borderlandshire District Council's offices, you'll see that Jillian's office has numerous locked units that meet all the authority's insurance criteria. As part of the negotiations with the Royal Palaces Collection, we had to send photos and detailed specifications of the safe where the recipe book would be stored until its display."

Stoyle paced the marquee, browsing the other exhibits.

"Abigail, you mentioned earlier about a missing butcher and a ransom note."

Abigail stepped forward. "Yes—"

"But there were strict instructions not to involve the police," Aldermaston interrupted. "Weren't there, Ms Mayedew?"

Abigail placed her hands on her hips. "If there's criminal activity taking place, the police have to be informed. I expect Chief Constable Stoyle to act."

Stoyle peered closely at a wooden bowl exhibit. "My wife is looking for something just like this for the sideboard in our dining room. Be ideal for her collection of fir cones." He paused, then turned to Abigail. "Which butcher are we talking about?"

"There are two," Aldermaston advised. "Jock Trotter and Seth Shepherd. Both wives told me categorically not to involve the police."

"That's fine, Your Lordship. Leave that with me." He stepped closer to them both. "And how long have they been missing?"

Abigail turned to Aldermaston. "I'm not too sure…"

"This morning. Jock Trotter went out for a walk this morning before seven, but didn't return. I saw Seth this morning just before eight o'clock in Mortiforde Woods. He's not been seen since."

Stoyle winced. "About eight or nine hours, then. Abigail, you mentioned something about a ransom."

"Mrs Trotter found Lord Mortiforde at lunchtime. She showed him the note. If they don't offer their beefburgers to the public for free from ten o'clock tomorrow morning, then it was clear the result would be fatal for Mr Trotter."

"And Mrs Shepherd received a similar threat?" Stoyle enquired.

Aldermaston nodded.

Stoyle took the cap from under his armpit and placed it on his head. "I'll talk to Mrs Trotter first." He checked his watch. "Going to be a late night."

"Come to Tugford Hall," Aldermaston offered. "Cartwright can sort you out a room. We're hosting a meal tonight for the Borderer's Guild. You're most welcome to join us."

Stoyle smiled. "Thank you, Your Lordship. That's extremely kind of you."

Aldermaston smiled. "I assume, Chief Constable, you'll need to examine Jillian's office." He turned to Abigail. "Perhaps you could show him round. It'll give you an opportunity to see more of your estate."

Stoyle nodded. "That would be helpful, Abigail." He turned to Aldermaston and shook his hand. "I'll see you later tonight, Your Lordship. Abigail, shall we?" He indicated to the marquee door.

She smiled at Stoyle, then scowled at Aldermaston, stepping to within an inch of his ear. "If I find out you're holding back anything from Chief Constable Stoyle's investigation," she whispered, "I will make sure this is the last Mortiforde Food Festival. *Ever.* Got that? Remember. This is *your* father's legacy, not mine."

∽

Lisa was washing their mugs when her mobile phone rang. It was Aldermaston.

"Hi, Aldermaston. How did Jillian's big moment go?"

"It didn't. It's a disaster. I've made a terrible mistake. Where are you?"

"At home. Why?"

"I need you to search Jillian's office NOW!"

Lisa switched her mobile to speakerphone, placed it on the

table and put her coat on. "What am I looking for?"

"The recipe book. Both it and Jillian are missing."

"WHAT?"

"I'll explain later. Abigail's got the Chief Constable here. She's really going for it big time now one of her council employees has gone missing. They're heading for Jillian's office to look for any clues. Hopefully, the recipe book is still locked in Jillian's safe. If the safe is locked, we'll have to assume it's still in there. Have a look round for anything else while you're there."

"Like what?"

"Anything. Nothing makes any sense at the moment."

Lisa grabbed her phone off the table. "I'm on my way now. I'll meet you at the King James Hotel at five."

∼

Basildon plumped the pillows on his four-poster bed. The crisp, white, Egyptian cotton sheets dazzled his eyes as he smoothed the Ralph Lauren Weston Park duvet cover, with its decadent patterns of neutral colours.

He stepped back, nearly tripping over the dirty laundry he'd stripped from his bed earlier. He'd take it down to the laundry rooms soon. Felicity's boar meat would be here soon. He wanted to be below stairs for that.

His eyes lingered on the freshly made bed. What else would a woman like Lavinia want? Not that he knew Lavinia would make it this far, after joining him for dinner tonight, but budding intelligence officials should always be thinking ahead.

He pictured the scene… Lavinia draped across his bed, wearing only her underwear, and running her hands through…
ROSE PETALS!

Basildon dashed to the door. Never had Tugford Hall's rose garden ever been of interest to him. But now…

Sheila looked up from her reception desk. "You're going the wrong way for a Friday evening, Lisa. It's nearly five. Most people are going home now."

Lisa smiled at the receptionist, even though she disagreed with that statement. During her six months in post, she'd soon learned that to most local authority staff Friday was POETS day — Piss Off Early, Tomorrow's Saturday. "Need to check something for the festival. Shan't sleep if I don't take a look."

Sheila slipped her arms through the sleeves of her green coat as she waited for her computer to shut down. "You're far too conscientious for your own good."

"Shan't stop long."

Sheila stepped out from behind her reception desk, her coat label visible, the seams stood proud, and the beige internal lining on the outside. "The work will still be here Monday morning. The fairies don't come in and do some overnight." She sighed. "More's the pity."

"Have a good weekend," Lisa called, leaving Sheila to determine why she couldn't find her coat pockets.

About halfway along the main corridor, she turned left into a side corridor with four offices, two on either side, and went to the one on the far left. *Jillian Jones, Chief Archivist*, declared the name plate.

Lisa knocked, grabbed the handle and pushed, praying it wasn't locked. The latch clicked, and the door released.

She slipped inside, muffling the sound of the door closing as best she could. The room was eerily quiet. A bank of four-drawer filing cabinets filled one wall, while the opposite wall mirrored those, albeit with low-slung, wide-drawer cabinets topped with Perspex displays, all filled with archive material.

Against the opposite wall was Jillian's paper-strewn desk, illuminated by a vast office window, although the blinds had been partially closed to keep out the harshest of sunlight. Piles of papers, files, and documents, teetering precariously at various angles, towered above her computer display, which was still switched on.

The rest of the desk was strewn with agendas, reports, historical maps and various minutes of groups she'd never heard of. Tentatively, Lisa moved some paperwork, looking to see what it covered. More paperwork. Lisa jumped when she uncovered a plate with a half-eaten jam doughnut, its bright red jam oozing ominously, as if a Middle Ages specialist had recommended some blood-letting for health purposes.

She covered it with another sheaf of papers, revealing as she did so a hand-scrawled to-do list, with many of this morning's activities crossed off:

— *meet Bœuf Boucher and Lord Mortiforde for lunch,*

— *review Food History Marquee displays,*

— *take recipe book from locked safe and place in display (leave open at recipe for Boor Pie),*

— *rehearse speech,*

— *print off information leaflets for press,*

— *be at Food History Marquee for 3pm.*

So, Jillian had disappeared before lunch. Her finger tapped the third item on the list. *Take recipe book from locked safe…*

She glanced around the room and spotted a huge, thick-walled metal safe in the corner adjacent to the bank of four-drawer filing cabinets. It was the height of two-drawers and had a two-drawer filing cabinet standing on top of it.

Lisa pulled the circular-shaped handle in the middle of the door. It creaked, squealed, and slowly opened wide, revealing … an empty safe.

"Sod it!"

She returned her attention to Jillian's desk, looking for anything that might be useful. Issues of *History Today*, *Archaeology Today* and *Trenchdiggers Monthly* littered the space, many folded back on themselves at a specific article, which Jillian had scribbled over.

Pushing them aside, a paper file dropped off the edge of the desk to the floor, spilling its contents.

She tutted as she crouched down to pick up everything.

The file was labelled *Trace Your Ancestors Evening Class*. On the front was a list of student names. Inside, she found a section of a map. Near the centre, in a particularly dense section of the wood labelled *Dead Man's Hollow*, Jillian had put a small, red cross.

She glanced at her watch. She was supposed to be meeting Ajay and the others at the King James Hotel in five minutes. Hurriedly, she grabbed more papers from the floor, one of which comprised several sheets of A3 paper taped together. It was a family tree of gigantic proportions, going back several generations. Lisa's eyes widened as she noticed some dates. This went back to the seventeenth century.

She carefully folded it and added it to the file. Only two more sheets of paper remained on the floor. One was an agenda for the Borderer's Guild Food Festival debriefing meeting scheduled for next Tuesday evening. The other was a blank sheet. She turned it over and gasped. It was Jillian's handwriting. *This is retribution for your forefathers' sins.* Weren't they the words of the note in Jillian's first package earlier this morning? Underneath, in huge capital letters, Jillian had written: *I'm related to a murderer!*

CHAPTER THIRTEEN

"Just sign here, mate."

From the shadows under the back stairs, Basildon watched Cartwright sign for the large cardboard box resting at his feet at the tradesmen's entrance. He slipped his fingers into his right jacket pocket to check the phials were there. "Ouch!" he hissed.

Cartwright turned, looked down the long corridor to the stairwell, then shook his head.

Basildon pulled his fingers out of his pocket, along with a couple of orange rose petals. A rose thorn punctured the tip of his middle finger. He pulled it out and a bead of blood appeared. Basildon sucked his fingertip as Cartwright collected the box and kicked the tradesmen's door closed behind him, then disappeared into the kitchen.

Sounds of packing tape being torn off the cardboard box, followed by further knocks and bangs, echoed along the corridor. Moments later, Cartwright came out of the kitchen.

Basildon slipped back into the shadows, as Cartwright approached the stairs and trod purposefully up to the ground floor. A door banged.

He peered around the stairwell and glanced up through the banisters. Silence. Slipping out of his hiding place, he hurried to the kitchen.

There, on the large preparatory worktop, was a large cool box, the lid of which now lay beside it, and next to that was a clear plastic box containing Felicity's boar meat.

Basildon grinned.

He unlatched the plastic lid. From his left pocket, he retrieved the two phials of clear liquid. Removing the tops, he checked over his shoulder, before pouring the transparent contents of both phials onto the pink meat.

Hurriedly, he slipped the empty phials back into his pocket and replaced the lid on the plastic box. Then he picked it up, turned it upside down, and shook it.

A door clanged in the distance.

Basildon returned the box the right way up and replaced it exactly where Cartwright had left it. Then he dashed to the kitchen door.

Cartwright's slow, steady, foot-stepped descent echoed in the stairwell.

Basildon turned left out of the kitchen and slipped out through the tradesmen's entrance, with a huge grin on his face. Mission accomplished.

～

Aldermaston stepped through the front entrance of the King James Hotel, ducking slightly, as he did so. His fingers ran along the dark oak panelling of the entrance hall, tracing the grooves and ridges originally carved into it, now perfect for collecting the dust of history.

"Afternoon, Lord Mortiforde." The receptionist beamed. "The festival's going well, isn't it?"

He nodded. "So far, so good," he lied. "Business good?"

"Full occupancy for the weekend. And the dining room is fully booked all weekend too."

"Excellent. That's why we put ourselves through all of this madness."

He made his way through to the lounge at the hotel rear, which was a collection of linked alcoves and corners, populated with a mixture of brown and green leather armchairs and occasional tables, perfect for sitting in and relaxing with the papers.

"Psst."

Aldermaston turned and spotted Daniel and Ajay huddled in a dark corner alcove. A large pot of tea, with cups and saucers, filled the table.

Daniel peered at his watch. "Lisa's late."

Aldermaston slipped into a high wingback chair. "Sent her on an errand. She shouldn't be long."

Ajay leant forward. "Is it true, Your Lordship? About Jillian."

Aldermaston's stomach churned. "I hope not, but I fear the worst."

Lisa suddenly stumbled across them. "Sorry I'm late." She collapsed into the remaining chair and removed her coat.

"Any luck?" Aldermaston enquired.

Lisa bit her lip and shook her head.

Ajay leant forward. "I'll be Mother, shall I?" He distributed the cups and saucers, the noise of the clattering china, helped shield what he wanted to say from any passers-by.

"Daniel has the file detailing the short measures case between ourselves and a company called Foraging Mortiforde. I can explain the intricacies of the case later to you, but in essence, Jock Trotter bought produce from Foraging Mortiforde that was of a lower weight than the figure declared on the packet. That is against regulations. Jock brought it to our attention at Environmental Health and Trading Standards, and so we investigated. We found the Trotters' claim to be valid. Foraging Mortiforde were blatantly misleading the public, selling produce that did not meet the weight requirements according to the packet."

Aldermaston nodded. "A clear breach of regulations, then."

"Exactly." Ajay poured milk into each of the cups. "But this all kicked off about six months *after* I'd met with Jock Trotter here in the King James Hotel one evening."

Aldermaston leant closer. "Could Jock have fixed the case in some way?"

Ajay picked up the teapot and poured. "No. Our investigations were completely independent. We proved Jock Trotter's allegations were valid."

Aldermaston sipped some tea. "So why did Jock meet you here six months before his complaint?"

Ajay pulled out a small, dishevelled, black notebook from inside his coat pocket, and placed it down on the table. He thumbed through the pages, eventually stopping about halfway through, tapping the page in question.

"Here we are." He checked nobody else was within close earshot. "This notebook is my personal property, which is why none of this appears in the official file that Daniel has. Sometimes, information that can't be used in a legal case can help with some context."

Ajay's finger ran down the page of scrawl. "He wanted to know about the legalities of foraging in Mortiforde Woods. Foraging Mortiforde had been in business for a few months and the butchers were intrigued whether it was legal."

Daniel frowned. "I thought you could forage anywhere, as long as it was for personal use."

Ajay pointed at him. "Exactly. The 1964 Theft Act permits foraging on land you don't own, as long as what you pick is for personal use. It's a completely different issue when there's a commercial gain."

Aldermaston stroked his chin. "So, was Foraging Mortiforde foraging illegally on a commercial basis?"

Ajay shook his head, then sipped some tea. "It is possible to forage on a commercial basis, on land you don't own, as long as you have the landowner's permission."

"Mortiforde Forestry, in this instance," Aldermaston clarified.

Ajay nodded. "And Foraging Mortiforde *had* their permission. I made discreet enquiries soon after I met with Jock."

Daniel flicked through the short measure case file. "How did Jock know Foraging Mortiforde existed and what they were up to?"

Ajay leant forward. "Back of the file. There's a photocopy of a front page news story in The Mortiforde Chronicle."

Daniel skipped to the back of the file, and skimmed through its pages, stopping at a black and white photocopy. *Foraging for Success* screamed the headline. *New local business supplies top London restaurants with wild plants.* It was accompanied by a close-up photo of wild leaves and fungi in someone's cupped hands.

"Let me see, please." Lisa held out her hands for the file.

"But I thought Mortiforde Forestry was a commercial enterprise itself these days," said Daniel, handing the file over. "Why give another company permission to do something that they could themselves exploit?"

"Fair point," Ajay replied. "At that time, Mortiforde Forestry had only recently changed from a Government Agency to a private enterprise model, so they didn't have the manpower to create a foraging enterprise themselves. Secondly, about a decade beforehand there was a case down south somewhere, where someone was foraging commercially, mushrooms I think, and the forestry body took them to court under the Theft Act. They lost. The judge threw out the case because, although the forestry body was the legal landowner, the land in question was also common land."

"As is Mortiforde Forest," Aldermaston stated.

"It is," Ajay continued, "but it still doesn't give everyone free rein to pull up what they like. Things like the Wildlife and Countryside Act, and the Countryside Rights of Way Act, still complicate matters further. The upshot of all of this is that Mortiforde Forestry felt the sensible action was to grant Foraging Mortiforde a licence to forage, which they could review regularly."

Lisa tapped the file and caught Aldermaston's attention. "This is dated about four months before The Powys Gazette story you asked me to look into."

Aldermaston's eyebrows rose. That was interesting. He turned to Ajay. "What made you jot all this down in your notebook?"

Ajay turned a page. "A question Jock asked."

Aldermaston leant forward. "Which was?"

Ajay's finger ran along the handwritten sentence in his notebook. "If the law allows you to forage on a personal basis, what are the personal legal limits?"

Aldermaston leant back in his chair and drained his teacup. "So do you think Jock Trotter was looking to forage in Mortiforde Woods?"

Ajay snapped shut his notebook. "I can't prove anything," he said, "but I wouldn't be surprised if all three butchers were illegally foraging on a commercial basis."

Aldermaston leant forward again. "All three?"

Ajay nodded and skipped forward a few pages in his notebook. "About a month later, I had a phone call one evening from Seth Shepherd on my work mobile. He asked me outright about the legalities of foraging. And then a few weeks later, Peggy's husband, Walter, got in touch and asked me the same question."

Daniel rubbed the back of his head. "Why would the butchers be interested in foraging?"

"Diversification," Aldermaston explained. "We've seen the accounts in those Shopfront Grant scheme applications. Ever since the supermarket opened, all three butchers have been under pressure."

Ajay held out his hand towards Lisa. "There's another press cutting in the file I think you might like to see."

Lisa handed it to him.

"Although the case was reported in The Mortiforde Chronicle, it wasn't a front-page story. It slipped into the business section near the back. But it made the news in *The Caterer*, the trade magazine most of the top London restaurants have."

Ajay opened the file at the page and held it up. *Foraging Mortiforde Fleece Top London Restaurants*.

"So," said Lisa, now perched on the edge of her seat, "even if Foraging Mortiforde had managed to survive the financial consequences, there was no way their customers were doing business with them again."

"Exactly." Ajay slipped his notebook back inside his jacket pocket. "Jock's complaint completely ruined their business and their reputation."

Aldermaston stared at the teapot in front of them. "It seems Foraging Mortiforde are exacting their revenge on the butchers, doesn't it?"

∽

Tibby placed a couple of loose onions into the wooden crate and stepped back. "Didn't take as long to clear the stall as I thought it might."

"We've sold so well there's hardly anything left." Ashton placed his hands on his hips and bent backwards, then twisted his torso, left, then right. "Can't wait to get in a bath."

Tibby passed him the crate of remaining vegetables. "Don't get too comfortable. Mrs Hargreaves is expecting you soon to help make tomorrow's burgers."

Ashton took the crate and sneered. "Enjoy your posh meal at Tugford Hall. Remember us serfs slaving away in the kitchen, won't ya?"

Tibby wagged a finger in his face. "Er, someone snuck off twice today, leaving me on my own, remember?"

Ashton shrugged. "They were emergencies. Nobody knows when an emergency will crop up."

Tibby untied her apron and threw it on top of the crate Ashton was holding. "I'll go to Mrs Hargreaves' now. We'll get a good batch of burgers made before I have to leave for Tugford Hall tonight."

Ashton harrumphed and threw the crate onto the rear of his black pickup truck, now parked behind their stall.

Tibby surveyed the market. Most tourists had drifted away now, filling the town's bars and restaurants, leaving a sense of calm across Market Square as the other traders packed away.

The evening sun threw the castle's ever-growing shadow further across the market. Tibby shivered, suddenly aware of the coolness in the October evening air.

Ashton slammed the rear door of his truck into place. "Right, Oi'll be off then. I'll dump this lot at HQ and see you here in the morning."

"What time shall I tell Mrs Hargreaves you'll be joining her?"

Ashton wrinkled his nose. "Seven-ish. Got a few jobs to do at home first." He jumped into the driver's seat and then stretched to reach for the door handle. "See ya tomorrow."

As he pulled the door closed, his wallet fell from his trouser pocket onto the tarmac.

Tibby waved. "Ashton! Your wallet!"

The diesel engine cranked into life and Ashton pulled quickly away.

Tibby rushed forward and grabbed the battered brown leather pocket wallet. When she looked up, Ashton's pickup truck had already disappeared.

She grabbed her pushbike, leant against the rear of the stall. The Society's HQ was adjacent to the allotments on the edge of town. Ashton's truck was too wide for Morte Bridge, so he'd have to take Ford Bridge and turn right onto the Birrington Road. But as a cyclist, Tibby could cut along Curtain Wall Road and drop to Morte Bridge and join the Birrington Road there. She might catch him up.

She threw his wallet into the wicker pannier basket and pushed off, dodging remaining stallholders as they packed up their stalls for the evening, and was soon freewheeling down Curtain Wall Road towards Morte Bridge. Ten minutes later, she was on the narrow lane of Birrington Road, and ahead, she spotted Ashton, pulling out of the allotment site.

Blast! He'd been quicker than she thought. She waved frantically, trying to catch his attention, but within seconds he'd shot off down Birrington Lane, leaving a cloud of exhaust fumes in his wake.

Tibby screeched to a halt, stuck out a steadying foot, and caught her breath. Now what? She could always leave the wallet with Mrs Hargreaves. She grabbed the wallet from the basket and opened it. Where did he live? If he wasn't far, she could drop it off. Perhaps he'd introduce her to his precious family.

Her fingers searched the pockets for a driving licence. She found it caught between a wodge of faded receipts. His bulbous face stared back at her from the photograph. She saw the address. *Truff Cottage, Birrington Lane, near Birrington, Mortiforde*.

Couldn't be far, then. She threw the wallet back into her pannier basket and pushed off. Perhaps if she handed it back to him personally, he'd be more of a team player on the stall tomorrow.

~

Ajay drained his teacup and stood. "I'll make a move, Your Lordship."

Aldermaston shook his hand. "Thanks for your help, Ajay. You've clarified a lot for us."

Ajay acknowledged Lisa and Daniel, then slipped out towards reception.

Aldermaston pulled his chair closer to Lisa and Daniel and turned to Lisa. "Please tell me Jillian's safe was locked and the recipe book may still be in it."

Lisa shook her head. "Empty. I grabbed some paperwork from her desk. Not sure if any of it is useful." She half pulled a wodge of paper from her bag. "I'll go through it later."

"Let me know if you find anything of interest." Aldermaston sighed. "We seem to be learning lots, but not getting anywhere."

Daniel held up the short measures file. "This, along with what Ajay's just told us, proves that there's bad blood between the butchers and Foraging Mortiforde. You saw Seth this morning walking a pig. We know Jock Trotter has a conviction for criminal damage caused by what we think was him training a pig to forage."

"Peggy Farmer has a pig too," Aldermaston confirmed. "I saw it this morning."

"And there's this," Daniel continued. He pulled the memory bracelet from his pocket and held it up.

Aldermaston frowned. "What's that?"

Daniel searched for the specific charm. "A woman flew out of Shepherds this morning, knocking me to the ground. I found this on the pavement, and I swear she was wearing it until we collided."

Aldermaston's eyes narrowed. "And?"

"When I went into the shop, there was a mysterious package on top of the counter."

"What time was this?" Aldermaston asked.

"About ten to ten. I believe the woman I collided with had delivered the package and ran into me as she hurried away." Daniel held up the charm he'd been looking for. "The owner's initials are MB."

Aldermaston took the bracelet from Daniel's fingers. "Evie called me *after* the official opening, when I was at home getting changed. That's when she told me about Seth's disappearance and having received his moustache."

Daniel tapped the short measures case file. "And MB are the initials of Foraging Mortiforde's owner in this short measures case. Miss M Bryan. It's got to be the same woman."

Lisa gasped, then clicked her fingers. "Give me the file."

Daniel handed it to her. "You all right?"

Lisa's fingers frantically flicked through the paperwork.

"What are you looking for?" Daniel looked at her quizzically.

She stopped. A huge beam broke across her face. "Yes! It didn't register when I first looked, but when you mentioned it."

"Mentioned what?" Daniel asked.

"The bracelet." Lisa held up the file, showing The Mortiforde Chronicle's feature on Foraging Mortiforde.

Daniel squinted. "What am I looking at?"

"That!" Lisa pointed to the photograph of two hands cupped together, holding an assortment of foraged items. "What can you see around the wrist?"

"The bracelet!" Daniel whistled.

Aldermaston handed the bracelet back to Daniel. "We need to find her."

Lisa held up her finger. "Hang on. This doesn't prove the woman you bumped into delivered Seth's moustache to Evie."

"But it proves I bumped into Miss M Bryan outside Shepherds this morning."

Daniel sighed. "But how do we track her down?"

Aldermaston turned to Lisa. "Electoral Roll. Fancy nipping back into the office? We're running out of time, but we could pay her a visit early tomorrow morning."

Lisa grabbed a pen and a notebook from her bag. "If I search the Electoral Roll computers, it'll leave a trace, won't it? Do we want to give Abigail any more ammunition to fire at the Guild?"

Aldermaston tapped his forehead. "Cautious Colin. Ignore the computers. Colin Rainner is the Returning Officer and manager of Electoral Services. Hates technology. Became obsessed with paper backups after the fear generated by the Millennium Bug. Colin produces a hard copy of the electoral register, which he keeps in a cupboard in his office." He grinned. "Assuming you leave the office as you found it, you won't leave any trace of your search."

Daniel shuffled in his seat. "Are the butchers in any *real* danger? It strikes me that this Miss Bryan simply wants to ruin the butchers financially, as they did her. Forcing the butchers to give away their burgers free tomorrow means they'll be hit hard financially, just like she was. Surely, the death threats are a bluff?"

"Hang on," Lisa pointed her pen at Aldermaston. "Why hasn't Peggy disappeared? She had a note too, this morning."

"*Yet*," Aldermaston reminded. "She's not disappeared yet."

"We should warn her," Daniel suggested.

Aldermaston shook his head. "But I want you to keep track of her."

"Me?"

"You haven't forgotten about that tracking I want you to do in Mortiforde Woods tonight, have you?"

Daniel sighed. "Something about a boar, you said. Where does Peggy Farmer fit in with that?"

Aldermaston grinned. "Because Peggy Farmer will be taking one for a walk."

"Peggy Farmer has a boar?" Daniel's eyes crossed at the thought.

"She has a pig *and* a boar," Aldermaston clarified. "Although the boar isn't hers. It's Jock's."

"How has she got Jock Trotter's boar?" Lisa asked.

"Says she found it wandering in the woods this morning." Aldermaston leant forward. "Daniel, I need you to stalk Peggy. She'll leave by the rear entrance. It's dark by seven. She may not leave until much later, but you need to be ready for when she does make a move. Text me as soon as she leaves. I'll join you as soon as I can get away from tonight's function."

Daniel nodded. "Why do all the butchers keep pigs?"

Aldermaston leant back in his chair. "You need to remember this is all about foraging. What are pigs known for being good at foraging for?"

Suddenly, Lisa's eyes widened. "Truffles!"

CHAPTER FOURTEEN

Felicity hobbled into Cartwright's basement kitchen and squealed with delight when she saw the boar meat. She pulled the torn recipe sheet from her pocket and looked at the other ingredients.

Cartwright wandered in, a small trug basket hanging over his arm. "I've just seen the most peculiar thing, My Lady. All the flower heads in the rose garden have disappeared."

Felicity leant against the worktop. "It's not Harry. He's been attached to his games console since he got home from school. Has to be my brother-in-law. It has the whiff of Basildon about it."

Cartwright took a large glass mixing bowl from a cupboard and placed it on the worktop. "It's rare for your brother-in-law to end up smelling of roses, My Lady."

He grabbed a chopping board from another cupboard, selected a small knife from his magnetic rack collection, and handed them to Felicity.

"If you could finely chop the lovage leaves and add them to the bowl, Your Ladyship, I'll sort out the other ingredients." He disappeared into the pantry.

Moments later, he returned with most of the other ingredients on a tray. "I suggest we mix all the ingredients together in the bowl and let the meat marinade overnight."

Felicity stopped chopping. "Overnight? As long as that?"

Cartwright nodded. "It allows the flavours to blend more effectively."

"But my entry needs to be in the Bake Off tent by two o'clock tomorrow."

Cartwright tapped the recipe. "There's plenty of time tomorrow morning. This needs baking on a medium to high heat for about an hour. Although, the meat will need browning off in a frying pan first."

Felicity waved the knife in front of Cartwright's face. "Bœuf mentioned something about browning the meat first." She smiled. For the first time today, she felt she might actually achieve something edible. Aldermaston will be astounded. Ah. Aldermaston. She hadn't told him she'd sourced some boar meat.

"Is everything all right, My Lady? You've gone quiet."

Felicity shuffled, wincing with the pain. "I've suddenly remembered that I asked His Lordship to find me some boar meat, and I've completely forgotten to tell him you've found some for me."

Cartwright passed Felicity an onion to chop. "In my experience of His Lordship, and if I'm honest, of the Seventh Marquess, too, forgetfulness of what they might deem as minor items is part of their DNA."

Felicity sniggered.

"It is the reason all the great houses of England have a Head Butler. We exist so the aristocracy can forget. That's what my father used to say. Now, let me go and find the measuring jug, and we can sort out this pottle of cider."

Cartwright disappeared into the pantry again.

Felicity's giggling continued, but her jollity suddenly

subsided. Cartwright had called her aristocracy. Nobody had said that before. Her eyes watered. She didn't feel aristocratic. She still felt like Felicity, the marketing manager. Her past life now. She put the knife down and wiped away the tears. Bloody onions.

∼

Ten minutes later, Tibby reached the hamlet of Birrington. She'd gone too far. According to the address, Ashton's cottage was on the Birrington Road, but closer to Birrington than Mortiforde.

The October air cooled her glowing cheeks as she peered at quaint cottages set back from the lane. The hamlet comprised only a dozen cottages, a mixture of timber-framed and brick structures, some with tiled roofs, others thatched.

What had once been forest workers' dwellings or farmhand houses were now mainly retirement homes of commuter properties for those who didn't mind the hour's commute to Shrewsbury or Hereford.

Set mainly around a small village green, she spotted the spire of Birrington Church behind the grandest property in the hamlet, the Rectory, a two-storey brick-built Georgian property with an Audi estate parked on the drive.

The bells of Birrington Church chimed the quarter-hour. Tibby checked her watch. Five forty-five. She headed back along Birrington Road, grateful of the downhill ease, towards Mortiforde.

She'd have to go with Plan B. Leave Ashton's wallet with Mrs Hargreaves, and then she could pass it on to him tonight when—

She grabbed her brakes and screeched to a halt. Her tyres skidded briefly on the woodland debris littering the edge of the lane. Was that…? Still seated, she walked her bike back a few metres to the narrow track on her right. She hadn't noticed it before on her journey into Birrington.

She squinted, for the failing evening light made it difficult to see through the tunnel of trees. But there, about a hundred yards into the woods, parked in front of a wooden garage, was Ashton's pickup truck. She'd found him!

Tibby dismounted and wheeled her bike a short distance along the woodland track. She stopped and leant the handlebars against an oak tree. Seconds later, the bike slipped and disappeared into the undergrowth. She ignored it, captivated by the sight before her. There stood an idyllic cottage in a clearing on her right, completely hidden from the lane.

The two-storey timber-clad building was rectangular, with two small, box-shaped single-storey extensions added. One, on the gable end, looked like it housed a bathroom. The other was a conservatory stuck on the front. A stone square chimney pierced the thatched roof in the centre of the building.

Tibby's nose twitched. Woodsmoke.

She was about to head towards the front door when she spotted the garden boundary in all of its glory. Hidden from the lane by the trees, the front garden was separated from the surrounding woodland by a six-foot-high holly hedge. Running along the top were two pigs and one, two, three… a dozen piglets, all neatly trimmed out of the hedge. Topiary pigs!

She wandered along the hedge, admiring the skill and design of the shapes. The adult pigs were clearly defined with big, round bodies, two ears, and a protruding snout, and an open mouth. They even had curly tails at the back. The piglets were smaller nodules of holly-hedge, with snouts and ears and short, stubby tails, yet to grow and curl.

Tibby frowned. Why would Ashton live in a property with an ornately trimmed, topiary pig hedge? Not that vegetarians couldn't be animal lovers, of course. In fact, many society members were vegetarians *because* they were animal lovers.

Enthralled, Tibby tiptoed along the full length of the holly hedge, and then gazed back along its entire length. Visually, it was stunning — an entire piggy family prancing about on top of a hedge. Ashton had a sense of humour.

Tibby froze. A strange sound puzzled her. Muffled. There it was again. She turned, scouring the undergrowth. The pitch of the noise rose. Tibby edged along the hedge, back towards the track, but the noise became frantic. She stopped and edged back towards the far end of the hedge, furthest from the track.

Only when she stepped past the hedge did she see where the noise was coming from. Tucked between two larger holly bushes was a four-foot tall wooden store. Half was open to the elements on one side and used for drying chopped wood. The other half was enclosed, with a padlocked door.

Tentatively, Tibby edged closer. The muffled moaning began again. The door shook violently, and the padlocked jangled. Tibby clasped her hand to her mouth. Two-thirds up the wooden door was a knothole. It blinked. Tibby craned her neck closer. The hole blinked again.

"Hang on!" Tibby cried. She ran to the door and pulled at the padlock. The metal-hinged clasp was rusty, but strong. Frantically, she searched for something to break it.

There had to be an axe in a wood store, surely? Her hands scurried over wood blocks, moving, searching, shifting, desperate to find something. In their feverish hunt, she stumbled across a wedge-shaped piece of wood. About an inch wide at the bottom, it splayed to six inches wide and deep at the top. Sanded down and polished, it would have made an ideal door wedge.

She grabbed it and wedged the thinner end behind the metal clasp. Then she grabbed another log and hit the broader end several times, forcing it further between the clasp and the wooden frame. Then, placing both hands around the thicker end of the wedge, she pulled.

The tendons in her arms tightened, sweat erupted on her forehead, and her feet sank into the soft earth as she struggled to force the metal clasp off the door. The sweat on her fingers increased, and suddenly, she lost her grip and fell backwards.

Staggering to her feet, she spotted a large circular disc of tree trunk, yet to be chopped into firewood. She strained to lift it off the ground. Summoning all of her energy, she raised it above her head and then screamed as she flung it down hard on top of the wedge.

Something splintered, cracked and clanked, as the heavy weight dropped to the floor with a thud. The wedge fell to the ground at the same time as the metal clasp and padlock.

Tibby's fingers scrambled around the square wooden handle and pulled. The door flung open wide and a woman in beige clothing fell out, face down. Her ankles and wrists were bound with thick black tape. Tibby clambered across and rolled her over. The woman's mouth was sealed with tape, but her eyes were wide open.

Despite the tape, the woman squealed and squirmed, her eyebrows jumping, indicating something behind Tibby.

Tibby recognised her. Jillian Jones.

CLICK.

Tibby froze. Somebody was behind her. Jillian's eyes were wide with horror.

Slowly, Tibby rose to her feet and turned round.

"Oh, Tibbs. What have *you* done?"

It was Ashton. With a shotgun. And he was pointing the barrel directly at her.

Aldermaston collapsed onto the bed. He'd been up for thirteen hours, and there was still an hour before the formal festival dinner. He rubbed his eyes and propped himself up on his elbows.

In the corner of the room beside his full-length mirror was his mahogany valet stand. Cartwright had already seen to his evening wear. His single-breasted, black wool, fine herringbone dinner jacket, with silk peaked lapels, had been dry-cleaned. His white evening shirt, with turndown collar, bib and double cuffs had been freshly pressed, as had his single-row braided black trousers. His patent lace-up shoes, on the bottom shelf, gleamed in the light. Beside them were a pair of black socks and a white pressed handkerchief, ready for the jacket's left breast pocket.

There was a knock on the bedroom door.

"Come in." Aldermaston sat upright.

Cartwright entered. "Chief Constable Stoyle has arrived, My Lord."

Aldermaston's head fell into his hands. "Cartwright, I'm *so* sorry. I meant to tell you. I've offered the Chief Constable a room for the night. And, therefore, it only seemed appropriate I should extend an invitation to tonight's festival dinner, too. I hope you don't mind."

"It's not my place to mind, Your Lordship."

Aldermaston stood. "Look, you must be running frantic at the moment, trying to sort out dinner and everything. I'll see to Stoyle, you carry on in the kitchen."

Cartwright bowed. "As you wish, My Lord."

Aldermaston walked towards the door. "Do you know where Felicity is?"

"The kitchen, My Lord."

Aldermaston stopped abruptly. "Is that wise, Cartwright?" he whispered. "Only, we both know the extent of her culinary skills."

Cartwright's face remained expressionless. "With some gentle coaching, My Lord, I think you'll find she's capable of great things."

"You haven't let her loose on tonight's meal, have you?"

Cartwright shook his head. "Her Ladyship is focussing on her Bake Off entry for tomorrow." He paused, then said, "If I may be so bold, My Lord, if I were to offer any advice regarding this evening's dining event, might I suggest you refrain from partaking in the canapés? Your brother has been in charge of that department."

Aldermaston tapped the side of his nose.

Cartwright bowed and stepped backwards out of the room.

Aldermaston followed him out of the bedroom and came face to face with a photo of his parents on the landing sideboard. Taken a few weeks before their fatal accident, it showed them standing on Tugford Hall's main entrance steps.

He ran a finger down the side of the frame. What would his father think of the mistakes he was making? How differently would he have done things?

Aldermaston dropped downstairs and took the secret doorway connecting their private East Wing quarters with the main central hall of the house. From the main hall, the door was disguised as a bookshelf.

Aldermaston swung the door wide open to see Chief Constable Stoyle inspecting the vast JMW Turner landscape painting of Mortiforde Castle surrounded by the densely wooded Mortiforde Forest, commissioned by the Third Marquess of Mortiforde.

"Colin, good to see you again."

Stoyle removed his cap and slipped it under his arm. He had a laptop bag slung over his shoulder. "It's kind of you to offer me board and lodgings for the night."

"It's the least I can do, in light of what's going on."

Aldermaston gestured towards the main staircase in front of them.

Together they headed through the main entrance hall, lined with glass cabinets gleaming with china and silverware, and headed into the grand hallway. In front of them, a large wooden staircase rose majestically and then split, with both sides turning 180 degrees to continue their upward journey.

"May I enquire how things went with Ms Mayedew?" Aldermaston ventured.

Stoyle sighed. "She'll struggle out here. For people like her, England outside of London is another time zone."

Aldermaston chuckled. "Yes. Somewhere in the 1950s, probably. Communications aren't as robust here as they are in London."

Stoyle raised an eyebrow. "Policing numbers are not as robust as she's used to in London, either."

At the top of the stairs, they turned right along a corridor with windows overlooking the front of the Hall.

Aldermaston hesitated. He didn't want this to sound like an interrogation. "I wonder… have you had a chance to speak to Mairi Trotter and Evie Shepherd?"

Stoyle pursed his lips. "Chat wouldn't quite be the word I'd use. Both women were forthright in the statement they issued. Although, I think they were both directing their anger at Ms Mayedew rather than at myself."

"They're still determined the police aren't involved?"

Stoyle nodded. "And there's not a lot I can do. Both their husbands are grown men, who've been missing for barely twelve hours yet. Seth Shepherd could be classified as vulnerable because of his age. I'll complete a Missing Person's report on them both, so they're on the system."

Aldermaston gestured to a door. "This is your room. The Disraeli Suite."

They entered a large room with a four-poster bed on a dais,

three armchairs around an unlit fireplace, and a Chippendale dressing table in front of one of the two huge sash windows.

Aldermaston headed straight to a door in the far corner and opened it. "The en suite is through here."

Stoyle took in his surroundings, including the ceiling's ornate plasterwork. "The strange thing was, Mrs Shepherd was most adamant she didn't have a ransom note."

Aldermaston rubbed the back of his neck. "I took it. Here…" he rummaged in his jacket pocket and pulled out the message.

Stoyle read it. "I see. And you say Mrs Trotter received something similar?"

Aldermaston nodded. "She categorically stated no police involvement, too."

"I got that message, loud and clear." Stoyle held up the note. "But, now I've seen this, it may help me draft in further resources. If I were to have the co-operation of both butchers, that would be a different story. As for the Council's Chief Archivist, I do find that more disturbing."

"Oh?"

Stoyle slipped his laptop bag off his shoulder and dropped it into one of the armchairs. "Ms Mayedew and I checked her office. The safe was empty. We can be certain the recipe book is missing." He bent over and unzipped his bag, sliding out his laptop. "I can complete a stolen property report, and potentially a Missing Person's report on Jillian Jones."

He looked at the floor. "How well do you know Jillian Jones, Your Lordship?"

Aldermaston rubbed his chin. He'd need to shave before dinner. "Extremely well. Known her for years, and we worked closely securing the recipe book from the Royal Palaces Collection. Why?"

Stoyle switched on his laptop. "Ms Mayedew is convinced

that Jillian Jones has been kidnapped. But as a police officer, I have to consider *all* possibilities."

"Such as?"

"That Jillian Jones has stolen the recipe book and is on the run. I spoke with the Royal Palaces Collection before I arrived. They believe it's worth nearly half a million pounds. Possibly more on the black market."

Aldermaston shook his head. "No. Jillian wouldn't do that."

Stoyle shrugged. "It's a possibility, not a probability."

"Of course. I'll leave you to get on. There are tea and coffee facilities on the unit over there, and dinner is at seven downstairs in the dining room. You'll be fine in your uniform. Should you need anything else, press that button on the wall there and Cartwright will attend to you as soon as he can."

"That's extremely kind of you, Lord Mortiforde, thank you."

Aldermaston closed the door on his way out and leant back against it. Jillian wouldn't have run off with the recipe book, would she? No. She wasn't like that. Anyway, why would she do that? Like the butchers, she, too, had received a threatening note this morning. Oh. A thought crossed his mind. One of hope. What if Jillian hadn't been kidnapped? What if she'd gone into hiding with the recipe book somewhere, instead?

∽

Abigail peered over the bonnet of her white Audi TT as she negotiated the narrow, cobbled section of Castle Street, where the bollards kissed the double yellow lines. This was worse than negotiating a London suburban street with parked cars on both sides.

She sighed with relief as she passed the narrowest section before pulling into the loading bay next to the independent boutique and switching off the ignition.

The Buttermarket was directly ahead, all quiet now the tourists and festival-goers had left for the evening. In fact, looking around, the town was practically deserted. So, this is what a Friday night in the Welsh Borders looked like. Great!

She glanced at the displays in the boutique window, and her heart sank. Not quite as cutting edge as Thameside's boutiques. Fashion trends round here had some catching up to do. About sixty years' worth.

Her figure-hugging, rich navy-blue dress, with a square-cut neckline and short trail, would not sit well in that window display. Abigail wriggled in her driver's seat. It didn't sit well in here either.

The bells of St Julian's chimed the quarter-hour.

"Come on, Tibby. Where are you?" Abigail checked her rearview mirror. From which direction would she be coming? Where did Tibby live? Castle Street back to Watling Street was empty.

She grabbed her black clutch bag from the driver's door pocket, pulled out a pair of sapphire and diamond bell-drop earrings, and popped them in.

With no sign of Tibby, she stepped out of the car door, gingerly hitching up her dress so it didn't drag along the cobbles, and then hobbled across to the front of the Buttermarket. Southgate Street was empty. There was nobody climbing the long hill into the centre of town. Abigail hurried far enough along Castle Street to see the stalls in Market Square. That, too, was empty, save for a few teenagers gathered on one of the empty stalls, sharing a bottle of cider.

She pulled her mobile phone from her clutch bag and called Tibby's number. It rang. And rang.

"Come on, Tibby. Answer."

Eventually, it cut to voicemail.

Abigail glanced up at the clock beneath the Buttermarket's cupola. Five to seven.

"Hi, Tibby. Abigail here. Look, I'm not sure what's happened, but I've been waiting for ten minutes, and I can't wait any longer. Hope you're okay. I'll catch up with you later. Bye."

She terminated the call and returned her phone to her clutch bag before slipping back into her car. She turned the ignition with one final glance in her rear-view mirror.

"What is it with the bloody yokels round here?"

CHAPTER FIFTEEN

Lisa glanced both ways along the first-floor corridor of Borderlandshire District Council's offices. Her second visit in one evening outside core office hours was stretching the authority's flexitime system to the extreme.

Softly, she knocked on Electoral Services' door. She wasn't expecting anyone to be working this late on a Friday evening, but Electoral Services staff were fastidious, often working late to ensure all the right boxes were ticked. Most wet themselves with excitement on polling day.

With no reply, she slipped inside and found the light switch. The flickering strip bulbs burst frenetically into life, then settled.

It was a small room, with space for four desks, each with a computer. From the pocket of her purple trench coat, she pulled out a small notebook.

Glancing round the office, she spotted a door in the far corner. Probably just a glorified stationery cupboard, despite authority guidelines insisting no department maintained its own stationery stock. In an attempt to cut the amount of stationery staff stole for personal use, departmental quotas had been issued. Once exhausted, no further replenishments could be ordered until the new financial year. All this had achieved was an exploding black market for Post-it notes and highlighter pens. Yellow ones of both items were prohibitively expensive.

When Lisa opened the door, it wasn't stationery she saw, but a room larger than the office she was standing in. Across the far wall was a bank of shelving units bearing row upon row of ledgers. Thank you, Cautious Colin.

Her fingers traced the ledger spines as she searched for the volume Bryan might appear in. On the second shelf, she found it. She grabbed the two-inch thick ledger and returned to the better-lit office.

After five minutes of finger-licking page flicking, she located the page with surnames beginning *Bry*. Seventeen people were on the closed electoral register with the surname *Bryan*, four with the initial *M*. Only two were female. She checked their ages: 24 and 32. Daniel had said the woman he'd bumped into was probably older than him, but younger than her. Better safe than sorry. She grabbed her notebook and pen and jotted both details down.

Miss Madeleine Bryan, 2 Arboreal Way, Mortiforde, Borderlandshire, 24.

Mrs Megan Bryan, The Glebe, Ashford Morte, Mortiforde, Borderlandshire, 32.

Was one of these women holding the butchers and Jillian hostage?

∼

Aldermaston stepped onto Tugford Hall's portico entrance and took his position beside Felicity, on the top step. The October evening air was crisp.

"There you are!" Felicity remained focussed on the driveway ahead. "For a moment, I thought I was hosting tonight's Borderer's Guild dinner. Good job Harry wasn't relying on you to feed him, too."

Aldermaston cringed. It wasn't just the air that was frosty. He pecked her chilled cheek. "Sorry, dear. Been pretty full on today, what with the festival and everything."

He admired her light green silk dress, which splayed out below the knee and practically touched the floor. A dark green, leaf-patterned silk shawl protected her bare shoulders from the evening air.

"You look stunning. How's your day been?" He glanced downwards. "How's your foot?"

Felicity turned. "Bloody agony, if you must know. I suppose I should be grateful you've finally asked. It's only taken you…" She glanced at her watch. "… ten hours."

Aldermaston winced. "Sorry. When I said it's—"

"Yes," she interrupted. "We've *all* had one of those days. I was in A&E first thing this morning. You could have called, or—"

A black BMW turned in through the main gates, its tyres crunching the gravel underneath. Cartwright descended the steps to greet the arriving guest, as the car swung round in a curve to the main entrance.

Aldermaston fixed his proud host expression. Appearances were important.

Cartwright had also added a sense of occasion to everything. He'd switched on the front floodlights, basking Tugford Hall's imposing façade in a soft, flaxen glow. Along the drive, at five-metre intervals, were burning braziers, their golden flames dancing high in the light breeze, sending light and shadow dancing across the grounds.

The BMW drew to a halt at the bottom of the steps. Cartwright was perfectly positioned to open the rear passenger door.

"I meant to tell you," began Felicity, "had you deigned to call and enquire about my health—"

"It really *has* been one of those…" Aldermaston caught the glare from the corner of his eye.

"About the boar meat I asked for—"

"I'm still—"

"Mr Bœuf Boucher!" Cartwright declared loudly, as if addressing the entire county. He directed the celebrity chef towards his hosts at the top of the steps.

Felicity stepped forward first to greet the black-tied chef as he danced up the steps. "Mr Boucher. How lovely to meet you again."

Bœuf stopped in his tracks. His eyes widened, then his hands clasped his cheeks. "*Mon dieu*! It is Vee-lis-itee, is it not?"

Felicity held out her hand. "You remembered."

Bœuf lightly kissed the back of her hand. "Your Ladyship, I am 'orrified that a clumsy old chef asked such a distinguished lady to help me in my moment of distress this morning. Had I known, I would not have imposed my idiocy upon you." He bowed deeply, then stepped back and looked towards her feet. "And here you are on duty, when you must be in so much pain, too. How is your foot, may I ask?"

Felicity briefly scowled at Aldermaston, then returned her attention to Bœuf. "How kind of you to ask."

Aldermaston held out his hand. "Mr Boucher, I'm so glad you could make tonight, and thank you again for making this year's food festival so special for us."

They shook hands.

"Your Lordship, it is an honour to be here."

A white Audi TT crunched its way along the drive. The black BMW Bœuf had arrived in moved away.

Aldermaston pointed to the main doors. "Do go through. We'll join you shortly."

Bœuf nodded and disappeared through the Hall's huge wooden doors.

The white Audi pulled up at the bottom of the steps. Cartwright opened the driver's door and extended a hand. A long arm emerged first, the elegant fingers wrapping themselves around Cartwright's hand for stability. This was followed by a blue dress, hiding two legs and feet, which swung out and planted themselves firmly on the gravel drive. Then the rest of the blue-dressed body rose from the vehicle.

"Oh my God," whispered Felicity.

Aldermaston frowned. "What? Is it your foot?"

Felicity swiped his arm. "Don't start acting all concerned now."

"Well, what then?"

Felicity leant closer and whispered in his ear. "It's her!"

Aldermaston's brows furrowed. "You know her?"

"I know *of* her."

"I don't understand. This is…"

Cartwright turned to face them, and declared, "Ms Abigail Mayedew."

Abigail glanced up and acknowledged them both, then hitched up her dress to negotiate the steps carefully.

Aldermaston continued whispering, "This is the new Chief Executive of Borderlandshire District Council. She's from London."

"I know. I've read about her."

Abigail reached the top of the steps and offered her slender hand to Felicity. "Lady Mortiforde. How wonderful to meet you. I'm the new Chief Executive at Borderlandshire. I start on Monday. His Lordship kindly invited me to tonight's event, in my capacity as a new member of the Borderer's Guild." She turned to Aldermaston, and continued, "However much longer that may be for."

Aldermaston peered round Abigail. "Is your guest not with you?"

She shrugged her shoulders. "I waited for her at our agreed location, but she failed to turn up. Is this lackadaisical approach to commitments a Welsh Border thing, Your Lordship?"

Aldermaston stuck his tongue in his cheek. "Perhaps you should report her missing to Chief Constable Stoyle."

It was difficult to be sure in the darkening sky and the orange glow of the floodlights, but Aldermaston thought he saw Abigail's face flush. "It's probably a simple misunderstanding." He extended a hand to the main door. "Do go through. We'll join you in a moment."

Abigail strode purposefully towards the main doors.

Aldermaston turned to Felicity. "What do you mean, *read about her*?"

"Follow me." They headed inside, ignoring the waitresses holding trays of champagne for the arriving guests in the main hall, and turned into the drawing room.

Felicity grabbed the copy of *Country Life* lying on the coffee table and flicked through the pages. "Here." She handed him the open magazine. "Top right."

Aldermaston took the publication and scanned the page.

"Four months ago," Felicity continued, "the Earl of Dartbury left her standing at the altar."

∼

Upstairs in his West Wing apartment, Basildon arranged his precious canapés on six solid silver platters. There was a knock at the door.

"It's open, Lavinia." Basildon placed the final canapé down on the last silver tray.

"My, you have been a busy boy, haven't you?" Lavinia

stepped into the kitchen, wearing a dusty red satin dress with matching shoes, and an elegantly sparkling pearl and diamond tiara.

Basildon's eyes popped. "Darling, you look abso-bloody-lutely scrumptious!"

Lavinia's laugh ricocheted off the surrounding cupboards. She mock-slapped Basildon's arm. "This little number? Mummy picked it up at a charity dinner event at Windsor Castle a few months back. Thought tonight was the night to give it an outing."

Basildon took Lavinia's hands in his and studied her. "Seriously, darling. You look absolutely spiffing!"

"Basildon, dear."

"Yes, darling."

"Your tongue is hanging out." She lifted his jaw with her index finger. "That's better." She air-kissed him on each cheek. "Now, then. What's the plan for tonight?"

Basildon inhaled deeply. Technically, there were two plans. Plan A involved distributing the canapés and then seeing what information he could extract out of the Borderer's Guild members. Such information might not only be useful, but hopefully prove his truth-serum canapés had potential as an MI5/MI6 weapon.

Plan B involved Lavinia and his bedroom.

"Well, Lavinia, darling. I thought we could distribute these canapés to the guests downstairs." He touched the side of his nose. "You know what's in them."

Lavinia crossed her arms. "Do I look like I'm dressed as a waitress?"

"No! But the essence of being a spy is about subterfuge. Once we've handed these out, it then gives us the opportunity to mingle with the guests and ask probing questions. The sodium thiopental will do its magic and, hopefully, offer some tasty morsels of interesting information."

Lavinia reached out and plucked a smoked salmon and horseradish canapé off the nearest tray. She opened Basildon's mouth with her other hand and popped the canapé inside.

As Basildon consumed it, Lavinia strolled round the kitchen and picked up two of the silver platters. "I couldn't help notice your bedroom door was open as I strolled in," she began. "So, Basildon, I'll ask you again. What's the plan for tonight?"

Basildon was overcome by the strangest sensation. A fuzziness in his brain. "I… I've told you," he stuttered, trying to control the information. "To… to hand out the canapés to the guests and ask pr… probing questions."

Lavinia cocked her head to one side. "And?"

"To bed you," he blurted.

The corners of Lavinia's mouth rose a smidgen. "Basildon! That's a bit forward, even for you. This is the first time you've invited me somewhere as your plus one."

"No, it isn't! You came with me to Tommy Byng-Fairfax's birthday bash."

Lavinia's right eyebrow rose. "We were four years old." She frowned. "Actually, wasn't that the last time you pulled down my knickers?"

Basildon crimsoned. "I'd dropped a pink wafer biscuit on the floor. One merely bent over to pick it up, but overbalanced. I grabbed something to steady myself and caught—"

"My knickers." Lavinia finished. Her eyes narrowed. "How long does the truth serum's effect last for?"

"About fifteen minutes," Basildon replied.

Lavinia checked her watch. "Ten more minutes to ask you some probing questions. Shall we walk and talk? The guests should all be here now."

Basildon grabbed the remaining silver platters and followed.

She paused outside his partially open bedroom door and

glanced over her shoulder at him. "Peach rose petals. My favourite." She winked.

～

The single street lamp's yellow cast barely reached Peggy Farmer's back gate. Daniel tiptoed along the alleyway, sandwiched between five-foot-high brick walls, until he reached it. He placed his gloved hands on top of the wall and pulled himself up high enough to peer over.

A shaft of light streamed out through the opaque window of Peggy's back door. There was a continuous chatter of snorts, grunts, and rustling noises. Daniel needed somewhere comfortable to sit and wait for Peggy to make her move.

In the dim light behind him, he spotted the brick-built frame of an outbuilding belonging to the opposite property. It was single storey and looked flat-roofed. To one side stood a wheelie bin.

He checked both ways along the alley, then snuck across to the wheelie bin. The bin wobbled as he clambered on. Gingerly, he rose onto his knees, grabbed the top of the outbuilding roof, and heaved himself up.

The vantage point was perfect. Sitting back from the outbuilding's edge, he was ensconced in complete darkness. The downward glow of the street lamp illuminated enough of the alleyway for him to see anyone coming. At this height, he could also see over Peggy's rear wall, with a clear line of sight to her back door.

Satisfied he was safe, he slipped off his rucksack, pulled off his gloves, and took out a small flask.

He hadn't finished unscrewing the top off his flask when he heard running. Light-footed, but quick paced. A dark, hooded, slender body appeared in the lamplight. It stopped, checked both ways along the alleyway, then stepped closer to Peggy Farmer's rear gate.

Daniel's eyes widened as the night runner pulled themselves up and peered over the gate for a few seconds, before dropping back down and running off into the darkness.

Daniel's chest pounded. He wasn't the only one keeping watch on Peggy Farmer tonight.

∽

Aldermaston sipped some orange juice as he glanced around the library. In a large bay window, Abigail chatted to Stella Osgathorpe from the Historic Borders Agency. Martin and Jane Crookmann were huddled together with Gerald Lockmount, and Cissy Warbouys had cornered the Revd Makepiece. From her handbag, she pulled her knitted gift for Bœuf. The Revd Makepiece's eyes widened and the hairs in his ears stood upright.

"You can't give him that, woman!" Revd Makepiece admonished.

Aldermaston intervened. "Cissy, is that your gift for Mr Boucher?"

"No good will come of it," the Revd Makepiece declared. "You mark my words! Such worshipping of the flesh should not be condoned, Your Lordship!"

"What *are* you going on about?" Cissy cried. "It's a fruit holder. This one holds two oranges and a banana, and this one," she continued, pulling another knitted garment from her handbag, "holds two peppers and a cucumber." She returned them both to her handbag.

The Reverend's cheeks flushed, and he sipped some champagne, turned and walked away. Aldermaston put his hand behind Cissy's back. "Perhaps now might be a good time to give your gifts to Mr Boucher," he suggested.

"Can I?" Her eyes sparkled in anticipation.

Bœuf and Felicity were chatting privately in the corner nearest the door to the dining room.

"Mr Boucher," Aldermaston interrupted. "You remember Cissy from earlier this morning, don't you?"

Bœuf took Cissy's freehand and kissed it. "'ow could I forget such a talented woman?"

Cissy giggled at Aldermaston. "He is lovely, isn't he, Your Lordship?"

Aldermaston smiled. "Cissy has a small gift for you, Mr Boucher."

"*Pour moi*? I am such a lucky man." He placed his champagne flute down on a nearby Thomas Elfe mahogany table.

Cissy handed her champagne flute to Aldermaston and opened her handbag. "I thought these might help you tidy your fruit bowl, or salad drawer," she declared, handing them over.

Bœuf took each gift and held them by the tip of their longest part.

"That one holds two oranges and a banana," Cissy explained, "which is why the orange pockets are orange and the banana pocket is yellow. And that one holds two red peppers and a cucumber."

Bœuf's eyes widened. "You clearly 'ave bigger cucumbers in England than we 'ave in France."

"Canapé, anyone?" Basildon barged through, lowering a silver platter supported by his upturned, splayed out fingers into the centre of the group.

Aldermaston's head shake was barely perceptible, but enough for Felicity to nod her understanding.

"*Mais oui!*" Bœuf declared, shoving each of Cissy's creations into his jacket pockets. He selected a quail's egg with dill mayonnaise and tomato pickle, all delicately perched on a Berkswell cheese disc.

His eyes closed as he savoured the flavours. He brought his fingertips to his lips and kissed them. "*Magnifique*!" He turned to Cissy. "Mademoiselle, I am sure you would enjoy ze flavours."

Cissy giggled. "Don't mind if I do!" She took one and popped it into her mouth. Her hand clasped her chest as ecstatic moans escaped her tight-lipped mouth.

Basildon offered the platter to Felicity. "Your Ladyship?"

Felicity waved her hand in the air. "Thank you, Basildon, but I'm saving myself for the dinner."

"Your Lordship?"

Aldermaston smiled. "I'm with Her Ladyship on this one, Basildon. But they look stunning."

A loud cacophony of laughter enveloped the room, and everyone turned to its source. Across the room, Gerald Lockmount raised his glass, acknowledging everyone's attention, then continued talking to the Crookmann's.

"That reminds me," began Aldermaston, turning to face Bœuf. "Gerald, over there, told you earlier about his little gîte in Saint Benno."

Bœuf nodded.

"You said it was on the Mediterranean coast, but Gerald says it's in Brittany."

Bœuf's face reddened. "Alas, my geography knowledge is not what it should be."

"But you specifically mentioned you'd dined there several times," Aldermaston recalled. "It seems strange you would recall the place with such affection, yet place it on entirely the wrong ocean."

The redness of Bœuf's cheeks intensified.

"Forgive my husband," Felicity interjected. "For his geography is not perfect either. This is the man who thought…"

"I'm not French!" Bœuf suddenly blurted in a clear

southern English accent. Shock etched every wrinkle and line on his face.

Basildon beamed. "Ding dong!"

Aldermaston glowered at his older half-brother. "Time to mingle elsewhere." His gazed remained fixed on Basildon until his brother sauntered off.

Felicity leant closer. "You're *not* French?" she whispered, checking over her shoulders.

Bœuf looked down at his shoes and shook his head.

Cissy burst out laughing. "Isn't he clever? He's only been over here for a day, and he can do a British accent better than most of us."

"Tell you what, Cissy," said Aldermaston, "why don't you go and try some of Basildon's other canapés?" He tried pushing her towards Basildon, who was now offering his delicacies to Abigail and Stella.

"No, Your Lordship. This sounds far more interesting."

Outwardly, he smiled, but inwardly he seethed. He turned back to Bœuf. "But you *are* the famous French chef, Bœuf Boucher, aren't you?"

Bœuf picked up his champagne flute from the mahogany table and downed the remaining contents. "Yes, and no."

The lack of French accent was disturbing. Aldermaston was puzzled. "But the festival crowds know you as Bœuf Boucher."

"I am Bœuf Boucher," Bœuf explained, "but before that I was Barry Ballingham from Basingstoke." He shook his head and frowned. "You're the first people I've ever told and… I… I don't even know why I'm telling you."

Cissy giggled. "People frequently open up to me. You'd be surprised what some have told me over the years. They see a woman knitting, but I'm also listening." She tapped her ear with a finger.

Felicity placed a comforting hand on Bœuf's forearm. "How did Barry become Bœuf?"

He sighed. "Remember the horse meat scandal?" He held both his hands up in surrender. "Wrong place at the wrong time."

Cissy frowned. "Basingstoke?"

"I ran a restaurant in east Hampshire. Business was going well."

"But I thought the horse meat scandal was more to do with processed meat," Felicity sipped some champagne.

Bœuf chuckled. "My mistake was having a dish containing horse meat on my menu. It was called *Pot-au-feu de Cheval*."

"Horse stew?" Aldermaston clarified.

Cissy shook her head. "Nah, you wouldn't catch me eating horse stew. Not natural, is it?" She pulled a ball of green wool and two size eight knitting needles from her handbag and cast on. The wool dropped to the floor.

Bœuf nodded. "It's a popular dish in France. One I've eaten there many times. Thought I'd try it on my menu. That was about the week before the scandal broke. I advertised in the local press. Picture the scene," he began gesticulating. "The same day my new advertisements go in the local papers is the day the horse meat scandal broke. I was besieged by tabloid newspaper journalists all keen to sample it and write about it. And although they all commented that the horse meat was clearly labelled on the menu, and I wasn't deceiving anyone, business dried up. I became the chef who cooked horses. Who'd want to eat there?" He shrugged his shoulders.

Felicity squeezed his arm. "That's awful."

"So I moved to France. Bought a small holding. Kept a few cows. I cooked beef dishes and sold them locally. Despite the French not being big beef eaters, my dishes went down well. Well enough for me to open a small restaurant. I was the chef who kept cows. Locals called me the Beef Farmer."

Aldermaston smiled. "*Bœuf Boucher.*"

"Exactly. I was a novelty. Got me a couple of slots on a French television programme. Then I was offered my own show. Bœuf Boucher stuck as a name, and the rest, as they say, is history. Honestly, Your Lordship, I am not here under false pretences. I changed my name by deed poll. I am Bœuf Boucher, a French television chef and, having lived in France for so long, I've acquired a French accent."

Aldermaston glanced across the room at Basildon. "Look, Bœuf. As far as I'm concerned, it's only you, me, Felicity and Cissy who know your secret. I'll talk to Basildon later." He turned to Cissy. "And we can rely on your discretion, Cissy, can't we?"

Cissy nodded, wide-eyed. "Of course, Your Lordship."

Aldermaston smiled. "Good." He turned to Bœuf. "See? Nothing to worry about. Just carry on as you have, and nobody will know."

Cissy giggled, as her needles clattered, a second row beginning to appear. "Quite common, really, when you stop and think about it."

"What is?" Aldermaston asked.

"Changing your name."

"Is it?"

Felicity stared at her husband. "Women do it all the time when they marry."

"No, that's not what I meant." Cissy tugged at her wool. "A family round here did it a few years ago." She stopped knitting and gazed up at the ornate plasterwork ceiling. "Come to think of it, it was more than a few years ago now. Gosh, it must be nearly thirty years." She giggled again. "*Truff.* That was it."

"Why the change?" Aldermaston enquired.

Cissy shrugged. "Can't remember." She paused. "Although, was it to do with…" She shook her head. "No. Can't think. It'll come to me when I least expect it."

Bœuf chipped in. "The Deed Poll Office can ask why you want to change your name, but you do not have to justify your reasons."

"What did they change it to?" Felicity enquired. "Perhaps that might clarify a reason."

Cissy tapped the ends of her knitting needles against her lips. "What was it now? What did it begin with? A? B? C?"

Aldermaston's head dropped. She was going through the alphabet. Please let it not begin with a Z.

"Harcourt!" Cissy declared. "That was it. The Truffs changed their name to Harcourt."

CHAPTER SIXTEEN

"Walk. NOW!" Ashton bellowed.

A sharp prod in Tibby's back knocked her off balance. She stumbled, sniffling. Her mouth was sealed by elephant tape, her hands were tied behind her back, and her ankles secured with a short rope restricting her stride.

"And you!"

From the corner of her eye, Tibby saw Jillian stagger forward alongside her, similarly constrained.

The forest track was wide enough for a vehicle. Tibby negotiated the left wheel rut, Jillian the right. Ashton's size eleven walking boots clomped heavily along the raised middle ground behind them. The only light was from the head torches he'd strapped around their foreheads.

Jillian stumbled frequently. Her breathing was laboured. Tibby sensed her fear.

"STOP!" Ashton bellowed.

Tibby and Jillian froze.

"Turn left nincty degrees."

Their torch beams swept the landscape in front of them.

Tibby's torch latched onto a narrow path, no more than an animal track, with bracken and brambles tumbling into it on both sides. It was only wide enough for single file.

"Go first, Tibbs."

Nervously, Tibby edged forward.

"Now you, Jillian."

Jillian's legs brushed through the undergrowth. The taller fronds of brambles caught and snagged her skirt.

Tibby edged forward slowly. The path dropped, and the drop steepened. Around her, silhouetted, perpendicularly regimented tree trunks towered above them. A tawny owl hooted.

Suddenly, Tibby's foot kicked a tree root. She stumbled and fell head first into the surrounding bracken. A squeal of fear escaped through her nose. She hit the ground hard, winding her. Her heart pounded against the forest floor.

She heard bracken stalks ripping, tearing, crushing, as Ashton smashed his way towards her. Two huge hands forced themselves under Tibby's armpits, and suddenly, she was hoisted upright, high into the air, before landing on her feet.

Tibby steadied herself. A browning frond of bracken dangled in front of her face, its stem caught in her hair. There was another prod in her back.

"Move!"

Tibby edged forward. Jillian was soon behind again.

After a couple more minutes, the ground levelled, and they entered a clearing.

"Stop!"

Tibby froze. Jillian drew beside her. Stars shimmered in the circular clearing above. Ashton pounded past, then stopped and threw a large rucksack to the ground with a thud. He loosened the cord around the top and pulled out a large halogen torch. Depressing the switch, a wide beam of light burst from its ten-inch lens. He shone it directly into their faces.

Tibby scrunched her eyes shut and turned away. Jillian moaned.

"Now then, ladies," Ashton drawled. "Welcome to a special part of Mortiforde Woods. This particular spot has immense historical significance. To the town. To my family. And to Jillian's family."

He dropped the torch from their faces and stepped closer to them. "Do you know *exactly* where you are, Jillian?"

She shook her head.

"Dead Man's Hollow."

Jillian's muffled scream cause Tibby to recoil.

Ashton chuckled. "So you *do* know the spot, then." He lunged, grabbed her by the arm, and dragged her forward several feet.

Tibby shook uncontrollably in fear.

Ashton pointed the torch at Jillian's feet, then started walking away. Jillian sobbed as she fell to her knees.

Tibby tried blinking away her frightened tears. Through the watery blur, she could make out the cause of Jillian's fear. A shallow grave.

Behind her, a metal lock snapped shut. Tibby spun round, but all she could see was darkness. To her right, feet shuffled. Bracken crackled. Undergrowth moaned. Metal clicked.

Tibby's eyes widened. Her trembling body exploded into convulsions. She knew what was coming. Her head shook.

BANG!

Tibby flinched, physically leaving the ground. Slowly, she turned, and all she could see were the soles of Jillian's court shoes poking up out of the shallow grave.

∽

"Cartwright, that was delicious." Aldermaston leant back.

The Head Butler took the starter plate and dirty cutlery from Aldermaston's place setting.

The two waitresses, who'd served champagne earlier, cleared the other guests' plates along the candlelit table.

Abigail sipped some water as she looked at the oil paintings hanging on the dining room walls.

Aldermaston pointed to the far corner nearest the huge bay window. "That's my father, the Seventh Marquess of Mortiforde. My grandfather is over there," he pointed to the opposite wall, "and my great-grandfather, the Fifth Marquess, is above the fireplace behind you."

Abigail twisted in her red velvet chair, and looked up at the six-feet-square canvas of a grey tweed-suited gentleman, with white hair, a ruddy complexion and a couple of golden retrievers sitting at his feet.

"He was standing over there when it was painted." Aldermaston pointed to the bay window.

Abigail turned to look. "The aristocracy's need to trace their lineage and put it on display always amuses me."

Stella Osgathorpe pulled her napkin straight on her lap. "Many people have a thirst for knowing where they come from. It's not an aristocratic thing at all. Genealogy is a popular pastime. Jillian Jones runs a popular *Trace Your Ancestors* evening class every Tuesday evening."

"How quaint." Abigail smiled politely. "Sounds like the highlight of some people's week. From what I saw of Mortiforde town centre earlier, Friday evenings don't have much going for them."

Stella adjusted the silver cutlery around her place setting. "Actually, it was at Jillian's *Trace Your Ancestors* evening class that we first learned of the Mortiforde Royal Recipe Collection. Jillian is teaching the class how to trace their ancestors by showing them how she's tracing her family history. About two years ago, she discovered she's related, on her mother's side, to

Oswyn Cooke, who was the castle's royal chef between 1626 and 1639."

Aldermaston leant forward. "Jillian said she had a personal connection to the recipe book, but I didn't realise she meant a direct family connection."

Abigail smirked. "Worried her family ancestry goes back longer than yours?"

"Once we knew that," Stella continued, "the evening class spent a couple of sessions going through the castle's archives. That's when we found a reference in a letter from one of the castle's kitchen suppliers proudly declaring his ingredients were regularly listed in Oswyn Cooke's recipe book."

Abigail returned her glass to the table. "So how did the recipe book end up in the Royal Palaces Collection archives, rather than those of Mortiforde Castle?"

Stella smiled. "When the castle passed into private ownership in the nineteenth century, the royal household took anything relating to the Royal family with them. When we approached them to see if they still had it, it took them several months to locate it."

Abigail frowned. "Surely these things are digitally catalogued?"

"It depends what they're catalogued under." Stella leant back as a waitress carefully placed a bowl of lobster bisque in front of her. "We thought Oswyn's book was simply a collection of recipes. But the Royal Palaces Collection had catalogued it as a diary."

Abigail tutted. "Human error, I suppose," she said as her vegetarian soup appeared before her.

"Not exactly," Stella continued. "Oswyn used the front half as a diary and simply recorded the recipes at the back of the book. Whoever catalogued it probably only looked at the first few pages."

"I always found history boring at school," Abigail sighed.

"Never have been interested in the past." She looked at the paintings hanging on the dining room walls again. "Do you like having all of your ancestors staring down at you while you eat, Your Lordship?"

The corner of Aldermaston's mouth rose. "Dining by candlelight has its advantages. But it's a powerful reminder of one's sense of duty. My responsibility is to keep things going for the next generation, as well as the people of Mortiforde."

Abigail picked up her soup spoon. "But why continue a system that doesn't meet with today's modern society?"

Aldermaston's hand gestured around the table. "The Borderer's Guild incorporates representatives from the local community. I merely facilitate the Guild's actions. The Food Festival was my father's idea, but the Guild made it happen. The local community wanted it to happen. If we didn't exist, your Economic Development Unit would be tasked with creating events like this to stimulate economic activity in the town. Do you have the manpower?" He brought his soup spoon to his mouth and blew gently on his lobster bisque. "Don't answer that now. Wait until you're officially in post." He savoured the bisque. "But, as I learned from that man up there," he pointed to his father's oil painting, "*who* facilitates the local community to achieve their goals and aspirations isn't as important as *how* those goals and aspirations are achieved."

Stella nodded. "The Borderer's Guild keeps us as a tight-knit community."

Abigail leant back in her chair. "But Mrs Trotter's pig-headedness, sorry, stubbornness, not to involve the police about her husband's kidnapping and ransom, is deeply disturbing. A society that does not trust civil agencies—"

Stella wiped her mouth with a napkin. "I think you'll find those civil agencies have abandoned us." She turned to Chief Constable Stoyle on her right. "Even you acknowledge that the

Marchlands Constabulary has practically withdrawn from the town. PC Norten is merely a token gesture."

Stoyle shuffled in his seat. "Mrs Osgathorpe, if I had a larger budget I could afford to—"

"Budget balderdash!" she snapped. "You chose to station one policeman here. You have officers. You decide where to deploy them. You chose to deploy one here. I'm sorry, Chief Constable, but you *chose* to abandon us."

Abigail leant forward. "Stella makes a valid point."

Stoyle cleared his throat. "It's not quite that simple. Budgetary considerations are more complicated. For example, although we don't have a team of officers here in Mortiforde, I have been able to access other resources. We've an All Ports Alert issued for—"

"And what happens," Abigail interjected, "when Mr Trotter's ransom isn't paid and his dead body is found dumped in Market Square? What happens then?"

Stoyle took a deep breath. "Naturally, we'd then have to divert the necessary resources from elsewhere."

Stella threw her hands in the air. "So there is a budget, but it's only for dead people. Great!"

"That's a bit harsh coming from you." Abigail sipped some water. "Your entire organisation spends money on the past. Without dead people, the Historic Borders Agency wouldn't have a business."

Aldermaston leant forward. "Surely, the point of history is to allow us to learn from the past, so we don't make the same mistakes."

Abigail returned her glass to the table. "Yes. I made a mistake dallying with the aristocracy in the past, and I'm not going to make it again!" Her face flushed as she toyed with the stem of her glass and ignored everyone's gaze.

At the other end of the table, Basildon waited until the waitress placed the last bowl of lobster bisque in front of Felicity. Then he picked up his soup spoon.

"Zis looks," Bœuf bent closer to his bowl and inhaled, "and smells wonderful."

"Enjoy the food now, old chap, because who knows what you'll taste in the Bake Off tent tomorrow!" Basildon slapped the celebrity chef hard on the back. Bœuf's face plummeted into the bisque.

"Oh, good heavens!" Felicity grabbed a napkin.

Lavinia burst into laughter, its frequent clipped tones sending shock waves across her bisque.

Bœuf brought his face out of the bowl and allowed the excess bisque to drip off his nose back into the bowl.

"Here, let me." Felicity wiped Bœuf's face with the napkin. "It didn't scold, did it?" She wiped the last of the bright orange bisque from his face.

Cartwright appeared instantaneously, removed the contaminated bowl and replaced it with another.

Bœuf shook his head. "*Non*. A bisque should not be piping hot. It was spot on."

Basildon offered his hand. "Sorry, old chap. No hard feelings, heh?"

Bœuf smiled and shook hands. "If nothing else, I shall always remember my visit to Tugford Hall." He chuckled.

Basildon tucked into his bisque. "And how is Her Ladyship's Boor Pie coming along?"

"Fine, thank you, Basildon." She glanced briefly at Lavinia.

"Just the one category you're entering in the Bake Off, is it?"

Lavinia turned to Basildon. "The President of the Ladies' Legion is confident enough to put all of her eggs in one basket."

Felicity smiled. "I'm simply learning to walk before I start running, Lavinia."

Bœuf looked quizzically at his fellow guests. "Zis boar pie, is it a local dish?"

"Oh yes," said Lavinia, jumping in quickly. "A historic dish, and a tricky one at that. It's getting the balance of flavours right."

"*Mais oui*," Bœuf agreed. "Ze boar meat 'as a strong flavour, so other ingredients are easily overwhelmed."

Felicity smiled. Nervously.

Lavinia's grin broadened. "So when Her Ladyship speaks of learning to walk before she can run, she may not have chosen the most suitable of dishes."

Bœuf placed a hand on Felicity's arm. "I am sure the chef knows what she is doing. The proof of ze pudding is in the eating, is it not?"

Felicity finished her bisque and patted her lips with a clean napkin. "That is why the recipe I am following recommends marinating the meat overnight."

"A wise move," Bœuf concurred. "Tell me, do wild boar still roam the local woods?"

Felicity shook her head. "They used to. And were a staple of the local diet, hence the recipe."

Cissy dropped her spoon into her empty bisque bowl and picked up her knitting needles. "You can see boar in Mortiforde Woods, if you know where to look."

"Can you?" Lavinia queried. "I thought we'd poached the wild boar to extinction."

Cissy's knitting needles clattered as she added additional rows to her current project. "My Stanley saw one only the other morning in Mortiforde Woods."

Basildon leant forward. "Really?"

Cissy nodded. "My Stanley might be eighty-four, but he doesn't need glasses, and he's got all his faculties." She tapped the side of her head. "Lost all his teeth, mind you, but a woman can't have everything."

Lavinia whispered in Basildon's ear. "A woman could go all weak at the knees on a rose-petalled bed for a man she thought was a successful hunter-gatherer. Especially one who manfully captures her a wild boar."

Basildon's heart beat faster. "Lavinia, darling. If you want a wild boar from Mortiforde Woods tonight, you shall have one."

∽

Lisa clutched the knife in her hand and stabbed the plastic film frenetically. The crisp, piercing pop was satisfying. She placed the ready-meal into the snug's microwave and programmed the first two-minute heating.

Esme's tail pounded the sofa from her horizontal position across all three cushion seats. Lisa rubbed her ear. "There's something wrong here. You're lying on the sofa like a lady of leisure, Mark is out there serving three-course meals to our B&B guests in the dining room, the Borderer's Guild is at Tugford Hall having at least five courses, and I'm having…" She picked up the cardboard sleeve. "… sweet and sour chicken with thirty per cent reduced fat."

The microwave pinged. Lisa removed the piping hot container, ripped off the plastic film, stirred the steaming contents with a fork, and returned them to the microwave for another two minutes.

She perched herself on the edge of the sofa and spread out the documents from Jillian's office on the coffee table in front of her. Leaning forward, she hooked her jet black hair behind her ear and picked up a sheet of paper.

It was a photocopy of an Ordnance Survey map. In the centre was a small, bright red cross. Next to it was written *Dead Man's Hollow*. She studied the rest of the map. A small, narrow road ran along the bottom of the sheet. There was a small cottage set beneath that, opposite which was a track heading into the woodland. It wound its way deep into woodland. But there was no path marked on the map, linking this track with the red cross.

At the top edge of the page, at an angle, was some printed text. ...*nalls Coppice*. Vinnalls Coppice? Was this Mortiforde Woods?

The microwave pinged.

Lisa retrieved her meal, slipped a plate out of a cupboard, poured the contents onto it, and left it on the worktop to cool.

Returning to the sofa, she picked up Jillian's large family-tree document. Once fully unwrapped, it overhung her coffee table on all four sides. She touched each generation line as she counted … eighteen generations.

At the bottom of the sheet, written in calligraphy, were the words *Jillian Jones*. She'd traced the ancestral line through the generations to the sixteenth century.

Lisa stood and grabbed her plate of sweet and sour chicken, and forked some into her mouth. Esme shuffled against her on the sofa.

She studied the top of the document. If anyone could trace their family history back eighteen generations, it was Jillian. A name near the top had been circled. *Oswyn Cooke*.

Underneath, in Jillian's handwriting, were the words *See Recipe collection*.

Lisa finished her sweet and sour chicken, then placed the plate on the floor. Esme leant over the edge of the sofa and stretched her neck far enough, enabling her to lick the plate without relinquishing any more of the sofa to Lisa.

Rummaging through the documentation, she stumbled across the sheet she'd seen earlier in Jillian's office. *This is retribution for your forefathers' sins*. Underneath, were Jillian's words: *I'm related to a murderer!*

Lisa glanced at the family tree, and Oswyn Cooke's circled name. Were these clues to Jillian's, Jock's and Seth's disappearances? And were there more clues in the recipe collection? If so, what had Jillian done with it?

∾

Aldermaston tucked into his roast venison main course. He turned to Abigail. "How's your grilled asparagus risotto?"

Abigail nodded, and she finished her mouthful. "It's superb. I must thank your staff for the trouble they've gone to, considering you only invited me some nine hours ago."

"I will pass on your appreciation. One thing I've learned since becoming Marquess is that without good staff, an organisation is nothing. We'd be lost without Cartwright."

Abigail paused her next forkful of risotto. "I think that goes for any organisation."

Stella poured some more water into her glass. "That's why we were so ecstatic to find the Mortiforde Royal Recipe Collection. To discover a document written by a member of the castle's staff is sensational. To have such a personal and real account of the period is rare." She sipped some water. "And then to find out that it was from 1632, well… that's the icing on the cake."

Aldermaston frowned. "What's so special about 1632?"

Stella leant back in her chair and looked shocked. "It's one of the castle's biggest scandals."

Aldermaston felt Abigail's eyes upon him.

"Tut tut, Your Lordship," she teased. "And there was me thinking you knew everything that went on in the town."

Aldermaston ignored her. "Enlighten our guests, Stella, if you will."

Stella made herself comfortable. "It was in 1632 that one of the castle's suppliers was brutally murdered in Mortiforde

Woods. It's always been rumoured that some of the other castle's suppliers were responsible. Quite feasible when so much of the castle's supplies came from the adjacent woods. It was not unknown for suppliers to wander into the territory of other suppliers and face the consequences."

Aldermaston placed his cutlery on an empty plate and patted his lips with his napkin. "You make it sound like some sort of turf warfare."

Stella laughed. "That's putting it mildly. There was money to be had becoming a castle supplier, especially one that was a royal residence. Woe betide anyone who didn't supply high-quality produce."

"That's it!" Cissy pointed a knitting needle at Aldermaston. "That's why the Truffs changed their name. It was the nursery rhyme we used to sing at school."

Aldermaston frowned. "What nursery rhyme?"

Abigail smirked. "Did they not teach you that at public school, Your Lordship?"

Aldermaston smiled politely at Abigail, then turned to Cynthia. "Do you remember it?"

She nodded.

"We still teach it when we do school tours at the castle," said Stella. She gestured to Cynthia. "After three?"

Cynthia put her knitting down and nodded.

Stella counted them in, "One, two, three…"

Together, to the tune of 'Yankey Doodle Dandee', they sang.

"Tobias Truff was such a duff, he found the King some truffles, but drunken Truff was huff and puff, 'cos they were rotten apples."

Cynthia burst out laughing, as the rest of the guests around the table applauded.

Stella turned to Stoyle sat beside her. "To have a historical event that transcends into social folklore so much that there's a nursery rhyme local children still sing today is fascinating. But we don't know how much truth there is behind it. That's what we were hoping the diary element of the Royal Recipe Collection might clarify. Are you any further forward in locating it?"

Stoyle shook his head. "We've no clues at the moment."

Stella sighed. "We hoped Oswyn Cooke might have noted some details of the event. Only then might we learn the full story of the murder of Tobias Truff."

"Sorry?" Aldermaston leant forward. "What was that name again?"

"Truff," Stella repeated. "Tobias Truff."

∽

Daniel shivered as the stars sparkled in a clear October sky. With over twenty-five miles to the nearest major conurbation, Mortiforde got more than its fair share of frosts at this time of year.

A patter of tarmac-slamming running shoes caught Daniel's attention. The runner had returned. They stopped outside Peggy's rear gate and peered over into the backyard.

The light through Peggy's opaque rear door window cast sufficient luminance to see both the pig and the boar were there. The runner dropped to the ground and ran off to Daniel's right.

Peggy was definitely being watched. Daniel slipped his mobile phone out of his pocket. He ought to let Aldermaston know.

Seconds later, Peggy's back door opened. Both animals squealed with delight as she slammed it shut. She wore a thick coat. This wasn't a goodnight kiss then.

He squinted. From the coat pocket, she pulled out what could have been a lead or some rope.

Peggy pulled something else from another pocket. Both animals squealed and snorted, and suddenly the pig jumped up on its hindquarters and peered over the top of its brick sty. But Peggy wasn't looking at the pig. Her attention was elsewhere.

A high-pitched squeal rang out and then suddenly it calmed, as Peggy handed it whatever was in her hands. As she did so, she bent over and caught its collar, and affixed the rope to it.

Silently, Daniel slipped backwards along the outbuilding roof, away from the alleyway, as Peggy wandered to the back gate. Two bolts slid against the woodwork. She checked the alley was clear, then stepped out. Daniel's mouth dropped when he saw the boar on a lead. Swiftly, she swung her back gate closed, and they toddled off to Daniel's left.

Time to move. Daniel woke his phone and thumbed a text to Aldermaston. Then, checking nobody else was about, he jumped to the ground. Hugging the alleyway shadows, Daniel followed Peggy. The chase was on.

∽

Cartwright entered the dining room carrying a tray of desserts. He placed a damson millefeuille in front of Stella, Chief Constable Stoyle, Jane and Martin Crookmann.

"Ms Mayedew, I noted the damson millefeuille contains gelatine, so I hope this pink dragon fruit layer cake will be acceptable." The three-layered dessert, topped by the brightest of pink jellies, sandwiching a raspberry chia jam between it and its buckwheat sponge base, was garnished with pink rosebuds. A collective gasp echoed around the room.

"That looks divine." Abigail's eyes began its devouring.

Cartwright slipped behind Aldermaston and placed a small silver platter in front of him. "For you, Your Lordship."

Aldermaston's platter contained not a tempting dessert, but his mobile phone.

"A text, Your Lordship. From Daniel. Seemed urgent." Cartwright woke the screen to display its message.

Lavinia rose from her chair and walked along the table towards Cartwright and Aldermaston. "Sorry, Cartwright. Where can I powder my nose?"

"Through the door, first on the left."

"Thank you."

Aldermaston glowered at Lavinia, who was staring at his phone's screen. "Thank you, Cartwright." He took the phone from the silver platter.

Peggy going walkies with boar now. I'm following. Heading to Mortiforde Woods.

Aldermaston turned to his guests. "Ladies and gentlemen, I'm afraid you'll have to excuse me. Something urgent has cropped up, to which I must attend." He gestured to Felicity at the end of the table. "I will leave you in the capable hands of Lady Mortiforde."

Her scowl was long enough for Aldermaston to spot, but immediately replaced with a dutiful beam as everyone around the table turned to her.

Abigail tapped the tablecloth to attract Aldermaston's attention. "Not news of Jillian, is it?"

Aldermaston shook his head. "No, this is another matter." He smiled at them all, then left the room.

⁓

Basildon pulled the napkin from his neck and placed it on the table as Lavinia returned to her seat beside him.

"What was that all about?" He nodded towards the top of the table where Aldermaston's empty chair sat.

Lavinia grabbed his arm and pulled him closer. "Something about a woman taking a boar for a walk."

Basildon's eyebrows rose. "A boar, you say?"

Lavinia's finger stroked the back of his hand. "I've always admired a man who can hunt. To trap an animal at night would show such skill."

Basildon's eyes lingered on her pouting mouth. His fingers forced a gap between his neck and his shirt collar. He'd suddenly come over all hot and flustered. "Darling, once this dinner is over, you should retire to my apartment and make yourself comfortable."

Lavinia seductively licked her lips. "Why? What are you going to do?"

Basildon beamed. "I'm going on a wild boar hunt!"

CHAPTER SEVENTEEN

Daniel stalked Peggy and Jock's boar along the alleyway and into Market Square. He glanced furtively, checking they weren't being followed, while also marvelling at Peggy's brazenness. She seemed unfazed, like a farmer driving a flock of sheep to market.

The bells of St Julian's pealed nine.

Peggy disappeared down a small path beside Mortiforde Castle. Daniel dashed across to the Crimean War cannon guarding the castle's entrance. He spotted Peggy again, as the path dropped and veered round the castle walls to the left.

Daniel held back, so as not to alert her to his presence, as he followed her for twenty minutes, around the castle and down towards Curtain Wall Road. She was heading for the river.

By the time he reached the road, Peggy was crossing Morte Bridge. He was about to pursue when a noise behind distracted him. He stared into the darkness. Nothing. Perhaps he was hearing things.

He dashed over Morte Bridge. Peggy had already taken the

stepped path into Mortiforde Woods. He had to keep up. Peggy would have a choice of several routes at the top.

As he reached the bottom, Peggy neared the top. Two more steps and she was there. She stopped and bent over. Was she talking to the boar?

Cautiously, he crept up the embankment steps until he was about ten feet behind her. Above the noise of a happy, grunting boar, Daniel heard words. She *was* talking to the boar.

"Come on, Tess. Where does Daddy take you? Show Aunty Peggy. There's a good girl!"

The boar squealed and dragged Peggy deep into the woods. Daniel followed. Tess was in complete control. For ten minutes, her snout pulled her along the path and sometimes she'd veer off through thick bracken and woodland undergrowth.

Behind him, a twig snapped. Daniel froze. Only his eyeballs moved as he searched for the source of the noise. All he saw was darkness. His heart pounded.

A squeal pulled his attention back to Peggy in the distance. Stealthily, he edged closer. Tess became more excited, agitating the soil.

Suddenly, a hand came from behind and clamped itself tightly across Daniel's mouth, pulling him backwards into the undergrowth.

~

Aldermaston zipped shut the door of his hide in Mortiforde Woods and then switched on his head torch. He brought his finger to his lips and allowed Daniel's eyes to adjust to the light.

Daniel clutched his chest. "Bloody hell! You scared the sh—"

"Sorry," Aldermaston interrupted. "I planned on coming straight to the hide and then try finding you. But I spotted you on the main path. How long's Peggy been here?" He nodded to his right.

"A few minutes," Daniel whispered.

Aldermaston lifted the covers of his hide's mesh windows.

"How are we supposed to see anything?"

"Same way I saw you." Aldermaston planted some night-vision goggles into his assistant's hand.

Daniel peered in Peggy's direction. "These are incredible!"

Aldermaston pulled another pair from his rucksack. "They're not army grade," he whispered, "but they're good enough for spotting wildlife at dusk."

"Tess is definitely excited about something," muttered Daniel. "She's rootling around and churning up lots of soil."

Aldermaston agreed. "Time to take some action, then."

"What are you doing?"

Aldermaston unzipped the hide door. "You stay here. Keep watch. I'm about to give Peggy the fright of her life."

Before he stepped out of the hide, a painful, high-pitched squeal penetrated the dense forest, followed by frenzied snorting and grunting.

Simultaneously, something crashed through the undergrowth, pounding past the hide, then hurled itself through the air at Peggy.

"Someone's attacking Peggy!" Daniel yelled.

Aldermaston bolted out of the hide and launched himself towards the elderly butcher's assailant. "Leave her alone!"

The hooded attacker turned, glanced in Aldermaston's direction, then pushed Peggy to the ground and ran off. "Watch them, Daniel!" Aldermaston yelled.

He bounded over clumps of knee-high bracken, his head torch spotlighting where Peggy had fallen.

"Tess! Come back!" Peggy yelled, just as Aldermaston tripped over a log and kissed the woodland floor beside her.

"Peggy, are you all right?" He spat bracken and soil from his mouth.

"Lord Mortiforde? Is that you?"

"Are you okay, Peggy?" He helped her to her feet.

"Tess has run off!" Peggy cried.

"We'll catch her soon, Peggy. First, you have to tell me something. What did she find? What did Tess find for you?"

Peggy dropped her head. Then, she slipped her hand into her coat pocket and pulled out three black, golf-ball sized knobbly spheres. She looked up into his eyes and sighed. "Truffles, Your Lordship. Autumn truffles. Or, as Jock Trotter calls them, Black Gold."

⁓

"Coffee, Ms Mayedew?" Cartwright stood beside a small walnut table near to the two armchairs in the Drawing Room where Abigail and Felicity were sitting.

"Thank you. Black, please."

Cartwright poured two small cups and handed one to Abigail and the other to Felicity.

"Thank you, Cartwright," said Felicity. "Leave the pot there. I'll circulate with it later."

Cartwright nodded, then disappeared into the Dining Room.

Abigail smiled. "Nice to see a marchioness still willing to get her hands dirty." Her hand covered her mouth. "Please, forgive me," she stuttered. "That was rude of me. I don't know why…" She blinked her glistening eyes.

Felicity leant forward and squeezed her arm. "There's nothing to forgive. If anyone should be offering forgiveness, it's the Earl of Dartbury."

Abigail crimsoned and sipped some coffee. "You know."

"If it's any consolation, your fiancé—"

"Ex-fiancé," Abigail interrupted.

Felicity nodded. "Your ex-fiancé has been shunned by society. Even his staff have acquired jobs elsewhere, such is the shame to be seen to be working for him."

Abigail replaced her coffee cup on the saucer. "Never imagined I'd be the subject of conversation downstairs, as well as upstairs."

"The staff have standards, even if the Earl doesn't. It never crossed my mind that staff would take that stance until Cartwright mentioned it." Felicity sipped her coffee. "I still have so much to learn."

Abigail returned her cup to its saucer. "I know you all thought his brother would inherit the title, but surely, you had some idea of what you were getting involved with when you married His Lordship?"

Felicity chuckled. "The heir and the spare are more of a royal thing." She gazed at a spot on the Persian rug underneath the card table, where Gerald and Martin were attempting to play Bridge with Stella and Bœuf. "No, for Aldermaston and me, it was supposed to be a relatively normal life. I thought I would continue with my marketing career, while Aldermaston would help run the estate so that Basildon could go and do all the Marquess stuff. We lived in a small three-bedroom house on the estate. Until the tragic accident, we were Aldermaston and Felicity, and assumed we always would be. Everyone expected Basildon to become the Eighth Marquess of Mortiforde."

Abigail brushed a speck of dirt off her dress-covered thigh. "It seems our titled aristocracy is completely adept at shafting us." She closed her eyes and dropped her head into her hands. "I'm sorry, I've done it again. I didn't mean to—"

Felicity smiled. "You have a lot to be angry about. Both Aldermaston and I get angry sometimes. Especially when we're in difficult situations… situations we shouldn't really be in because we were never destined to be in them." She brought her cup to her lips. "You'll get over the Earl. Perhaps not as quickly as you'd like, but you will. Is that why you're here? In Mortiforde."

"Running away, you mean?"

"Wouldn't blame you."

Abigail tutted. "Hasn't worked, has it? Moved to the middle of nowhere and the first decent conversation I have is all about the lying, cheating Earl of Double-crossing Dartbury."

Felicity returned her cup to the saucer in her hand. "Nobody here is judging you. In fact, I doubt anybody else in Mortiforde knows. It's probably just me, Cartwright, and Aldermaston."

"His Lordship knows?"

Felicity nodded. "He won't judge you for it."

"It's not that," Abigail explained. "I owe him an apology. I've been treating him as though he's an aristocratic twat."

Felicity giggled. "You carry on, dear. He is!"

They both burst into laughter and raised their coffee cups.

∿

Aldermaston's head torch spotlighted Peggy's face. "Stay here! Daniel will come and get you. DANIEL!"

"What about Tess?" Peggy stared into the darkness.

"We'll find her. What worries me is somebody knew you'd be up here. With Tess. Somebody came to kidnap you."

Peggy's eyes watered. She bit her lips and nodded.

Daniel appeared beside them.

"Take Peggy back to the hide," Aldermaston instructed. "There's a flask of coffee in my rucksack."

Daniel nodded.

"Which way did Tess go?" Aldermaston scanned the woods with his head torch.

Daniel pointed. "Through there."

Peggy reached out to Aldermaston. "Remember what I said this morning. Don't chase her. You'll frighten her. Follow the trail."

Aldermaston nodded. Upturned leaf litter and decaying woodland debris surrounded them. It looked like a herd of wild animals had passed through. But in the direction Daniel had pointed, there was a clear line of trampled bracken and undergrowth.

"Follow that boar!" Daniel grinned, pointing deep into the darkness.

∾

Twenty feet from Aldermaston's hide, hugging the protective trunk of a Douglas fir, was Basildon, watching events through his own military-grade night-vision goggles strapped to his head. He'd no idea what was going on, but Lavinia was right. Aldermaston was hunting boar.

He raised himself up on his elbows, bent his hand over his shoulder and picked his weapon of choice, strapped to his back. A tranquillizer gun.

He rummaged in his chest pocket for one of the three tranquillizer darts he'd primed in preparation, loaded it, and then aimed.

Even with this enhanced military-grade night-vision goggles, locating the boar through all the undergrowth was challenging. He latched onto some movement. He couldn't see the boar, but the bracken stems danced as something stimulated them. His finger caressed the trigger. His eyes squinted, guesstimating where he thought the boar's rear hind quarters might be. It was now or never. He pulled.

∾

Aldermaston bounded through the overgrown woodland floor, as best a man who'd been up since five o'clock this morning could. Brambles tugged his khaki trousers, as his heavy walking boots challenged his leaping of bracken tops. Occasionally, among the broad beech tree trunks, and the intermittent Douglas fir, he thought he saw someone ahead.

He squinted, trying to focus on the black blob that was in front of him. Peggy's attacker? His heart pounded. It had to be. Who else would be in Mortiforde Woods running through thick undergrowth at ten o'clock at night? Tess would have to wait. Whoever he was now chasing was nimbler than Tess.

Suddenly, he heard a *Pffft* sound. There was a muffled shriek, and something ahead of him crashed heavily to the ground.

∼

Basildon frowned. He'd hit something, but the dense foliage in front of him still danced and swayed as it was forcibly tugged by something large pushing its way through. Perhaps he'd hit a tree stump.

His fingers retrieved the second dart from his chest pocket, and he reloaded the tranquillizer gun.

This time, he trained his sight just ahead of the movement, not easy because this boar wasn't running in a straight line. Perhaps it was MI5-trained. A random zigzagging movement was a classic sniper-avoidance tactic.

Spurred on, Basildon concentrated, his eyes narrowing further. He slowed his breathing and edged the tip of the rifle ahead of the movement. Once more, his finger stroked the trigger, waiting for the moment that would come any second…

Pfft.

∼

A piercing, searing pain shot through Aldermaston's right buttock. Instinctively, he grabbed it with both hands while his feet continued running. Something was stuck in him! He pulled, and another excruciating stinging sensation pulsated through his cheek muscle.

"Aaarrrggghhh!"

Aldermaston's eyes watered, making it difficult to scrutinise what he'd pulled from his right buttock. There was a long, thin, metal needle with a wider tube attached. A bright red ball of fluff exploded from its top.

His feet stumbled, and he struggled to stay upright. Everything swayed, and then his foot caught something soft. He glanced downwards at the blurry mass at his feet. Was that a dark hooded jacket?

The dart fell from his hand as he instinctively braced for impact.

∽

Basildon frowned. What the…? That wasn't the scream of a boar. It sounded familiar. Something about the tone that… His eyes widened. Aldermaston!

Basildon bit his lips to stifle any laughter. He'd only gone and tranquillized his little brother. His stomach spasmed, trying to force out a giggle, but Basildon was strong. He'd shot an old bore. Just not the sort Lavinia wanted.

The thought of Lavinia, lying on his rose-petalled covered bed, refocussed his attention. There was still a boar out here running free, and he was determined to make Lavinia's wish come true.

He surveyed the bright-green landscape before him, as his night-vision goggles enhanced every detail. There! About thirty degrees to his right was a small clearing. A snout pushed its way through the dense bracken.

Basildon beamed. This had promise. All he needed was for the boar to take a couple more steps forward, and he would have a clean shot.

Stealthily, he slipped his hand into his jacket pocket and took out his third, and final, tranquillizer dart. He reloaded and rested the gun on his shoulder in preparation.

He heard the boar snorting happily, as its nose rooted through the soft soil, churning its top layer like a minesweeper clearing a path. Then it happened. The boar took two steps forward, and suddenly its right shoulder was in clear view. Basildon didn't hesitate.

Pffft!

The boar squealed and shrieked in pain, jumping violently, trying to throw off the dart. Its red, bushy tail, having exploded from the rear of the canister on impact, confirmed the deployment of its sleep-inducing chemicals.

It staggered from side to side and then disappeared into thick undergrowth again.

Basildon smiled. He wasn't worried. It wouldn't get far. But best of all, he'd just demonstrated to Lavinia the lengths he would go to give her what she wanted.

~

Daniel flinched at the scream. He grabbed the night-vision binoculars and peered through the narrow window slit in the hide. Nothing. Just trees and undergrowth. And stillness.

"Can you see anything?" Peggy whispered.

Daniel shook his head. "I'm going to look for Aldermaston," he decided. "He sounded in pain." He hung the night-vision binoculars around his neck and turned to face Peggy. "You stay here. Whatever you do, don't move!"

Peggy scowled. "Like hell I will! There's some nutter out

there trying to kidnap me, and you want to leave me on my own? I'm coming with you."

∽

Aldermaston hit the ground with a thud, partially winding him, yet he continued moving. He tumbled over and over again. The force of his somersaulting down a steep embankment threw his arms and legs wide, slowing the speed of descent. His mind was mushy and fogged as his co-ordination disappeared. Over and over, he continued, until finally, he came to stop at the bottom, on soft soil.

Groggily, he tried opening his eyes. It was dark. His nose was squashed against something soft. Was he face down? He tried pushing himself up, only managing to raise his chest and head a few inches. His head spun. Where was he?

The ground underneath him was soft. Velvety soft. Not the rough, brambled woodland floor he'd just been running through. This was cultivated.

Tiredness and wooziness washed over him. He struggled to remain conscious. His hands sunk into the soft soil and touched something. A tree root? No. He squeezed his fingers together, and he caught something. Material? Cloth? He shook his head and regretted it.

He winced, fighting to stay awake. His fingers clenched the soft material. He pulled. So loose and fine was the soil that his quarry was soon revealed. An arm and a bare hand.

Woozily, he pushed and pulled with both hands, trying to sweep away the soft soil, to reveal the top of an arm and a shoulder. His head struggled to stay in control, to stay conscious of his action.

He pushed his fingers deep around the shoulder and then forced them underneath. With an almighty roar, he pulled. The shoulder turned, and as it did so, it brought up a head and a face. Jillian's face. Jillian's dead face.

Then it went black.

∼

Basildon jumped to his feet, threw the tranquillizer gun over his shoulder, and scuttled towards the clearing. When he arrived, he scanned the edges, looking for clues as to where his prize specimen had stumbled. She wouldn't have gone far. In fact… he cocked his head to one side. Yes. There was a faint snorting.

Cautiously, he crept through the thick bracken, in the direction of the noise, and soon found its source. Lying on her side, her stomach rising and falling with the soft rhythm of sleep, was the brown-haired body of Tess. Basildon beamed. Lavinia would be smitten. With him, hopefully, not the boar.

His fingers rummaged in his trouser pockets and pulled out some string. He set to work.

The easiest way to carry her would be across his shoulders. He tied her rear feet together, then repeated the exercise with her front feet. His hand stroked the side of her wiry-haired flank. Now all he had to do was to get upright with her on his shoulders.

He laid down, resting the back of his head on her flank. His hands grabbed her trussed feet and pulled them over his shoulders, like rucksack straps. Then he rolled over onto his knees, struggling with the weight of the boar across his shoulders. Slowly, he straightened his back until he was upright, then, drawing upon all his strength, pushed himself up onto his feet.

Suddenly, somewhere, a woman shrieked. Basildon glanced in the direction, but only saw darkness. He needed to get out of here.

Pushing downwards, he slowly rose into an upright stance. He wobbled precariously while he secured his balance.

He jiggled his shoulders, adjusting Tess's weight. That was better. Now all he had to do was march the couple of miles to Tugford Hall, where he would present his offering to his darling Lavinia, as she lay seductively on his bed of romantic rose petals.

He closed his eyes and let his imagination run wild. Meanwhile, the tranquillizer relaxed more of Tess's muscles, and she emptied her bladder down Basildon's back.

∽

Peggy shrieked. "I've kicked something soft."

Daniel looked through the night-vision binoculars. There, at her feet, was a body dressed in jogging bottoms and a hooded top. "Shit."

In the top of the thigh, he spotted a dart with a feathered end. He bent down and pulled it out. "Looks like a tranquillizer."

Carefully, he turned the body over. Was this the jogger he'd seen running along Peggy's alleyway? Their face was smothered with camouflage paint. He stuck his fingers against the victim's smooth-skinned neck.

"There's a pulse."

"Is it Lord Mortiforde?"

"No." He scoured the woodland floor.

"No? What do we do now?" Peggy enquired.

Daniel's eyes latched on to a broken, long, thin branch, about five feet long, lying on the ground. He picked it up and impaled one end into the soft soil.

"Do you have a handkerchief, Peggy?"

She rummaged up her sleeve and pulled one out. "What are you doing?"

He tied it round the top of the branch. "Marking the spot so we can find it again. We need to find Aldermaston first. Whoever this is, they're safe at the moment. Come on."

He grabbed Peggy's hand and pulled her away as they continued their search. The ground undulated underfoot, and the damaged undergrowth became more obvious to Daniel. A few steps later, they reach a large hollow in the ground. Daniel brought the night-vision binoculars up to his face again.

"The ground slopes away here, Peggy, so be careful and… there's Aldermaston!" Daniel spotted his boss lying face down in the soil at the bottom, and… Was that another body?

Together, they edged down the slope, stopping a few feet before they reached Aldermaston. "Hold this." He pulled his phone out of his pocket and placed it in Peggy's hands. He swiped the screen and selected the torch app.

Brilliant white light flooded the area. Peggy gasped.

Daniel stepped across to Aldermaston, then turned him over. Instinctively, he felt for a pulse. There was one. He let out a deep breath. He slapped Aldermaston's cheek. "Aldermaston! Aldermaston. Wake up!"

"Is he all right?" asked Peggy.

"I think so. He's alive."

"What about her?" Peggy's voice wavered. She pointed at the arm, shoulder and partially covered face a few feet away.

Fingers trembling, Daniel tentatively brushed away the loose soil from the woman's face. "Oh God." He jumped up, and backed away.

"Who is it?" Peggy stepped forward for a closer look.

"It's Jillian Jones. She's dead."

His eyes remained fixed on Jillian's white face as he backed away from it. Suddenly, he lost his footing, and fell backwards onto the ground.

Peggy shone the phone torch in his direction. "Are you all right?"

Daniel nodded. He tried pushing himself up, but his hands sank into the soft soil. "Eeuurrgghh!"

"What's the matter?"

Daniel shook. "There's something under here."

Tentatively, he pulled his hands out of the soft soil and brushed more of it away. A white hand suddenly appeared in the dark soil. Daniel flinched and backed away again.

Peggy held Daniel's phone higher, casting the light further.

Daniel's quivering hand reached out and grabbed the cold wrist, still partially submerged in soil. He pulled.

An arm rose out of the ground, as loose soil simply dropped away. The more he pulled, the greater the movement of earth, until suddenly, the upper torso and head sat upright.

Daniel freaked out and released his grip. The body fell back to the ground as he scuttled back to Peggy's side.

"We need to call Lisa," Daniel stammered. "I don't know who that is."

Peggy clasped her hands over her mouth. "I think…" she muttered, "… I think it's Tibby Gillard."

CHAPTER EIGHTEEN

Lisa hurtled along Birrington Lane in her red, battered Land Rover Defender, its diesel engine hammering away as her headlights illuminated the way ahead. Suddenly, Daniel jumped out of the tree-lined verge in front of her, frantically waving his arms. She stood on her brakes so hard her bottom rose off the seat. Daniel indicated to a lay-by on his right.

Lisa swung into it, switched off the engine, but left the sidelights on. As she jumped out of the vehicle, Daniel threw his arms around her and sobbed, uncontrollably.

She stroked the back of his head. "It's the shock." She leant back and clasped Daniel's head in her hands. "You're sure it's Jillian?"

He nodded.

"And Tibby?"

"Peggy reckons so."

"But Aldermaston's okay, albeit tranquillized?"

Daniel nodded.

"And there's someone elsc?"

"Yes," Daniel blurted between sharp breaths. "Don't know

who. Someone tried to attack Peggy. Could be them. Could also be an innocent bystander."

Lisa wrinkled her nose. "Off the beaten track, at gone ten o'clock at night? I doubt it."

"What do we do?" Daniel wiped his eyes.

Even in the partial moonlight, Lisa could see how scared he was.

"Hello?"

Lisa jumped, then turned to see Peggy standing near the Defender's bonnet. She hurried across and put an arm around Peggy's shoulders. "Mrs Farmer, are you all right?"

Peggy nodded. A tear ran down her cheek.

"Come on, let's get you in here." She opened the front passenger door. "I had the heater on full blast, so you'll be warmer in here."

A wall of heat engulfed them as Lisa helped Peggy into the front passenger seat.

"You stay there. Daniel and I will sort things out."

Peggy nodded.

Lisa shut the door.

"So what do *we* do?" Daniel enquired.

Lisa pondered briefly. "We need to get to Aldermaston and this other mystery person for a start."

Daniel glanced into the woods. "What about the police?"

Lisa leant against the side of the Defender. The thought of calling PC Norten… No. She grabbed Daniel's shoulder. "Jillian and Tibby aren't going anywhere just yet. Let's wait until Aldermaston is conscious and see what he says."

She bit her bottom lip. Hopefully, he wouldn't be out for the count for too long.

Sweat streamed down Basildon's forehead as he reached Tugford Hall's tradesmen's entrance. He shifted Tess's weight on his shoulders for the final stretch of his journey.

He twisted the door handle and peered through an inch gap to check the coast was clear. A clock chimed the half hour. Ten-thirty. The Guild guests should have departed by now. Cartwright would be tidying up.

He pushed the door wide, slipped in sideways, then shut it gently with his foot, only moving forward once he'd heard the reassuring latch click.

Basildon shuffled along the smooth tiled floor to the rear staircase and began the climb. The pain in his thigh muscles seared with each rise. He thought of Lavinia undressing herself in his bedroom, slipping under the soft, silk sheets, and awaiting his bountiful return. He struggled on.

Twenty minutes and three floors later, he reached his apartment door. He kicked it open, stumbled inside, and fell against the side wall. Tess's snout shifted a Stubbs oil painting off-centre. He kicked the door closed, but the latch failed to engage. Blast. He'd come back to sort it.

"Lavinia, darling. I'm home!" he sang, his mind imagining her delightful welcome. "Look what I've caught, especially for you!"

He staggered along the hallway, then hovered outside his bedroom door to compose himself. He puffed out his chest, then strolled manfully into his bedroom.

The silk sheets of his four-poster bed remained petal-strewn and neatly made. He glanced around the room. "Lavinia? Darling?" He staggered to the end of the bed and peered through the en suite bathroom door. Empty.

She wasn't there. "Buggering hell!"

The pain in his shoulders was unbearable. He desperately needed sleep. Finally, Basildon succumbed. He fell backwards onto the bed, sandwiching Tess between the pillows and his head. Rose petals shot high into the air, and then fluttered back down, raining like silk butterflies.

He let go of Tess's feet, slipped his hand into his pocket, and pulled out a penknife. First, he leant to his right and cut the twine around her front legs. Then he leaned left and sliced the binding round her rear legs.

Tiredness washed over him. His eyes closed, and deep, rejuvenating sleep was thrust upon him.

∽

Cartwright brought Abigail's white Audi TT to a halt beneath the steps of Tugford Hall's main entrance.

Felicity held out a hand. "It was lovely to meet you, Abigail. I only wish my husband were here to say goodnight to you."

Abigail shook her hand and smiled. "I'm sure he's grateful for any excuse to avoid meeting me."

Felicity clasped Abigail's hand in both of hers. "I'd say the Earl of Dartbury did you a favour."

Abigail frowned. "Doesn't feel like it at the moment."

"One day soon, hopefully." Felicity smiled.

Cartwright cleared his throat.

Felicity acknowledged Cartwright. "And that, Ms Mayedew, is Cartwright's way of telling you he's getting cold holding your door open."

They air kissed each other's cheeks.

"Thank you for our chat." Abigail dropped a couple of steps. "It was useful." She turned and dropped to her waiting car before elegantly slipping inside.

Cartwright shut the door, took two steps back and then placed his hands behind his back.

Felicity waved as Abigail drove off, the crunch of gravel filling the night air.

"That's the last of our guests, My Lady. Chief Constable Stoyle has retired to his room."

"I'm off to check my son is asleep and not still playing computer games. You might as well lock up, Cartwright."

"And His Lordship, My Lady?"

Felicity shrugged. "Cartwright, your guess is as good as mine."

∼

"Is that snoring?"

"It had better be Aldermaston." Daniel offered his hand to Lisa, as they dropped into the woodland dip. "I propped him up against that embankment over there." Daniel shone his torch at Aldermaston.

Aldermaston's head had lolled to one side. His mouth was open.

"Mind where you tread!" Daniel instructed.

Lisa stopped mid-step and looked down. Her head torch illuminated Tibby's face and shoulder in the earth, then Jillian's further along.

"Come round the edge," Daniel suggested.

"So, how are we going to do this?" Lisa asked.

Daniel grabbed Aldermaston's arms and pulled him onto his side. "Grab his feet."

Lisa grasped Aldermaston's ankles.

"Ready?" Daniel enquired.

Lisa nodded.

"After three, then. One… two… three."

Together they lifted him, his bottom barely leaving the ground. Cautiously, they edged along the bottom of the hollow until Lisa suddenly lost her footing. She screamed and dropped Aldermaston's feet.

"You okay?" Daniel lowered Aldermaston to the floor and hurried over to her.

She nodded. "My foot sank in this soft soil."

"Here, let me." Daniel grabbed her calf muscle and pulled. The toe of her shoe snagged on something. He pulled again, slowly revealing her foot, and the tied handles of a supermarket carrier bag caught on her shoe.

He unhooked it and pulled the whole bag out of the ground.

"What is it?" Lisa rubbed her shin.

Daniel ripped the carrier bag apart and pulled out a large ledger. "The recipe book!" He flicked through the pages. "Does this mean Jillian stole it? But why bury it? This is worth a fortune. Even more on the black market."

Aldermaston groaned.

Both Lisa and Daniel spun round, their head torches spotlighting his face. Lisa crouched down beside him.

"Aldermaston. Can you hear me?"

He turned towards her voice, but his eyes remained closed.

"Come on," she said, standing. "He's coming round. We need to get him back to the Land Rover quickly."

Daniel nodded. If Aldermaston was coming round now, what about the hooded attacker?

∾

Basildon's nose twitched. Something was tickling his face. His cheek tingled as a softness stroked across it.

"Wake up, sleepyhead," sang a voice.

He beamed. Lavinia! His eyes opened to see her fingers gently tracing around his face with a rose petal.

"Darling, you're here! How spiffing!" He blinked away the sleep from his eyes.

Lavinia nodded, but frowned. "Basildon. Men who promise the earth and then fail to deliver disappoint me immensely."

He propped himself up on his elbows. "I say, dear. That's a bit harsh."

Lavinia leant back, and for the first time he noticed what she was wearing. Or rather, what she wasn't wearing.

His eyes widened. "Where were you earlier?"

Lavinia slid off the bed, giving him a full view of the opulent black basque, with lace cups and front panel. "Slipping into something more comfortable." She posed seductively, draping herself around one of the bottom posts of his four-poster bed.

Basildon gulped. If she was disappointed, he certainly wasn't. He forced his eyes wider.

Lavinia pouted. "But Basil Baby, you promised me a wild boar."

Basildon nodded frantically. "I did!"

Lavinia's bottom lip protruded further forward. Then she held her hands up in the air. "So where is it?"

Basildon chuckled with relief, then froze. He spun round on the bed. Tess wasn't there.

"But…"

He picked up each of the four pillows on the bed in turn and threw them onto the floor. "It was here!" He stared at Lavinia, dumbfounded. He pointed to the space where the pillows had once been. "I swear to you, darling. It *was* here!"

Lavinia stepped over and grabbed two of the pillows from the floor. "You put a wild boar on the *bed*?"

Basildon nodded.

She placed her hands on her hips. "What were you thinking of? A threesome?"

Basildon rose to his knees with outstretched arms. "No, darling. Of course not. But…" He stopped and turned to the empty sheet at the top of the bed where the pillows once were.

"Oh, God." He sat down on the mattress.

"What?"

He gazed directly at her. "I promise you. I caught you a boar, with a tranquillizer dart, and brought it back here for you."

Lavinia threw her hands in the air, each still holding the pillows. "So where the hell is it?"

∼

"Will Peggy be all right with Aldermaston?" Lisa hurried after Daniel, as he led her back into Mortiforde Woods.

"Probably grateful to have someone else in your car," he replied. Daniel surveyed the woods with the night-vision binoculars. "It was round here somewhere."

Lisa's head torch illuminated little in the mixed woodland. "Didn't you mark the spot?"

"Yes!" Daniel snapped. He sighed. "Sorry."

Lisa gripped his shoulder. "We've all had a long and stressful day."

"I stuck a tall branch in the ground, tied one of Peggy's handkerchiefs to the top. It stood a good foot above the bracken. We should be able to see it… There!" The relief in his voice was overwhelming.

Daniel dashed ahead, but soon came to a crashing halt. He spun round several times, then grabbed the branch with the handkerchief tied to it and bashed the surrounding the bracken.

Lisa caught up with him. "What's up?"

"They're gone."

"Gone?"

Daniel nodded. "Look." He pointed to the ground. All Lisa saw were the flattened, broken stems where a body had once lain.

"Bugger!" yelled Daniel, thrashing out and whacking the branch against a large clump of bracken.

Lisa grabbed his arm. "You said you came across this person first, before you found Aldermaston."

Daniel nodded.

"So we're assuming, whoever they are—"

"Peggy's attacker, probably," Daniel interrupted.

"Okay," Lisa continued, "but my point is, you came across them first. So, if Aldermaston is just coming round now, then chances are the attacker came round before Aldermaston."

Daniel turned and stared at her. His mouth dropped open. "What is it?"

"If the attacker regained consciousness, Peggy could still be in danger."

∽

Felicity lay in bed, seething. Where the bloody hell was he? She looked at the bedside clock radio. Half eleven. She turned over and punched the pillow a couple of times before resting her head back on it. The Borderer's Guild was his domain. He shouldn't have left her to do his entertaining tonight. Next time she had a Ladies' Legion meeting here at the Hall, she'd abandon them to him. See how he liked it.

What was that? She stopped breathing, straining to hear. Silence.

She pulled the duvet tight and snuggled underneath it. It was no good. She'd have to lay down some ground rules about what was deemed acceptable behaviour when hosting events. Disappearing halfway through when—

There it was again! A scratching sound? Or was it scraping?

Felicity propped herself up on her elbows. The bedroom was dark, but she could make out the curtained window, the door to the en suite, the door to her dressing room, and Aldermaston's tall dressing mirror, beside his large cupboard unit. There was no dark human shadow wandering around the room. She seethed. If it had been Aldermaston, he'd have had a piece of her mind. A big piece.

It wasn't Harry either. He was fast asleep when she checked in on him earlier. She settled down again. Tomorrow she would finish her Boor Pie and enter it into the Bake Off tent, and—

There! She sat bolt upright again. That was a definite scratching noise. She cocked her head to one side and froze. She hadn't noticed it earlier, but their bedroom door was ajar. Not just an inch, but a good two feet. The nightlight outside Harry's bedroom at the other end of the corridor cast a faint shadow against the bedroom wall.

Felicity gulped. *Something* was in the room. She stretched out her hand, searching the wall for the bedside light switch in wide, sweeping arcs. Suddenly, her hand knocked it and both bedside lights came on, although it took the low-energy lightbulbs nearly a minute to produce any beneficial light.

Another scratching noise came from the foot of the bed. Felicity pulled the duvet close around her neck. Something was in the room. A rat? She shuddered.

She was about to throw back the duvet and swing out her legs to investigate when there was a loud snort, followed by a rhythmic scratching noise.

Warily, she leant forward and crawled to the bottom of the bed on her hands and knees, fearful of what she might find.

First was the hairy snout, its nostrils twitching as they savoured every scent in the air. Then she saw the long face, and the two swept-back, black hairy ears. Felicity gulped. There, at the foot of her bed, was a boar, sat on its rear end, scratching its flank with its hind leg.

She screamed. Her ear-piercing screech frightened the boar, causing it to squeal in a competitive response. It fell backwards in fright, then fought desperately with the carpet, until it finally found its grip and hurtled out through the open bedroom door.

∽

Aldermaston collapsed into the soft-cushioned sofa in the snug of Lisa's B&B. He winced. Esme climbed beside him, licked his face and wagged her tail, excited so many people were here late at night.

"Bum still sore, Your Lordship?" Peggy grinned.

He wagged his finger at her. "You have some explaining to do."

The grin dropped from her face.

"There you go, you two." Lisa passed them both a mug of coffee. "How are you feeling?"

Aldermaston yawned. "Not so groggy. Weirdly, I feel as though I've had a good few hours' kip."

Daniel sat cross-legged on the snug floor between Peggy and Aldermaston. "I reckon you were only out for about an hour. What are we going to do about Tess?"

Aldermaston sipped his coffee. "Not much we can do. We'll just have to hope she turns up somewhere. Unless she's been kidnapped."

Peggy clasped a mouth over her hand.

Lisa wrapped her hands around her mug of coffee and sat on the arm of the sofa, next to Esme. "What? So, whoever attacked Peggy was actually after Tess?"

Aldermaston rubbed the back of his head. "I'm not sure, but…" He rummaged in his camouflage jacket pocket and pulled out the tranquillizer dart. "Whoever hit me with one of these was probably aiming for Tess."

Daniel placed his mug on the coffee table. "Why is Tess so important?"

Aldermaston looked at Peggy. "Perhaps you'd like to show them what you showed me earlier."

Peggy slipped a hand into her pocket and pulled out three black truffles.

Daniel took one and looked at it, quizzically. "What is it?"

"A truffle," Peggy clarified. "An Autumn Truffle."

"I thought truffles were French." Daniel's eyes crossed as he scrutinised it.

Peggy toyed with her wedding ring. "France has a good supply of truffles, but they exist here, too. Have done for centuries. They thrive in the right conditions."

"Which includes Mortiforde Woods," said Aldermaston.

"Jock realised first," Peggy explained. "He was researching his ancestors, and discovered that during the sixteenth century, as well as supplying meat to the castle when it was a royal palace, his ancestors also supplied truffles found in Mortiforde Woods. When that supermarket opened on the outskirts of town, we were all hit financially. Then, when that foraging company set themselves up, Jock wondered if he could find truffles again. The top restaurants in London pay good money for prime specimens. So, he borrowed a pig."

Daniel choked on his coffee. "He what?"

Peggy nodded. "We're butchers. We know where to find pigs. The French use pigs all the time. They have a great sense of smell, and their snouts are perfect for breaking up the top layer of soil without damaging the truffle. Dogs have great noses, but their paws are not so careful. Today, truffle hunters use dogs to sniff out the truffle, then sit when they've found one. The truffle hunter extracts it from the ground. But pigs can do it all with their snouts."

Daniel brought the truffle to his nose and sniffed. "Cor! Pongs a bit."

Esme sat up on the sofa, her nose twitching.

Peggy snatched it back. "Pungent is the term often used. Sometimes there's a hint of garlic."

Lisa leant forward. "How much? For that one in your hand?"

Peggy pursed her lips. "This smaller one. Fifty pounds."

"Fifty quid!" Daniel shrieked. He glanced at the others in Peggy's lap. "So what Tess found for you there is about…"

"Getting on for two hundred pounds."

Daniel whistled.

Aldermaston clutched his coffee to his chest. "Useful cash when your traditional butchery business is struggling. Even more so when you haven't won the Best Borderlandshire Burger competition for several years."

Peggy nodded. "I thought this could save us. All we needed was something to keep us afloat financially until we won the Best Borderlandshire Burger competition. But the Trotters have done that for three years running, and…"

"And what?" asked Aldermaston. "Tess?"

"Yes! Bloody Jock Trotter discovered that while pigs are fantastic truffle hunters, boar are better."

Aldermaston sat up. "Where'd he find her?"

Peggy sighed. "They're prolific down in the Forest of Dean. Somehow he caught a youngster, tamed it, then trained it. Seth and I are still bumbling around with pigs. I'm lucky if I find one or two truffles a week. We all go out most nights, or early mornings. And look!" She held all three truffles in her hands. "This is what Tess found within a few minutes. Heaven knows how many more she'd have found had we not been interrupted."

Aldermaston drained his coffee mug. "There's a reason you all do it under the cover of darkness, isn't there?"

Peggy avoided eye contact, choosing to stare at the truffles in her hands. "I told you, Your Lordship. Pigs can be dangerous. When they're off on a scent, they can knock people flying. Safest at night when nobody's about."

Aldermaston nodded. "Nothing to do with the fact that harvesting foraged foodstuffs for commercial gain requires a licence from the landowner?"

Peggy crimsoned. "We approached Mortiforde Forestry."

Aldermaston's eyebrow rose. "They granted you all permission to forage for truffles for commercial gain, did they?"

Peggy bit her bottom lip and shook her head. Her eyes welled up. "Don't judge me, Your Lordship. We're just trying to survive!"

Aldermaston leant across the coffee table and took Peggy's hands in his. "Peggy, there are two dead bodies in the woods, and we haven't found Jock and Seth yet. And, in one way or another, it's all to do with truffles."

CHAPTER NINETEEN

Cartwright hurtled down the hallway in his green Black Watch tartan nightwear, clutching the matching nightcap with white pompom. It was unusual for Her Ladyship to call him after hours. Slipping through the connecting door into the East Wing, he thought he saw Basildon disappearing round the far corner of the corridor.

Approaching the bedroom, Cartwright noticed the door was open. He paused, straightened his nightcap, and knocked twice. "Everything all right, My Lady?"

Felicity appeared at the doorway, slipping her ruby red dressing gown over her pink satin nightwear. "Oh, Cartwright! Thank heavens you're here."

"Whatever's the matter, My Lady?"

She frowned. "Didn't you just see it?"

"See what, My Lady?"

"The boar."

Cartwright was perplexed. "The what, My Lady?"

"BOAR. I've just seen a bloody boar in my bedroom."

This didn't make any sense. Unless… "My Lady, did you partake in any of Basildon's canapés this evening?"

Felicity pulled her dressing gown tight. "No. Aldermaston warned me not to. What was in them?" She placed her hands on her hips. "I'm not bloody hallucinating, Cartwright! There was a wild boar sat right there," she pointed to the end of her bed, "scratching its underbelly." She shuddered. "The thing's probably got fleas. Now the bedroom will be infested."

A perplexed smile crossed Cartwright's face. "I'll investigate, My Lady."

"Make sure you chase it off the premises." She turned and slammed the door in his face. The bobble on his nightcap bounced.

He looked along the corridor. At the far end, a boar trotted past. Cartwright rubbed his eyes. It was gone. Now *he* was seeing things.

Suddenly, Lavinia hobbled into view at the end of the corridor in her basque.

Cartwright's eyes bulged. His face crimsoned. So much naked flesh. His mouth opened to speak, but… He shook his head and rubbed his eyes. Then he opened them again. The end of the corridor was empty again. He sighed.

An ear-piercing squeal ricocheted around the corner, followed by an angry boar now bolting towards him. Cartwright flattened himself against the wall, as it careered past, quickly followed by a half-naked Lavinia. Seconds later, Basildon dashed past.

All three hurtled through the open connecting door into the main hall. Cartwright sighed. He took a deep breath, straightened his nightcap, hitched up his nightgown, and gave chase.

∾

Aldermaston terminated the call on his mobile. "Chief Constable Stoyle says he'll draft in officers from Worcestershire to come and deal with the bodies." He looked at each of them, sat in Lisa's snug at the B&B, then stroked Esme, lying on the sofa beside him.

His eyes moistened. "I made a grave error of judgement here. Abigail was right. I should have called the police earlier. I let Jillian and Tibby down. Badly." He pulled a handkerchief from his trouser pockets and wiped his face.

Peggy put the truffles down on the coffee table and took Aldermaston's hands in hers.

"You are not to blame," Peggy began. "For Jillian's death. Or Tibby's."

He grimaced in disagreement.

Peggy's grip tightened. "Did *you* kill them?"

"No, of course not, but—"

"Whoever killed them is responsible, not you!"

"I should have thought about that note more, first thing this morning, when that package arrived. That was a direct threat to Jillian. And Tibby's too. I bungled it. I…"

"You're not responsible for everyone's safety in this community," Peggy continued. "You're not to blame."

Aldermaston ran his fingers through his thinning hair. "I could have handled things differently. My father wouldn't have made such an error of judgement. He—"

Peggy wagged a finger in Aldermaston's face. "Stop it! Your father made plenty of mistakes at the start of his tenure, believe you me. My Walter nearly punched him once, because of his stubbornness and refusal to listen to the community. And remember, your father knew he would become the Seventh Marquess. He was schooled and coached for that moment. You? You've had this thrust upon you."

She leant back in her chair. "Your father made mistakes. You'll make them too. We all will. We're human. But *how* he remedied his mistakes is what made your father the man he was. You have that choice too, Your Lordship. You can't change what you have or haven't done. But you can change what you're going to do about it."

A tear abseiled down Aldermaston's cheek. He nodded. His hereditary title put him in a position of leadership. One he hadn't asked for. And even though he'd led them to this point of failure, they still trusted him. They were still looking to him now, waiting for, and wanting, his leadership. He had to resolve this.

"In that case," he began, "we've got a killer to catch and, hopefully, two butchers lives to save."

∽

Basildon's eyes latched onto Lavinia's seductively shimmying bare buttocks as she bolted along the corridor. Much better than a boar's hairy rear end.

In the distance, a door opened, and Basildon spotted Chief Constable Stoyle step out into the corridor, in full uniform, with his briefcase.

"STOP THAT BOAR!" Basildon bellowed.

Stoyle flinched, then stared in horror at what was charging down the corridor.

"Do something!" Basildon hollered.

Stoyle dropped his briefcase and assumed a rugby tackle stance, feet apart, bent knees and arms outstretched.

The boar dithered briefly, unsure of how to deal with this new threat. Stoyle shuffled on his feet. The boar opted for the direct route and shot straight between his legs.

Stoyle snapped his arms together, ensnaring only himself. He wavered slightly, then fell forward face first. Somehow, Stoyle turned his head-first fall into a face-saving forward roll, kicking his legs and jumping back up onto his feet.

He pulled taut his uniform jacket cuffs and savoured a moment of smugness. Seconds later, Lavinia smashed into him, and together they fell onto the red-carpeted corridor floor.

As Basildon drew nearer, his eyes latched on to Chief Constable Stoyle's hands tightly clenching Lavinia's still-shimmying bare buttocks.

"Let her go!" Basildon repeatedly smacked each of Chief Constable's hands until he released Lavinia's now-reddening cheeks. Then he hooked his hand under the small strap of basque material between Lavinia's shoulder blades and pulled.

Lavinia screamed as she unexpectedly flew backwards into the air, into an upright position. Basildon stared at Stoyle lying on the floor. No prospective MI5 candidate could tolerate such inappropriate manhandling of his plus one.

Basildon stepped astride the Chief Constable and planted his face a foot away from Stoyle's now-trembling face. "How dare you manhandle Lavinia in such a brusque and degrading manner."

Stoyle shook his head. "It was an accident."

Basildon drew back his right fist. "So's this." The downward force of Basildon's fist colliding with the bridge of Stoyle's nose created a crunching noise that would satisfy any Friday evening brawler outside The Nooseman's Knot at closing time.

Stoyle screamed as blood poured down over his top lip.

Basildon stood upright and looked at Lavinia, her eyes wide with wonder and admiration.

"Oh, Basildon," she sighed, her voice husky in her deep breath. "You old-fashioned gentleman."

Stoyle rolled onto his side, desperate to protect his nose from any further assault.

Basildon gawped at Lavinia's heaving chest, as she stretched out a hand and cupped his chin.

"Which way did the boar go?" he asked, gazing deep into

her cleavage.

"Left," she whispered.

A penetrating, falsetto squeal echoed around the corridors of Tugford Hall, as the boar came charging back round the corner into the corridor, trailing a body.

Basildon's jaw dropped as Cartwright's one-handed defiant grip on the boar's stubby, wire-haired tail caused the butler immense pain, as his body was dragged, face down, around the corner at breakneck speed. Cartwright's Black Watch tartan pyjama trousers were around his ankles, as the bare cheeked butler fought desperately with his other hand to retrieve his pyjama bottoms and restore order and dignity to the household, his profession, and his genitalia.

Basildon winced. Cartwright had to be suffering from the worst possible carpet burns. Still, staff were staff, and should do as instructed.

"Whatever you do, Cartwright, don't let go!" he yelled, just as the boar turned the corner.

"No, sir," came the reply, just before the butler disappeared.

∾

Aldermaston shuffled on the sofa. "Did you get anywhere with that address, Lisa? From the electoral register."

"Yes!" She grabbed some paperwork from the top of a sideboard. "There were two potential names. Here we go." She handed Aldermaston her notebook.

Miss Madeleine Bryan, 2 Arboreal Way, Mortiforde, Borderlandshire, 24.

Mrs Megan Bryan, The Glebe, Ashford Morte, Mortiforde, Borderlandshire, 32.

He handed it to Daniel. "How old would you say the MB of your bracelet is?"

"Nearer to twenty-four than thirty-two," he said.

"And Arboreal Way," Aldermaston continued, "is just the other side of Morte Bridge. Whereas Ashford Morte is what, five miles away?"

Daniel agreed. "Arboreal Way backs onto the woods, too."

"Could Miss Madeleine Bryan be the attacker you found in the woods earlier?" Aldermaston asked.

Daniel shrugged. "I didn't get a good look at their face, and they were wearing camouflage paint too." He paused. "They had a similar athletic build. Earlier, while I was watching Peggy's backyard—"

"You were what, young man?" Peggy snapped.

"I asked him to," Aldermaston chipped in. "Probably as well I did. Go on, Daniel."

"Well, this runner came up and down the alley a couple of times and peered over Peggy's rear gate. That could have been the same woman I bumped into outside Shepherds. The woman we think is Madeleine Bryan. She'd be fit enough to overpower you, Peggy."

Aldermaston sat upright. "We must pay Madeleine Bryan a visit. The earlier, the better. Shall we meet on Morte Bridge, in the morning, at five-thirty?"

"Doesn't give us much sleep," yawned Lisa.

"Sleep's a luxury Jillian and Tibby no longer have." Aldermaston raised his eyebrows.

Lisa grabbed her other paperwork. "Talking of Jillian, this is what I found from her office. There's a map here, with a cross in the middle and words *Dead Man's Hollow*."

Daniel passed the paperwork across to Aldermaston. "Is that Mortiforde Woods?"

Aldermaston nodded. "That's Vinnalls Coppice in that corner." He paused, then shook his head. "Stella said something about *Dead Man's Hollow* at dinner this evening." He shook his head again. "Brain's still fogged from that tranquillizer."

Daniel snatched the map from Aldermaston. "Hang on a minute." He rotated the sheet. "Yes, there's the road. There's the track... Bloody hell!" He tapped the paper. "*Dead Man's Hollow.* That's where we found Jillian's and Tibby's bodies."

Lisa frowned. "Why would Jillian have a map in her office of where she would be buried? I also found these on her desk." Lisa unfurled Jillian's huge family tree out over the coffee table, covering the truffles. "Here's Jillian, right at the bottom, and look. If you follow this maternal line, you reach Oswyn Cooke, whom she's circled."

Daniel whistled. "That's some family tree."

Aldermaston suddenly sat upright. "Stella mentioned Oswyn this evening, over dinner. She said that Jillian discovered her family connection with the castle's chef a couple of years ago."

Peggy shuffled in her seat. "So Jillian is a direct descendent of a chef who worked at Mortiforde Castle some four hundred years ago. It's not just us butchers who can trace our ancestry back that far, then."

"Yes, but," said Lisa, finding another piece of paper. "What does Jillian mean here?" She pointed to Jillian's handwritten note at the bottom of the page. *See recipe book. Now it all becomes clear!*

"Bugger!" snapped Aldermaston. "I'd forgotten about the recipe book."

"We found it!" Daniel bent behind the sofa where they were sitting. "Look." He picked up the carrier bag they'd found in the woods earlier.

Aldermaston took out the padded envelope, and then carefully extracted the food diary. His shoulders relaxed. It appeared intact and undamaged. He flicked through the pages. "The answer to everything is in here, it seems. Who's good at reading Latin?"

He stared at their blank faces in turn. Great.

Felicity hobbled along the corridor of the main hall, wincing at the pain in her toes. Yesterday had been a long day, and it didn't seem to be over yet. It had gone midnight and Aldermaston still wasn't back. Where *was* he?

She turned the corner and shrieked as she came face to face with a bloodied Chief Constable Stoyle coming the other way.

"What happened?"

"That brother-in-law of yours needs locking up," he seethed, spitting blood. Literally.

Felicity linked her arm through his. "Don't let me stop you," she muttered. "Follow me. We'll go downstairs to the kitchens."

Behind his bloody façade, Stoyle looked confused.

"It's where the better first aid kit is," Felicity clarified. "I have one in our private apartment, but it's mainly plasters for when Harry grazes a knee." She looked up at his nose. "And you're going to need more than a plaster that says 'I've been a brave boy today' across it."

She led him to the stairs, and they began their slow descent. The swelling under his eyes impinged his ability to see, curtailing his speed of movement to that of Felicity's.

Ten minutes and two storeys later, the two invalids turned into Cartwright's huge kitchen. Felicity flicked a switch and the bank of fluorescent lights cranked into life. Stoyle winced at the brightness and the pain it induced.

"Come to the sink." Felicity ran the hot tap and dampened a cloth, then squeezed the excess moisture away. Gently, she raised it to Stoyle's face and lightly touched his top lip.

He flinched.

"Sorry." She wiped his chin instead, which was just as bloodied, but less painful when touched. She pointed to the bloodstains on his shirt uniform. "You'll need to get that dry-cleaned."

He nodded, then wished he hadn't.

"You're going to need hospital treatment."

"Probably broken," he suggested.

Felicity nodded. "I'll get Cartwright."

As she turned to press the call button to summon Cartwright, she came face to face with something large and hairy staring at them both. It stood, defiantly, in the kitchen doorway, staring up at them. Its snout twitching, smelling blood, its feet scraping at the tiled floor, preparing to act.

Felicity edged backwards, bumping into Stoyle, whose gaze remained transfixed on the animal.

The boar snorted, grunted fiercely, then charged. Using her good foot, Felicity jumped backwards, launching herself up onto the draining board by the sink, and swung her legs out of the way. Stoyle shot behind Cartwright's preparatory island unit.

The boar attempted turning the corner. Its front legs maintained a grip on the tiled floor, but momentum carried its rear legs out from under its body. It squealed in anger as it battled to regain an upright position.

Stoyle ran around the island, his eyes fixed on where he thought the boar might be. He failed to see Lavinia running in.

"Look out!" Felicity screamed.

Stoyle collided with Lavinia, knocking her to the floor, and then fell on top of her. The boar careered around the corner and ran into the entwined couple, its snout and head smacking into Stoyle's bottom. Stoyle yelled, spraying blood in all directions. Together they rolled across the kitchen floor as Lavinia struggled to push the Chief Constable off her, and Stoyle desperately fought off Tess.

Basildon appeared in the kitchen doorway. He brought the sight of his tranquillizer gun up to his eye. "KEEP STILL!"

Felicity screamed. "Basildon, don't!"

Basildon's focus remained fixed on the boar. He pulled the trigger.

Pffft!

A high-pitched scream bounced off the stainless-steel surfaces. Lavinia kneed Stoyle in the groin. He slumped against the side of the island unit, unsure of whether to clutch his groin or his nose.

Lavinia stood and glanced at the red feathered dart sticking out of her left buttock. "Basildon! You shot me!" she screamed. Suddenly, her eyes widened, then rolled back, and she passed out, collapsing to the floor.

The boar, frightened by Lavinia's scream, bounded towards Basildon.

Felicity suddenly saw her chance. Carefully, she slipped to the ground and hobbled over to the larder, where she unlatched the door and opened it wide.

Basildon dropped the tranquillizer gun to the floor and roared, pounding his chest hard with his fists. The boar swerved this threatening ape and backtracked around the large preparatory island in the kitchen centre. As it turned the corner, it saw the safe darkness of the larder, and charged.

Felicity slammed shut the door and leant back against it, her heart pounding. There was a huge crash as the boar collided with several sacks of potatoes and onions at the back of the larder.

Suddenly, the door pounded, nearly knocking Felicity to the floor. "Basildon, do something!"

Basildon skidded across the kitchen and joined Felicity, crashing against the larder door. Together, their bodies jolted each time the boar head-butted the larder door.

"We need something heavy," Basildon suggested.

Cartwright appeared in the kitchen doorway, his tartan

nightwear now properly in place, although the white pompom on his night cap looked a little dishevelled.

"Something heavy, did you say, sir?"

"YES!" Basildon bawled, as their backs lurched forward several inches with each battering.

"Allow me." Cartwright wandered towards the kitchen waste bin near the larder door. He pushed the bin aside to reveal Felicity's first Boor Pie creation. Cartwright leant against the adjacent kitchen unit and wedged his feet on the blackened Boor Pie brick. Pushing hard against the kitchen unit, he straightened his legs, his feet struggling to inch the Boor Pie forward millimetres at a time.

Eventually, inertia gave way. Cartwright howled as he finally pushed it against the bottom of the larder door. "Okay, My Lady," he coughed, between inhaling huge lungfuls of air. "Step away, slowly."

Basildon nodded in agreement, and she edged away from the door. It jolted suddenly as the boar rammed it from the other side. Basildon recoiled, but the door held. Tentatively, Basildon leant forward, removing his weight from the door. The larder door rocked once more, the top corner flying open three inches, but the door remained solid.

Basildon stepped back a few paces. "What is *that*, Cartwright?"

"One could call it an experiment, sir, where the results were not those as expected," Cartwright offered, without glancing at Felicity.

Basildon wagged a finger at him. "You see, Cartwright. You mock me for all of my little wheezes and japes, and yet here you are trapping a wild boar with one of your cooking disasters."

"Did someone say wild boar?" Aldermaston stood in the kitchen doorway and folded his arms.

Felicity scowled. "Where the hell have you been?"

The larder door suddenly jolted again. Everyone flinched.

"What's in there?" Aldermaston stepped forward.

Basildon walked up to his younger brother and slapped him on the back. "Do you know, old chap, you'll never guess."

Aldermaston paused as he looked down at Lavinia, splayed out across the floor, the red tranquillizer dart still penetrating her pert buttock. "Who did that?"

Basildon chuckled and pulled a face. "I was trying to tranquillise our captive in the larder over there, but poor Lavinia got in the way. It'll wear off soon. I'll take her upstairs and make her comfortable."

Aldermaston turned and grabbed Basildon with both hands by the throat. "It was you!" His nostrils flared as he stared intently into Basildon's eyes.

Basildon shook his head, not that it moved much in Aldermaston's grip. "What was?"

Aldermaston released one hand, slipped it into his camouflage jacket pocket, and pulled out a red feathered dart. "I think this belongs to you. I pulled this out of my bottom earlier, you cretin!"

Basildon laughed nervously. "Oh, did I hit you too, old bean? Whoops!"

The top corner of the larder door clapped in its frame as the prisoner continued its efforts to escape.

Aldermaston released his grip on Basildon and stormed across to the larder door. He grabbed the latch and lifted it.

"No!" screamed Felicity. "Don't!"

Aldermaston pulled at the door and then spotted the blackened brick at the bottom. The door shuddered again. "Alright, Tess. Calm down."

Felicity frowned. Did he just call that thing Tess?

"Cartwright, help me move this," Aldermaston instructed.

Together, both men leant against the opposite cupboards and pushed with their feet until the blackened brick scraped a few millimetres out of the way. Then they threw their weight against the larder door.

"After three, I want you to move away," Aldermaston instructed.

Cartwright nodded.

Felicity raised herself up onto the kitchen worktop again.

"Is this wise, Your Lordship?" Stoyle spluttered.

Felicity watched Aldermaston slip his hand into his other jacket pocket and retrieve something.

"Okay, Cartwright. One… two… THREE!"

Cartwright jumped away from the door. Aldermaston stepped back a pace, opened the larder door briefly and threw something inside.

Alarmed squeals and grunts escaped until Aldermaston slammed it shut again. The squealing subsided. Moments later, there were calm grunts of appreciation. Tentatively, Aldermaston opened the larder door wide enough and slipped inside.

All that escaped now was a series of happy grunts and snorts.

"That's it," Aldermaston soothed. "You like these, don't you, Tess?"

Felicity looked at Cartwright, then Basildon, and then Stoyle.

"Let me put this back on you," Aldermaston soothed.

Slowly, the larder door swung wide, and Aldermaston stepped out with Tess, on her lead, contentedly chewing something. Aldermaston beamed at Felicity.

"Darling. You asked me to get you some boar meat."

CHAPTER TWENTY

Aldermaston shook his head as he leant against the rear of the ambulance parked outside Tugford Hall and watched the female paramedic clean Chief Constable Stoyle's nose. "What did my brother think you were doing to Lavinia?"

Stoyle glanced at the paramedic. "Probably a misunderstanding."

Aldermaston scratched the back of his head and yawned. "I don't understand, that's for sure. I come home to find you with your nose bashed in, Lavinia tranquillized and wearing... not a lot, Cartwright being treated for carpet burns on his... you know what, and a boar trapped in my larder."

Stoyle's mobile phone beeped. He raised it high in the air, so the paramedic could continue working on his nose. "My chaps are at the scene, Your Lordship. They've sealed off the site."

Aldermaston nodded. At least Jillian and Tibby were being dealt with formerly now.

"Ow!" Stoyle yelled at the paramedic. "Careful!"

"Sorry," she soothed. "That might need manipulating to get it back into shape."

"Great," Stoyle moaned. He turned to Aldermaston. "We'll need a statement from you about tonight's events. Someone will be in touch tomorrow."

Aldermaston nodded, waved at them both, and then shut the rear door of the ambulance.

He rubbed his bottom as he watched the ambulance disappear up the driveway. Perhaps he should have got the paramedic to check out his puncture wound. That was going to be painful tomorrow morning. Then he remembered: it already was tomorrow morning.

∽

Basildon gazed longingly at Lavinia's sleeping face, as he carried her across his threshold, in his arms. In his bedroom, the peach-coloured rose petals still littered the soft satin sheets on the four-poster bed. He gazed at her face once more. Only the comfiest, softest furniture would do for his sleeping beauty.

He carried her around the side of the bed, pulled back the rose-petal-strewn bedding, and gently placed her down onto the soft mattress: a beautiful vision in the black basque.

He kissed her lightly on the forehead. "Goodnight, sweetheart. Sleep well."

He walked out of his bedroom, closed the door, and headed for the chaise longue in his drawing room. It was the gentlemanly thing to do.

∽

Aldermaston collapsed onto his side of the bed, fully clothed.

"The least you can do is get undressed." Felicity switched

off her bedside lamp. "Tell me you weren't wearing that jacket when you fell into Jillian's and Tibby's shallow graves."

He leapt off the bed. "Sorry." He emptied his pockets, placing three truffles on his bedside cabinet, along with several screwed up scraps of paper.

"You could have told me Cartwright had sourced you some boar meat," he said, getting changed. "I sent Daniel round all the butchers looking for some."

Felicity stared at him. "I would have if I'd known you'd delegated yet another job to Daniel." She sighed. "If I want anything doing round here, Cartwright is the man to go to. At least *he* doesn't desert me during dinner."

Aldermaston perched on the edge of the bed. "I wouldn't normally leave you hosting a Borderer's Guild event, but when Daniel texted to say Peggy was on the move with Tess—"

"You left me to host so you could chase an elderly woman take a wild pig for a walk in the woods!"

Aldermaston buttoned up his blue and white-striped nightshirt. "We found these, too." He picked up a truffle from his bedside table and threw it on the bed.

Felicity shrieked. "What is it?"

He picked it up and rotated between his fingers. "Jock Trotter calls this black gold."

"Looks disgusting to me."

"It's a truffle. That's what Peggy was after, with Tess."

"Where is Tess now?" Felicity took the truffle and examined it.

"Cartwright put her in one of the old stable blocks. She'll be safe there." He pressed buttons on the alarm clock radio.

"What are you doing?"

"Setting the alarm."

Felicity's eyes narrowed. "For what time?"

"Five o'clock."

"It's just gone one o'clock now! Why do you need to be up that early? Not another early morning photo shoot?"

Aldermaston swung his legs under the duvet and relaxed into the bedding. "Dawn raid."

Felicity inspected the truffle. "Can I keep this?"

Aldermaston closed his eyes. "Do what you like."

Felicity reached across and placed it down on her bedside table. "Before I forget. This fell out of your camouflage jacket pocket earlier." She bent down and picked something up off the floor and threw it at him.

He opened one eye and stared at the thick wodge of paper now resting on his stomach. Suddenly, he opened the other eye. It couldn't be? He grabbed it and brought it up to his face. It was! He'd forgotten Jillian had given it to him — the English translation of the Mortiforde Royal Recipe Collection.

Aldermaston sat up and opened the envelope.

"I thought you were settling down." Felicity plumped her pillows.

"Not now," he replied, turning the pages. "This holds the clue as to why Jillian was murdered."

∼

Basildon flinched as the boar hurled all eighty kilograms of its body weight right at him. The large snout loomed closer, the mouth gaped open, and Basildon's eyes fixed on the two huge canine teeth protruding from the bottom jaw. Fear coursed through his body as the boar's serrated jawline flew closer to his exposed neck and jugular. He screamed as he felt a weight on his right shoulder.

"Basildon, wake up."

He blinked rapidly. Sweat pooled on his forehead, and his heart pummelled his chest. Lavinia squeezed his shoulder.

"You were having a nightmare."

Basildon propped himself up on his elbows on the chaise longue.

Lavinia's thumb stroked the side of his face. "Come to bed."

The corner of Basildon's mouth rose as a fantasy filled his imagination.

Lavinia held out her hand. "You needn't have given up your bed for me."

He stood. "It was the least I could do."

Lavinia placed a finger on his lips. "Shhh! You promised me a wild boar from Mortiforde Woods, and you delivered. It's time for me to deliver my promise to you."

Basildon's heart somersaulted.

Lavinia paused in the bedroom doorway. "Your nightmare. What was it?"

"Attacked by a wild boar. Going right for the jugular—"

Lavinia's hand grabbed the back of Basildon's neck and pulled his lips onto hers. Eventually, she broke the kiss. "Your nightmare is my fault. I sent you off hunting boar. We must do something to turn tonight into a wonderful memory. That will make your nightmare disappear for you. And mine." She turned towards the bedroom.

Basildon grabbed her wrist. "You had a nightmare too?"

Lavinia pursed her lips together and nodded. "Horrible. We were chasing this boar around the hall when somebody shot me in the buttock with a tranquillizer dart."

"No!" Basildon hoped his shock appeared genuine.

Lavinia rubbed her buttock. "My cheek even feels sore."

Basildon gulped. "Perhaps I should kiss it better."

Lavinia pouted her lips, then practically dislocated his shoulder as she pulled him onto the bed.

Aldermaston dropped the recipe book onto the duvet. Now, it all made sense! If only he'd read this when Jillian had first given it to him. If only he'd started searching for Jillian when she failed to turn up for lunch with Bœuf yesterday. If only…

He sighed. If only's… If only his parents hadn't been driving along the Mortiforde bypass on that fateful day. No matter how many times he thought, *if only*, nothing changed. And it wouldn't change Jillian's and Tibby's deaths. Peggy was right. All he could change was the here and now.

He stared at the recipe book. Did Jillian know what it contained when she asked him to help her trace it and secure it for the food festival?

He glanced at the screwed up bits of paper he'd placed earlier on his bedside table. The ones from his jacket pockets. He unravelled them. The kidnap notes, the threatening messages and… what was this one? A reader's pass. That's right. It had fallen from the recipe book when Jillian had first unpacked it. He stared at the name written on it. *A Truff*. Perhaps its importance might have registered sooner if the reader had used his other name. But *A Harcourt* knew exactly what he was doing.

He was about to turn off the bedside light and settle down when he saw the time: four forty-five. He switched off the alarm. No point waking Felicity unnecessarily. He swung back the duvet and jumped out of bed with a spring in his step. Today he was going to catch a killer and solve a four-hundred-year-old mystery.

∽

Aldermaston leant on the lichen-smattered stone wall of Morte Bridge. The moonlight reflected in the waters of the River Morte as they carried a few mallards and the occasional swan under the seventeenth century stone arches. On his left was a huge shadow of trees, forming the edge of Mortiforde Woods. He was used to having this world to himself at this time of the morning. Although, he was usually in a hide somewhere, with his camera poised to capture some photographs.

To his right, perched above a wooded embankment, the crenelated outer walls of Mortiforde Castle formed a huge black wall, punctured only by the moonlit sky where an arched window, or arrow slit, broke its structure.

Aldermaston pondered the castle's significance. Four hundred years ago, it was the centre of a conflict that would result in murder, which, in itself, had sown the seeds for yesterday's murders.

"Lord Mortiforde! There you are!" PC Norten's head torch acted more like floodlighting, such was the height of the policeman's forehead. He sidled up beside him and mimicked Aldermaston's pose, albeit the length of his arms meant he had to stand in the middle of the bridge to achieve it. "This had better be good, Your Lordship. Chief Constable Stoyle doesn't like paying overtime rates. When I put five-thirty on my timesheet, I have to put it in the night shift column."

"I'm sure the Chief Constable won't mind." Aldermaston brought PC Norten up to speed with events from last night.

The policeman crossed his arms, achieving a knot Cissy Warbouys would have been proud of with any of her knitting needles. "Blimey. Who'd have thought a wild boar could kill two people and bury them in the woods?" He shook his head. "We don't give animals the credit they're due sometimes, do we, Your Lordship?"

Aldermaston stared at the copper. "You're right, Constable. There are definitely some animals out there that have more intelligence than some people in this town."

PC Norten perched against the top of the bridge parapet. "So, why do you need me here?"

"We're going to chat to someone this morning, and having

a member of the constabulary with us might encourage them to talk."

PC Norten tapped the side of his nose. "I like you're thinking, Your Lordship. Always happy to help."

Aldermaston waved to Lisa and Daniel, their torches illuminating the path in front of them, as they approached the bridge from town. "Morning, you two," he stifled a yawn.

Lisa pulled a sheet of paper from her shoulder bag and shone her torch on it. "Madeleine Bryan lives at number two Arboreal Way, which is the middle one of those three cottages just over there." She pointed to a terraced row of cottages on the other side of the river, just visible through the trees lining the river. "She's lived there for the last five years, and lives alone."

Aldermaston clapped his hands, trying to warm them up more than anything. "That should make it straightforward. Come on."

They crossed the bridge and followed the single track lane round to the right.

"Does the cottage have a rear door?" Daniel enquired. "These look as though they're built into the hillside." His torch beam picked up a dense tree canopy behind the roofline.

PC Norten nodded, the light from his head torch dancing on the tarmac lane ahead. "Yes. Old Mrs Townsend, the cat burglar, used to live at number one."

"How old was she?" asked Daniel.

"In her nineties," PC Norten replied.

"What? And she stole from other people's houses?"

"Blooming good she was, too."

Daniel whistled. "Never imagined a ninety-year-old woman could climb drainpipes."

"Climb drainpipes?" PC Norten repeated. "No, she was housebound."

"You said she was a cat burglar."

"She was," PC Norten confirmed. "She stole other people's cats."

Aldermaston stared up at the outline of the cottages. "No lights on. Good. Seeing as you know about the rear gardens, Constable, perhaps you could make your way round to the back door, just in case Miss Bryan decides to leg it out the back."

PC Norten nodded and slipped away, easily striding over the neighbour's fence on his way round to the rear of the property.

Aldermaston gave him a few minutes to get into position. He turned to Daniel. "Did you bring it with you?"

Daniel nodded.

"Ready?" Aldermaston hammered his fist against the cottage's wooden front door. A dog barked in a neighbouring cottage. He waited a few more seconds, then pounded on the door again.

A light came on in the hallway, followed by the shooting of bolts at the top and the bottom of the door. A bleary-eyed woman, wearing a faded T-shirt as a nightgown, pulled the door ajar and peered through. "What do you want? Do you know what time it is?" She blinked at Aldermaston.

Daniel stepped forward and thrust his hand closer to the occupant's face. The silver bracelet hung from his fingers. "I thought you might like this back."

"Shit!" The woman tried slamming the front door, but Aldermaston's foot blocked it. Abandoning her efforts, she disappeared inside.

Daniel shouldered the door wide open and ran after her.

"Are you all right?" Lisa asked.

Aldermaston flexed his foot. "Tough leather on these walking shoes." He nodded towards a staircase. "Check Jock and Seth aren't up there."

As they stepped into the small, cosy, stone-walled living room, someone out the back screamed.

Daniel entered the living room from the kitchen door. "Somebody didn't see the long leg of the law stretched across her back door. She's just gone flat on her face."

"Ger' off me, you lanky lummox!"

PC Norten backed his way into this living room, struggling to get under the low cottage door frame. Eventually, he pulled the woman, her hands already handcuffed behind her, backwards into the living room.

There was a wood-burner, two sofas covered in beige throws surrounding it, a narrow wooden staircase opposite, and a small, paper-strewn dining table in the window.

PC Norten pushed the woman onto one of the sofas, forcing her to sit on her handcuffed hands.

Aldermaston sat opposite. "Morning, Madeleine. It is Madeleine, isn't it?"

"Sod off, the lot of you!" she spat.

PC Norten clipped the back of her head with his hand. "Don't talk to Lord Mortiforde like that."

Lisa came downstairs and caught Aldermaston's eye. She shook her head.

Aldermaston shifted on the sofa. "Tell me something, Madeleine. When you collided with Daniel here, yesterday morning, outside Shepherds, had you just delivered a package to Evie Shepherd? One that contained Seth Shepherd's moustache?"

Maddie screwed her face up. "Don't know what you're talkin' about."

Daniel leant forward and placed the charm bracelet on the arm of the sofa. "I found it on the pavement. This little disc has your initials on it."

Maddie crimsoned and looked down at her feet.

Aldermaston leant forward. "Madeleine, I need you to

listen to me. I'm sure you know what's going on with the butchers around town, but I don't think you know *everything*. I—"

"She's my bloody thief!" PC Norten exclaimed. "Look! Here are all my posters." He stepped across to the dining table and picked up several sheets of WANTED posters with Jock Trotter's face on them. "I could arrest you right now for theft."

Aldermaston stared at her. "You might be able to arrest her for double murder, Constable."

"What? I ain't murdered nobody!" Madeleine looked at them one by one. "What if that bracelet is mine? It don't prove nuffin'."

"Maybe it doesn't," Aldermaston continued, "but when my assistant here collides with someone dashing out of a butcher's shop immediately after a ransom demand has been left there, it raises several questions. Like, who has a big enough grudge against the butchers to want them to endure financial hardship? Who used to run a business that was closed down because the butchers made an official complaint?"

Lisa pulled some documents from her shoulder bag. "These council documents, Madeleine, show that you ran a small business called Foraging Mortiforde. Had a unit on the trading estate, didn't you, where you packaged the produce you'd foraged in Mortiforde Woods? You supplied local restaurants and some further afield too."

Aldermaston crossed his legs. "Must have been frustrating when the butchers started foraging in the woods."

"Yeah, and they didn't have no permission! They just—" She stopped and closed her eyes.

"Go on, Madeleine. It's for the best. Tell me what you know," Aldermaston encouraged. "Murder carries a long sentence."

"What's he keep going on 'bout murder for? I ain't murdered no one," she glanced at Daniel. "If you's trying to frame me, I ain't having it. I ain't done no murders. I swear!" Fear filled her eyes.

"Two bodies were found in the woods last night," said Aldermaston. "Jillian Jones, Chief Archivist at Borderlandshire District Council, and Tibby Gillard, President of the Vegetarian Society."

Madeleine's jaw dropped. "T… Tibby's dead? Are you sure?"

Lisa nodded. "We found her body last night."

"I don't know nothing about those, I swear!" Maddie pleaded.

Daniel stood. "But you were in Mortiforde Woods last night, weren't you? You attacked Peggy Butcher."

Maddie shook her head defiantly.

Daniel stepped closer to Maddie. "Stand up."

"Sorry?"

"Stand up!" Daniel instructed.

"No, I won't!"

Daniel leant over, hooked his arm through hers, and pulled her to her feet.

"You're hurting me!"

Daniel nodded to Lisa. "Check her right thigh."

Lisa frowned. "Excuse me?"

Daniel twisted Maddie round so that her right leg was facing Lisa. "Lift her T-shirt up to hip level."

Lisa slid the hem of Maddie's saggy T-shirt up her muscular thigh. She nodded. "Yes, it's there."

"It's an insect bite of some sort," Maddie blustered.

Daniel turned to Aldermaston. "That's where I pulled the tranquillizer dart from the attacker I found in the woods last night."

PC Norten took his notebook and pen from his uniform shirt pocket. "In that case, Miss," he began, "I have no choice but to arrest you on the suspicion of the murder—"

"What? No! I ain't killed no one!" Maddie screamed.

Aldermaston stood up and grabbed PC Norten's notebook and pen. "You're wasting your time, Constable. She didn't kill Jillian or Tibby. But I know who did."

∼

Felicity peered tentatively into Cartwright's kitchen. All seemed quiet compared to six hours ago. Cartwright wasn't about yet, although, at six-thirty, it wouldn't be long before he showed his freshly shaved face.

She retied her dressing-gown belt, as if girding her loins, and entered Cartwright's domain.

Limping over to the fridge, she let out a sigh of relief when she saw her marinading boar meat was still there.

She grabbed the glass bowl from the fridge shelf and placed it on the worktop. Her nose twitched. A heady aroma of lovage, boar, and cider enveloped her. It smelt divine.

Her hand slipped into her dressing-gown pocket and pulled out the truffle Aldermaston had shown her last night. Why shouldn't she adapt the recipe slightly? Make it her own.

She searched several drawers for a grater, then grabbed the truffle and… how much should she add?

As she rubbed the truffle against the grater, a fine dust showered the marinading meat below. There was a lot of meat here. She grated a bit more. Once she'd grated half the truffle, she stopped, grabbed a wooden spoon from the top drawer and mixed it well. She paused. It looked okay. She bent closer and inhaled. It smelt good. Better not overdo it. She didn't want to ruin it. She slipped the remaining truffle back into her dressing-gown pocket.

Felicity was about to put the mixture back in the fridge when she paused. No. There was no reason why she couldn't continue. She grabbed her blind-baked pastry case from the larder and then spooned in enough of the boar meat mixture.

Suddenly, a door banged. Footsteps. Hurried footsteps. Felicity frowned. Not Cartwright's. Too light. Hurriedly, she opened the fridge door, and returned the glass bowl with the unused marinading meat to the middle shelf. Then she grabbed her pie and searched for somewhere to hide. The larder.

She limped inside, slipped the pie dish onto a shelf, and covered it with a fly mesh. Then she turned and pulled the larder door to, leaving the slimmest of gaps to see through.

Footsteps entered the kitchen. She eased the door open another millimetre and — Lavinia! Still wearing the basque. What was she doing in the kitchen?

Lavinia's fingers stroked the worktop surface as she strolled beside the island unit. She paused when she saw the fridge.

The fridge door seal broke, and Lavinia grabbed the glass bowl with the remaining marinading boar meat and placed it on the worktop.

Felicity pursed her lips. Then her jaw dropped.

Lavinia's fingers delved deep into her cleavage and extracted a short plastic syringe containing a clear liquid. She squirted the contents over the remaining marinading meat. She returned the spent syringe deep into her cleavage, then picked up the glass bowl and swirled the contents around to help them mix before returning it to the fridge.

The fridge door closed. Lavinia hurried to the kitchen door and dashed back upstairs.

Felicity fell against the larder door frame. Lavinia thought she'd sabotaged her Bake Off entry. Well, if Lavinia wanted to play dirty, then two could play at that game.

CHAPTER TWENTY-ONE

Aldermaston paced in front of the wood-burner in Maddie Bryan's cottage. "When you ran Foraging Mortiforde, who else was in business with you?"

Maddie frowned. "Uncle Ashton. Why?"

"And how did he take the business collapse?"

Maddie shrugged. "How d'ya think? It was our livelihood. Gone."

Aldermaston crouched down in front of her. "Anyone would be angry. But *how* angry was your uncle? Angry enough to seek revenge?"

"We was all angry!" Maddie spat. "I wanted to move. Make a fresh start. But…"

"But your uncle had other ideas?"

Maddie shuffled on the sofa. "Wouldn't let it drop. Kept saying it was history repeating itself."

Lisa scribbled down some notes. "What did he mean? History repeating itself?"

Maddie shrugged. "He told me once about something that happened like, hundreds of years ago, but…" She sighed. "Never was any good at history."

Aldermaston stood. "But what he suggested to you was revenge for what the butchers had done recently."

Maddie looked at her feet and nodded. "But, I tell you. I ain't killed no one."

Daniel chipped in. "So, what was the plan? Kidnap the butchers during the festival weekend and what? Make them give away their burgers for free?"

Maddie smirked. "Yeah. See how they like being ruined financially. Took both me and Uncle Ashton to kidnap Jock Trotter yesterday morning. He's a big bloke. We lost his boar in the struggle. Then a couple of hours later, I managed to grab Seth Shepherd on my own. Getting his pig was a bonus."

PC Norten cleared his throat. "In that case, Miss, I'm arresting you for the kidnap and—"

Aldermaston held up his hand. "Hang on, Constable." He turned to Maddie. "Where are Jock Trotter and Seth Shepherd?"

Maddie shrugged.

Daniel threw his hands in the air. "Course she bloody knows!"

"I don't!" she scowled at Daniel. "I was to grab 'em and pass 'em over to my uncle."

"Where does your uncle live?" Aldermaston asked.

Maddie avoided his gaze.

Aldermaston looked at PC Norten. "Constable, I think it's time you took over. See how she likes being processed for kidnap and murder."

"I TOLD YOU!" Maddie screamed. "I ain't murdered no one!"

Aldermaston bent down and planted his face inches from hers. "Your uncle has played you for a fool. You should have listened to his history lessons, Madeleine. Because that's what this is *really* all about. The murder of Tobias Truff in 1632. These kidnappings were only ever meant to be a distraction to deflect the authorities from the murder of Jillian Jones. At the moment, you're an accessory to murder. I strongly suggest you help us all you can. Where does your uncle live?"

Maddie trembled and nodded her head towards the front door. "Further along this road. Couple of miles. Get to Birrington and you've gone too far."

Aldermaston grabbed Maddie's arm and pulled her upright. "We won't go too far because you're coming with us. And heaven help you if Jock Trotter and Seth Shepherd aren't there."

He paused and turned to Lisa. "Nip back and get your Land Rover. We're going to need a set of wheels."

Lisa nodded. "Give me ten minutes." She slipped her notebook away and shut the front door behind her.

Daniel whispered in Aldermaston's ear. "Won't Ashton be there?"

Aldermaston checked his watch. It was nearly six-thirty. His eyes narrowed as he fixed his gazed on Maddie again. "He won't be there, Daniel. He'll be truffle hunting with Maisie. But he'll be back by daylight." Aldermaston checked his watch again. "That gives us less than an hour."

∼

Basildon shuddered as cool air brushed against his bare skin. The mattress beside him moved. He stirred from his slumber. Lavinia kissed him lightly on the lips.

"Where have you been?"

"Bathroom," she whispered, adjusting her basque. "This puts extra pressure on a woman's bladder."

Basildon turned towards her. His hand stroked the lace curves of her body. "Perhaps you should take it off."

"You are naughty," she purred, stroking his face. "I might get cold."

"I can think of ways to keep warm." He rolled on top of her and stared into her eyes. The eyes of a liar.

"Did the toilet flush okay?" he quizzed. "Only the handle doesn't always seem to catch properly."

"Seemed fine to me."

Basildon grinned. "You've obviously a knack for grabbing a handle and pulling."

She arched her eyebrows, and her hand suddenly grabbed him. "Oh, yes!"

Basildon kissed her, and yet, try as he might, he couldn't hear the cistern clanking away, as it always did when it had been flushed. Wherever Lavinia had been, it hadn't been in his bathroom.

∼

"On the right here." Maddie nodded.

Lisa eased off the accelerator.

"There!" Aldermaston whispered from the front passenger seat. He pointed to a narrow track almost hidden by the trees.

Lisa pulled up alongside. A narrow tunnel of trees led to what looked like a black hole. "Now what?"

Aldermaston looked ahead. "Find a discreet lay-by. We don't want Mr Harcourt seeing he has visitors."

Lisa nodded.

Aldermaston jumped out and opened the rear Defender door. PC Norten, Maddie and Daniel climbed out.

"After you, Maddie," Aldermaston gestured. He signalled to Lisa to move off.

The Defender pulled away, leaving them in semi-darkness, as Lisa's rear lights diminished and eventually disappeared.

Nearby, a fox screeched.

Maddie led them along the narrow tree-lined track, the

semi-darkness enveloping them as much as the overhanging branches.

She stopped. "That's my uncle's pickup truck there, and that's his cottage."

Aldermaston took in the two-storey timber-clad building with its two small, box-shaped single-storey extensions.

Daniel pointed to the shadowy outline of the holly hedge in front of the property. "Are those what I think they are?"

Aldermaston twisted to see.

"Ooh, little piggies!" cried PC Norten. "That's clever."

"Strange to go to all that work, and yet nobody can see it from the lane back there," Daniel muttered.

Aldermaston shook his head. "It's an ancestral reminder, isn't it, Madeleine?"

Maddie kicked at some leaves. "Dunno what you're talking about."

"So where's your uncle hiding Jock and Seth?" Aldermaston asked.

Maddie shrugged.

Aldermaston glanced around. "Any outbuildings?"

Maddie nodded. "A greenhouse and shed out back. And some old pigsties."

"Show us."

PC Norten pushed her forward. She scuffed her feet through the leaves as she led them around the side of Ashton's pickup truck, down a narrow path beside the garage, and round into the rear garden of the property.

Daniel shone a torch around, adding detail to the tall shapes and shadows. A healthy vegetable patch occupied most of this woodland clearing, along with the small greenhouse and shed. To the rear of the garden plot stood a terraced row of five brick pigsties.

"You check the first," Aldermaston instructed.

Daniel nodded and hurried across to the first sty. He

jumped the chest-high brick wall and landed with a squelch. "Eeuurrgghh!"

Aldermaston stifled his smirk as he dashed over to the second sty. Using the torch app on his mobile phone, he illuminated the interior.

He stepped back in shock, covering his mouth with his hand. The flagstone floor was littered with leaf debris, and blood. In the middle sat a pig's body: headless, heartless, and legless. A rat scurried across the floor and out through a small drainage hole in the rear wall.

"Looks like we've found Farmer Bell's missing pig," Aldermaston muttered. Did this make it a full house on his porcine bingo card?

"IN HERE!" Daniel yelled from the next sty along.

Aldermaston took a short run up to the sty's wall, leapt up, and threw his arms over the top. He hauled himself over and the laws of physics pulled him over the other side.

"Whhhoooaaaa!"

The landing on his back was soft. The loud squelch, followed by pig excrement spraying in all directions, made Aldermaston cringe. He gagged at the nauseous aroma. Daniel held out a hand while pinching his nose with the other.

"Thanks." Aldermaston grabbed it and pulled himself upright. He shuddered as a fresh aromatic wave of pig excrement wafted around them. "In here?"

Daniel nodded. "Not pretty."

Cautiously, Aldermaston stepped forward, peered over the half door, and shone his phone torch inside. Two pairs of eyes blinked. Frantic muffled sounds emanated from taped mouths. Aldermaston recognised Jock's rotund shape. And in the far corner was Seth's unmistakable blue eyes, minus his handlebar moustache.

"You're up early, My Lady." Cartwright clattered some saucepans on the gas oven.

Felicity leant against the worktop in her jeans and pale green cashmere crew-necked jumper. "That's what happens when your husband disappears at five o'clock in the morning."

Cartwright shook a frying pan vigorously. A hiss of spitting oil exploded around them. "Will be with you shortly, My Lady. Just got to finish this."

Felicity waved away the apology. "I didn't realise we still had guests in the main hall."

Cartwright glanced over his shoulder at her and nodded. "His Lordship's brother has a guest. They're too exhausted to make breakfast themselves."

Felicity cringed. "Actually, I was in here earlier. Did the next step with the boar pie." She stepped across to the larder, and slipped inside, reappearing with the pie dish. "As far as I'm concerned, I just need to put the pastry top on. Crimp around the edges, egg-wash it and put it in the oven."

Cartwright smiled. "You're getting the hang of this, My Lady."

Felicity beamed. "Only, I remembered we made a second pastry case, didn't we? A spare."

"You know how society likes a spare, My Lady," Cartwright commented. "If you're baking one, you may as well bake two."

She stepped back into the larder and brought out the spare pie case, and placed it down on the worktop, next to the filled pie.

From the fridge, she selected the pastry to make the pie lid, and the glass bowl with the remaining marinading boar meat. She dusted the worktop with some flour, and flattened the ball of pastry, and then cut it in half. She put half to one side and rolled out the other, gradually rotating it, and rolling it out into a circle. "About a quarter-inch thickness for the lid, would you say, Cartwright?"

"Perfect, My Lady."

Felicity beamed. This was going well. When the lid was big enough, she rolled it up over the rolling pin, picked it up and unravelled it over the pie dish. A sense of satisfaction overwhelmed her.

Cartwright placed a small bowl of egg-wash next to her.

"Thank you, Cartwright." She crimped the edges of the pie, then brushed it with egg-wash, before adding two tiny slits in the centre. She stood back and admired her creation.

She grinned. One down, one to go. Lavinia's pie. Because Lavinia was getting a taste of her own medicine.

~

"Brace yourself, Seth." Aldermaston picked at the corner of the black duct tape sealed across his mouth. "Ready?"

Sat on the flagstone floor with his legs crossed, Seth nodded.

Aldermaston yanked it. Quickly.

Seth's scream frightened a flock of roosting jackdaws into flight from a nearby tree. His chin, cheeks and upper lips were red raw.

"On the bright side, Seth, you won't need another shave until next month. Might take a while for your moustache to grow back."

His eyes watered from the pain. "Mig teegth. I need mig teegth."

Aldermaston frowned.

Seth nodded to the duct tape in Aldermaston's hand, and the set of dentures hanging from the sticky side.

"Sorry!" Aldermaston eased them off the sticky surface and then popped them back into Seth's mouth. "There you go."

"My hands are taped too," Seth muttered.

Jock screamed as Daniel ripped the tape from his face.

Jock's breathing raced as he tried to speak. "Thank heavens you found us, Your Lordship. I thought we were a gonna, then."

Aldermaston took a penknife from his dirty camouflage pocket and sliced through the multi-layered tape binding Seth's wrists.

"You sort Jock out." Aldermaston handed the penknife to Daniel. "Right Seth, let's see if we can stand you up."

He bent over, slipped his arm under Seth's armpit, and then pulled him upright. Seth's hands clung tightly to Aldermaston's arm as he wavered unsteadily on his feet. "Take your time."

"Oh, that's heaven," said Jock, rubbing his free wrists. "What time is it? What day is it?" Jock rolled over onto his hands and knees and then pulled himself upright, using the wall.

"Saturday," Daniel confirmed. "About seven o'clock."

Jock nodded. "Good. If we can get back to the shops in the next half an hour, we'll be ready for opening. There's still one more day of festival trading," he panted.

"Yow's not going anywhere!" Ashton roared. He released the safety catch and pointed the shotgun at them. Then he waved it to one side. "Everybody out, with your hands in the air."

Ashton stepped backwards, giving them room to manoeuvre. Daniel led, followed by Jock, Seth, then Aldermaston. In the rear garden, Aldermaston saw Maddie holding the blade of a garden spade at PC Norten's throat. His hands were handcuffed behind his back.

"Sorry, Your Lordship. He had a gun." It was PC Norten's turn to shrug his shoulders.

"SHUT UP," Ashton bellowed. "We're going for a little walk. Follow Maddie." He nodded at her. "Holly hedge."

Ashton stepped behind Aldermaston and rammed the

shotgun barrel in his back. "One wrong move, Your Lordship, and little Harry becomes the Ninth Marquess of Mortiforde before breakfast. Got that?"

Aldermaston nodded. They traipsed, single file, around the garden and the side of the garage, to the front of the property.

"Right, you. Over there!" Ashton instructed, pulling the shotgun from Aldermaston's back and waving it at PC Norten, then pointing it at the largest holly pig.

"Now you." He forced Seth next to the constable, under the first topiary piglet.

Ashton stepped forward and pushed Daniel in the back, knocking him off his feet. "You, under that one. Now you, Your Lordship."

Aldermaston stood with his back to the hedge and looked up. The day was dawning. Above him, a robin sat on the topiary piglet's snout, singing its heart out. Then it pooped on his forehead.

"And last, but not least, Mr Trotter," Ashton's Black Country accent drawled, "over there." He waved the shotgun at the fourth topiary piglet.

"PUT YOUR HANDS IN THE AIR." Ashton waved his shotgun at each of them in turn. Maddie joined her uncle.

"Firing squad, is it?" Aldermaston asked. "Did Uncle Ashton tell you about this part of the plan, Maddie?"

"Shut up!" Ashton stepped forward, waving the barrel in Aldermaston's face. "Everybody has to meddle, don't they?" he spat. "Interfering busybodies. The lot of you. All my family has ever tried to do is earn a living. Why are we never allowed to get on with our lives? Somebody, somewhere, always wants a slice of the action."

Ashton paced up and down, looking at them in turn. He pointed the shotgun at Jock. "And you! If you hadn't…" Ashton sneered.

"I didn't do anything!" Jock screamed.

"Didn't do anything?" Ashton stormed across and shoved the shotgun barrel under Jock's chin. "How dares you! That makes things a hundred times worse, knowing you have no idea what you've done." Ashton's snotty nose was millimetres from Jock's.

"Tell him," said Aldermaston. "He deserves to know."

Maddie stepped forward with the spade. "He's not going to kill you. That's not the plan, is it, Uncle Ashton?"

Ashton spun round, pointing the shotgun at her. "Shut up, little girl!"

Maddie screamed, backing away.

"I told you, Maddie," said Aldermaston. "Your uncle tricked you." He turned to Ashton. "Why didn't you tell Madeleine what you were really up to?"

Maddie shook her head. "No! Uncle Ashton wouldn't do that to me. Would you?" She looked at Ashton, confused.

Ashton stormed back towards Maddie. "Stay wheres you is, and do as I tells ya, otherwise I'll shoot!"

Aldermaston nodded. "He's killed two so far, Madeleine."

Maddie ran backwards, her eyes fixed on the shotgun in front of her.

Ashton lunged, ripping the spade from her hands, and threw it into the undergrowth.

She shrieked and fell to her knees. "Don't kill me! Please don't kill me!"

"Shut up and listen!" He kicked her to the ground. "I'm gonna tell you a story."

~

Abigail's phone buzzed and levitated across her bedside table. She stirred, her hand sliding out from under the duvet in time to catch it as it leapt over the table edge.

She brought the screen close to her half-asleep eyes. Stoyle's name and number. She swiped her thumb.

"Chief Constable, good morning."

"I wish it were, Abigail."

She propped herself up on her elbows. "What's happened?"

"I'm sorry to inform you that, last night, two bodies were discovered in Mortiforde Woods. One of them was Jillian Jones. I thought, as the new Chief Executive, you ought to know."

Abigail sat upright and brought the phone closer to her face. "How awful. Do we know the cause of death?"

"Shotgun wound. Square in the back."

Abigail cupped her mouth to her hand. "Oh, God." She paused. "We'll have to cancel the food festival out of respect. And the recipe book?"

"We didn't find anything with the bodies." Stoyle confirmed.

"Who was the other person? Do we know?"

She heard Stoyle turning paper. "I don't think it's anyone you knew," he muttered. "Local woman. Here we go. Tibby. Tibby Gillard."

The blood drained from Abigail's face. "Oh my God."

"You *did* know her?" Stoyle was confused.

"Yes—" Her mind flicked back to yesterday when they'd both been in her office, eating the vegetarian burger. She could taste it now. "Do we know when she died?"

Stoyle sighed and turn more paper. "Initial investigations suggest they may have been dead for about four to five hours. And we were at the scene soon after midnight."

Abigail did the maths. "Sometime between seven and eight o'clock last night, then."

"Roughly. Why?"

Abigail took a deep breath. "Tibby Gillard was supposed to accompany me to the dinner last night at Tugford Hall."

"Really?"

Abigail heard Stoyle writing on a hard surface.

"What reason did she give for not turning up?"

A tear ran down Abigail's cheek. She wiped it with the back of her hand. "She didn't."

"Didn't give a reason, or didn't get in touch?"

Abigail ran her hand through her hair. "I'd agreed to meet her outside the Buttermarket at a quarter to seven. She never showed up. I waited ten minutes, then left. That's why I was the last to arrive last night."

"You didn't try calling her?"

"I did, but there was no answer. I assumed she'd changed her mind. I…"

"You weren't to know," said Stoyle. "Even if you had raised the alarm, we had no reason to search the woods where she was found."

Abigail sobbed. "I should have done something."

"Honestly, Abigail, there is nothing you could have done to save her."

"But…"

"I'll be in touch when we have more news."

Abigail wiped her cheeks. "Thanks." She terminated the call, brought her knees up to her chest, and washed the brilliant white duvet cover with her tears.

She'd failed Tibby last night. But she could do something today. She wiped her face and picked up her phone. They had to cancel the food festival out of respect for Tibby and Jillian. She scrolled through her contacts for Aldermaston's number, but… she didn't have it. She frowned. How come she'd not sorted that yet?

Suddenly, she saw Gerald's name. He'd given her his business card. He was on the Borderer's Guild. She'd need them onside. She selected the number and brought the phone to her ear.

"Morning, Gerald. Abigail Mayedew here." She shook her head. "No, I'm not calling about lunch, or to view a property. I need you to gather the Borderer's Guild. I don't have Lord Mortiforde's number, so can you sort it? It's urgent. Nine o'clock. Yes. *This morning*." She disconnected the call.

With two dead bodies, Aldermaston and the Borderer's Guild would have to listen to her now.

∽

Ashton waved the shotgun at Aldermaston. "Kidnapping those two numbskulls was not a cover. I meant to damage their businesses financially, in the same way they ruined our business."

"But you couldn't tell Madeleine the real reason for doing this," Aldermaston suggested. "She would never have agreed to help you."

Ashton stepped towards Aldermaston. "I told her all she needed to know."

Maddie remained on the ground, tears streaming down her face, her head shaking in disbelief.

"I grew up here as a young boy. Lived here, until my teens. Then we moved to Dudley. Strange 'ow I picked up the accent, really, but it meant people round here didn't think I was local when I came back." Ashton turned round and looked up at the timber-framed cottage. "I'm probably more local than most of Mortiforde. My family has lived here, in this precise spot, for over four hundred years." He spun round and focussed on the butchers. "I knows these woods likes the backs of me hands. I knows where to find the wood sorrel, the wild chestnuts, the rose-hips and the sloes. I knows where the best wild garlic flourishes in spring, and where to find the most succulent chanterelle mushrooms, and the best beech nuts, wild raspberries and strawberries and…" he sidled up towards Jock Trotter. "And I knows about these." He slipped his hand into his stockman wax jacket pocket and retrieved two black truffles.

He leant closer to Jock's face. "My grandfather told me where to find these, just as his grandfather showed him and his grandfather showed him. So, when my niece, over there, comes up with the idea of starting an official foraging business, supplying restaurants with natural, wild products, I thought *Yes!* This is in our blood."

He stepped towards the house, the shotgun still primed. "After nearly three decades away, I came back. To the family home my parents had left me."

He spun round. "And Maddie and I, we chats to all the right people at the authorities, and we get permission to forage. And at first, them top London restaurants, they loves our supply of truffles. But then, you guys comes along." He pointed at Jock and Seth. "And you… you plunder these woods. The most profitable element of our foraging business, and you steal it from under our noses."

"But you didn't know it was the butchers, at that time, did you?" Aldermaston interrupted. "You panicked when the supply of your most profitable foraged product dwindled to next to nothing. So, you economised with how much produce you were putting in the packets."

"WE WAS DESPERATE," Ashton bellowed. A globule of saliva shot out onto the floor. "Suddenly, we found ourselves trying to survive by flogging a few limp sorrel leaves and some beech nuts."

Aldermaston took a step forward. "So when did you discover it was the butchers helping themselves to the truffles?"

Ashton sneered. "I had my suspicions when we learned from the court paperwork that it was Jock Trotter who'd complained about our short measures to the Council," he began. "But about three years ago, while I was doing some other research, I came across his arrest for criminal damage in The Powys Gazette." He flung a finger in Jock's direction. "And I knew then. Only an animal like a pig could do the damage that he did to Offa's Dyke. And only someone looking for truffles would let an animal do that sort of damage."

Jock quivered. "I was training Tess at the time. It was too risky training her here."

"And then, a year ago, I sees *him* in the woods, with a Gloucester Old Spot." Ashton focussed on Seth.

Seth struggled to keep his arms in the air. He dropped them to a pleading position. "Mortiforde is a close community," he implored. "When I heard Jock was supplying truffles to some of his upmarket clients in London and Edinburgh, I was intrigued. So I followed him. Secretly, mind. Saw him with Tess. And I thought, well, if he can do it, so can I. Did a bit of research. Turns out Gloucester Old Spots are good truffle hunters. One of my regular suppliers gave me Maisie as a piglet, and I trained her right from the start."

Ashton sneered. "You's already got your own businesses. Why ruin ours?"

Aldermaston lowered his hands, but kept them in front of him, where Ashton could see them. "Butchery isn't the cash cow you might think it is," he said, remembering Peggy's plight. "But it's not the first time the butchers have ruined things for your family, though, is it, Mr Harcourt? Or should I call you Ashton Truff?"

Both Jock and Seth looked puzzled.

Ashton's eyes narrowed, and his nostrils flared. His breathing became heavier and his face reddened. "I hated my parents when they changed our name. Embarrassed, they was, of our history. That bloody nursery rhyme. Weren't just school kids singing it. People would see us walking down the street and just launch into it. Drove my parents mad! So we changed our name and relocated. But you can't run away from history." He sighed. Deeply. "I swore then to return, and when the time was right, reinstate the family name."

Aldermaston stepped forward, tentatively. "People look at families like mine and know they've been here for centuries. But so, too, have others. Walter Farmer's bloodline stretches back over four hundred years, as do Jock's and Seth's."

Aldermaston turned to Maddie. "All three independent butchers in Mortiforde can trace their ancestry back to when Mortiforde Castle was a royal palace. There aren't many families who've remained in the same line of business for four centuries. But your Uncle Ashton knew that, Madeleine. Always has done. What he didn't know, until he started attending Jillian Jones' *Trace Your Ancestors* evening classes, was the truth behind the mysterious murder of Tobias Truff, the Royal Truffle Hunter in 1632."

Seth turned to Aldermaston. "But that's the point, Your Lordship. Nobody knows who killed him. It's all been lost in folklore."

"Everyone knows he was an alcoholic," Jock dismissed. "He probably tripped over in the woods because he was so drunk and hit his head. That's what my grandfather always told me."

"HE WAS MURDERED!" Ashton sneered. "And your families were culpable!" He raised his shotgun to his shoulder and aimed it squarely at Jock.

"No! Don't shoot!" Jock held up his hands in surrender.

Ashton's chest heaved. "He was *my* ancestor, and he was the official truffle hunter for Mortiforde Castle. Until he was murdered. Killed by the butchers of this town. Murdered by your ancestors."

He pointed the shotgun at the large topiary pig above PC Norten's head. "This little piggy got murdered."

BANG!

A sudden clap of pigeon wings and crows squawking

accompanied the gunfire echo as it reverberated through the woods. A shower of holly leaves fluttered to the ground.

Ashton primed his shotgun, readying for the next shot.

"Except it wasn't the butchers who delivered the fatal blow, was it?" Aldermaston intervened.

"They bloody tried. Left him for dead in Dead Man's Hollow because that's what they wanted," Ashton snivelled, striding towards Aldermaston. He suddenly stopped and swung the barrel of the gun in Jock's direction.

"No!" Jock squealed. "Please, no!"

"Your ancestors thought they was clever, luring Tobias to The Nooseman's Knot one evening. Plied him with so much ale he could hardly stand."

He twisted and pointed the gun at Seth. "Took all three of the butchers, your ancestors, to carry him to the woods, where they kicked the living daylights out of him. When they thought he was dead, they left him to rot, ready to divvy up the forest between them, so they could forage for truffles instead."

Aldermaston edged closer to Ashton. "But he wasn't dead, was he? According to the diary section of the Mortiforde Royal Recipe Collection, someone observed the whole thing. The chef at Mortiforde Castle, Oswyn Cooke."

Ashton's grip on the shotgun tightened as he hissed through gritted teeth. "Murdering bastard!"

"The butchers had left him for dead," Aldermaston explained, "for that's what they'd set out to do, but he wasn't. That night, Oswyn had followed them. And he wrote in his diary how Tobias suddenly reared up from the ground, clutching a rock, ready to strike back. Oswyn Cooke grabbed the nearest branch and whacked Tobias across the back of the head. That was the fatal blow."

"So it wasn't our ancestors, then?" Jock cried.

Ashton raised the gun sight to his face and aimed at Jock.

"No! Please don't shoot!" Jock fell to his knees and sobbed.

"Yow's ALL guilty!" Ashton spat. "Your ancestors wanted him dead. They thought they *had* killed him!"

The gun barrel was inches from Jock's face. "Please, no," he whined.

"And that's why you killed Jillian, wasn't it?" said Aldermaston. "Because as you sat there at her evening class and helped her trace her family history, you discovered the woman teaching you was a direct descendent of the castle's chef, Oswyn Cooke. At the time, that meant nothing to you. But when the evening class found references to Oswyn Cooke's diary and recipe collection of 1632, the same year as Tobias Truff's murder, the hunt was on to trace the Mortiforde Royal Recipe Collection. Would that hold any clues to Tobias Truff's murder?" Aldermaston stepped closer to Ashton. "You hunted down the document at the Royal Palaces Collection, didn't you? You got to it first. And that's when you read Oswyn Cooke's confession."

Ashton swung the gun away from Jock and stormed towards Aldermaston. "Couldn't believe it when I read that. But there it was, in black and white."

"And in Latin," Aldermaston commented.

"Easy enough to get it translated," Ashton sneered. "Them staff at the Royal Palaces Collection was very amenable." He paused. Then squinted at Aldermaston. "How's yow know I saw the Latin version of the text?"

Aldermaston slipped his hand into his camouflage jacket pocket and pulled out a Royal Palaces Collection reader's pass. "It fell out yesterday morning when Jillian opened the recipe collection. It has your name on it. Your true name. A Truff."

"ARMED POLICE!" bellowed a voice behind them. "Drop your weapon and put your hands in the air."

Ashton spun round, pointing the still-cocked gun at Chief Constable Stoyle.

A gunshot rang out. Maddie screamed. The colour from

Ashton's face dissipated, and then he dropped to the ground. Dead. All went quiet, save for a gentle breeze helping the tree branches wave goodbye. Maddie ran across to him as two armed police officers reached Ashton's body.

Stoyle approached Aldermaston. "Are you all right, Your Lordship?"

Aldermaston nodded. "Not sure about Seth and Jock." He pointed to the butchers by the hedge. "Our missing butchers."

"Excellent," said Stoyle.

Behind Stoyle stood Lisa, her face white with shock. Stoyle turned and shook her hand. "You did the right thing. Well done."

He strode over to where his armed officers were dealing with Ashton's body.

Aldermaston stared at Ashton's dead body, cloaked in his aged brown wax jacket, blending in with the leaf-strewn debris on the ground. The woodland was swallowing him up, like it had Tobias.

Daniel ran across to Aldermaston and Lisa.

"Are you all right?" Lisa asked.

He nodded. "I think so."

Aldermaston turned to Lisa. "After that first gunshot, I wondered where this was heading."

"By the time I'd hidden the car and snuck back here," Lisa explained, "I saw Ashton aiming the gun at you all by the pigsties. I knew we'd need reinforcements, so I ran to where we found Jillian's and Tibby's bodies. Chief Constable Stoyle was there getting an update from his officers. I was explaining what I'd seen when we heard the first gunshot."

Aldermaston squeezed Lisa's shoulder. "Who knows what could have happened if you all hadn't arrived when you did?" He yawned. "Time to go home and grab a few more hours' kip, I think."

Lisa bit her bottom lip. "Not just yet."

Aldermaston's shoulders dropped. "What now?"

Lisa pulled her smartphone from her pocket and showed him the screen. "Text message from Gerald Lockmount. Abigail's called an urgent Borderer's Guild meeting at nine o'clock."

CHAPTER TWENTY-TWO

Felicity stood back and admired her second Boor Pie. "Do you know Cartwright, I'm really proud of how these have turned out."

Cartwright peered over her shoulder. "It's marvellous what a little coaching can do, My Lady. Forgive me, but the decoration on that second pie. Is it a vase?"

Felicity rotated the pie. "It's an outline of two faces looking at each other. See? Chin, mouth, nose, eyes, forehead."

"Of course, My Lady. How naïve of me not to notice."

"It's my symbolic interpretation of the heir and the spare," she said emphatically. "And this is the spare pie."

"I see," said Cartwright.

Felicity smiled. In reality, it depicted the two faces of Lavinia Farquhar-Cordell.

~

Abigail sat at the far end of the table in the meeting room above the Buttermarket. She banged the tabletop with the palm of her hand.

"Ladies and gentlemen, if I can call this meeting to order." She shuffled some paperwork on the table in front of her and moved her mobile phone to one side.

"Excuse me?" Cissy stopped knitting momentarily and held up her hand.

"Yes?" Abigail snapped.

"The Marquess usually chairs the meetings when he's here. And, he is here… even if he pongs a bit." She wafted her hand in front of her nose.

Aldermaston placed his hand on her forearm. "It's fine, Cissy. Ms Mayedew called the meeting. I'm happy for her to chair."

Abigail nodded. "Thank you, Your Lordship."

She clutched both hands together and rested her forearms on the table. "I'm sure, by now, you've all heard of the tragic deaths of Jillian Jones and Tibby Gillard, both horribly murdered last night in Mortiforde Woods. Please join me in a minute's silence as we remember their contribution to this town."

She stood, her chair scraping heavily against the wooden floor, as she touched her mobile phone screen.

Everyone followed suit, with their chairs adding to the crescendo.

Silence fell, except for the constant clattering of knitting needles. Aldermaston nudged Cissy and coughed. Cissy's fingers froze. She peered around the table at each pair of eyes watching her, then bowed her head.

Outside in the streets below, tourists gathered, as stallholders prepared for the second and final day of the festival, due to start in thirty minutes' time.

Aldermaston clenched his hands tight behind his back as he furtively glanced around the room. Abigail was not going to shut his food festival down now. It was too late. Out from the corner of his eye, he spotted Chief Constable Stoyle, with his head bowed and his heavily bandaged nose. What would he have to say on the matter? Stella Osgathorpe would support him. The Historic Borders Agency couldn't afford the day's loss of income for hosting some of the event in the castle grounds. Cissy and Gerald would probably support him too.

His eyes fell on Revd Makepiece, who appeared to be asleep, something he was adept at doing in a vertical position, particularly when standing in the pulpit. The Crookmanns, though. They might vote either way. Neither Daniel nor Lisa had any right to vote.

Suddenly, Abigail's phone beeped its alarm. Her finger swiped the screen.

Abigail's head rose from its deferred bow. "Thank you, everyone." She sat, as did everyone else.

Abigail looked at them all in turn around the table, except Aldermaston. "In light of recent events, I think it goes without saying that the food festival should be cancelled with immediate effect."

Shocked intakes of breaths and hushed voices echoed around the large-windowed room. Sunlight brightened the chamber, if not the mood.

Stella Osgathorpe leant forward. "Whilst we at the Historic Borders Agency are deeply saddened to hear of both deaths, we feel it would be inappropriate to cancel the festival at such short notice now." She stretched her hand out to the nearest window. "Can't you hear? The tourists are gathering already. Far better for us to stop and reflect after the event to see how best we honour their lives."

Abigail stared at Stella. "Worried about losing a day's takings? Two people died last night. One of whom was supposed to be accompanying me to dinner last night at Tugford Hall …" Her voice caught. She stopped, looked down at her notes, took a deep breath and composed herself.

Aldermaston stepped in. "Blaming ourselves for the actions

we did not take will not bring them back, Ms Mayedew. We *both* made mistakes yesterday. Mistakes we'll have to live with for the rest of our lives. Shutting down everything now won't change that. My view is that the food festival goes ahead, subject to any conditions Chief Constable Stoyle may have."

Stoyle shuffled in his seat, his eyes widening as he tried to look around his bandaged nose at the paper in front of him. "Perhaps I should bring the Guild up to speed with events over the past few hours."

He looked for Abigail's permission.

She nodded.

"Following the kidnapping of two butchers yesterday, His Lordship here successfully located them in the early hours of this morning, at a private residence not far from Birrington. Thankfully, both butchers were safe, albeit shaken and shocked from their horrendous ordeal."

Stoyle moved a sheet to one side. "At approximately seven forty-five this morning, my armed officers shot a man, Mr Ashton Harcourt, the resident of said private residence, whom they thought was about to open fire. Regretfully, he was pronounced dead at the scene."

Cissy tugged at her wool. "Why did this Mr Harcourt kidnap the butchers? Ooh! Your Lordship! *Mr Harcourt*. He's the man I told you about last night. The family who changed their name."

Aldermaston nodded. "That information, Cissy, was immensely useful."

"Was it?" Cissy's chest puffed as she double the speed of her knitting.

Stoyle picked up a pen. "Actually, Your Lordship, I'll need a statement from you at some point, so we could make this the first draft."

Aldermaston smiled and nodded. He pulled out the English

translation of the recipe book from his camouflage jacket pocket. "Last night's tragic events all began in 1632, when Mortiforde Castle was a royal residence."

"Oh, come on!" Abigail threw her hands up in the air. "You're telling me that this authority lost its Chief Archivist because of something that happened four centuries ago?"

Aldermaston turned to Abigail. "The catalyst dates back to that period, Ms Mayedew. Whatever *you* may think of the past, we should always remember that it can't be undone. But we do have to live by its consequences."

Abigail swallowed and averted her gaze.

"As a royal residence," Aldermaston continued, "its kitchen was a significant purchaser of food provisions. Indeed, all three of the town's current independent butchers can trace their family and butchery businesses back to this period, when they were all regular suppliers to the royal kitchens. This recipe book tells us so." He held up the English translation.

"But," he continued, "those butchers were experimenting with a little sideline. Truffles. Using local wild boar they'd captured in the woods, they foraged for truffles, and then offered them to the royal kitchens. Quite understandably, this upset the castle's official truffle hunter, Tobias Truff."

"Truff?" Cissy queried. "That's the name the Harcourt's changed their name from, isn't it?"

Aldermaston smiled in acknowledgement. He flicked through the recipe collection's pages. "On the seventeenth of September 1632, Oswyn Cooke, the head chef, writes, *Tobias lost his temper with me today for buying truffles off the butchers again. He dislikes it when I tell him theirs are cheaper.*"

Aldermaston looked up at his audience. "Tobias accused the butchers publicly of destroying his livelihood. The castle was his only customer. If they didn't buy his truffles, he had no income. What little money he earned he spent in The

Nooseman's Knot, getting drunker by the day. Indeed, ten days later, on the twenty-seventh of September, Oswyn wrote, *Tobias was so drunk today he tried telling me the dirty apples in his basket were truffles the butchers had missed.*"

Jane Crookmann chuckled. "Still happens today. I take Martin into The Nooseman's Knot for a drink and two hours later he comes out thinking he's God's gift to women."

Gerald Lockmount burst out laughing. Cissy dropped a stitch and cursed.

Aldermaston continued, "Tobias' drunkenness made matters worse. One night, he stole all three butchers' boars and set them free. The following day, Oswyn noted, *Tobias is in a cheerful mood today. He brought me truffles, and the butchers didn't. Without their animals, the butchers cannot hunt for truffles.*" Aldermaston paused for dramatic effect. "It turned out to be a fatal mistake."

Aldermaston nodded to Lisa, who passed round printouts of a map of Mortiforde Woods. "A week later, Tobias is found dead in a hollow, here in Mortiforde Woods."

Stella recognised the spot. "Dead Man's Hollow."

Aldermaston nodded. "I'm sure that's how the name originated."

Stoyle frowned as he examined the map. "But this is where…"

"Yes," Aldermaston confirmed. "We have documentation that proves Jillian understood the significance of the spot where she was killed."

He turned to the recipe collection again. "Oswyn Cooke recorded in his diary the following day, *Truff's body was found in the woods today, bludgeoned to death by a tree branch. The town is rife with gossip about the butchers. Especially after they were seen buying Tobias drinks in The Nooseman's Knot earlier. When Tobias was completely inebriated, the butchers carried him to the woods and attacked* him. I know, for I secretly followed. They kicked and punched him until he was covered in his blood, and then buried him under a pile of autumnal leaves. They left him for dead, for that is what they wanted. As soon as they turned their backs, Tobias rose from the ground with a rock in his hands. I grabbed a nearby fallen tree branch and struck it hard on Tobias' head from behind. He dropped to the ground, motionless. He was dead now."

Abigail scrutinised the map, then threw it on the table. "The history is fascinating, Your Lordship, but what has this four-hundred-year-old supplier spat got to do with yesterday's murder of Jillian and Tibby and the kidnapping of the butchers?"

Aldermaston leant on the table. "Here in the Welsh Borders, we're all interconnected."

Martin Crookmann chuckled. "Inbreeding. Shallow gene pool. PC Norten is the result."

"That's not what I meant, Martin," Aldermaston defended. "Families have roots here. Roots stretching back centuries. We understand how we fit into the landscape, and how it moulds our lives. It's what the food festival is about. Sharing our love of local produce. Sharing our knowledge garnered over the centuries. That knowledge is passed from generation to generation. Sometimes, grudges get passed on that way, too."

Aldermaston turned to Lisa. "Can you pass round those short measures file notes, please?"

Lisa distributed several sheets of paper around the table.

"A few years ago, Borderlandshire District Council brought a case against a new start-up company called *Foraging Mortiforde*. It was run by an uncle and niece team, Mr Ashton Harcourt and Miss Madeleine Bryan. They were found guilty of selling underweight produce. Packets of foraged produce, such as wood sorrel or wild garlic, were being sold as one hundred gram packets, despite containing fewer than ninety-five grams.

They were fined the maximum penalty, and they went out of business."

Abigail leant back in her chair and waved the sheet of paper in the air. "Lord Mortiforde, first you tell me a four-hundred-year-old story, and now you're telling me about some packaged produce that's short of a few leaves. How does this relate to Jillian's and Tibby's deaths?"

Aldermaston smiled at her. Awkwardly. "The Council instigated its investigation based upon a complaint by Jock Trotter."

Lisa chipped in. "It takes a business involved in weights and measures to understand the regulations."

"Exactly," Aldermaston confirmed. "And the reason *Foraging Mortiforde* were selling underweight produce was because of the butchers. A few years ago, the supermarket opened on the edge of town. There was uproar at the time, and many independent retailers were hit with a drop in trade, including all three of our independent butchers. But the butchers looked for new markets. Or rather, Jock Trotter did. Just like his ancestors, some four hundred years ago, Jock started a new sideline. Truffle hunting." Aldermaston nodded to Lisa. "He'd been inspired by this article."

Lisa distributed copies of The Mortiforde Chronicle feature announcing the launch of Foraging Mortiforde.

"It didn't go well at first, though," Aldermaston continued.

Lisa then distributed copies of The Powys Gazette article.

"Jock gained a criminal record when he taught his boar to hunt for truffles along Offa's Dyke, churning up an ancient scheduled monument. But after many months, his training paid off. He began harvesting truffles from Mortiforde Woods, supplying them to some of the top restaurants in London. It became a useful income stream. Now, what one butcher does round here, the others tend to follow, and sure enough, both

Seth and Peggy began using pigs to scour Mortiforde Woods for truffles."

Stoyle held up his hand. "Sorry, Your Lordship. Do we know whether any permissions had been granted for this foraging?"

"*Foraging Mortiforde* had permission for commercial foraging from Mortiforde Forestry. The butchers did not."

Stoyle scribbled down the information. "So why didn't *Foraging Mortiforde* complain?"

"At the time, they didn't know what the butchers were up to. The butchers foraged secretly in the dark," Aldermaston clarified. "Foraging is reliant upon what you find. As far as Harcourt and Bryan knew, the truffle yield was falling. As their most expensive foraged product, it affected their income significantly, hence why they started selling underweight products. They were trying to make the most of what little foraged material they had until they could resolve the issue. After all, who weighs a one hundred gram packet to check it's one hundred grams?"

Cissy giggled. "Jock Trotter, clearly"

Aldermaston smiled. "Yes, Cissy. And it led to Foraging Mortiforde's downfall. But it wasn't until a year or so later that Ashton Harcourt discovered the truth. While researching his family history, he found The Powys Gazette piece and knew immediately what the butchers had done."

Stella leant back in her chair. "History repeating itself."

Aldermaston nodded. "Exactly. The murder in Dead Man's Hollow of one of his ancestors is a story Ashton Harcourt learned at an early age. It's been passed down from generation to generation. For the man whose ancestor was murdered by the butchers who wanted to take away his business, discovering that yet again it was the butchers who'd taken away his and Maddie's business was too much. He sought revenge."

Stoyle scribbled furiously. "Hence the kidnapping of Jock

Trotter and Seth Shepherd, the ransom notes and the instruction to give away their burgers free of charge, which would have a significant financial impact on their businesses."

Aldermaston nodded.

Stoyle paused writing. "So why wasn't Mrs Farmer kidnapped?"

"We interrupted that process last night," said Aldermaston. "We determined this morning that Madeleine Bryan had been out in Mortiforde Woods last night following Peggy, as we were, too. It was lucky for Peggy that we were there."

Abigail rose from her chair and stood by a window, leaning her bottom against a windowsill. "Okay, I understand why Mr Harcourt wants revenge on the butchers for destroying his foraging business, but what's this got to do with Jillian and Tibby?"

Aldermaston turned to Lisa. "Have you got the family tree and Jillian's *Trace Your Ancestors* evening class list?"

Lisa nodded, pushed the evening class list across the table to Aldermaston, and then began opening out Jillian's huge family tree document.

Aldermaston held up the evening class list. "Jillian ran a popular weekly evening class called *Trace Your Ancestors*. And if you look at this list of students here, you'll see a certain A Harcourt." He tapped the paper.

"Jillian used her family tree to show others how to trace their ancestors. As you can see from this, if we follow her maternal line," Aldermaston leant across the table and traced the line with his finger, "it takes us all the way to here. Oswyn Cooke."

Stella gasped. "It was while we were researching castle archives that we learned of the Mortiforde Royal Recipe Collection." She paused. "Hold on. The evening class never saw the recipe collection. You know how difficult it was for Jillian to get the Royal Palaces Collection to agree to lend it to us for this weekend. Jillian was the first person in Mortiforde to see the recipe collection in four hundred years. So, how did Mr Harcourt know what was in it? How did he know that Oswyn Cooke, Jillian's ancestor, killed Tobias Truff?"

Aldermaston nodded. "Because Mr Harcourt travelled to London and visited the Royal Palaces Collection in person." He slipped his hand into his jacket pocket, retrieved a small slip of paper and placed it on the table.

"Yesterday morning, when Jillian first unwrapped the Mortiforde Royal Recipe Collection, something dropped to the floor. I picked it up." He pointed to the pass. "A Royal Palaces Collection reader's pass, for A Truff. He told us this morning, that he detested his family's decision to change their name, but it's what made it possible for Ashton to learn so much from Jillian, without her realising who he truly was."

Abigail stepped away from the window ledge and put her hands on her hips. "Well, that ties a lot up neatly, but it doesn't explain Tibby Gillard's death, does it? Nor does it explain why the Vegetarian Society also received a threatening note yesterday and a pig's heart, which Tibby came to see you about. And *you* ignored."

Aldermaston bit his lips. "Yes, it didn't make sense, and I was wrong to ignore it for as long as I did."

Stoyle held his pen in the air. "Why did the Vegetarian Society get a threatening note and pig's heart when they weren't involved in this in any way?"

Aldermaston returned to his seat. "When Tibby gave me that pig's heart, she told me it was Ashton who had discovered the package on their stall when he'd arrived in the morning. I'm sure he placed it there himself, to help bide him some time. We found the remains of Farmer Bell's pig, in one of pigsties at the rear of Ashton Harcourt's property. All four limbs had been removed, as had the head, and the carcass had been ravaged for the heart. Ashton needed this to look like a spat between the butchers and the Vegetarian Society. How Tibby came to be with Jillian, I have no idea. Perhaps we'll never know."

Stoyle looked through his paperwork. "Our current line of enquiry suggests she was simply at the wrong place at the wrong time. One of the butchers… Mr Trotter… said he heard two female voices near the property yesterday evening, one of which he recognised as Tibby's. Then he heard Mr Truff shouting at them. About twenty minutes later, both he and Mr Shepherd heard two gunshots in quick succession, from somewhere in the nearby woods. During our search of the property's grounds this morning, we found Ms Gillard's bike lying in the undergrowth. Mr Harcourt's wallet was in her pannier basket. We're not sure why. We also found threads of clothing from both Jillian Jones' and Tibby Gillard's clothing on the door frame of a wood store shed beside the property. Again, why Tibby was there, we just don't know yet."

Abigail's gaze remained fixed on Aldermaston. "I still think we should cancel the food festival."

Stoyle put his pen down and checked his watch. "There are ten minutes until the castle gates re-open. You can already hear the crowds gathering outside. If you tell thousands of people, some of whom have travelled a good distance to get here, that the event is off, you run the risk of public disorder and antisocial behaviour. Ashton Harcourt is dead. We have Madeleine Bryan in custody. Jock Trotter and Seth Shepherd are safe, as are the public."

Aldermaston jumped in quickly. "All those in favour of closing the festival raise their hand."

One hand rose. Abigail's.

"And those in favour of continuing."

The remaining Borderer's Guild members all raised their hands, albeit Cissy's was still clutching a knitting needle.

Aldermaston sighed. "Motioned carried. The festival continues."

Stoyle put his pen down and leant back in his chair. "You do have one small problem, Your Lordship."

Aldermaston frowned.

"The butchers," Stoyle commented. "We shall be chatting to them all today about the events of the past twenty-four hours and also the unlawful commercial foraging they've been undertaking in Mortiforde Woods over the past few years. None of the butchers will be trading today."

"Blimey!" Daniel exclaimed. "How did you manage to get Mairi Trotter to agree to that?"

"Being the Chief Constable of the Marchlands Constabulary gives me the authority," he explained. "And she was grateful to have her husband returned to her, alive and well, too."

"That gives us a problem," Gerald Lockmount declared. "The Best Borderlandshire Burger competition has been an integral part of the food festival since its inception. We've got to have a winning burger. If today's visiting public can't buy them to taste and score, what do we do?"

Aldermaston tapped the side of his nose. "Leave it with me. I may just have an idea."

∼

The bells of St Julian's chimed four o'clock. Felicity stood in the corner of the large Bake Off tent, fanning her face with the competition programme, as Bœuf judged the entries. The tent doors were closed, and the air was stuffy. Only entrants were allowed in during the judging process.

Heidi Yail sidled up beside Felicity, fanning herself with her clipboard. The breeze pushed her half-moon glasses further up her nose. "Is it a good sign if Bœuf took two bites from my cherry Bakewells, and only one from Margaret Hillbrow's?"

Across the marquee, Felicity caught sight of Lavinia on Basildon's arm.

Aldermaston whispered in Felicity's ear. "Is that Lavinia on Basildon's arm?"

"Yes," Felicity smiled through gritted teeth. "I believe they are an item."

Aldermaston inhaled deeply. "She might help him settle down."

"I think she has an ulterior motive."

"Oh?"

"She wants my job."

Aldermaston sniggered. "To have your job, she needs to be married to me."

Felicity thumped Aldermaston on the arm. "Not everything is about being Lord of the bloody Manor, you know. No. She wants to be President of the Ladies' Legion."

"Here we go," Aldermaston whispered. "Bœuf's moving on to the Boor Pie category. How many entries were there?"

"Four."

Harry tugged at Felicity's arm. "That's not the black brick, is it, Mummy?"

Felicity's toes throbbed. "No, darling. Mummy wouldn't be that stupid."

Bœuf picked up each Boor Pie entry, scrutinised its pastry, turned it over, knocked the base, and then replaced the pie on its stands.

"Who made the others?" Aldermaston whispered.

"Mrs Hastings, Mr Simpson and Lavinia," said Felicity.

"Lavinia? I didn't know she was entering the Bake Off."

"Neither does she." She winked.

Bœuf cut into each pie and inspected the meaty contents. Then he forked a piece from the first entry into his mouth.

Felicity's stomach churned as he savoured the sample and closed his eyes in ecstasy. He paused, as if relishing the flavours on his tongue, then scribbled copious notes on a clipboard, finishing with a flourish.

Next, he selected a similar sized piece from the second pie and placed that into his mouth. His face was less animated, and his notes were brief. The third entry pleased his taste buds more than the previous entry, but then he paused, placed a finger and thumb into his mouth and pulled out a long brown hair.

Felicity shuddered.

Finally, Bœuf turned to the fourth entry. His eyes widened expectantly as he popped the morsel into his mouth. Immediately, his eyes bulged and cheeks reddened as he choked. He spotted a small wastebasket under a trestle table and lunged.

Felicity spotted Lavinia glance across at her, biting back a smirk, as Bœuf's retching echoed around the tent.

A festival volunteer rushed up to him with a glass of water, which Bœuf downed in one.

Once composed, Bœuf moved along to the next category, the Mortiforde Sponge. Bœuf enjoyed judging this category, pushing every crumb into his mouth. He stepped back and jotted down some thoughts on his clipboard. The hushed atmosphere in the marquee began to falter as excitement among the entrants effervesced.

Finally, he stepped up to the small podium at the end of the marquee.

"Ladies and gentlemen," he began. "Eet 'as been an honour and a privilege to taste and judge your entries in the Mortiforde Ladies' Legion Bake Off tent."

The entrants cheered and applauded.

"I 'ave the results of my judging here." He turned to his clipboard and announced his decision in the marmalade and jam categories.

Lavinia and Basildon edged around the crowded marquee,

eventually slipping beside Aldermaston and Felicity.

"Basildon's got high hopes for his Mortiforde Sponge," Lavinia beamed.

Bœuf read out some winners' names. A round of applause filled the room as the entrants collected their cups from Bœuf.

Felicity smiled. "Well, if he's used his mother's recipe, he should be onto a winner."

Lavinia chuckled. "Nervous about your category, Your Ladyship?"

"Of course. I've never entered anything like this before."

Basildon leant closer. "You can rest assured Bœuf won't lie, old gal." He tapped the side of his nose.

Felicity frowned. "What's that supposed to mean?"

"I added an extra ingredient to your meat dish." He sniggered. "Sodium thiopental."

"Sodium what?" Felicity looked horrified. "When?"

"Shortly after your boar meat arrived last night. It's tasteless and odourless, so it won't harm your dish. But Bœuf will feel compelled to tell the truth about its flavour and the chef's cooking skill."

Felicity's stomach gurgled with nerves.

Aldermaston turned to Basildon. "Is that what you put in your canapés last night? Is that why Bœuf declared his true identity?"

Basildon beamed.

"And now for ze Boor Pie category," Bœuf declared. He closed his eyes, pursed his lips, then kissed the tops of his fingers. "Mwwwaa!" he enthused. "Wow! Ze winner in zis category was outstanding. Never, 'ave I tasted such amazing flavours. Perfect pastry, tender meat and a hint of something exotic, I think. Ze winner in this entry is number twenty-three. And before I open ze envelope, I 'ave something else I wish to say. Whoever has cooked this marvellous pie has secured themselves a contract to supply me with three of these pies for every Garden Party I cater for at Buckingham Palace."

A collective "Oooh," rose from the assembled entrants.

A volunteer handed him an envelope. He slipped his thumb inside and tore it open. "And ze winner is… Oh, *mon dieur*! It is Lady Mortiforde!"

A huge round of applause erupted. Harry punched the air. Aldermaston kissed her reddening cheek. Basildon leant closer. "Remember my sodium thiopental. He's telling the truth, my dear."

Suddenly, Heidi Yail grabbed Felicity's wrist and pulled her towards Bœuf. They air kissed, and Bœuf presented her with a small silver cup and a rosette. And then he handed her a paper tube secured by a red ribbon. "Your contract, Your Ladyship."

Felicity thanked him, and leant closer to the microphone. "Congratulations to the other winners, and commiserations to the other entrants in the Boor Pie category."

Bœuf pulled a face. "Whoever baked entry number fifty-eight should never be allowed in a kitchen again. Zat pie was vile."

Basildon cupped his hands to his cheeks. "Tell us who it was, then. Who was entrant fifty-eight?"

Felicity waved her hands in front of the microphone. "It would be inappropriate of me to reveal who that entrant was. It's bad enough they have to live with the ignominy of their entry being classed as vile by one of the most famous chefs in the world."

Bœuf stepped down and chatted to a festival volunteer, who rummaged through a box and pulled out an envelope. He returned to the microphone. "Your Ladyship. While it may be inappropriate for you to name names, as a chef, I am adamant whoever cooked that entry should not go anywhere near a kitchen ever again."

Basildon leant closer to Aldermaston. "Me thinks Bœuf is still affected by the sodium thiopental."

The celebrity chef ripped open the envelope and pulled out the entry form. "Ze name on here is… Lavinia Farquhar-Cordell."

Such was the huge intake of breath, the tent walls were sucked inwards. All eyes turned to Lavinia, who vigorously shook her head.

"I didn't enter. It wasn't me!"

Felicity returned to Aldermaston and Harry, clutching her trophy and contract. Then she turned to Lavinia. "I entered it on your behalf."

"What?" Lavinia's mouth dropped.

"I saw you this morning." Felicity leant closer and whispered, "You tampered with the marinading boar meat you took from the fridge in Cartwright's kitchen."

Basildon looked at Lavinia. "So *that's* where you nipped off to this morning. I knew you hadn't been to the toilet."

Lavinia went to move, but Felicity blocked her. "I made two pies. The first was made before you contaminated the meat. The second contained the meat with your extra ingredient. That's why I put your name on it. Next time you plan to humiliate me in front of everyone, I suggest you think again!" She wagged a finger in Lavinia's face. "I never want to see you in Tugford Hall ever again."

Lavinia burst into tears and ran, knocking Felicity's shoulder as she fled the marquee.

Another round of applause rippled through the marquee.

"Oh, what spiffing good luck!" Basildon declared. "I've won! And with Mother's Mortiforde Sponge recipe too!"

"Ladies and gentlemen!" Aldermaston bellowed from the stage in the grounds of Mortiforde Castle.

The crowds supped their plastic pints of beer, nibbled a cheesy bread stick, chewed candyfloss or some toasted pistachios, as they readied themselves for the food festival's finale.

"On behalf of the Borderer's Guild, I would like to apologise that, due to circumstances beyond our control, we've not been able to run our Best Borderlandshire Burger competition in the usual manner this year."

A chorus of boos and hisses echoed around the castle's perimeter walls.

"But we do still have four fantastically flavoursome beefburgers to choose from, and a decision to make."

A huge cheer rose from the crowd.

"Instead, we're going to have a race. Can I ask my friends to bring out the runners and riders, please?"

From behind a temporary fenced off area, Lisa, Daniel, and Bœuf appeared, each with a porcine animal on a lead. Squeals of delight emanated from the crowd as well as from the runners. Lisa, Daniel, and Bœuf dug their heels in as they struggled to contain the excited animals whose noses sniffed the grass in the castle's outer bailey grounds. Strapped to the back of each pig was a brown paper bag containing a burger.

"Wearing the red collar is Miss Piggy," Aldermaston declared, "running for Peggy Farmer and her pork, thyme, oregano and wild garlic burger." Lisa waved a red handkerchief high above her head.

Another cheer rang out.

"Wearing the blue collar is Maisie," Aldermaston continued, "from Shepherds, for their lamb, rosemary, and wild garlic burger." Daniel waved a blue handkerchief in the air.

A third cheer erupted from the crowd.

"And for Trotter's Butchery, there's Tess the boar, running

for their beef, truffle, mushroom, burgundy wine, and pheasant burger." Bœuf waved a white handkerchief high above their heads.

An intrigued *Ooooh* rippled through the spectators.

Aldermaston grabbed the microphone from its stand and dropped down the stage steps towards the pigs. "In addition to the butchers, this year we've also had an entry from the Vegetarian Society."

Felicity rushed up to him carrying a vegetarian burger in a brown bag and handed it to him.

"So we have four burgers, but only three pigs," Aldermaston explained.

"That's okay, Your Lordship," bellowed Mrs Hargreaves. "We don't want a dumb animal running for us."

"What about the tall, lanky chap over there," jeered an onlooker, pointing to PC Norten standing beside the stage. Peals of laughter erupted across the gathering.

Mrs Hargreaves grabbed Aldermaston's microphone briefly. "I said we don't want a dumb animal running for us."

PC Norten frowned as the audience fell about in fits of giggles.

Aldermaston turned to PC Norten and handed him the vegetarian burger. "Would you mind holding this for a moment?"

"I'd be honoured, Your Lordship."

Aldermaston stepped back and surreptitiously slipped his hand into his pocket. His fingers selected a small piece of truffle.

He brought the microphone closer to his face. "The first burger to escape from the castle will be the winner," he pointed to the castle's main entrance, about two hundred metres away. The crowds turned and looked. Aldermaston slipped the truffle piece into PC Norten's back pocket.

Tess looked up and sniffed the air. Miss Piggy and Maisie also caught a whiff of truffle, too.

"After a count of three. Are you ready?"

The crowds clapped vigorously.

Bœuf waved at Aldermaston.

"Wait up, everyone," Aldermaston said, hurrying towards Bœuf. "It seems our celebrity chef wants a word." He placed the microphone in front of Bœuf's face.

"Ladies and gentlemen," Bœuf began. "I 'ave tasted each of zese burgers, and they are all magnifique! Ze winning beefburger will secure a contract from me for ze Royal Garden Parties."

The crowd cheered and applauded.

"Here, that pig keeps sniffing my bum!" PC Norten peered over his shoulder at all three porcine noses fervently interested in his back trouser pocket.

"Three!" Aldermaston bellowed.

"Two!" joined in the crowd.

"ONE!" everyone cheered.

Lisa, Daniel, and Bœuf let go of the leads they were holding. Tess jumped up and bit PC Norten's bottom.

"OW!" he screamed.

Maisie rammed her snout between PC Norten's legs.

"I'm being attacked!" PC Norten screamed. He ran, and the pigs gave chase. The policeman howled as two squealing pigs and a shrieking boar chased the long-legged copper across the castle grounds. Another cheer rose from the crowd as PC Norten was first to leave the castle grounds with the vegetarian burger.

Aldermaston brought the microphone to his mouth. "I do declare the Vegetarian Society is the winner of this year's Best Borderlandshire Burger competition."

But the crowds weren't listening. They were too busy

flocking out through the castle gates to see how long PC Norten would keep running.

~

A slumbering, dozy Sunday morning mist meandered around the lower trunks of the Douglas firs in Mortiforde Woods. Through the viewfinder, Aldermaston watched the moisture molecules rise, tumble, then rise again, as the sun's rays fingered their way through the canopy.

A sudden crack in the foreground broke his thoughts. A heavy foot. His right hand twisted the barrel of his zoom lens and, suddenly, there she was. A vision of beauty. Her wet, black nose reflecting the morning sunshine, two powerful puffing jets of air escaping her nostrils, the enigmatic gleam in the corner of her eye, and the unmistakable long hair.

Aldermaston licked his lips and readied his camera. His index finger felt for the shutter release. Timing was everything. He mimicked her breathing. In. Out. In. Out. His finger depressed halfway. The camera focussed. In. Out. In. Out—

A high-pitched whine pierced the silence as the zip to his hide rose forcibly upwards. Aldermaston turned, looking over his shoulder, as his finger simultaneously pressed the shutter button.

The door to his hide fell inwards and there, crouching down to peer inside, was Abigail.

"It's true what they say then." She stepped inside, bending at the waist. "You do hide in the woods, Your Lordship."

"Even a Marquess is entitled to some personal time, Ms Mayedew." Aldermaston turned back to his camera and placed his eye against the viewfinder.

"Anything interesting?"

Aldermaston's heart fell. Once again, his quarry had disappeared.

"I thought I had something then," he muttered quietly. "But it seems I was wrong."

"So you are wrong sometimes?"

He turned and spotted the new Hunter boots. Not a four-inch heel in sight.

"I wanted to come and say well done," she began, shuffling in her wellies.

He frowned. Was this an apology?

"Seems everything worked out well… in the end. Although, there are some things I haven't quite got my head around just yet."

Aldermaston nodded. "That's a rural community for you. It always comes together in a crisis."

Abigail smiled. "Even so, come nine o'clock tomorrow morning, there *will* be changes. I shall drag this authority into the twenty-first century. And our relationship with the Borderers Guild may have to change. The shambles of this weekend cannot be allowed to happen again."

"That a warning or a threat?" Aldermaston raised his eyebrows.

Abigail smiled. "A statement." She paused and looked down at her fidgeting fingers. "May I ask you something?"

Aldermaston shrugged. "Ask away."

She took a deep breath. "The Earl of Dartbury. It's not common knowledge round here, and I'd like it to stay that way."

Aldermaston nodded. "Nobody will hear anything from me. That's a promise, Abigail."

"Thank you." She smiled. "Aldermaston."

He nodded. Progress.

"I'd better leave you to it." She turned to leave, but caught a wellington boot on the hide's frame and tripped, falling flat on her face. He heard her spit woodland debris and detritus from her mouth.

"Are you all right?" Aldermaston called.

"Fine!" she snapped.

The hard thud of boots pounding the soft woodland floor slowly dissipated.

Aldermaston returned to his camera and pressed the button to display on the LCD screen the last image he'd captured, just as Abigail had arrived. He took a sharp intake of breath. For there, on the screen, was a beautiful image of the rare, long-haired fallow deer, surrounded by a thin veil of early October morning mist, and a glint in the corner of her eye.

The End

STAY IN TOUCH

If you'd like to be the first to know of new Marquess of Mortiforde mysteries as they're released then sign up to my free, occasional newsletter, *Writing from the Welsh Borders* at: http://www.simonwhaley.co.uk/newsletter/

Alternatively, follow me on social media via:

Facebook: facebook.com/SimonWhaleyAuthor
Twitter: twitter.com/simonwhaley

ENJOYED FORAGING FOR MURDER?

I hope you enjoyed reading *Foraging for Murder*. Please consider leaving an honest review (which can be as short or as long as you like) on the store from where you purchased it.

Thank you.

ACKNOWLEDGMENTS

My thanks go to the Tuesday Evening Zoom bunch, without whom I may never have had the motivation to push through the first draft of this novel (as well as some of the subsequent drafts, too). It always amazes me how some of my most completely and utterly bonkers friends can offer such practical support. Yet somehow you did.

Thanks also go to the other weirdoes at my writers' group, for not only supporting the first novel, but giving such useful feedback when I asked for it, and for their part in helping me choose the right cover for this book.

Writing a book is a writer's job, but bringing it to life involves others. My thanks also go to Catherine Clarke for another wonderful cover, and to eagle-eyed Helen Baggott for her proofreading services.

And, finally, thank you to my family who, once again, put up with my grumpiness on those days when the words didn't flow as well as I'd have liked them to.

ABOUT THE AUTHOR

Simon Whaley is the author of the Marquess of Mortiforde Mysteries and many other humorous non-fiction books (including the bestselling *One Hundred Ways For A Dog To Train Its Human*). His articles have also appeared in publications such as *BBC Countryfile*, *Country Walking*, *The People's Friend*, and *The Countryman*.

He lives in Shropshire, a county on the Welsh Borders that many UK residents struggle to locate on a map, and can often be found pounding the hills as he dreams up new ideas for more books.

You can find out more about Simon and his work via his website: www.simonwhaley.co.uk (and don't forget to sign up to his newsletter at www.simonwhaley.co.uk/newsletter/).

SIMON WHALEY'S NON-FICTION BOOKS

Books for Dog Lovers

One Hundred Ways For A Dog To Train Its Human

One Hundred Muddy Paws For Thought

Puppytalk: 50 Ways To Make Friends With Your Puppy

The Bluffer's Guide to Dogs

Books for Walkers

The Bluffer's Guide to Hiking

Best Walks in the Welsh Borders

Books for Community Project Fundraisers

Fundraising For A Community Project

Books for Writers

The Positively Productive Writer

Photography for Writers

The Complete Article Writer

The Business of Writing - Volume 1

The Business of Writing - Volume 2

The Business of Writing - Volume 3